The Twelve Dates of Christmas

The Twelve Dates of Christmas

JENNY BAYLISS

G. P. PUTNAM'S SONS
NEW YORK

PUTNAM
— EST. 1838 —

G. P. PUTNAM'S SONS
Publishers Since 1838
An imprint of Penguin Random House LLC
penguinrandomhouse.com

Library of Congress Cataloging-in-Publication Data
Names: Bayliss, Jenny, author.
Title: The twelve dates of Christmas / Jenny Bayliss.
Identifiers: LCCN 2020034966 (print) | LCCN 2020034967 (ebook) |
ISBN 9780593085387 (trade paperback) | ISBN 9780593085370 (ebook)
Subjects: GSAFD: Love stories.
Classification: LCC PR6102.A975 T84 2020 (print) |
LCC PR6102.A975 (ebook) | DDC 823/.92—dc23
LC record available at https://lccn.loc.gov/2020034966
LC ebook record available at https://lccn.loc.gov/2020034967
p.   cm.

Printed in the United States of America
1   3   5   7   9   10   8   6   4   2

Book design by Kristin del Rosario

To my family with love x

. . . . .

Expectations and Deflations

Kate Turner stepped gingerly on the crisp ice-dusted leaves and tried not to slip and land on her backside. She couldn't see where she trod because of the large plastic containers in her arms. The sky was so blue it looked like a scene from a children's picture book, and her breath plumed out in white clouds and rose up toward the pale winter sun.

She leaned against the door of the Pear Tree Café and it yielded. A friendly tinkle of bells above her head heralded her arrival. The café was full and warm and noisy. The smell of fresh coffee was rich in the air. Condensation dribbled down the windows and clouded the view of the frosted world outside.

A few people raised their heads from their cappuccinos and waved. Matt turned from the steaming black and silver coffee machine and grinned at her.

"Thank God, he said, banging hot coffee grounds out of the porta-filter and filling it back up with freshly ground coffee. "We ran out of caramel brownies this morning, I thought there was going to be a riot."

Matt's hair was permanently unkempt and right now was standing on end like one of those trendy hair styling adverts; he had a habit of running his hands through it when he was stressed, which only made it worse. Some might call his unruly mop ginger, but he insisted it was strawberry blond.

A voice from across the café called out:

"Did I hear someone say brownies?"

Matt cleared a space on the counter, and Kate put the boxes down with some relief. She could feel her cheeks burning red in the heat, and she unwound her scarf. Her newly straightened hair was already beginning to kink.

"Over here," she called. "Hot off the press."

There was a scraping of chairs as regulars clambered over sleeping dogs and Christmas shopping to claim chunks of Kate's cakes.

"I've brought some more mince pies, orange and chocolate chunk shortbread, and rocky road as well," said Kate.

"You're a lifesaver," said Matt. "Carla, can you come over here and take these cake orders, please."

He picked up a check pad and handed it to the young waitress, who was instantly encircled by a small crowd of sugar-deprived customers. Matt took up his post back at the coffee machine, and Kate sidled around the counter to perch on a stool next to the coffee grinder.

"What can I get you?" he asked.

Matt poured two shots of espresso into a wide-brimmed cup and added steamed milk; a flick of his wrist as the liquid reached the top made a caramel leaf pattern in the latte. He placed the cup on the counter behind him for Carla to deliver and began the next order.

"Just a flat white, please," Kate said as she slipped out of her coat and laid it across the back of a battered old sofa.

"Wow," said Matt. "You look . . . lovely. Where are you off to?"

Kate brushed her hands self-consciously over the floral tea dress and pulled her cardigan closer around her.

"Is it too much?" she asked.

"Too much for what?"

"You know," said Kate conspiratorially. She leaned forward and whispered, "For the first date."

Recognition dawned on Matt's face.

"Oh yes," he said. "I'd forgotten about that. Yes, it is too much, go home and put on baggy jeans and a turtleneck jumper."

Kate poked her tongue out at him.

"Well, well, well," said Matt. "The twelve shags of Christmas, eh?" He grinned and looked at her expectantly.

"Will you stop saying that," she hissed. "You know perfectly well it's the Twelve Dates of Christmas."

"That's not what they're saying on Facebook," said Matt, shaking his head in mock disapproval.

"Well, then you'd better get some classier Facebook friends," said Kate.

The Twelve Dates of Christmas was the brainchild of the Lightning Strikes dating website: twelve dates, in twelve different locations in the weeks leading up to Christmas. It wasn't cheap, but the choice of date venues was varied, and the more Kate had read about them, the more she had to admit that it might actually be fun.

It wasn't something she would normally have bothered with. Kate was not the kind of woman who needed a man, but equally she thought she might quite like one. Her last long-term relationship had fizzled out some time ago, and it was mostly down to laziness that she hadn't dated much since.

She supposed she had the opportunity to meet people when she was in the city, but that would mean having to go out and socialize after work, and really she just wanted to come home and eat pie in front of the telly. And as for meeting someone new in Blexford, people generally moved here to start a family or retire. There was a distinct lack of eligible bachelors buying up property in the sleepy village.

It was Laura, Kate's best friend, who had pushed the idea of signing up. Laura was head custodian of Blexford Manor, and the Lightning Strikes team had rented out function rooms at the manor for some of their dates. Laura had been relentless.

"It's perfect!" she said. "You don't need to lift a finger. You pick the activities you'd like to do and they'll put you with someone who matches your profile."

"It's not really my thing," Kate had protested. "And it's a lot of money."

"But once you've signed up, all your drinks and food are included," said Laura. "Twelve dates! And you don't even have to go out looking for them."

Kate had to admit that her regime of pajamas, toast, and telly by seven thirty every night was not conducive to establishing a satisfying sex life. And as much as she wanted to meet someone, she was a bit too happy in her own company. Kate had become her own best date.

"You can't have it both ways," said Laura. "You can't whinge about wanting to meet someone and then look down your nose at dating websites. This is the modern way!"

"How would you know, Mrs. Married with Children?" said Kate.

"I read *Cosmo*," said Laura. "*Cosmo* doesn't lie."

"Isn't there a catalog groom service? Maybe I could just order one in," said Kate. "Or is that another bastion of sexual inequality we have yet to conquer?"

Laura pushed the laptop forcefully toward Kate.

"Would you do it?" asked Kate.

Laura threw her arms in the air in exasperation.

"Yes!" she said. "God forbid, if Ben died, this is exactly how I would find a new man." She paused. "Although Ben has decreed that should he die before me, I'm to have him stuffed and placed in the bedroom, pointing at the bed," she went on. "He says any man who can still perform under those circumstances will be truly worthy of me."

Laura smiled dreamily. Kate shuddered.

"I'll have a think and get back to you on it," said Kate.

"The time is now," said Laura. "I have real concerns that if you don't change your ways, you'll slip into a cheese-and-crackers coma and I'll find you collapsed, with your face wedged in the pickle jar."

And that was how Kate found herself signed up, paid up, and now dressed up for the first of her Twelve Dates of Christmas.

"So is it a blind date?" asked Matt.

"Not exactly," said Kate, as she flicked through her phone. "They put us together with people whose profiles match our own and then they send us a photo so we know who we're looking for."

"So no need to wear a pink carnation in your lapel, then?" said Matt.

Kate screwed her face up at him.

"His name is Richard. He's something to do with hedge funds, though I never know what that actually means," said Kate. "He's a divorced, devoted father of two."

"How do you know he's devoted?" asked Matt.

"Because he said so in his profile," said Kate.

"Oh, well then it *must* be true," said Matt. "Come on then, show us a photo of Wonderman."

Kate flipped her phone around and showed Matt a picture of a smiling dark-haired man. He was clean-shaven and broad-shouldered and covered in mud as he stood in full rugby regalia, with a rugby ball under one arm.

Matt sniffed.

"He looks like a murderer," he said.

Kate laughed.

"He does not."

"I bet he's got cauliflower ear," he said, squinting at the picture.

"Well, I don't care about that stuff," said Kate. "I just want to meet someone nice. Who's not a maniac. And who doesn't turn out to be a money launderer and/or a drug dealer."

"Your track record is terrible," said Matt.

"I prefer to think of it as atypically galvanizing," said Kate.

"That's just a fancy way of saying freakish and terror-inducing," Matt pointed out.

"It's been more interesting than yours."

"You didn't meet my wife," said Matt.

Kate laughed. Barely anyone than other than Evelyn had met Matt's ex-wife. His short-lived marriage was the stuff of Blexford legend: whispered stories abounded about his mysterious bride, everything from cult member to jewel thief to—somewhat unkindly—buried beneath the patio.

Kate was in the happy position of having two best friends: Laura had been a stalwart, a constant in Kate's life that neither distance nor brimful calendars could hamper. Her friendship with Matt had evolved rather differently; he had been her childhood best friend, her bête noire, and then her best friend again. There was a time when Kate had vowed she'd never step foot in the café, let alone be baking for it.

"I've got to go," said Kate. "I'm meeting Richard on the bench on the green and we're walking up to the manor together."

Kate hopped down off the stool and slipped her coat back on, wrapping her scarf twice around her neck. She called her good-byes to the Pear Tree regulars, who waved back, their mouths full of cake.

"Have fun!" called Matt above the noise. He began to sing loudly: "On the first date of Shagmas . . ." Kate turned back and poked her tongue out at him.

"Hey!" he shouted, as she pulled the door open and let in a waft of spiky cold air.

Kate looked back, her eyes narrowed as she waited for another sarcastic comment.

"Catch," he called, and threw over one of the tartan blankets they kept for weather-hardened customers who liked to sit outside. "That bench will be freezing."

"Thanks," said Kate; she caught the blanket and stepped out into the cold.

"I don't want you getting piles!" Matt shouted after her. Kate shook her head, smiling, and walked across the white-tipped grass to the bench.

· · · · ·

The green was a small patch of land in the middle of Blexford Village, around which sat the café, the Duke's Head pub, and a small but princely stocked corner shop run by the ever-busy Evelyn, all surrounded by trees and cottages.

Kate stretched the blanket out. She laid one half on the bench and the other across her lap and waited. A large fir tree liberally strewn with fairy lights stood proudly in the center of the green, and several smaller sets of lights hung from brackets above shop windows. Even the trees that were mere skeletons of their summer selves were dripping in lights.

A bright red Santa hat had been placed atop the wooden sign that pointed in the direction of Blexford Manor, and it was in that direction that a steady stream of cars and cabs now headed. Kate guessed they were going to the first of the Twelve Dates; Blexford didn't usually get much through traffic. A couple of Range Rovers struggled with the narrow road, and more than one car pulled over near the corner shop to check their satnavs.

Kate felt glad she'd come back here to live. At first she'd missed city life, but now she felt she had the best of both worlds. She worked on her fabric designs at her kitchen table, looking out onto the long garden and the vegetable patch beyond. And when they were ready for printing she took the train up to her London office and soaked in the bustle of the city.

It hadn't been an easy decision to pull up stakes and move back to Blexford, but when her mother ran off to Spain with Gerry, the estate agent who was supposed to be helping her parents downsize for their retirement, her father, Mac, was distraught.

It was a shock to everyone; one minute they were looking at cozy cottages and the next her mum had dropped everything and disappeared off to Spain.

For some reason Kate had assumed her mum would calm down as she got older, learn to appreciate the gem she had in Mac. But age hampered neither her mother's ambition nor her libido.

It was Matt who'd called Kate to alert her to Mac's deteriorating mental health. He'd popped round to the house and found Mac slumped across the table, drunk, an empty bottle of whiskey next to him.

That phone call was the first time she and Matt had spoken in nearly ten years. They'd had a monumental bust-up at university and severed all contact thereafter. Her father's illness forced a tenuous contact, whereby they communicated over text and occasional phone calls to discuss her dad's progress. But these were cold, overly polite exchanges.

During those first few months Matt kept an eye on Mac during the week and Kate came down on the weekends. It was easy enough to avoid each other. But it soon became clear that Mac's pain ran deeper than melancholy. Eventually Kate felt she needed to be with him more than just Friday night to Sunday. That was four years ago.

Luckily her colleagues at Liberty were very understanding; she could Skype for meetings and email photographs of mood boards and new designs straight to the office.

Laura had been delighted to have Kate back in Blexford, especially since she had just discovered she was pregnant with Mina.

It had always been Laura's intention to move back to Blexford after university. Laura had been in love with Blexford Manor since she was a child. She was a history nut. She'd gotten a part-time job there as soon as she was old enough, and the lord and lady of the manor had all but promised her a job after university.

Neither Kate nor Matt, on the other hand, had ever intended to move back to the sleepy village of their childhood. But life has a way of tipping the seemingly unimaginable on its head.

· · · · ·

A robin flew down and perched on the armrest of the bench. It looked at her expectantly with onyx eyes, its head moving jerkily as though powered by clockwork.

"I don't have anything for you, I'm afraid," said Kate.

The robin jerked its head from side to side.

"My date is late," she told the tiny bird.

The robin took off suddenly, splatting droppings on the concrete slab around the bench. Kate looked at it and nodded.

"Yes," she said. "My sentiments exactly."

The bird landed on the holly tree near the entrance to Potters Copse. Its red breast glowed against the dark spiky leaves. Kate slipped her phone out of her pocket and took a photo of it. Her brain whirred into action: stiff cotton, the voluptuous curve of a feather-down chest, the bottle-green leaves arching outward, taut and shiny, needle sharp. Kate's fingers twitched for the feeling of her paintbrush between them.

At eighteen, Kate had been so desperate to escape the quiet village that she'd forgotten how beautiful the changing seasons of the countryside were. When she moved back—travel savvy and city hardened—she found fresh inspiration in everything around her, and her fabric designs reflected a new style and confidence that delighted her managers and earned her a promotion.

Slowly her father recovered, and when he was well enough he rented a smaller cottage by the green. He wanted a fresh start and Kate needed a place to live, so she took over the mortgage on the old family home and they both rubbed along quite happily.

The line of cars wending their way through the village had dwindled. Most people would have taken the faster A-roads to the manor, rather than the bumpy Blexford road, with grass growing along its middle like a Mohawk haircut.

Kate checked her watch. It was ten to four. She'd been waiting for twenty minutes. They'd have to get a stride on if they were going to make it to the manor for four p.m. afternoon tea. Her stomach growled. Lightning Strikes didn't display their clients' phone numbers on their profiles, so Kate couldn't even call Richard to see if he was lost. She thought about the roaring fires in the gigantic stone fireplaces at the manor and shivered, tucking her hands under the blanket.

Blexford Manor was built in the seventeenth century, and Blexford Village had grown up around it. The estate had been passed down through the Blexford family and once upon a time was the chief employer in the area.

As with most stately homes of that ilk, social and economic changes brought about by the world wars led to a scaling down of both staff and finances. The big high-society parties dwindled, and the balls that had once been the talk of the county became a mere memory.

By the mid-1970s the manor could no longer survive on revenue brought in solely from its farmland, and it was decided that Blexford Manor would be opened to the public. These days Lord and Lady Blexford lived mostly in the east wing of the manor and shared their home with tourists and wedding parties, and, for the next month, groups of hopeful singles on a quest to find love.

The light was already beginning to fade. The sky toned down as though on a dimmer switch, from brilliant blue to washed-out denim to cold gray. Windows festooned with Christmas lights flickered into life as the sky darkened and parents and children returned home from the school run. The branches of the old fir creaked as the wind began to pick up. Kate pulled the blanket tighter around her and wished she'd worn an extra pair of socks inside her boots.

A hand rested gently on her shoulder and she jumped, turning expectantly. It was only Matt. He held out a lidded paper cup.

"Hot chocolate," he said. "You must be freezing."

"Thanks," said Kate. "I am. I think I've been stood up."

"Maybe he got lost? Or had a medical emergency?"

"Or maybe he just didn't like the look of me," Kate said flatly.

"Well, then he must be blind," said Matt. "Or an idiot. Or both."

Kate smiled sadly. She clasped her hands around the cup to warm them.

"Why don't you come inside?" Matt suggested. "There's this woman that supplies me with great caramel brownies. You can have one. On the house."

"I'll just give him ten more minutes," said Kate.

"You're not going to go all Miss Haversham on me, are you?" Matt wrapped his arms around himself against the cold. He'd come out without a coat, and his flannel plaid shirt wasn't doing much to keep the chill out. The blond hairs on his freckly arms stood to attention.

Kate laughed. "Not just yet," she said. "But if all twelve stand me up, I might start to get a complex."

Carla called across the green. "Matt! Phone for you, something about duck eggs!"

"Coming!" shouted Matt. "I'd better go. Don't be out here too long. I don't want to have to chip you off the bench in the morning."

Kate promised. "Thanks for the hot chocolate!" she called after him. He waved but didn't turn back.

Matt had inherited the Pear Tree from his mother. For twenty years she ran it as a bakery and tea rooms until she was killed one night, along with Matt's older sister, Corinna, in a car accident on their way back from the wholesalers. Matt was just seventeen.

Mac had helped with a lot of the practicalities when Matt's mum and Corinna were killed. He ferried Matt back and forth to the funeral directors, and he and Evelyn, who'd been Matt's mum's best friend, took on the lion's share of dealing with solicitors and banks. Kate recalled her mum being annoyed at the amount of time Mac and Evelyn were spending together.

Their deaths changed Matt. How could they not? There was overwhelming grief and behind that, an anger that seemed to bubble beneath his skin. And behind that, silently festering, a kind of insolence, a sense that he was owed happiness, that life owed him. At least that was how it had felt to Kate at the time. It was to be a death knell to their friendship; there is only a hairsbreadth between adoration and animosity and when the gap closes, it is rarely pretty.

Evelyn took Matt under her wing and into her home. She guarded his interests—business, pastoral, and educational—like a lioness. Evelyn ensured that his family home was taken care of, until such time as he was ready to live there again. And she rented the bakery to an older couple, the Harrisons, who ran it until they retired.

By that time Matt was working in Manchester for a large accountancy firm with even larger prospects—he took the financial reins back from Evelyn and rented the shop out to another family. Unfortunately, they ran the business into the ground and left one night, having stripped the shop of anything of worth and leaving a string of debts behind them.

Matt didn't come back to Blexford to rescue the business—he was too busy with his whirlwind bride and high-flying career—nor did he try to rent it out again. Instead, he paid the debtors, closed the place up, and left it. A shell, or a shrine. The Pear Tree Bakery was a forgotten story, like an old book that would never be read again but equally couldn't be parted with.

Kate's mother—who even then, it seemed, had a keen interest in real estate—had tried to get Evelyn to encourage Matt to sell the building and recoup some of his losses. Evelyn, however, felt quite certain, despite all indications to the contrary, that Matt would find his way back to Blexford one day.

The Pear Tree lay empty for a few years. The windows were boarded up, the garden became a wilderness, and what little remained inside the shop was left to fall into ruin.

Kate would sneak over the back wall sometimes when she came to Blexford to visit her parents. She'd wade through the long grass and peep in through gaps in the shuttered windows.

Kate had wanted to capture some spark of the happiness she'd felt in that place, her childhood playground. As if memories were tangible things that could be plucked like dandelion clocks to turn back time. But she could never quite reach them.

After his divorce, Matt returned to Blexford and his family

home—just as Evelyn had predicted: it turned out he wasn't the city slicker he'd imagined himself to be—and spent the next year completely renovating the Pear Tree and finally reopening it as the Pear Tree *Café*.

He'd asked Mac to help him with the renovations, and Mac was only too pleased to help. Despite Kate and Matt's falling-out, her dad had always had a soft spot for Matt. And Kate was far enough away for it not to bother her too much; she was busy forging her career in London and her relationship with Dan, and she rarely came back to Blexford.

When Kate came back to nurse her father, the Pear Tree Café was a thriving business, firmly rooted in the hearts of Blexford's residents.

Matt rented out the newly refurbished kitchen to Carla and her mother to use in the evenings for their ready-meal business and offered discounts on drinks to book clubs and committee meetings. In such a small, close-knit community, the café had become a hub around which the village revolved.

Kate used to avoid the café like a turd sandwich. She'd drive down into Great Blexley when she needed a coffee fix and cross roads or dive into bushes if she saw Matt coming her way. Kate spent a lot of time hiding in bushes those first few months. A small fortune spent on a swanky coffee machine for her house fixed the caffeine cravings; finding ways to avoid Matt in such a small village was not such an easy problem to solve.

· · · · ·

Kate shivered. Another ten minutes had passed and the daylight had all but gone. Ice crystals glistened on car roofs and the stars were already diamond points in the sky. There were no clouds. It was going to get very cold.

Her phone blipped:

Where are you?

It was a text from Laura.

With numb fingers, Kate texted back:

Been stood up! Am sitting on the bench on the
green, freezing my tits off. Think my bum has frozen
to the wood. May need to be surgically removed.

Laura replied immediately:

What a dick! He doesn't know what he's missing.
Would you like me to hire a hit man?

Kate chuckled to herself and sighed.

Richard wasn't coming. *Brilliant*, she thought. *I can't even get a date
when I pay for one.* Kate was disappointed but not, she decided, as
disappointed as she was to have missed out on the tiny patisserie cakes
that would have been served at the afternoon tea; she texted Laura to
ask for a doggy bag.

Come up here and get it! Laura texted. You never know, you
might cop off with someone else's date, hee hee

Can't, Kate texted back. Too cold. Frostbite setting in. Need
care package containing many many small cakes to aid recovery.

Roger that! xxx, texted Laura.

Kate stood up mechanically, her feet and hands stiff with cold; she
couldn't feel her toes at all. She folded the blanket and laid it on top of
the wood basket outside the café door, where Matt would find it. She

wasn't really in the mood to be gloated at, even if it was meant lightheartedly. She kept hold of the cup to recycle back at home and started walking.

Someone in the Duke's Head was playing the old beat-up piano. The tinkling melody wafted around the square and mixed with the wind chimes outside Evelyn's shop; it reminded Kate of Tchaikovsky's "Dance of the Sugar Plum Fairy." The grass was turning silver under the glimmer of the streetlamps. Blackbirds chattered as they settled down to roost in the holly bushes that ran along the farthest end of the village square by Potters Copse.

The heat would be on and Kate determined to get the wood burner going in the kitchen and light the fire in the lounge as well. She warmed herself with these thoughts as she hurried home.

She had one of Carla's lasagnas in the fridge, half a bottle of good red wine by the stove, and a healthy stash of chocolate in a tin above the coffee machine. She smiled to herself, her cold breath clouding out before her; she didn't get the guy but she had a veritable feast and the BBC's *Pride and Prejudice* waiting for her at home. And it didn't get much better than that.

· · · · ·

Kate shivered as the warm air washed over her. She pushed her front door closed behind her and shut out the frozen evening. The answering machine on the hall table blinked a red number 3 at her. Kate pressed play and went to get the fire going in the lounge. A loud disembodied voice boomed out from the machine.

"Hello? Hello? Katy-Boo, are you there?"

It was Kate's mum. The message clicked off and another began.

"Katy-Boo, it's Mum. I picked up the parcels at the weekend.

Nothing for Gerry, I noticed. I do wish you'd try to make an effort, darling."

Kate frowned as she scrunched newspaper up and tucked it underneath the kindling. *Make an effort!* She snorted to herself, striking a match and dropping it into the paper nest. *He's lucky I wrote his name in the card.*

Gerry wasn't so bad, Kate supposed. He always made an effort when they visited—which wasn't very often. They had a studio flat in Chiswick, where they would hold court when in England—and Kate was always perfectly amiable toward him. But she wasn't quite ready to buy him Christmas gifts yet.

She'd sent a Christmas package to her mother three weeks ago to make sure it reached her in time. In it she had wrapped the latest release by her mum's favorite author, some perfumed body lotion from Elizabeth Arden that her mum had been dropping hints about since October, and a pair of slouchy knitted bed socks and matching scarf—she'd commissioned Petula to knit them for her—in purple and mint-green stripes. Even Spain got chilly in December, she had reasoned. And at the last moment, she'd bought a voucher for a slap-up meal for two in one of the restaurants on the marina, as a nod in Gerry's direction.

The little flames began to catch, spitting and popping as they grew in confidence. The machine beeped the end of the message and another one began.

"Kate Amelia Turner, call me! I have news! You'll never guess it! Call me on my mobile."

Kate sighed. She hoped her mother hadn't gotten herself into anything stupid; she had a habit of jumping in with both feet before seeing how deep the water was. Kate pressed her finger to her mum's phone number. Her mum answered after three rings.

"Katy-BooBoo, my darling!" Her mum's voice rang out from the speaker, shrill and excitable; she had a kind of frenetic energy, like a wild pony.

Kate had often wondered how her parents ever came to be married. Her mum was gregarious. She liked parties and bubbly and had two volumes: loud and louder. By contrast, her dad—Mac, short for Mackenzie, which he hated—was reserved. He liked Sudoku and tea and avoided parties like the plague.

"How are you, my sweet, sweet girl?" her mum cooed.

"I'm fine, Mum," said Kate. "How are you?"

Her mum laughed loudly. She had the laugh of a 1920s heiress hosting a soiree; it was raucous yet extraordinarily posh.

"Darling, you won't believe where I am!" said her mum.

"Not Spain?" said Kate.

It occurred to her that they might have come back to England for Christmas. That would make life awkward. Thus far Kate had always been spared the uncomfortable *picking a parent to spend Christmas with* issue.

"Not even close!" said her mum. "We're in Barbados!" Her voice had risen to a screech.

Kate moved the phone away from her ear.

"Can you believe it?" her mum went on. "Barbados for Christmas!"

Kate could believe it. She felt a prickle of guilt at the relief she felt.

"How did that come about?" Kate asked.

"Well," said her mum. "I sold a yacht for a gentleman last week and he said he had another one he's been thinking of selling, moored out in Barbados. Anyway, he showed me some photographs and I said Barbados was a bit out of our remit. And before I knew what was happening, he'd spoken to Serge—you remember Serge, don't you, darling? My boss? Took a shine to you when you came over last year. You could do a lot worse than Serge, Katy-Boo, age is just a number, you know, and men can go on producing viable sperm until the day they die . . ."

"Mum!" said Kate.

"Hmm? Where was I?" asked her mum.

"The boatman had spoken to Serge," Kate prompted.

"Oh, yes," said her mum. "So he spoke to Serge and I was personally commissioned to come out here and value it. We're staying on it to get a feel for it!"

"Wow," said Kate. "That's amazing. I bet Gerry was pleased."

"He's over the moon, darling. A free holiday! He hasn't worn trousers since we landed."

This was more information than Kate needed. She winced as a vision of Gerry in Speedos flashed before her eyes.

Gerry was in his midsixties, tall with terra-cotta skin and thick gray hair, immaculately styled like Barbie's plastic boyfriend, Ken. In Gerry it seemed her mother had finally met her match. He was dynamic, he always had a deal on the table, and he'd always spent the commission before it hit the bank.

Her mum's affairs had always been with men of Gerry's ilk, but for one reason or another his predecessors had always come up short; the bubbly was cheap and the fast cars were rentals. Her mum wasn't stupid; she wasn't going to throw in all her chips for someone who, beyond the dinner jacket, could only offer her the same life she already had with Mac. As soon as they invited her back to their three-bedroom duplex in Deptford, her ardor chilled quicker than the fake champagne on ice.

An outsider might assume that her parents' marriage had been unhappy, but in truth, it wasn't; unconventional, certainly, but not altogether unhappy.

Her dad knew about her mum's *dalliances*—not the details, of course, it was all very discreet—but somehow he lived with them on the understanding that she would always come home to him at the end of the night.

And her mum had needed Mac like a compass, or a buoy, to stop her from drifting into danger. His gravitational pull kept her centered and she was always happy to return to the safety of his orbit after a wandering. It was a state of denial that had suited them both, until Gerry cruised into their lives.

"The nights are so balmy, we've been sleeping on the balcony, completely naked!" said her mum. "There's a salon in the bay and a sweet girl gave me a Brazilian wax. Have you tried it, darling? It's so much cooler *down there!*"

Kate shook her head to try to erase the image and changed the subject.

"So when will you be back?" she asked.

"We fly back to Spain on the twenty-ninth," said her mum. "Why don't you come over and spend New Year's with us? You'd love it."

"Maybe next year," said Kate.

She could hear her mother pouting on the other end of the line.

"Oh, tut-tut, darling, you always say that!" said her mum. "What are you waiting for? I could set you up with a hundred different men out here. It's not much to ask that I have grandchildren before I'm too old to pick them up!"

"Mum!" said Kate.

"I'm just saying," she said. "None of us are getting any younger . . ."

"Mum!"

"Okay, okay," said her mum. "How's Mac?"

"He's fine," said Kate. "He's great, actually."

Kate wished she had something to say about her dad that would impress her mum, or make her think she might be missing out; she doubted his sprout trees, tall as they were, would do the trick.

Mac was a quiet doer. He'd retired from the civil service but kept his hand in on a consultancy basis. He grew things and he fixed things. He took long walks in the country and made notes for the RSPB on the birds that visited his handmade bird tables and feeders. These were things Kate loved about her dad, but they were not enough to light her mum's touch paper. And there, Kate supposed, was the problem; her mum had always been the rocket to her dad's Roman candle.

Kate was an absolute concoction of her parents. She had inherited her mum's drive to succeed and her dad's quiet determination. Her code of ethics and love of nature were all her dad, but the part of her that thrilled at a challenge was entirely her mum. And, though she didn't like to admit it, perhaps some of her reluctance to commit to relationships was congenital from her mother's side too.

Kate moved to the kitchen, still with the phone at her ear, and stoked the wood burner.

"Is he seeing anyone at the moment?" her mum asked.

"What do you care?" said Kate. It came out harsher than she had meant it to.

Her mum *tsked*.

"Tetchy!" she said. "You always were a daddy's girl."

"I just don't know why you're so interested," said Kate. "It makes no difference to you whether he is or he isn't."

"I want him to be happy," said her mum.

"Well, he *is* happy," Kate said. "So, what will you be having for your Barbadian Christmas dinner?" She thought it wise to change the subject.

"We're keeping it traditional, darling," her mum told her. "We've booked into a five-star hotel in the bay for dinner."

"Only five-star?"

"Don't be glib, darling," said her mum. "It's an unattractive quality in a person."

Kate pulled the stopper out of the wine bottle and poured herself a full glass. She took a gulp.

"I sent your Christmas parcel before we left," said her mum. "Let me know when you've got it."

"Will do." Kate placed her dinner in the microwave and started the timer.

"I'll be off now, darling," said her mum. "Gerry's making cocktails. Send my love to everyone. Love you, Katy-Boo!"

"I love you too, Mum."

The call ended as the doorbell rang. Kate answered it with her glass of wine in hand. It was Laura, holding a cardboard cake box and grinning.

"One emergency cake delivery."

"I love you," said Kate.

"I know." Laura's grin widened.

"You coming in?"

"I can't," said Laura. "Ben's mum's got the kids. She'll be about ready to hit the gin by now."

"Fair enough. How was it, anyway?"

"It was really busy, a great atmosphere. I wish you'd have come up."

"I didn't really fancy being the only person on a mass date without a date," said Kate.

"Oh, who needs that dick anyway," Laura scoffed.

"His name was Richard."

"He'll always be a dick to me," said Laura.

Kate waved Laura off, after pointing and laughing as she eighteen-point-turned her car in the narrow street and closed the front door on the cold evening.

The smell of lasagna filled the kitchen. Kate lifted the lid on the cake box. Ten beautifully crafted patisserie cakes lay side by side like tiny works of edible art. She smiled to herself as she pulled the curtains closed in the sitting room and queued up the BBC.

"Mr. Darcy, I'm coming to get you," she said.

·····

Christmas Cookery and Weeping Vegans

Two mornings later, the postman knocked, just as Kate was cleaning her brushes, after color-washing her early-morning sketches.

The sun rose a little before eight a.m. in December. Kate enjoyed the transformation of the landscape, as the winter sun crept across the fields in a voile of pale gold, chasing away the last vestiges of misty dawn; ice-crystalline blades of grass bent at the knees as the sun's scant warmth whittled the frost.

It was an enchanted time of day and, when she could, Kate made sure she was out with camera and sketchbook to catch it.

"Looks like a package from your mum," said Joe the postman.

"Looks like it," said Kate.

"How's she getting on these days?"

"Oh, you know," said Kate. "Causing a Spanish whirlwind."

"She's a character, all right," Joe said. And then: "Bummer about you getting stood up."

"Yes," Kate echoed. "Bummer."

"Just changed his mind, did he?" Joe went on. "Didn't like the look of you, maybe?"

"Maybe." She tugged the package out of Joe's hands a little more roughly than was necessary.

Kate made herself a coffee and opened the package. There had been an unfortunate incident three years ago, with a gift that—unbeknown to Kate—was a wheel of Cabrales cheese. After two weeks festering under the Christmas tree, in the warmth of the open fire, the smell was so pungent, Kate had begun to wonder if the builders had bricked a body up in the walls of her new kitchen extension.

A similar incident the following year with a selection of Spanish deli meats had taught Kate never to save her mother's gifts until Christmas Day.

She needn't have worried this year. The only edibles were the chocolate kind: a bar with cacao nibs and almond shards, a bag of chocolate-coated almonds, and a tin of drinking chocolate, all of which made Kate salivate.

As well as these, there were two self-help books: *Find Love before You're Forty* and *Is That My Body-Clock Ticking?*

Thank you, Mother, thought Kate. Beneath these was a bottle of Chanel perfume wrapped in what could only be described as porn-star lingerie: a push-up bra with see-through fabric where her nipples would be, and a pair of matching crotchless panties.

Kate texted her mum:

Thanks for the presents. Interesting underwear!

· · · · ·

"Don't be disheartened just because one wholly let you down." Laura's voice crackled through the phone loudspeaker.

"I'm not," Kate assured her. "I'm just going to finish off these mince pies for Matt and then I'll get ready."

"I still don't know why you didn't just come up anyway; the banqueting hall looked amazing, even if I do say so myself," said Laura. "What are you wearing?"

"What, now?" Kate asked. "Are you being pervy?"

"No, dumb-arse," said Laura. "For the date!"

Kate dusted the rolling pin with icing sugar and began to roll out the pastry.

"Jeans and that sequined jumper I bought when I was out with you."

"Jeans!" exclaimed Laura.

"It's a couples' cooking night, not a cocktail party, Laura."

"Okay, okay. So who are you coupled with tonight?"

Kate pressed the fluted cutter in the pastry and gently pressed the bases into the muffin tin.

"His name's Michael. He's a vegan. Divorced. No children. Works for an art gallery in Soho," said Kate, reeling off the scant details sent to her by the dating agency.

"Ooh, that sounds promising," cooed Laura. "What does he look like?"

Kate dusted her hands off and picked up her phone, flicking through her emails until she found the one she wanted.

"Blond hair, kinda foppish, cute smile, crinkles around his eyes," she said. "I don't know why I let you talk me into this; it feels like I'm shopping from a man catalog."

"Because you need a little push," said Laura. "You haven't seen anyone properly since Dan. I'm not saying you're going to meet Mr. Right at these things, but it'll help you to get back into dating again. And anyway, who's to say that the man of your dreams won't be at one of these events? It could be a Christmas miracle."

Laura and Kate had been friends since primary school. They went to university together and shared a house for three years, until Kate went off to go traveling and Laura came back to Blexford to take up her position as trainee curator at Blexford Manor and marry her childhood sweetheart, Ben.

Kate laid pastry stars onto the mincemeat, brushed them with milk, sprinkled them liberally with granulated sugar, and put them in the oven to bake. The first batch were cooling on a wire rack and the whole house smelled of citrus and spice. She got cleaned up and changed while they cooked; she would have to go on her date smelling of mince pies, but there were worse things to smell of.

She boxed up the cooled pies and put the hot ones on the rack. While she waited for them to cool, she leafed through some of the brightly colored sketches that were scattered over the battered kitchen table. She'd emailed photographs of her latest designs to the printers and would pick up the resulting test fabrics from her London office—a dainty spring design of nodding daffodils and cerulean hyacinths—when they were ready.

She scooped the papers into a rough pile and rinsed out her brushes and the jam jar they'd been sitting in. Then she boxed up the last of the mince pies, zhooshed her hair quickly in the mirror, and set off for the café.

The Pear Tree Café was so named because of the giant pear tree in the garden. It wasn't the only fruit tree in the garden, but it dwarfed the plum, cherry, and apple trees and made a mockery of the gooseberry bush.

Kate and Matt used to spend their summer holidays messing about in the garden, climbing the trees—when no one was watching to tell them not to—and making tents out of broken chairs and old curtains. Laura's parents weren't together, and so during the holidays she would go to her dad's house in France.

Kate's parents worked in the city, but her mum worked a three-day week during school holidays. With Matt's mum working full time in the bakery and tearooms, it made sense for them to pool their childcare resources.

On the days when Kate's mum was home, she would take them to the beach or rambling, or they'd spend the day in Fitzwilliam Park. And the rest of the time, Kate and Matt would stay at the bakery, with as much barley water and buns as they could manage from the tearooms at the front of the shop and free rein of the large garden at the back of the kitchen.

Come autumn, there were more pears than any one family could consume, even with Matt's mum preserving them in brandy and selling them in the shop or making them into jam. So she would invite the villagers into the garden for a "pick your own" party. It became a tradition. Blexford's very own harvest festival. And year after year it got bigger and bigger until it was an event in the village calendar; gazebos would be set up on the green for an American-style supper after the great pear harvest.

Patrick, from Old Blexford Farm, used to concoct a terrifying pear wine with his spoils. He'd dish it out at the Christmas caroling, hot and infused with cinnamon, cloves, and vanilla, guaranteed to keep you warm and give you a mild case of amnesia. Corinna would just happen to pass by with a tray of steaming glasses and leave them for her kid brother and his mates: the then fifteen-year-old Kate, Matt, Laura, and Ben, who would get merrily sozzled on the bench on the green.

When Matt's mum and sister died, the pear parties stopped. Some people suggested they should continue: a good way to keep their memory alive. But Matt couldn't face it; it was too soon, too raw, and nobody was going to argue with an orphan, especially one with Evelyn in his corner.

The Harrisons used to pile the windfalls into baskets and set them outside the front of the shop for people to help themselves. But the people after them didn't bother, and once the place was boarded up, the pears would rot where they fell.

Kate had suggested to Matt that maybe he could consider inviting people back into the garden in autumn to pick the pears. It wouldn't have to be a party, just a community get-together. So far, he'd been reluctant.

He had though, buckled under Kate's persistence and made good on the garden the year before last. With her dad's help, Patrick's cultivator, and Barry's muscle (Barry was landlord at the Duke's Head), the five of them had stripped the wilderness back to its former glory.

They laid new turf and gave the fruit trees a mercy prune, and Evelyn helped shape and fill new flower beds. At the far end of the garden Kate's dad built raised beds using the old boards that had been at the windows and then were left piled in the coal cellar. And Matt filled them with vegetables, herbs, and soft fruits.

The kitchen used to fill the whole back half of the building. But when Matt renovated the shop, he made the kitchen smaller and put in new customer toilets—previously the only toilet cubicle was the one in the garden next to the coal cellar—and a corridor that led from the café through to the garden.

Matt furnished the nearest end of the garden with sturdy wooden chairs and tables for customers. It was the first time the garden had been used for anything other than Matt and Kate's playground. It was a beautiful space, popular year-round, and increased Matt's seating capacity by almost double.

It was closing time when Kate arrived at the café. The music was turned down low and some of the chairs were already upturned on the tables, ready for the floor to be mopped.

A couple of die-hard customers skulked in the corner on easy chairs: always the last to leave, savoring the dregs of their coffees, determined to finish their newspapers before Matt finally put out the lights and turfed them out. They nodded at Kate over the tops of their glasses.

Louder music came from the kitchen along with the smell of something meaty being cooked in red wine. Carla and her mum were cooking up a storm. Kate's stomach growled and she made a mental note to check Evelyn's freezer to pick up one of whatever they were making back there.

Petula waved from the back of the café. Three tables were covered in polka-dot oilcloth covers and spread all over with bits of paper, craft knives, and all the glittery detritus left from Petula's handmade-card-making class.

Petula's cottage was far too small to fit her craft sessions in and so Matt let her use the café. It suited them both; Petula got the space she needed and Matt made money on all the coffees and cakes her class purchased while they crafted.

From now until Christmas the group would be making all manner of cards, decorative parcel labels, and place settings. Petula was one of the founding members of the Blexford Knitting Sex Kittens; her specialty was Christmas jumpers and Kate was her muse, a role that Kate, as a Christmas jumper enthusiast, was happy to fill. Petula was a multiskilled Sex Kitten; she could embroider and crochet and had been making her own greeting cards long before it was considered trendy. She also worked part time in the Pear Tree.

"Hello, darling!" said Petula. "I was hoping to see you. I was wondering if you'd help me with one of my Christmas craft sessions. I think your design expertise would be a real boon."

"I'd love to," said Kate. "When were you thinking?"

"I've got a class next Tuesday afternoon," said Petula. "I want to do natural Christmas cards and table settings using fresh and dried foliage."

"Great," said Kate. "Count me in."

"Oh, super," said Petula. "Oh, and Kate darling, I heard you got stood up by your first date. Don't let that put you off. Onward and upward!"

Petula smiled and went back to clearing up from her class.

Matt came out from the kitchen. He smiled when he saw Kate and smiled wider when he saw the boxes full of mince pies.

"Hello, you," said Matt. "Are those for me or are you just really hungry?"

Kate screwed her face up at him.

"As it happens, I *am* hungry," said Kate. "But I will remedy this by cooking a meal with my hot dinner date."

"Does he know you're really bossy in the kitchen?" asked Matt.

"I'm not bossy, I am assertive," said Kate. "And besides, I'm only like that with you because you're so slack."

"I prefer *relaxed*," said Matt.

"Slack," said Kate.

"My God!" said Petula from the other end of the café. "You two have been bickering like this since you could talk."

One of the die-hards stifled a guffaw from behind his newspaper.

Simultaneously Matt and Kate pointed to each other and said:

"She started it!" "He started it!"

Matt beamed and pulled a large plate with Christmas trees painted all around the edge from a stack above the sink. Kate helped him pile the pies onto the plate, and Matt covered them with the dome of a bell jar, ready for the next day.

Matt sang while they worked, "On the second date of Shagmas my true love gave to me, a bad case of VD."

Kate thumped him.

"I'll bet you spent all day thinking that up, didn't you," she said.

Matt grinned. "Not *all* day."

"I'm impressed that you think I'll take twelve lovers between now and Christmas."

"Well, you don't have to sleep with *all* of them."

"I don't *have* to sleep with *any* of them," said Kate. "But I might want to."

"Kate," said Matt. "Some of the men who sign up for these kinds of things aren't very nice."

"Matt," said Kate. "I'm a big girl. I've been around the block a few times. You don't need to be signed up at a dating agency to meet not-very-nice men."

Matt huffed. "I don't know why you feel the need to join a dating agency anyway."

"I didn't feel the need. *Laura* felt that I felt I should feel the need." Kate frowned as she mentally considered the sense of her sentence. "And anyway," she continued. "It's good to meet new people. And I would like to . . . you know . . . settle down maybe."

"I don't want to cast aspersions on your character, Kate," said Matt. "But you've never exactly been short of men."

"Yeah, but I can't seem to make any of them stick!"

"You mean they don't make the grade."

"I see nothing wrong with being choosy," said Kate.

"What about that James bloke? I liked him."

"Yes, Matt, but it's not really about whether *you* like them or not that matters, is it?"

"Or Harry!" said Matt. "Harry was great."

"Maybe you should have gone out with him then," said Kate. "I don't know." She sighed and began applying berry-red lipstick in the mirror above the fireplace. "Since Dan there hasn't really been anyone that's . . ."

"Rocked your world?" Matt finished for her.

"Exactly."

"You're always saying you don't need a man."

"I don't," said Kate. "I just think it would be nice to meet someone I could share my life with. Laura's got Ben. You've got Sarah . . ."

"Well, it's only been a couple of months," said Matt hastily. "We're not exactly ready for marriage."

"But you've got someone to kiss under the mistletoe," said Kate wistfully.

"If that's all it takes to make you happy, I'm sure I could rustle up one or two customers to give you a snog under the old love branches."

"That's exactly my point! I'm tired of *rustling up* men. I've had my fill of sprinters, I'm looking for someone who can go the distance."

"You're looking for a marathon runner?"

"Metaphorically speaking, yes."

"Come on, then, show me tonight's date."

Kate brought the picture up on her phone. Matt looked at it and frowned.

"Private school mummy's boy," he announced dryly. "I don't think he'll make the cut."

Kate let out an exasperated breath.

"I knew you'd say that," she said. "You took one look at his hair and made a judgment. It just so happens he works in an art gallery."

"Did he go to private school?"

Kate scrolled down Michael's profile. He had. Damn. "Yes," she admitted.

"I rest my case."

. . . . .

The date was being held in a cookery school. Kate parked her car and crunched along the gravel drive and through a stone archway decorated with ivy and twinkling fairy lights. She was met at the door by a Lightning Strikes rep who took her name and told her to head for workbench five.

The walls were hung with more swags of ivy and holly. A Christmas tree that must have been twelve feet high stood in one corner, the fairy at the top almost lost in the vast ceiling. The room was filled with workbenches, each with its own cooktop and oven beneath. Around the edges of the room were more worktops with food mixers and electric hand whisks, and hundreds of hooks with utensils swinging from them.

Two gigantic saucepans steamed at the back of the room and filled the place with the heady scents of mulled wine and cinnamon. Out of one, a rosy-cheeked woman ladled hot wine into glass-handled jars, and a similarly flustered-looking man did the same with the saucepan labeled *nonalcoholic*. Kate got herself a jar of the latter and took her place by bench five. She sincerely hoped her date turned up tonight.

All the benches faced toward a huge expanse of glass at the front, which lent a view of a generous walled kitchen garden, lit by floodlights. Just as the noise of excitable amateur chefs was becoming unbearable, a stream of youths in white chef tunics glided in carrying wicker baskets laden with vegetables and meats and fish. A rotund ruddy-faced woman waddled in with an air of authority, and the room hushed.

Kate felt someone brush her arm. She turned to see her very handsome date smiling at her, and she smiled back far too broadly.

"I'm Michael," he whispered as the head chef boomed instructions from the front of the room. "And you must be Kate."

He held out his hand and she shook it, still smiling. *This could be something,* she thought. *This could actually be something.* And her stomach gave a little lurch of excitement.

For obvious reasons Kate and Michael cooked a vegetable dish. *Kate and Michael, Michael and Kate.* She ran their names together around in her head, and she liked the way they sounded. *Oh, hi! This is Michael; we fell in love over a vegetable tagine.* She chided herself for being such a schoolgirl. But it was hard not to be, when you were in a classroom with the best-looking boy in the school.

Michael was very handy in the kitchen as it turned out, and they worked well together, chatting and laughing as they followed the extensive list of instructions. They were making a Thai vegetable curry—making the fragrant curry paste from scratch—with sticky coconut rice.

"If you don't mind me saying," said Kate as she stirred the bubbling pot of pale red sauce, "you don't seem like the sort of person who would need all this to meet someone." She gestured around the room with her free arm.

Michael carefully dropped handfuls of chopped baby corns and green beans into the thin but potent liquor. He smiled.

"I could say the same about you," he said.

"But it's different for me," said Kate. "I live in a tiny village; we don't exactly have a steady stream of attractive single men passing through. You work in an art gallery in the city."

"A bigger pool doesn't necessarily mean a better swim," said Michael.

He looked down at Kate and gave her a cheeky half smile, and she felt her cheeks—already glowing from the steamy pot—redden.

With their meals cooked, the couples plated their spoils and headed through to a candlelit converted barn to eat. It was cooler there, and Kate was glad of it. The seating was informal; two large banqueting tables ran the length of the barn with benches on either side.

Kate and Michael—she still loved how that sounded—sat opposite each other and began to eat. Invariably as their comfort with each other grew, the lighthearted conversation moved on to more serious topics.

Their backgrounds were very different, but their politics were the same. He made no bones about the fact that he had "father issues" owing to his dad's controlling nature, and Kate found herself confiding in him that her mother's affair with the estate agent had been far from her first indiscretion.

"I mean, no one likes to admit that their mother was a bit of a slapper," said Kate. "But unfortunately, my mother was a bit of a slapper."

Michael laughed.

"I genuinely think that my mother would have been much happier if she had had affairs," said Michael. "Instead of being a begrudging martyr."

"Why do people stay together when they're clearly so unhappy?" Kate asked. "It makes no sense."

"To save face?" suggested Michael.

"Maybe in the 1940s," said Kate. "But not now, surely?"

"In some social circles it would still cause a scandal," Michael said in such a knowing way that Kate determined to look his family up in Laura's high-society gossip magazines.

"So," said Kate as she poured them each another glass of water from the carafe. "The big question is, are our parents' inadequacies the reason we find ourselves midthirties and still single?" And she smiled broadly at what she thought was quite a humorous suggestion.

Michael didn't smile. He looked down at his plate and gently rested his cutlery across it. A curtain of dirty-blond hair fell over his eyes, but Kate could see by the way he bit his lip that he was fighting back tears.

Kate didn't know what to do. The noise in the barn burst through the conversational cocoon she'd been wrapped in, and she was suddenly very aware of people all around her laughing and shouting and preening at their dates, or the dates of others in some cases, and of her and Michael's awkward silence in the middle of it all.

"I'm so sorry," said Kate. "I didn't mean to upset you. I was just trying to be funny."

Michael sniffed. Kate handed him her napkin and he dabbed his eyes and wiped his nose.

"It's not you," he said. "It's just." He sniffed again. "It's just, that's exactly why I am single. When I got together with Morgan I was trying to piss my dad off. She was everything he didn't approve of. But then I fell in love with her. Real love. And then one night at a dinner party someone let slip the reason I'd first asked her out. And. And."

Michael took a moment to compose himself.

"And she left me!" he hiccupped.

His composure went out the window, along with Kate's hopes for a second date. Michael broke down in floods of tears: shoulder-shuddering, snot-bubbling, body-jerking tears that had probably bottled up over years of private schooling and stiff-upper-lip enforcement.

People began to stare. Michael's sobs became louder, accompanied every minute or so by a howling that would've driven wolves back to their dens. He'd blown his nose on his and Kate's napkins. The woman across from her—clearly a mother—handed Kate a packet of pocket tissues and gave her a sympathetic look. Kate smiled at her gratefully and mouthed, *Thank you!* Then she opened the pack and handed one to Michael.

Michael banged his fists up and down on the table, shrieking, *"Why! Why! Why!"* in time with every thud. *"Why, in God's name, WWWWWHHHYYY!"*

People began sliding surreptitiously along the bench, away from Kate and Michael, until there was a distinct gap around them. Kate wondered if it would be insensitive to eat her curry while consoling her date; she decided it probably would be. Soon the dinner plates were replaced with dessert dishes and Kate's mouth watered at the smell of brandy sauce rising up from her sticky Christmas pudding.

"Maybe it's not too late?" Kate asked. "Perhaps there is a way you two could be reconciled."

"HOW?" Michael groaned. "TELL ME HOOOOOWW-WWW!"

He threw his arms up into the air and wailed at the vaulted ceiling. People began to take their puddings through to the bar area. Michael seemed unaware of the scene he was causing.

Eventually he wore himself out. The Lightning Strikes team were clearing up around them. Michael's eyes were red-rimmed and blood-shot. He'd used an entire packet of tissues.

When he was calm enough and Kate was satisfied that he wasn't likely to start howling again, she began to reason with him.

"Have you actually tried calling her to apologize?" Kate asked.

"What's the use?" asked Michael. His lip wobbled.

"But have you?" Kate pressed.

"She said she never wanted to see me again." Michael hiccupped.

"So you haven't," said Kate.

"I'm not going to beg!" said Michael petulantly.

"Nobody said anything about begging," Kate told him. "But an apology is definitely in order."

A long pep talk ensued and finally, in the car park—because the cookery school had closed and everyone had gone home—Kate persuaded Michael to swallow his pride and call Morgan.

"You literally have nothing to lose," said Kate as Michael scrolled down to Morgan's number.

Kate sat with him on the steps to the school. Morgan answered on the second ring and Michael gripped Kate's hand as he apologized to Morgan over and over in a hundred different ways.

Morgan's responses were difficult to make out above all the sobbing, but the words *I love you!* tumbled out over and again from both of them and drifted off into the black December sky.

Kate wouldn't be going home with Michael tonight, or any other night for that matter, but she couldn't help feeling a certain rosy glow as she waved him good-bye. *This must be what guardian angels feel like*, she mused.

Her phone blipped as she got into her car. It was a text from her mum.

You're welcome, darling! I thought they might come in handy for your 12 dates. I've seen your underwear, you could use your knickers to catch apples with. What you want to be catching in them is a man, my dear. Love you xxx

"I'm trying, Mum. Believe me," Kate said out loud. "I'm trying."

· · · · ·

By the time Kate reached Blexford the roads glistened with ice. It was late. As she reached the green she saw Matt and Sarah leave the Duke's Head, arms wrapped around each other's backs. The lights in the pub went out and the couple were illuminated only by the moon and the thick white frost.

Kate pulled into a small spot next to some hedges and shut off the engine. Matt would recognize her car as she drove past, and she would be obliged to stop and make small talk, and he would ask how her date had gone, and although she knew it would be funny tomorrow, somehow she just wasn't in the mood to tell the tale right then.

She watched them amble along together, zigzagging in that way you do when you walk with your arms around each other after a couple of glasses of wine. The finest of snowflakes began to flurry down as if just for them, and they held their gloved hands out to catch them. Sarah rested her head on Matt's shoulder and he kissed the top of her head, and Kate's chest ached for a love like theirs.

· · · · ·

Ice Skating and Perfect Misses

The next couple of days were a flurry of activity, and Kate was happy to be immersed in things that kept her mind from wandering to matters of the heart, though as a single woman in her thirties, she brought out the matchmaker in every coupled person she knew.

The morning after her date with Michael, Kate caught the early train to London, with her portfolio and an overnight bag. It was her office Christmas meal that evening and she was going to crash at her friend Josie's place in the city.

When Kate arrived at her desk, having fought her way through the thronging Liberty hallways, she found a brown paper package waiting for her. She tore it open and pulled out the first of her spring samples.

It was a heavy jacquard material. Kate's daffodils and hyacinths were woven into the fabric, giving it a raised texture that felt both luxurious and sturdy. The egg-yolk yellows and bright blues studded with peridot-green leaves sang spring, when all around the office shrieked deep midwinter.

Finding her designs printed on a fabric, out of which like-minded strangers would create clothes or soft furnishings, never ceased to thrill Kate; it was like being part of a special club.

A part of her felt it was too good to be true, as if at any moment her colleagues would discover she was a fraud; after all, what did she really do? Paint flowers and draw patterns; nature came up with the goods and she shamelessly plagiarized it with her brushes and pens.

"You coming out tonight, Kate?" asked Mel, breaking Kate's reverie.

Mel was a genius with pattern and color; where Kate's designs were dainty and ditzy, Mel's were bold with a fluidity that danced out of the canvas.

"Yes," said Kate. "I'll be there."

"So will Pete," said Mel. She winked and her face cracked into a wide-toothed smile.

Kate slapped her forehead.

"I'd forgotten about Pete," she said.

Kate had indulged in some festive snogging with Pete from accounting at last year's Christmas do. Nothing had ever come of it, it was just one of those *party things*, but she'd had a hard time living it down.

"He's still single," sang Mel.

Mel was neither the first nor the last person to mention Pete to Kate that day. And it was while hiding from Pete that evening that Kate found herself sat on the drafty back stairs of a karaoke club, talking to Laura on the phone.

"So he cried all the way through dinner?" Laura shrieked with laughter.

"All the way through," said Kate.

"Dammit," said Laura. "I had high hopes for him."

"He was lovely," said Kate. "But his heart was well and truly taken."

"Was the dinner good at least?"

"I don't know!" said Kate. "I couldn't exactly chow down while Michael was in such a state; it seemed disrespectful of his angst. I was starving by the time I got home. I hoovered up half a loaf of cheese on toast in bed."

"Romantic, though." Laura sighed. "A man in touch with his emotions. Ben only cries at the football. Oh, and when Arnie dies in *Terminator 2*."

"I don't think I've ever induced a man to cry over the loss of me," said Kate.

"How would you know?" said Laura. "You might have left a string of weeping men behind you."

Kate shivered. The draft in the stairwell was becoming an icy breeze. "I've got to go," she said. "My body's going stiff."

"Get Pete to warm you up!" said Laura.

"That won't be happening again," said Kate.

"Couldn't you just give him a snog to pass the time?"

"Laura!"

"What?" said Laura. "Warble out a couple of Bonnie Tyler numbers, play a bit of tonsil hockey with Pete, and then get an early night."

Kate left the karaoke bar after a spectacular rendition of "Proud Mary" and managed not to snog Pete, although he seemed to be underneath mistletoe every time she saw him.

The taxi pulled up outside Josie's building and even from the ground Kate could see the orange flickering glow of candlelight at Josie's windows.

Josie was the first proper friend Kate had made in London, when she'd come back from traveling. Kate had found a job in a little greasy-spoon café in Camden, the wages from which just covered the rent on the tiny studio apartment above it.

Kate had earned her living making mugs of tea and cooking fry-ups and spent her evenings upstairs, working on her linocut designs. She bought packs of plain fabric tote bags at wholesale and printed her designs onto them.

Kate got to know the regular customers at the café, in particular Josie. Josie had a stall in the market, where she sold Indian print scarves, tie-dye skirts, and velvet jackets and smelled permanently of smoky incense.

Josie had offered to sell some of Kate's tote bags in her stall. They sold well and, soon, with Josie's encouragement, Kate began to paint her designs directly onto fabric: patterns and colors inspired by her travels, on silk scarves and squares mounted onto stiff card for greeting cards, to be sold alongside her bags.

As with so many things in life, coincidence played its hand, in the form of a Liberty buyer wandering through Camden Market on the hunt for a lunchtime burrito, who happened across Josie's stall and was instantly struck by Kate's designs. It was the start of her beloved career and a lifetime love affair with Liberty.

The sweet scent of smoky incense wafted up through the communal hall and then rolled over Kate like a sea fog of yellow scent when Josie greeted her at the door, wearing a tie-dye caftan.

"Happy winter solstice season!" said Josie. "You're just in time to help with the tree."

Kate was dragged into the small flat, handed a mug of organic mulled cider, and set to work.

Josie's Christmas tree was made from a series of long twigs fastened horizontally to a tall, gnarled branch that rose up out of a large clay pot. There was a wicker basket on the floor filled with small scraps of fabric, which Josie and Kate painstakingly tied to the tree until the branches fluttered with multicolored scraps, like a kaleidoscope of butterflies.

"Maybe you're not cut out to stay with one man," said Josie. "You're a free spirit! Embrace it!"

"I *have* embraced it," said Kate. "Now I'd like to embrace a lasting relationship."

"Come back to London," said Josie. "I could introduce you to the new Camden crowd. I'll bet I could have you hooked up in a heartbeat."

"Someone recently told me *a bigger pool doesn't mean a better swim*," said Kate.

"Was he the one who cried all through your date until you got him back with his ex?" asked Josie.

"That's not the point," said Kate.

"Come back to London," said Josie. "This is where it all happens."

"You ought to come to Blexford," said Kate. "You'd be surprised at how much happens there."

"Oh dear," said Josie, taking a long drag on her cigarette "It's happened just as I feared. You've gone back to being a country mouse."

Kate shared the spare room in Josie's flat with her stock for the Christmas rush; boxes of scented soy candles and chunky knit rainbow scarves and hats jockeyed for space with carved wooden elephants, velvet jackets, and the small single bed where Kate slept under a patchwork eiderdown.

Josie left with a cheery wave a little after five a.m. She liked to have her stall open early to catch opportunist Christmas shoppers on their morning commute. Kate left soon after, her clothes and hair infused with the scent of patchouli and her head muggy from too much organic cider.

Kate had to admit there was a certain magic to the early-morning city bustle: the roar of cars and buses and the air electrified with the sheer determination of human energy. But as the train left London behind and the landscape became studded once more with shivering forests and a miscellany of dark green and brown scrubby fields, Kate knew Josie was right: she was no longer a city mouse.

Blexford was still mostly functioning behind closed curtains when Kate arrived back in the village, hot beneath her layers from the walk up the hill. She saw Matt getting the café ready for opening and banged on the window, pressing her face against the cold glass in a variety of unflattering expressions until he let her in.

"You smell like a fire in a perfume factory," said Matt.

"I stayed at Josie's last night," said Kate, and yawned.

The coffee machine began to make noises like it was ready to start work, and Kate took up her perch at the counter.

"So, did you hear any more from the weeping vegan?" Matt asked as he heaped froth into Kate's takeaway cappuccino.

Kate narrowed her eyes; Laura must have told him. She made a mental note to poke her finger in Laura's cake before she gave it to her tomorrow.

"Not yet," said Kate. "But I'm sure I'll get an invite to their wedding."

"Only you could go on a date and end up fixing him up with his ex," said Matt.

"Shut up and give me my coffee," said Kate.

Matt handed over the cup.

"Never mind, it's number three tonight, isn't it?" said Matt. "You know what they say: third time's a charm!"

"Let's hope so," said Kate. "Or I'll be asking for a refund."

"You can't have expected them all to be Mr. Right," said Matt.

"I'd settle for Mr. Turns Up and Doesn't Cry."

"It's only a matter of time," said Matt. "You're an intelligent, talented—"

"Don't patronize me," said Kate.

"Slightly-better-than-average-looking woman," Matt finished.

"Slightly better than average," said Kate. "Cheers!"

"You told me not to patronize you," said Matt, holding his hands up.

"Yeah, but *slightly better than average*?"

"All right, then," said Matt. "You are beautiful, Kate, and these men should be dropping at your feet."

"Now you're just being stupid," said Kate.

"I give up," said Matt. "You know what your problem is?"

"Oh, do tell," said Kate. "I would love for *you* to tell *me* what my problems are!"

"You're spiky," said Matt.

"Spiky?" repeated Kate.

"Yes," he said. "You prickle when someone tries to pay you a compliment, but you equally prickle when someone understates your worth. Spiky."

"Perhaps it's only you who makes me spiky," said Kate.

Matt laughed. "Perhaps it is."

Kate riffled through her bag looking for gloves.

"Don't worry about paying," said Matt. "It's on the house."

"I wasn't going to pay anyway," said Kate. She pulled on her gloves and swept out of the café as gracefully as one can wearing a multicolored bobble hat over the top of skanky bed hair.

"Good luck with victim number three!" shouted Matt after her. Kate flipped him the bird with her free hand and heard him laughing as she walked away.

"Charming!" said Barry, who was leaning against the café's wall with a hammer in hand. Kate flushed.

"That was for Matt," she said by way of an explanation.

"Obviously," said Barry.

Barry was a bear of a man, as broad as he was tall, with a mass of long gray hair that matched his grizzled beard. He'd been a roadie back in the day and had bought the pub after an infamous guitarist from the seventies left him a sizable chunk of cash in his will.

"When's the next date?" asked Barry.

"Does everyone know about my dates?" asked Kate.

"Yes," said Barry.

Kate nodded. It figured. Nothing got past the Blexford residents.

"It's tonight, actually," said Kate.

"Not gonna make this one cry, are you?" Barry asked with a smirk.

Kate narrowed her eyes.

"I'll try not to, Barry," she said.

Barry bent down to Kate's height; his blue eyes twinkled beneath a draft-excluding monobrow.

"Any of these fellas gives you any trouble, you send 'em round the Duke's Head," he said.

Kate smiled.

"Thanks, Barry," she said.

· · · · ·

Barry strode off and Kate was alone in the village square. It was just past eight a.m. Now was the lull. The early birds had been out already for their newspapers, and soon front doors would be slamming and children would be skipping and scootering and cycling to school, with their parents running along behind them, bundled down with lunchboxes and backpacks. But for now, it was quiet.

Kate collected some pinecones and dropped them into an old tote bag she kept rolled up in her coat pocket for just such an occasion. Some she would drop into the hearth in her bedroom fireplace and some would be tied into Christmas garlands, along with cinnamon sticks and dried orange slices—which were currently finishing off in the airing cupboard—to be hung from the windows and the kitchen dresser.

She also needed to clear her head. She had designs to work on and a date tonight that she was less than enthused about. And the look of utter contentment on Sarah's face the other night in the snow was still tugging at her insides. Why was that?

Kate tried to remember herself being that happy; she was sure she must have been, certainly at the beginning with Dan and those first few weeks with Rhys. But for her, contentment waned quite quickly to become a faint questioning, which bloomed into nagging doubt and ultimately wholehearted assuredness that it wasn't right. Laura called it self-sabotage. Kate called it gut instinct.

"You can't give up at the first hurdle," said Laura, when Kate had ended her brief affair with James after he got mayonnaise on his upper lip while eating a burger. "That wasn't even a hurdle," Laura went on. "You dumped him for a small lip indiscretion!"

"It wasn't working anyway," said Kate.

"You didn't give it a chance," Laura objected. "You pressed the self-destruct button prematurely. This is a classic case of your self-sabotage."

"I disagree," said Kate. "A man is like an optional extra; you should only take one on when it is beneficial to do so. It's like refraining from the fourth plate at the all-you-can-eat curry buffet. Just because it's there, doesn't mean you have to have it."

· · · · ·

As she wandered home the snow had all but disappeared, small patches surviving only in the darkest recesses beneath the hedgerows. The weather had warmed by a few degrees and the silver frosts had turned leaf-strewn paths to mush and grass verges to bog.

Kate sucked the coffee froth through the hole in the lid, and the hot liquid followed it. She smiled to herself; the first coffee of the day was a joy unlike any other. She walked, swinging her bag of pinecones and stopping occasionally to pick up an amber or russet leaf, not yet withered to brown by the cold.

It was ten o'clock by the time she reached home. A wicker basket filled with carrots, parsnips, and a celeriac with alien tentacles sat on the kitchen table; her dad must have been up early too.

Part of the large garden was a devoted vegetable plot that Mac had nurtured since Kate could remember. Although he had his own garden at the cottage, he still came up to work the garden at the old house. Year round they were never short of vegetables. And when they had a glut the neighbors benefited too.

Kate grabbed her Polaroid camera and snapped the basket. She pinned the photograph to her ideas board. She shuffled out of her coat and hat, dropped her overnight rucksack and bag of pinecones in the corner of the kitchen, and grabbed a pencil and her sketchbook.

The feather-fronded carrot tops curled shyly around one another as their orange bodies kinked and curved with the pale parsnips that shared their bed. The celeriac sprouted leggy roots through its armored skin like one of H. G. Wells's monsters.

Hours later she was still drawing; pencil lines had been joined by washes of color and detail in black fine-line pen. Sketches were strewn about the table: flashes of green vibrant against shades of calm stone and amber. This was how a fabric design was born. Anything could inspire it. Just when she thought she'd no spark in her today, a basket of bent, muddy vegetables had come to the rescue.

Absent-mindedly she grabbed her coffee cup and swigged.

"Eurgh!" she exclaimed. Kate was not a fan of cold coffee, not unless it came with ice and a shot of Baileys at least. She got up and went to the cupboard, grabbing a coffee pod, and fired up the coffee machine. She realized she was still wearing her boots; she was just in the middle of wrestling them off when the phone rang. It was Laura.

"Hello, traitor," said Kate.

"What?"

"You told Matt about my date," said Kate. "He's named him 'the weeping vegan'!"

Laura laughed.

"That is brilliant," she said.

"Laura!"

"Oh, I'm sorry," said Laura. "I didn't think it was a secret. And anyway, you probably would have told him eventually. You know, when you can see the funny side of it."

"I *can* see the funny side of it," said Kate. "I just don't want him laughing about me behind my back."

"I don't think Matt is the type to laugh behind your back," said Laura.

Kate sighed.

"No, neither do I," she said resignedly. "Not when he can laugh at my face."

Kate's other boot shot off with force and slid along the floor, leaving a mud trail on the wood.

"Anyway," said Laura. "Why are we talking about Matt? I didn't call to talk about Matt. I've got about five minutes before Charley wakes up from his nap and Mina realizes I'm not watching CBeebies with her. What and who is tonight's date?"

Kate held the phone between ear and shoulder as she cleaned the floor. "It's ice skating and my date's name is Anthony."

"Ice skating?" screeched Laura. "You?" In the background a baby began to wail. "Why would you choose ice skating?"

"The alternatives were go-carting or mince pie making," Kate explained. "I make enough mince pies as it is, and driving the Mini is like go-carting."

"And it wouldn't hurt to be a damsel in distress on the ice," said Laura sardonically.

The wailing became more urgent.

"Oh shit!" said Laura. "Okay, talk fast, tell me about Anthony."

"Six foot three, dark brown hair, short but sort of quiffy at the front, brown eyes, fireman, two kids, single father, divorced," Kate reeled off.

"No wonder you wanted to ice skate."

The wailing was a siren now, shrill and relentless. Kate could hear Laura panting as she ran up the stairs.

"And a fireman!" she said. "Mummy's coming, Charley! Well, he sounds promising. Does he know you can't stand up on the ice?"

The wailing was close to the earpiece now; Laura had Charley in her arms. In the distance a little girl's voice sounded shrilly, "Muuuuummmmy! Where are you?"

"Oh my God!" said Laura.

Kate could hear the thud of her feet as she descended the stairs with Charley still yelling in her arms.

"I've got to go," Laura shouted. "Tell me all about it tomorrow. Love you."

The phone went dead and Kate made herself a coffee and set back to work.

It was true that she couldn't ice skate. At all. Of the many things she was good at, balance was not one of them; roller skates, ice skates, skateboards, even hopping caused her problems, although since leaving primary school hopping as a requirement to life skills had admittedly waned.

· · · · ·

Kate swigged her fresh coffee and looked over today's sketches. She had gotten a lot more done than she'd expected. She was tempted to add a little more detail; her fingers itched to deepen the shade along the edge of the celeriac, but she resisted. If she picked up her paintbrush now, she'd be lost for another hour.

Her phone pinged as she made her way up the stairs to have a shower. Her dad had sent her a photograph of a vegetable soup he'd made. She'd never imagined he'd become so good at being by himself, or so adept in the kitchen. How different things were now.

Four years, she thought as she lathered shampoo into her hair. In the last four years Laura had had two children and Kate had made senior designer. She had also rekindled a friendship she had thought was lost forever.

Kate had only been back in Blexford three months when one of the Knitting Sex Kittens was diagnosed with breast cancer—thankfully she recovered, but it rocked the Kittens. The Knitting Sex Kittens were a formidable group of women, all over age sixty and all single, by either design, divorce, or death.

They were on every committee in the village; in fact, they had started every committee in the village. When they weren't knitting, they were organizing, and when they weren't organizing, they were planning. There was *nothing* these women did not know about Blexford's goings-on. *Nothing!* They were like sleeper cells for MI6, planted surreptitiously all over the village, gathering intel from behind patchwork quilts and chunky-knit cardigans.

When Bella was diagnosed, the Kittens became a tour de force in their bid to raise money for cancer research charities. It was how they coped with the prospect of losing one of their own and how they kept Bella positive during her treatment.

There were six charity events arranged for six consecutive Saturdays. Kate declined their invitation to be Miss September in the Blexford naked calendar and also to model their knitted lingerie line for the catwalk show, but she did agree to bake for the bake sale.

Her caramel brownies became the talk of the marquee. Kate and Matt had still only shared the most meager niceties, when Matt, having no idea that Kate had made the brownies, declared that he *must* have them in the Pear Tree.

Kate had guffawed loudly when she'd heard.

"As if I'd sell my brownies to him," she said to Laura.

"It might be a good ice breaker," said Laura.

"I've done all right with the iceberg between us thus far," said Kate.

"But don't you think it would be nice to make your peace with him?" asked Laura. "It must be stressful having to worry about bumping into him every time you leave the house."

Kate frowned at her friend in the way she did when Laura was talking sense and Kate didn't want to hear it.

"At least think about it," said Laura. "We're grown-ups now, real ones. Give him a chance. I can vouch for him, he's been a good friend to me. And it would be nice if we could all be mates again, like the old days."

Kate had promised to consider it. Laura was a good judge of character and if she'd forgiven Matt his misdemeanors, then perhaps he really had grown up. And in a village as small as Blexford, sooner or later the impasse between them would have to be addressed.

As it turned out, it was sooner. As part of Mac's rehabilitation after his breakdown, Matt would call for him on Wednesday mornings—Kate stayed out in the kitchen—and take him for a coffee at the Pear Tree and a wander around the village.

On this particular morning, Mac had forgotten his key and Kate was forced to answer the door when they returned. To her annoyance, Matt seemed reluctant to leave the doorstep after he had safely deposited Mac into the house. Kate was too polite to close the door in his face, even though she enacted the scenario out in her mind and derived great pleasure from it.

Matt shifted his weight awkwardly from foot to foot as though he needed the toilet really badly. He smiled sheepishly at her and ran his hand through his hair so many times it stood on end ridiculously; he reminded Kate of a Muppet.

"Listen, Kate," he said finally. "We've been skirting around each other for weeks. But here's the deal. I was a shit back then."

Kate took a step back. She stood tall and jutted her chin out in defiance.

"Yes," she said. "You were."

"I handled things really badly and I'm sorry," Matt continued.

"You didn't handle things at all," said Kate.

"No," Matt agreed ruefully. "I didn't."

"I never denied it was a mistake," Kate told him.

"I know."

"It was the worst mistake I've ever made," said Kate.

"I deserve that," Matt allowed. "I was in a terrible place and I took it out on you because you were the closest person to me." He held his hands up in surrender before Kate had a chance to jump in. "I'm not excusing my behavior," he said quickly. "I'm just explaining it. But we both live in this village and it's time we buried the hatchet. Preferably not in my head."

"Are you saying all this just to get your hands on my brownies?" asked Kate.

"No," said Matt. "I'm saying *all this* because I want my friend back. *And* because I want your brownies in my café. *And* because I can't keep pretending not to see you when you hide in the bushes to avoid me!"

He grinned.

"I am sorry," he added.

His expression was utter sincerity. Kate could see the boy he had been, beneath the man he had become: the boy who had been her best friend in the world, the boy on whom she could never truly turn her back.

"Apology accepted," said Kate, resigned.

Laura was right; they were real grown-ups now and it served nobody for Kate to hold on to a grudge. That said, she wasn't about to dive right in and declare him a confidant; they would have to dig back down to the foundations and build up. But their mutual love for Laura, Ben, and Mac was a pretty solid platform to start from.

Kate ushered her disheveled father back into the kitchen for the second time.

"I know we can't just pick up where we left off," said Matt, as though reading her mind. "I'll take the smallest, shallowest friendship you've got, as long I've got something."

"I'm going to have a cup of tea," said Kate. "Stay for one, if you like."

She turned and walked toward the kitchen, leaving the front door open. She knew that Matt would follow.

"I'll make brownies for the café," she called without looking back. She could hear Matt's footsteps behind her.

"But I don't come cheap," she added. "And I'll expect free coffee for life."

She turned then and saw Matt smiling at her. Kate smiled back.

· · · · ·

It was a forty-five-minute drive to the ice rink. There was no time to straighten her hair, so she scrunched it up into a loose curly topknot. She wriggled into a pair of jeans and pulled on a red sweater—courtesy of the Knitting Sex Kittens—with silver Christmas trees around the neck, cuffs, and bottom. She applied a slick of red lipstick to complement the jumper, and after a squirt of expensive perfume she was ready to go.

Kate dashed out of the house without a second to spare. It was dark and cold and as the heaters blew furiously to clear the windscreen, she considered blowing off the date for a glass of red and some bad TV. But then she remembered how it had felt to be stood up, and she resigned herself to a night of looking like a tit on the ice.

Kate arrived as an ice hockey session was finishing up. The rep from the Twelve Dates team was slipping through the crowd of love-hopefuls that had converged at the gates and marking people down on her clipboard. Occasionally she would usher a disgruntled dater away from someone they clearly preferred the look of and deliver them to the date they had been assigned.

The rep—a girl young enough to be the daughter of some clients—ticked Kate off her list and pointed her toward Anthony, who looked relieved when he saw her and gestured to the skates he was holding by their laces. Kate smiled as she pushed through the expectant throng, some faces familiar from the cooking night.

"Hi," said Anthony. "I got you a six and half before they all went."

He handed the boots to Kate.

"That's amazing!" she said. "How did you know what size shoe I wear?"

He laughed.

"Don't worry," he said. "I'm not a crazy stalker. I guessed you'd be

around a size six from your profile stats and your build in the photo."
He shrugged. "You don't find many five-foot-five women with size
eight feet."

It was Kate's turn to laugh.

"Fair enough," she said. "Okay, I guess we'd better get these monsters on me."

"You don't sound too keen," said Anthony.

"I can't skate," she confessed. "At all."

"So you picked an ice skating date?" said Anthony.

"It was the best of the three dates on offer," said Kate. "And I never
shy away from a challenge."

"Neither do I," said Anthony.

His tone was suggestive. It made Kate feel a bit giddy, and she guffawed loudly and finished with a piggy snort. *Keep it together, Turner!*
she thought, and mentally shook herself by the shoulders and slapped
her face.

Anthony led her to a bench and began loosening the laces on the
skates.

"My main concerns are breaking my legs, breaking someone else's
legs, or causing an ice rink pile-up," said Kate.

Anthony chuckled, a low chuckle that seemed to rumble around
like thunder beneath his pectoral muscles.

"Don't worry," he said. "I won't let you fall."

He smiled. Kate blushed; it was quite the most romantic thing she'd
heard in years.

To her surprise, he took control of putting her skates on, taking her
feet in his large hands and gently pushing them into the stiff boots,
pulling the laces tightly to secure them. She hoped her feet weren't hot
and sweaty. She hoped they didn't smell.

Kate suddenly felt all hot, despite the cold of the place. She dearly wished she weren't wearing her Rudolph socks with glittery red noses. It was such an intimate act. She didn't know where to look. She'd never had this problem in Clarks shoe shop. When he'd finished he looked up at her with a wolfish grin, and Kate felt sure steam was rolling off her cheeks.

The hockey teams relinquished the ice and when the Zamboni had smoothed the rink to a glassy precariousness, the Twelve Dates gang descended onto the ice with whoops and screeches.

They were a distinctly mixed-ability bunch, for which Kate was greatly relieved. Although some couples instantly took off arm in arm like Torvill and Dean, there were plenty of wobblers, huggers-on-for-dear-lifers, and clingers, who inched their way around the edge, never releasing their white-knuckle grip on the rail; it was to this last group that Kate firmly belonged.

"I'll just go around the edge for a while," said Kate. "You can wave at me as you go past."

They had teetered their way to the gate and Kate found herself hanging onto the edge of the Perspex window, afraid to step out onto the ice.

"It's not really a date if we don't skate together," said Anthony. "How are we supposed to get to know each other if we can't talk?"

"I'll shout interesting facts about myself as you go by," said Kate.

Anthony laughed a deep, friendly laugh, like the Jolly Green Giant, only Anthony was much better looking. He put one arm firmly around Kate's waist and pulled her tightly into his side, almost lifting her from the ground.

"I told you," he said. "I won't let you fall. Trust me, I'm a fireman."

As Kate did her best not to dissolve into a puddle, Anthony pulled her onto the ice. True to his word, he held her so tightly to his side that despite her legs moving in opposite directions, she did not fall.

After a couple of laps Kate began to relax; she stopped squealing and began to enjoy the skating, or at least going through the motions of skating.

"If I'd known all I needed to skate proficiently was a six-foot-three fireman, I'd have done it more often," said Kate.

Anthony's laugh rumbled through her. After a couple more laps Kate felt confident enough to hold a conversation on the move and they talked a bit about their jobs and gave a brief précis of their respective singleness.

Anthony had the children Sunday night to Friday afternoon, and his ex-wife had them every weekend.

"That's unusual, isn't it?" asked Kate.

"It is," said Anthony. "But it shouldn't be. Her job is better paid than mine. She works longer hours and I've got a really close-knit family who help out when I'm on shift. She doesn't have anyone. It makes sense for me to have them more. But it doesn't mean she loves them any less."

"No, of course not," said Kate.

Dammit! This was just the sort of gender equality she was always harping on about, and as soon as she actually found some, she questioned its validity. She felt instantly ashamed. Her feminist self pinched her judgmental self hard.

"It sounds like you have a very healthy relationship with your ex," said Kate.

"That's mostly down to her," Anthony replied.

Self-deprecating, pro-women, and a sexy six-foot fireman, thought Kate. She was crushing so hard on this guy she was having palpitations.

"I'll bet you're a hit at the school gates," said Kate.

Anthony laughed.

"I'm not going to lie," he said. "I've had offers."

I'll bet you have.

"So why sign up for this?" asked Kate.

"Because I don't have the time or the energy to go out in the hopes of meeting someone," he said. "And between work and school runs I'm unlikely to meet anyone by chance. How about you?" he asked. "You're smart and sexy, even in reindeer socks, and you've got a great career. What's holding you back?"

"Oh, I'm just *really* lazy," said Kate. And Anthony laughed, a deep gravelly laugh that made Kate want to rip all her clothes off.

· · · · ·

When the rep's voice boomed over the loudspeaker that it was half-time hot chocolate break, Anthony tucked Kate under his arm with ease and skated—with Kate's heavy-booted feet dangling uselessly—to the gate. He set her gently down on the rush carpeting and waited for her land legs to return before releasing her. Kate could not deny that she was giddy, and not just because of the skating.

They sat at a sticky plastic table; Kate spooned the whipped cream off the top of her drink into her mouth and listened to Anthony talk about his children.

"Here," he said. "Do you want to see some photos?"

Kate nodded and Anthony took out his phone. The screen lit up and two adorable children grinned out at her. They had dark hair like their dad. An unexpected pang traveled up through her stomach and settled in her chest; she wondered what color hair her children would have.

"You have beautiful children," said Kate.

"Thanks," said Anthony. He seemed pleased as he put his phone back into his pocket. "It's hard to date when you've got kids," he said. "I want to meet someone special, but in the back of my mind I'm always thinking, do they like kids? Will they like my kids? Will my kids like them?"

"It's a lot to consider," agreed Kate. "But when you get to our age, you sort of expect that some people will have kids already. I mean, it doesn't worry me, you know, dating someone who's got kids."

Anthony sighed as he stirred his chocolate.

"But it adds certain expectations," he said.

"What do you mean?"

"Well, people assume that because I've got kids and I'm still relatively young that I'll want more," said Anthony.

Kate tried to keep her voice level. She wanted children. Whether with a partner or by herself, she knew children were in her future.

"But you don't want more kids?" she asked carefully.

"No," replied Anthony. "I've got my kids. They're perfect. I adore them. But I don't want to have any more. I've done all that, you know? The sleepless nights, the teething . . . And I'd worry that if I had children with someone else, they'd feel they were being replaced."

"Well, surely that's down to how you handle the situation," said Kate. "I mean, you might meet someone who makes you change your mind. Never say never . . . right?"

Anthony drained his mug and rubbed his hands together.

"Nope," he said. "Not me. I know myself. When I make a decision, that's it." He gestured to the rink. "Shall we?" he asked.

Kate nodded, smiling, and attempted to keep her deflation hidden. Anthony held out his arm and she ducked under and squeezed herself back in her nook beside him. As he lifted her onto the ice, she made a conscious decision not to let melancholy rule. Instead she vowed to enjoy the rest of her perfect first and last date with the handsome fireman and chalk it up to experience.

And it was perfect. They had so much in common, if you put ice skating to one side. But Kate wasn't about to get into something that would ultimately lead nowhere; she deserved better than that. She deserved to be with someone who wouldn't ask her to compromise on something as big as having kids.

Anthony helped Kate out of her heavy ice skates and into her coat and together they made their way out to the car park. Kate was parked in the farthest corner and Anthony walked her to her car. *Chivalrous to the last!* thought Kate. And for a second, she doubted her resolve.

Anthony cleared his throat.

"Can I see you again?" he asked. "I'd really like to."

Kate wavered but recovered herself.

"I'd love to," she said. "But . . ."

"Please, not a 'but,'" said Anthony. "I really like you and I think you like me."

Kate stood taller.

"But here's the thing," she continued. "One day I'd like to have children. I'm not suggesting I'm on some kind of baby-daddy mission with this Twelve Dates thing. In fact I'm not saying there has to be a man involved in my family at all. But at this point in my life, I don't want to start something with someone I might really like when it's bound for doom because eventually I will want kids and you won't."

"Wow," said Anthony. "I thought you never shied away from a challenge."

"This isn't a challenge," said Kate. "It's a dead end. I'm not for turning and I don't think you are either. You said it yourself: when you make a decision, that's it."

"Brutal but fair," said Anthony.

Kate shrugged.

"You were honest with me," she said. "I'm just returning the compliment."

"And I appreciate it," said Anthony. "You're right. I don't want more kids. Period. I won't deny I'm gutted, though. I think things could have been really simple with us."

"I think so too," said Kate.

Kate held out her hand for him to shake. Instead, Anthony slipped his arms around her waist and pulled her toward him.

"With your permission," he said. "I'd like to leave with a taste of what could have been if things were different."

"Permission granted," said Kate.

It was a good kiss. The kind of kiss you feel all the way down to your toes and back up again. But still, as he walked away from her, she knew she'd made the right decision.

She was still thinking about the kiss when she pulled back into the Blexford village square. As she swung in, her headlamps illuminated the Pear Tree Café and Matt, swinging precariously off a ladder as he stapled a string of icicle fairy lights to the fascias.

Kate pulled over and got out.

"What in God's name are you doing?" she asked.

"What does it look like I'm doing, Kate?" said Matt, his voice strained as he stretched and stapled in another length of wire.

"Yes, but why are you doing it now, at eleven thirty at night?"

"Because I don't have time during the day," said Matt. "And if I did, every bugger in the village would have a helpful suggestion as to how I could do it better."

"You missed a bit," said Kate.

Matt looked down and grimaced at her.

"Smart-arse," he said. "You gonna help or make wisecracks?"

"Make wisecracks," Kate decided.

At that moment Matt leaned too far and the ladder tipped up onto one foot. Kate grabbed it and steadied it.

"And help," she added.

Together and without incident they managed to run the icicle lights underneath the roof of the café and attach a jolly Santa and sleigh to the roof itself. By the time they'd finished, Kate's fingers were numb with cold.

"Just stand out here for one more minute while I go in and turn them on," said Matt. "And then I'll make us a hot chocolate."

Kate waited, blowing into her hands while Matt disappeared into the blacked-out café. A moment later the outside was illuminated by hundreds of glittering icicle threads, swaying gracefully like jellyfish tentacles. Above them, the jolly Santa's cheeks glowed poppy red; Kate expected him to take off from the roof at any moment with a whoosh and a *Ho Ho Ho!*

Matt came out to join Kate, and they both stood admiring their handiwork in the silent village square.

"Come on," said Matt, after a minute. "I've got the milk on the stove."

Kate followed Matt through the unlit café and into the kitchen. There was something hopeful, expectant almost, about the café at night, empty and dark as it was, as though it were only sleeping, waiting for the morning to bring it to life again.

The only lights on in the kitchen were the ones above the hob, where Matt stood, heaping cocoa and sugar into the saucepan of milk, stirring it furiously with a small balloon whisk.

Matt turned to the kitchen island and poured the cocoa into the waiting mugs. He handed one of them to Kate.

"Sex Kitten special?" he asked, motioning to her jumper.

"How did you guess?" said Kate. "One of Petula's beauties. I think this was two Christmases ago."

"What's this year's like?" asked Matt.

"I don't know," said Kate. "She's being cagey about it."

Kate blew on her drink and took a sip.

"Ooh, that's good," she said. "Touch of cinnamon?"

Matt nodded, pleased.

"Cinnamon stick," he said. "Added to the pan while the milk's still cold."

Kate mmmm'd appreciatively.

"So how did the date go?" asked Matt.

"It was perfect," said Kate.

"Perfect?" said Matt. "That's a strong word."

"He would have been a strong contender," said Kate.

"But?"

"But I won't be seeing him again."

"Don't want to talk about it?" asked Matt.

"Not really," said Kate.

They sat quietly for a little while, thawing out over cocoa.

"Remember when we used to sneak in here after Mum had shut the shop and make ice cream sundaes?" said Matt.

"And when we used to steal the pain au chocolats from the cooling racks," said Kate.

Matt laughed.

"Yeah," he said. "Sneaking in through the back door on our hands and knees and swiping them when Mum's back was turned."

"You could hear her bellowing all the way down the end of the garden." Kate laughed.

"*Those bloody kids!*" mimicked Matt, shaking his fist.

"With hindsight, we were little shits," said Kate.

"Undoubtedly," said Matt. "We had fun, though."

"Undoubtedly," said Kate.

"We should try to synchronize our child rearing," said Matt. "I'd love it if my kids and your kids could grow up together like we did."

"You might have a long wait if you want to synchronize with me," said Kate.

"That's okay," said Matt. "I'm in no hurry."

They finished their drinks and Matt put the empty cups in the sink.

"I'd better get back," he said. "Sarah's at my place, she had a load of paperwork to get done. She'll be wondering what happened to me."

"Yep," said Kate. "I've got to get some work done first thing in the morning, I need my bed." She could feel her leg muscles beginning to ache already from the ice skating.

Matt waved her off as she pulled away. He was standing there still as she turned the corner.

.....

Cocktails and Kisses

"Does it have to be the Pear Tree?" asked Kate. "Can't we go into town? There's a new place opened up near Fitzwilliam Park."

"I've been up all night," said Laura from the other end of the phone. Her voice was forced calm. "Charley's teething. And when Charley wakes up, Mina wakes up. The only person who doesn't wake up is Ben. Do you have any idea how hard it is to wrestle two cranky children into car seats, and then have to listen to nursery rhymes while they scream all the way to town?"

Kate was about to speak, but Laura continued.

"Don't make me stay indoors. I need coffee. I need to be in a place with other grown-ups. With coffee. Coffee is vital."

"You can't have caffeine, you're still breastfeeding," said Kate.

"I like to have decaf and pretend," said Laura. "For the love of God, help me, Kate!"

"What about the tearooms at Blexford Manor?" Kate asked. "Don't you get free drinks if you're a staff member?"

"My kids don't conform to tearoom etiquette," said Laura. "The Pear Tree has toys, it's child friendly, and Matt can't throw me out because he's the kids' godfather. Don't let me down, Kate," she warned. She was a woman on the edge today. "I need a safe environment where I can drink decaffeinated coffee and my children can't shame me."

An hour later they had penned themselves into the sofa area in the far corner of the Pear Tree Café. Mina had created a sort of toy village on the large two-seater armchair, and Charley watched her progress eagerly from his pushchair. Delighted to have a captive audience, Mina gave Charley a running commentary on what each toy was doing, in the style of a children's TV presenter.

Laura pushed her empty cappuccino cup across the low coffee table and pulled the next one toward her. Kate had just finished filling her in on her ill-fated fireman date.

"You didn't even give him your number?" said Laura.

"What would be the point?" asked Kate.

"Booty calls?" suggested Laura.

"If I only wanted sex, I wouldn't have paid out all this money to Lightning Strikes!"

"How much is high-class man-hooker?" Laura asked.

Kate ignored her.

"So who's next?" Laura asked.

"Next is Sam," said Kate. "Sam is thirty-eight and a motorcycle enthusiast."

Laura pulled a face.

"Please tell me you won't get on the back of his motorbike," she said. "You can barely control a bicycle. At no point should you ever try to ride a bike with an engine."

"Don't worry." Kate laughed. "I know my limitations."

The sound of smashing crockery from behind the counter caused the entire café to raise their arms in unison and cheer. Matt took a bow and the regulars went back to their noisy conversations.

"What else?" asked Laura. Mina was still cheering, and Charley copied.

"He's a graphic designer," said Kate.

"Tick!" said Laura, making the gesture in the air.

"He says in his profile he'd like children."

"Tick!" said Laura again.

"And he's passionate about conservation," said Kate.

Laura clutched at her heart.

"Oh, perfect! Perfect!" exclaimed Laura. "Picture, please."

Kate flicked to the photograph of Sam and handed the phone to Laura. His hair was closely shaved, mostly blond with a spattering of white at the sides. His clean-shaven, angular face came to a chiseled chin and his eyes crinkled at the edges where he was smiling.

"Oh, ding-dong," said Laura. "Surely this is game over. He is beautiful."

"Isn't he?" agreed Kate.

Charley's eyes were beginning a slow droop that even Mina's lively commentary couldn't remedy. Sensing that she'd lost her audience, she squeezed past the pushchair and toddled off up the café in her tutu and wellies.

She walked over to Matt, who had just set down a tray of cakes for a table of six eagle-eyed customers, and put her arms out to him. Matt picked her up and began to make a fuss over her. Mina squeezed his cheeks and made him laugh.

"Looks like Matt's found his intellectual equal," said Kate.

"Don't be so rude," said Laura. "Mina is way more intelligent than Matt."

Matt strode over to the sofa. Mina sat contentedly on his hip licking the icing off a cupcake.

"Oh, thank you so much," Laura said with daggers in her eyes. "You gave my overactive daughter more sugar. You must have known how little I like sleep."

Matt smiled.

"It's in the *Good Godparents Handbook*," he said. "Besides," he went on, "it's all nonsense, isn't it? It never did me any harm."

He crossed his eyes and smiled goofily at Kate and Laura, letting his tongue loll out of the corner of his mouth.

"I will set birds on you," said Laura. "I will find some and I will set them upon you."

Matt didn't like birds. Even sparrows. Robins on Christmas cards made him shudder.

"Don't you like birds, Uncle Matt?" asked Mina.

"Not the feathered kind," said Kate.

He looked at Kate and poked his tongue out.

"Is it hard being the second-favorite godparent?" he asked.

"I wouldn't know," said Kate. "Is it?"

"Don't start!" said Laura. "Two children is quite enough."

"So," says Matt. "What's the next date of Sha—"

Laura cut him off.

"Don't you dare!" she said. "She repeats everything she hears at the moment, and if she gets kicked out of nursery for using bad language, I'll be delivering her here for daycare instead!"

Matt looked at Mina.

"Uncle Matt's been told off by Mummy," he said.

Mina giggled and kissed his nose, leaving a blob of pink buttercream behind. The doorbell jingled and Sarah walked in looking rosy-cheeked and fresh from the cold, her dark hair bouncing against the shoulders of her green tweed jacket.

Kate saw her first and waved.

"Hi, Sarah!" she called.

Sarah waved and came over.

"Hi," said Sarah cheerfully.

Sarah always had that delicately windswept English rose look about her, like she'd just finished making daisy chains beside a babbling brook. Which was odd because by her own admission, she hated the countryside.

"Hey, babe," said Matt.

Matt went to kiss Sarah. She backed away.

"Got a little something on your nose there, honey," she said, and wiped it off with a napkin. Then she kissed him on the lips. Mina puckered up and Sarah gave her a kiss too.

"Sarah," said Laura. "I've been meaning to ask you, when do I need to apply for Mina's school place?"

Sarah was the headmistress at Great Blexley Primary School down the hill in Great Blexley, commonly referred to by Blexford locals as "the Big Town."

"You came to the open day, didn't you?" asked Sarah.

Laura nodded. "And we put Mina's name down on a list."

"Well, in that case you're already on our mailing list," said Sarah. "You'll get a letter after Christmas telling you what you need to do."

Laura and Kate had gone to the church school in the village, but regular church attendance was required for a place, and Ben point-blank refused to go to church for anything other than baptisms, weddings, and burials.

Laura had initially felt a bit sad that her children wouldn't attend the same school she had, but Sarah's reputation as an outstanding head teacher took precedence over her budding relationship with Matt. She had joined the school a couple of years back with excellent credentials, and word quickly spread around toddler groups and nurseries that Great Blexley Primary was *the* school to go to.

"So which date is next?" asked Sarah. Kate and Laura scrunched up on the sofa and Sarah nestled in beside Kate.

"This is date number four: cocktail making," replied Kate.

"Sounds dangerous," said Sarah.

Kate laughed.

"I wouldn't rule out extreme drunkenness," said Kate.

"I remember drunkenness," said Laura with a faraway look in her eye.

· · · · ·

Kate's dad pulled up outside the cocktail bar at seven thirty p.m.

"Thanks, Dad," said Kate. "I feel like I'm sixteen again, getting you to drop you me off."

"Well, just because you're all grown up doesn't mean you stop being my little girl," said Mac. "Now are you sure you don't want a lift home? It's no bother."

"No thanks, Dad, I'll get a taxi," said Kate. "Oh, I nearly forgot. Evelyn gave me a fruitcake for you, when I went in earlier for some milk. She said it was in exchange for the veg you gave her."

Mac smacked his lips.

"Ooh, one of Evelyn's fruitcakes!" he said. "She's a smashing cook, is Evelyn."

Evelyn had been widowed in her early fifties and had run the shop by herself ever since. It was more of an emporium than a shop, really; Evelyn liked to keep enough stock to cater for an apocalypse or a month of snow, whichever came first. The usual tinned and packet goods were provided, along with chest freezers full of home-cooked ready meals—courtesy of Carla and her mother's cottage-industry catering company—local farm fruit and veg, and an impressive wine selection. She was also a newsagent, pharmacy, and purveyor of eccentric chunky knit socks and jumpers created by Blexford's own Knitting Sex Kittens. If you were cold or hungry, Evelyn was your woman.

Kate waved good-bye to her dad and followed a flashing sign down the stairs to a vast basement cocktail bar. Inside, the bar had a nineteenth-century French feel; Toulouse-Lautrec prints lined the walls, and wingback chairs of tan leather and round mahogany tables with ornately carved legs dotted the opulent bar. One whole wall was taken up with gray-painted bookcases that reached as high as the great glass chandeliers, whose crystal petals twinkled as they swayed.

There were two long bars, each backed with mirrors that gave the impression of an even bigger space beyond and were more than a little disconcerting after a few glasses of wine.

Cocktail shakers, glasses, and an unholy number of ornate bottles containing brightly colored spirits ran along each bar, and slowly the fourth-daters found their partners and took their places beside them.

Kate spotted Sam—her date for the evening—deeply engrossed in conversation with a woman wearing a very small red leather skirt. Kate pulled at her leaf-patterned corduroy tunic-dress and wondered if she'd judged her outfit wrong. Standing on the other side of Red Leather and clearly being ignored was a good-looking Indian chap with a lumberjack beard and an awkward look on his face. Kate guessed he must be Red Leather's date.

Kate moved closer to Sam and tried to get into his line of vision by craning her head in a sort of meerkat fashion. Sam didn't seem to notice her, but Lumberjack Beard smiled knowingly, tapped him on the shoulder, and pointed in Kate's direction.

Her date excused himself from Red Leather and came over, holding his hand out and smiling warmly.

"Hi!" he said. "I'm so sorry, how rude of me, I was just talking off-roading with Clarissa . . . but you don't want to hear about that. I'm Sam and you must be Kate."

Kate shook his hand and accepted his apology. As they made their way across to their allotted bar space, she noticed that Sam looked back at Clarissa and her red leather miniskirt three times. They hopped up on to their bar stools and checked out the cocktail ingredients and laminated recipe cards, which read like a hooker's sales pitch: Sex on the Beach, Screaming Orgasm, Slow Comfortable Screw, and Slippery Nipple.

Kate tried not to look prudish in front of the handsome man she had only just met, but her burning cheeks were letting her down and her corduroy dress didn't exactly scream *sexy*. They giggled about the silliness of the cocktail names and made small getting-to-know-you talk, while Sam kept one eye firmly across the room.

After about five minutes Sam stood up.

"I'm sorry about this," he said. "But I just have to check something."

And with that he strode across the room to the nearest Lightning Strikes rep and engaged in a clandestine conversation with her. After a couple of minutes—and some expressive protestations from the rep—Sam and the rep walked over to where Lumberjack Beard was talking amiably to a sullen-faced Red Leather. Kate watched the peculiar farce play out with incredulity, and moments later, Lumberjack Beard and the harassed rep arrived at her cocktail station.

"Um, hi there," said the rep.

She was overly smiling in a way that begged, *Please don't hate me, I just work here.*

"This is a bit awkward," she continued. "But Sam and Clarissa feel they've made a connection and they'd like to continue the date with each other."

She glanced at Lumberjack Beard, who smiled and shrugged.

"So, with that in mind," said the rep, "I was wondering if you two, as their dates, would mind pairing instead?"

"Fine with me!" said Lumberjack Beard.

His smile was warm and his posture relaxed, and Kate thought there probably wasn't much that rattled him.

It was down to Kate now. The rep looked at her with a cross between hope and pleading. It would be churlish to make the rep's life difficult and pointless to force Sam to continue their date when he clearly wanted to be with someone else.

"Of course," said Kate graciously. "No problem at all."

The rep visibly relaxed.

"Thank you!" she said, and introduced them. "Oliver, this is Kate. Kate, Oliver."

And she scurried off before they had the chance to change their minds.

Oliver sat down.

"Hello," he said, holding out his hand. "I'll be your consolation prize for the evening."

They hit it off instantly.

"This isn't really my thing," said Oliver. "My mates signed me up for it because they're fed up with my, and I quote, lackluster love life."

"Oh dear." Kate laughed. "Is it that bad?"

"Put it this way," said Oliver. "Lackluster would be an improvement."

Kate considered her own love life. It had been so long since she'd had sex, she worried her hymen might have grown back. Kate raised the shot glass that the barman had just filled with blue liquid.

"Here's to an end to lackluster love lives," she said.

"Amen to that," said Oliver.

They clinked shot glasses, knocked back the blue liquid, and coughed and spluttered on the strong liquor.

Oliver was into rock climbing and, ironically given his choice of clothing, was a tree surgeon by profession. He was impressed that Kate knew her way around a climbing wall—thanks to Dan—and even more impressed by her design credentials; their shared love of nature made for easy conversation.

"It seems to me," said Kate after her second Slippery Nipple, "that there are two distinct camps at these events."

"Go on," said Oliver, draining a Sex on the Beach and checking the ingredients for the next cocktail.

"Well, there's the 'just haven't found the right one yet' camp and the 'found the right one and lost them' camp," she said.

"Actually," said Oliver, "there are three. You're forgetting the 'I'm just here for a shag' camp. And don't go thinking that's just a bloke thing," he went on. "On my first date we didn't get on *at all*! We both agreed we didn't want to see each other again. And then she suggested that we might as well have sex anyway so it wasn't a wasted evening."

"Wow!" said Kate.

"On my life." Oliver handed her a glass. "Screaming Orgasm?" he asked.

Kate took the drink and sipped it.

"Don't mind if I do," she said. "At least your date turned up. My first couldn't be bothered." She hiccupped and almost slid off the stool but recovered herself.

"Aw, that sucks," said Oliver. "He was clearly an idiot." And he poured himself a double measure of something green.

An hour and a half later and Kate and Oliver were well and truly hammered. They had fixed themselves something that loosely resembled the recipe for a Sex on My Face and retired to a couple of leather arm-chairs in the corner.

"So you're a found- 'em-and-lost- 'em," Kate slurred. "And I'm a jus-aven't-found-the-righ-one-yet. *Hic*."

"Yep," said Oliver. "I am a self-confessed idoit, I mean indoit . . ."

"You mean idiot," said Kate helpfully.

"Yes," he said. "I am an idiot! I let the love of my life slippery through my flingers because I was too proud to let her dream job dicta-tion where we lived."

Kate shook her head.

"That's soooo sad," she said, flopping her hand on Oliver's knee.

"I thought I'd be compromolising my own happiness by going with her," said Oliver. "But it turned out, breaking up with her compro-molised my happiness anyway."

"You should tell her!" said Kate, swinging her glass in the air as she spoke. "You should tell her that you've comonise. Cosmonprised. Ru-ined your happiness."

"No," he said. "She deserves better. She's gelling along with 'er own life again. I can't jus' bowl in there and tell 'er I made a mislake. She deserves to be *hic-hic-hic*-happy."

"You're sooooo lovely," said Kate. "Sooooo romantic." She leaned her elbow on the table and rested her chin on her hand. "You're like a book I read once," she told him.

"Wha was it called?" asked Oliver.

"I dunno," said Kate. "Maybe . . . *Book*."

And whal abou' you?" asked Oliver. "Why are you always the brise-maid and never the brise?"

"Because I'm picky," said Kate. "And spiky! Like a cactus!"

Kate made claws of her hands in an attempt to look cactus-ish.

"I don't think you're spiky," said Oliver.

"You don't?" asked Kate.

"No," he assured her. "And you're not green."

He had leaned down across the table so that his face was level with hers. "I think you're great," he said. "And really, really pretty."

"No, I'm not," said Kate. "I wore the wrong dress. This dress is not sexy. Corduroy is not sexy like leather. I should have been sexy! Even my date did'n' like the look of me!"

"I think you're very sexy," said Oliver. "I think corduroy is a very sexy fabric. Leather is made from a cow."

Kate laughed. She tried to shake her boobs but sloshed her cocktail over herself. Oliver leaned over and haphazardly wiped at the spilled drink with a napkin.

"I'm mopping your boobs," said Oliver.

"They don't mind," said Kate.

"I think you're the prettiest girl in the bar," said Oliver. "I'm very pleased that I got to be your consololation prize."

"Aww, thanks, Oliver," Kate replied. "I think you're pretty too."

"I going to kiss you now," said Oliver. "I've been wanting to kiss your face for about an hour."

He leaned closer to Kate and their lips met. Kate was drunk and relaxed and Oliver tasted delicious. He pulled her around the table toward him and wrapped his arms around her, and Kate let herself be blissfully swept into his embrace.

They kissed for a long time. It was good. He was a good kisser. It had been a long time since Kate had been kissed like that. The rest of the night was a perfectly lovely blur.

· · · · ·

It was Sunday morning. Kate opened her eyes and closed them again quickly. She groaned. The sounds of crockery being clanked together down in the kitchen forced her to become more alert. She sat and held her head. She kicked off the patchwork eiderdown that covered her. She was fully clothed, right down to her shoes.

"Oh God," she moaned, and peeled herself off the bed. "Dad, is that you?" she called softly as she shuffled down the stairs.

She kept a tight hold on the banister and shielded her eyes from the brilliant winter sun that flooded the kitchen.

"I may have gotten shamefully drunk last night," she said, flopping down onto a dining chair. "Don't judge me."

She laid her head on the cool pine table and kept her eyes closed.

"Oh, I'll judge you, young lady," said Matt.

Kate shot up from the chair, lost her balance, and keeled over face first and headlong into the sofa by the French doors.

"Why are you here?" she grumbled into the cushion. "How did you even get in?"

"You called me up at three a.m., remember?" said Matt.

Kate's eyes snapped open and with supreme effort she pushed her face up out of the cushion and her body unglamorously onto all fours on the sofa, where she stayed, swaying like a cow in a strong breeze.

"Why would I do that?" she asked.

She had no recollection of calling Matt.

"What did I say?" she asked.

"You said you'd been kissing a sexy lumberjack for three hours and you couldn't get into your house," said Matt.

Kate remembered Oliver's body pressed up against hers. That was definitely a good memory. She didn't remember much else. Things were blurry. She had a hazy recollection of them being asked to leave the bar. She couldn't remember where they'd gone next. His place? Hers? No, she would have remembered that. A vague image of Oliver helping her into a taxi swam into her mind. She felt like she had beard burn. She wondered if her face was red.

Kate grimaced and shuffled backward off the sofa in an ungainly fashion, pulling herself up to standing and assuming the haughtiest air she could muster.

"I see," she said. "Is that all?"

Her eyelashes were sticking together with last night's mascara and she knew her hair must look as if it had been backcombed, ready for a beehive.

"No," said Matt. "You also told me you'd had sex on the beach— which must have been very cold—and a screaming orgasm."

Kate raised her eyebrows and pursed her lips and tried to retain a regal unamused posture, which was not easy when the room wouldn't stop spinning.

"Anything else?" she asked nonchalantly.

"Only that if I didn't come over at once and help you get into your house you would die of exposure," said Matt.

"Well," said Kate, smoothing down her corduroy dress and finding an alarmingly sticky blue stain down the front of it. "It *was* very cold," she reasoned. "Why are you still here?"

"Because I didn't want you to choke on your own vomit in the night," said Matt. "And you did vomit, Kate. You vomited an inhuman amount. How on earth did you get into that state? You were paralytic!" His voice was serious. "Especially on a blind date. You don't know these men! They could be rapists or murderers!"

Kate put her hand to her ear mockingly and said, "Is my mother here? I think I can hear her lecturing voice."

"I'm serious, Kate," said Matt.

Kate sighed and flopped back down on the sofa.

"I know, I know," she said. "Bad Kate. Stupid Kate. But so far as I remember Oliver was an almost perfect gentleman, if that's any consolation."

"It isn't," said Matt. "You were lucky."

He took Kate's hand and pushed a large mug of coffee into it.

"I've got to go," he told her. "Sarah's opened the café for me." He kissed Kate on the top of her head. "Stop being an idiot," he said.

The door slammed too loudly behind him.

THE FIFTH DATE OF CHRISTMAS

·····

Slinky Salsa
and Shivers

Laura was perched on the sofa in the kitchen with a takeaway coffee in her hand.

"So, you got on really well and you kissed him *a lot*, but you're not going to see him again."

"Correct," said Kate.

Laura leaned back and crossed her legs. She shook her head.

"I don't understand you," she said.

Mina was painting at the table next to Kate, who was color-washing some winter berry sketches. Charley lay dozing on a mat on the floor.

"I can't see the point of starting something with someone who is still clearly broken up about their old girlfriend," replied Kate.

"But you could be that person who makes him forget her!"

"In which case I would be the rebound fling who helps him over his ex and then he'd break up with me, all fit and ready to marry someone else," said Kate. "I don't want to be the rebound, I want to be *the One*."

"Geez, you're cynical," said Laura.

"Cynical!" Mina parroted.

"It's all academic anyway," said Kate. "We didn't swap numbers. At least I don't think we did. So I couldn't call him even if I wanted to."

"Matt was spitting feathers," said Laura.

"Matt can do what he likes," said Kate. "It's none of his business."

Laura tapped her nails against her mug and gazed out the French doors.

The sky had turned a grayish mustard color; it looked heavy, closer to the ground somehow, like a theater backdrop. Perhaps it would snow again.

"Are you sure," Laura began with trepidation, "that you're not making excuses to avoid meeting someone?"

"I signed myself up for the Twelve Dates thing," said Kate. "Why would I sign up for something—that wasn't cheap, by the way—if I wasn't serious about meeting someone?"

"You tell me," said Laura.

"There's nothing to tell," said Kate. "I'm being sensible, that's all, strategic even. I am not going to pursue someone who has a dead-end sign flashing above their head."

· · · · ·

Laura left and Kate cleared up the mess inevitably left behind by two children under the age of five.

Kate opened a cupboard in the dresser and pulled out a Tupperware container filled with leaves she'd foraged the day before: the last of the russet autumn spoils, which had been hidden from the elements beneath dark hedgerows. She'd painted them liberally on both sides with thick PVA glue to preserve them; they wouldn't keep indefinitely, of course—over time the vibrancy of the reds and golden greens would fade—but it gave her a few days' grace.

She upturned the box and let the leaves float down onto the kitchen table: feathery oak leaves the color of jack-o'-lanterns and beetroot blood, mottled moth-winged birch leaves, and fanned horse chestnut leaves with rust spots creeping over their skeletons.

Kate reached for her sketchbook and a fine-line pen and began to work. When she had five pages of leaf studies, she began to mix paints to capture their colors: poppy red and satsuma for flaming maple leaves, toasted gold and egg yolk for the leaves of the poplar tree.

When the studies were dry Kate would cut them out and arrange them on different-colored backgrounds until she found a design that pleased her. Sometimes it would be quick; the first arrangement gave her the thrill in her stomach that signified success. Other times the process seemed to take an age; she'd fiddle with the composition, she'd go away and drink coffee and consult her mood boards, but she couldn't submit a design until that tickle in her stomach made itself felt.

Perhaps—she mused as she pushed an oak leaf to overlap a horse chestnut—that was why her relationships hadn't lasted; maybe she was waiting for her stomach to thrill with a man the way it did with her work.

· · · · ·

"So, what's the next date?" asked Evelyn.

Kate had popped in to the shop to get one of Carla's ready meals and a bottle of wine. She raised her eyebrows.

"Does the *whole* village know about my twelve dates?" she asked.

"Oh yes, dear," said Evelyn merrily. "We're all very excited for you."

Kate shook her head and picked up a chocolate bar. There was a sign on the counter that read *Order your late Christmas tree here.*

"Have you gone into business with Patrick?" Kate asked, pointing at the sign.

Patrick rented extra land from the Blexford estate to grow Christmas trees.

"Didn't you hear?" asked Evelyn, delighted that she had news. "Patrick's run out of trees!"

"You're kidding," said Kate.

"I'm not," said Evelyn. "Fresh trees have become all the rage; everyone wants one. He ran out on Friday, so we're doing a little business venture together; we're going up to Covent Garden market on the fifteenth with his van to buy a load and we'll sell them from the shop here."

Evelyn was a canny businesswoman. There was a list with names on it by the sign. Kate hadn't gotten around to getting a tree yet, so she wrote her name and the size tree she'd like on the list.

She noticed Matt had his name down for two trees. She couldn't imagine where he'd fit them; the whole of one corner of the Pear Tree was already taken up with a large Norwegian spruce, dripping with ornaments and gaining more each day as children brought in more homemade baubles to hang on it.

"Well?" said Evelyn.

"I'll have one seven-footer, please," said Kate.

"Not the tree," said Evelyn. "The date!"

"Oh, yes. Sorry." Kate laughed. "The next date is salsa dancing."

"Oh, well, Kate, that's marvelous," Evelyn gushed. "You're on safe ground there, dear. Gosh, I remember you on Saturday mornings, always rushing off to the Big Town for ballet lessons, and you did tap too, didn't you?"

"Yup. And jazz, and I tried my hand at contemporary modern when I was at university," said Kate.

"Have you ever salsa danced?" Evelyn inquired.

"I have, actually," she said. "I signed up for classes when I first moved to London; there was a great salsa club just off Regent Street that I used to go to quite a bit. You should try it! It's great for keeping you limber."

Evelyn pondered as she rang Kate's shopping through the till.

"Maybe I will," she said. "I'll see if there are any evening classes in the Big Town. Does Mac dance?"

· · · · ·

The club was forty-five minutes away. Her dad had offered to take her, but Kate wanted to drive. After the overindulgence of the last date, she had decided to stick to lemonade this time. The snow had held off, but the temperature had dropped and the night sky was thick and starless.

She was supposed to have received details and a photograph of her date via email, but the Lightning Strikes website had gone down. Instead they had tweeted to say that the date was still going ahead and that the reps would assign them their dates when they arrived.

In the foyer, three tables had been hastily set up and three nervous reps handed out name tags with a slip of paper attached to each, which had the name of their date scrawled on it in ballpoint pen.

Kate handed her coat and jumper in at the cloakroom and shivered in her strappy vest top and skinny jeans; she expected to get hot later from dancing, but for now, with the door to the foyer constantly opening, she felt goose bumps burst out over her arms.

Latin beats furled out from the club entrance, and Kate felt her hips twitch as she waited in line. The closer she got to the door, the more distinct the sounds; the siren call of saxophones and the sexy throb of bongos pulled at her body. Kate spotted her name tag and the scrap of paper attached that read *Drew*. She scooped them up and pushed at the red velvet doors to the club.

The sound swept over her. The bass pounded through the soles of her feet and thrummed up through her body. It was impossible to stay still and Kate found herself wiggling where she stood. She ripped off the piece of paper that read *Drew* and fastened her name tag to her vest top.

The club was dark and hot. The dance floor was beginning to fill; couples locked into each other and moved with the music, swaying and grinding together as if under the spell of a snake charmer.

Around the edges of the dance floor other couples looked on nervously, biting their lips and shifting their feet. Many people were still wandering around checking name tags, looking for their date. Some had rooted themselves resolutely at the bar; their dates would be disappointed if they had hoped for a night of steamy salsa dancing. Kate looked around and hoped her date wasn't one of them.

The bar front and back was a colorful patchwork of Mexican tiles, floral repeating patterns in vibrant royal blue, rich saffron, and sangria red that echoed their larger counterparts on the surrounding floor. Some parts of the walls were exposed brick; others were painted turquoise and fiery ginger. The curved wall that ran behind the DJ was a mural of Day of the Dead dancing skeletons.

Kate headed to the bar to order herself a drink.

"Kate?"

Kate spun round to see a man holding up her name on a scrap of paper. He pulled at his close-fitting short-sleeved shirt to show her his name tag. It read *Drew*. Kate was delighted.

Drew was tall, black, and athletically built, and she had no trouble believing he had a six-pack hiding beneath his shirt. He looked like he could dance too. His hair was swept back off his face, which was nothing short of beautiful; his eyes were framed by perfectly arched brows. He was clean shaven. His nose came to a perfect point with just the right amount of turned-up to be desperately cute, and his lips formed a perfect cupid's bow.

Kate wondered if her outer self was grinning as hard as her inner.

"Lovely to meet you," he said over the noise of the music, and kissed her chastely on both cheeks.

"Likewise," Kate said. She couldn't hold back her smile.

"I think there's been a mistake," said Drew.

Kate's smile faltered.

"How so?" she asked.

"It's nothing personal," he said. "You're just not my type, I'm afraid."

"You don't even know me!" Kate was affronted.

"I don't need to." He smiled.

A swarthy man with sweat sticking his shirt to his pecs walked by. Drew pointed at him.

"Because he's my type," said Drew.

Kate's disappointment instantly dissolved.

"Oh no!" She laughed. "Poor you! Shall we go and see the reps?"

Drew shook his head.

"I don't think they'll be able to help," he said. "They've got no access to the website files and I don't fancy approaching every man in the club to ask if they happen to be gay and dateless."

Kate looked about her, her laughter subsiding. She didn't know what to do next. Tonight was clearly a washout as far as meeting her potential soul mate, but she had been looking forward to dancing.

"Can you salsa dance?" asked Drew.

"Yes," said Kate. "Can you?"

Drew smiled devilishly.

"Like a young Patrick Swayze," he said. And he grabbed her by the hand and led her out onto the dance floor.

He wasn't lying. He was one of the best dance partners she'd ever had, and the sexiest too; such a shame he was more into Kevins than Kates, she thought. They danced until they were both breathless and dripping with sweat, and Kate had to admit to herself that she needed to do more exercise.

To one side of the bar was a doorway that led into a chill-out area where canopied banquettes lined the walls and candles flickered in sconces. And it was here that Drew and Kate retreated to, breathless and glistening. They collapsed onto a cerise velvet banquette.

The throbbing beat from next door still made itself felt, but the music here was slow salsa and a lower volume, though no less provocative judging by the silhouettes of some couples hidden behind the veiled canopies.

"So, besides wiggling your hips like Shakira," said Drew, "what else do you do?"

Kate laughed.

"I design fabrics for Liberty and I bake for a local café," she said.

"Liberty!" he exclaimed. His eyes grew wide and Kate was pleased she'd impressed him. "I knew you had to have soul if you could dance like that."

"What about you?" Kate asked.

"I'm a banker," he replied, raising his eyebrows. "Cue jokes and innuendos."

"I wasn't going to say a thing." Kate held her hands up in innocence. "Have you met anyone special on any of the dates?" she asked.

"Well, there was one guy," said Drew a little shyly. "I don't want to jinx it, but his name is Steven and he works as a translator for the Home Office. He seemed nice; tired of all the dating bullshit, and he wants to settle down."

"He sounds perfect," said Kate. "I take it that's what you want?"

"I'm thirty-six," said Drew. "If I want to start a family, I need to get a move on."

"Tell me about it," said Kate. "I'm thirty-four. Don't get me wrong, I'm happy to go it alone if the right guy doesn't come along, but I just always had this romantic idea about being with someone special and starting a family together."

Drew sighed.

"You and me both," he said, and he put his hand on Kate's and gave it a squeeze. "What about you? Met anyone with potential?"

Kate thought about Anthony and Oliver. Both had potential, she thought; just not with her.

"Not yet," said Kate. "But I remain hopeful."

"I'm surprised a fine filly like you is single anyway," he said. "What gives?"

"Did you just call me a filly?"

"Don't avoid the awkward question," said Drew. "Spill it! I want the full heartbreaking details."

Well, thought Kate, *he did ask!* And so, Kate gave Drew a brief overview of her love life thus far.

"That's quite a list," Drew said.

"I prefer to think of it as research," said Kate.

Drew raised his eyebrows.

"Longest relationship?" he asked.

"Dan," said Kate. "Four years."

"That's longer than any of mine," he mused. "Greatest heartbreak?"

The image of an all-too-familiar face swam unbidden into Kate's mind. Her breath caught, but she recovered herself quickly and pushed the image back into the recesses of her mind, where she kept painful things.

"I don't think I've had my heart broken by an actual boyfriend," said Kate.

"Oh, that's very deep," said Drew. He rested his chin on his hands and fixed Kate with an intense stare. "But you've been heartbroken," he said.

"Yes, I think I have," said Kate. "But it was fixed a long time ago. What about you?"

"Longest relationship was Conner; eighteen months."

"And was he your greatest heartbreak?"

"No," said Drew. "That would be when Take That broke up!"

Kate laughed. "Please tell me how a sex bomb like you can have trouble finding guys."

"It's not the finding them I struggle with," said Drew. "It's the keeping hold of them."

"You and me both," said Kate. "Maybe you've been dating the wrong kind of men?"

"Are you suggesting I'm shallow?"

"No!" she said. "But maybe you should broaden your horizons, try a different type, someone you wouldn't normally go for."

"I signed up for this, didn't I?" he said. "And look who I ended up with!" He gestured toward Kate.

"Well," said Kate, laughing. "You have to admit, I'm not your usual type."

· · · · ·

After a cold drink and some respite, they went back to dancing: hot, sticky sensual dancing punctuated by cozy chats and cooling lemonade, minus unreasonable expectations, nerves, and pressure to conform to a hopeful stranger's ideals.

Salsa night turned out to be the best date yet, despite there not being the ghost of a chance of a relationship. It was the most fun she'd had in a long time. Kate and Drew had a lot in common. They'd swapped numbers and Kate hoped they would keep in touch; it shouldn't be too hard for them to schedule in a lunch or a drink after work when she was in London.

Drew was catching the train back to the city; the station was only a five-minute walk from the club. Even with her coat on, the cold smacked her hard when they finally left the thrumming music behind and Drew walked Kate to her car. After being so hot for so long the chill seemed to bite through to her bones. There was a thin crunchy layer of snow on the ground and the flakes were gathering momentum.

"Will you be all right driving home?" Drew asked. His brow was furrowed as he looked up at the sky and pulled his gloves on. "I think this is just getting started."

"I'll be fine," said Kate. "We have a tendency to get snowed in where I live, so I'm used to driving in far worse than this."

"If you're sure," said Drew. "I don't mind shouting you a taxi. I'm sure I could talk the club management into letting you leave your car here."

"Honestly, I'll be fine," Kate assured him. "I'll take it slowly. The main roads will be clear and the gritters will be out."

Drew kissed Kate on both cheeks. He smelled delicious: sweat and expensive aftershave.

Kate watched him turn out of the car park. He turned back and shouted a final good-bye.

"Sorry I wasn't your dream man!" he called.

"Sorry I don't have a penis!" Kate called back.

She heard Drew laugh loudly as he crossed the road.

Kate gave one last wave and climbed into her car. Her teeth were chattering. Where she had been damp with sweat not twenty minutes before, she now felt icy, borderline numb. She blew on her hands and turned the key in the ignition. The engine coughed lazily and choked.

"Oh no no no," she said. "Don't you dare. It's not that cold; everybody else's car managed to start."

She turned the key again. It bayed mournfully like an old bloodhound and died.

"Shit," said Kate.

There were only two cars left in the car park now and the surge of people leaving the club had dwindled to a drizzle. Her whole body was shaking. Sleeping in the car was not an option.

She got out and headed back into the club. The snow was coming down fast now and her original footprints had already been wiped out. There was no one in the foyer, so she pushed through the doors into the club.

As with most nighttime establishments, the magic and mystique was lost when the lights went up. The salsa club was no exception. What had seemed sensual and luxuriant in the dark was stark and a bit tacky under the white glare of the spotlights.

Two people were clearing up behind the bar and another three collected glasses from around the club. There were no punters, save one drunk man with a quiff and a cheap suit shouting into a mobile phone and demanding to know where his "bloody taxi" was.

Kate approached the bar.

"Hi," she said. "I'm sorry to be a pain but I don't suppose anyone's got any jump leads? My car won't start."

Nobody did. Apart from one girl who'd walked the fifteen minutes from her house, they all commuted in by train and were eager to get cleared down and gone before they missed the last connection.

They offered her the use of the phone to call a breakdown service, but Kate hadn't bothered to get it renewed when she set up her last insurance. She'd decided to shop about for cheaper breakdown coverage but never got around to it. The manager said she could stay in the club until they closed down, and Kate was grateful.

It was too late to call her dad, and she didn't want to bother Matt and Sarah. She looked up train times on her phone, but the last connection to Great Blexley had been and gone. The drunk man stumbled out of the club shouting, " 'Bout effing time!"

"I'm just going to give it another try!" Kate called to the bar manager. He nodded and carried on working.

It was bitter. The snow had almost filled in her second set of footprints. The chessboard roof of her old Mini Clubman was covered in a white frosty fur. She climbed into the icemobile and tried the engine. It gave one quiet wheeze and gave up.

"Shit shit double shit!" shouted Kate.

The snow was creeping up the windscreen. She slammed the door and tramped back over to the club. The doors were locked.

"Shiiiiit!" she said. They must have gone out the back way and thought she'd gotten her car started.

The club was on an industrial estate and at this time of night it was empty and eerily quiet. Through the muffling of the snow she heard a train pull into the station and hoped the bar staff had made it in time.

She shuffled back to her car and climbed in, pulling her coat tightly around her. Kate jabbed a stiff finger at an app on her phone and music began to play. She kept the volume low; she didn't want to advertise her status as lone-woman-Popsicle.

She couldn't feel her toes at all. Her limbs, so supple and pliable on the dance floor just hours ago, felt brittle. She pulled the tartan throw—usually draped over the backseat for esthetics—up over her nose and mouth. *I'll give it ten minutes and see if it'll start, and if it doesn't then I'll really panic.*

After a few minutes she turned the music off; she didn't want to run the battery down, just in case. A pair of foxes padded lightly across the car park, coming in from different directions. They saw each other and stopped. Kate wondered if there'd be a fight, but they seemed to think better of it and turned back out the way they had come; one stopped to nose around the bins before leaving.

Two men, drunk by the sounds of them, walked past the car park, talking in shouts. One declared he needed to "take a piss!" Kate watched as he doubled back and stumbled into the car park.

He zigzagged toward the car. Kate slunk down in her seat, hoping he wouldn't see her. The man stopped a stone's throw from the Mini and began to urinate against the wall. Steam rose up as he melted the snow.

"Come on!" yelled the man outside the car park. "I'm freezing my nads off here!"

"Coming!" shouted the other man, doing up his fly.

Kate sat very still, breathing shallowly. The man stumbled back out again and their noisy commentary resumed. She breathed out, relieved.

After another five minutes she tried the key in the ignition again. It turned over once and then choked.

Kate banged her head against the steering wheel. "Oh bloody, shit, shit, shitters!" she shouted, pummeling the dashboard with her fists. She didn't hear the car pull into the empty car park.

There was a knock on her driver's-side window. "Fuck!" she shouted; she jumped so high, her bottom left the seat and she banged her head on the ceiling.

"Sorry!" said a man's voice. "I'm not going to hurt you. I just wanted to check if you were all right? See if you needed any help?"

The man backed away from the car with his hands up like a

surrender. The window was misted with her breath. She opened the window a crack. "My car won't start," she shouted through it.

The man walked slowly toward her.

"I've got jump leads in my car," he said. "I can help you get it started. I was on tonight's date," he went on. "I came back to see if I'd left my phone in the club."

He was tall and broad, made all the broader by a heavy ski jacket. The hood was up and his face was half in shadow. He reached the car, still with his hands up, as though trying not to frighten off a wounded rabbit. He knelt down by the window.

Kate didn't open it any wider, but she wiped her sleeve across the glass to clear the mist.

"Kate?" said the man, squinting through the glass. "Are you Kate?" He pulled his hood down.

"It's me, Richard!" he said. "From the Twelve Dates of Christmas."

Kate peered at him through the glass. Dark hair, square jaw; minus the rugby ball, but that was to be expected.

"Richard the rugby player who stood me up?" asked Kate.

"The very same and the very sorry," said Richard. "I've been trying to persuade the Twelve Dates guys to give me your number so I could call you, but it's against their company policy."

Kate rolled down the window another two inches and craned her neck to get a better look at him.

"It *is* you," she said incredulously.

"Listen," said Richard. "Why don't you get into my car, which has heating, and I'll get your car started. It's the least I can do after shamelessly ditching our afternoon tea date."

"You had me at *heating*," said Kate. With the tartan blanket still wrapped round her, Kate extricated herself from the Mini and climbed up into Richard's SUV.

"Do not murder me," Kate warned him once she'd gotten settled in her seat.

"I wouldn't dream of it," said Richard, smiling.

He shut the passenger door, went around to the driver's side, and started the engine. It purred and immediately warm air began to fill the car. Richard tapped his finger to the touchscreen dashboard and the heaters began to roar.

"Sit tight and warm up," he said. "I'll get the jump leads and see if I can get your engine started."

Kate was only too pleased to do as she was told, while Richard set about manhandling Kate's car so that their bumpers were almost nose to nose. Richard's car smelled of man: a mixture of aftershave and deodorant. It was quite intoxicating, sort of woody notes and black pepper; Kate found herself strangely aroused, but she put this down to gratitude and relief.

She watched as he attached the red and black lead clamps to her car battery. Then he doubled back around and opened the driver's door of the SUV and switched the engine off. As he did so, a flurry of snowflakes swept into the car; they perched delicately on the seat like resting butterflies before the heat from the car disappeared them.

Richard deftly attached the remaining leads to his battery and then climbed in beside Kate and switched the engine and the heaters back on.

"I should explain," Richard began. "My son, Nathanial, was rushed into hospital the night before our date and, I'll be honest, I forgot all about it. It just went out of my head. I remembered about two days later, when everything had calmed back down. I called Lightning Strikes to see if I could get your number, but they couldn't let me have it because of data protection."

"Is he all right?" Kate asked. "Nathanial?" Kate recalled Richard's profile: two children, a boy and a girl. Richard had joint custody with his ex-wife.

"He's fine," said Richard. "Thank God! He made a full recovery. It started off as an ear infection. The doctor said it was viral and would go away on its own, but then when he was at my place his temperature spiked and I . . . well, I just panicked."

"Of course," said Kate. "You must have been terrified."

"I was beside myself," said Richard. "Not very manly, I know."

"More manly than not being worried," said Kate. "Men seem to have this idea that showing emotion is a sign of weakness, when really, the opposite is true."

As her bones warmed in the heat of the car, so did her feelings toward Richard.

"Huh," said Richard. "A wise woman indeed! Anyway, they put him on some strong antibiotics and kept him in overnight. I stayed up there with him. I know I should have emailed the rep to let them know I couldn't make it, but it just went out of my head."

"Honestly," said Kate. "Don't give it a second thought. You've more than made up for it by rescuing me from a night in my car."

"Don't thank me yet," said Richard. "I haven't got it started yet. In fact, I'll give it a try now."

Richard climbed out of the SUV, and Kate watched him crunch through the snow and round to her Mini, which was accumulating quite a head of snow on its roof. She smiled to herself as Richard folded his enormous frame almost in half to crush himself into Kate's tiny car. Next to him it looked like a child's toy.

She heard her engine turn over a couple of times and then wheeze to a stop once more. Richard got out and came back to sit with Kate. Snow had settled on his black hair.

"We'll give it another few minutes," he said. "I'm not ready to give up on it yet."

"It's not really built for someone as big as you," joked Kate.

"You're not kidding," said Richard. "I thought I was going to need a shoehorn to get me out of it!"

Kate laughed.

"Thank you for this," she said.

"I couldn't leave a damsel in distress," he replied.

"How funny it was you who found me," said Kate. "I didn't see you in the club."

"Nor I you," he said. "I'm not one to go misty-eyed over coincidence, but it is a hell of a coincidence."

Kate agreed.

"So how was your date?" she asked.

"Fine, I suppose," said Richard.

"Do you think you'll meet up again?" Kate asked.

"I don't think so," said Richard. "She's quite a bit younger than me. We didn't have much in common really, aside from sport. How about yours?"

"I had a great time," said Kate. "And I would definitely like to see him again, but only as friends."

"Oh?" said Richard. Kate could see a smile working around his mouth; she thought he looked pleased.

"They got our dates mixed up," said Kate. "My date was gay. I'm all for giving things a fair crack of the whip, but in this case, it would be a lost cause."

Richard laughed. "Less competition for me."

"Who says you're still in the race?" asked Kate.

"After a false start, I'd like to put to myself back in the running," he said. "If that's all right with you?"

He looked at her and Kate felt a tickle of excitement in her stomach. "I'd like that," she said.

They sat quietly for a few minutes, watching the snow tumble down outside; the soothing whirr of the engine and the blowers pushing out hot air made Kate feel suddenly very sleepy. She yawned.

"Oh, I'm sorry," she said, as another yawn chased the first.

"It's late," said Richard. "I'm going to give the car another try."

This time her Mini spluttered into life and stayed that way. Kate was almost disappointed. Richard sat, like Gulliver in her driver's seat, revving the engine until it was clear it wasn't going to flake out again. After a few minutes he disengaged the wires and came around and opened the passenger door of the SUV.

"Your chariot, such as it is, awaits," he said.

"Such as it is indeed!" said Kate, allowing Richard to help her down from his monster vehicle. He smelled delightful; there was a hint of engine oil mixed in with his eau de cologne now that made her feel quite silly.

"She is small but perfectly formed," said Kate.

"Like her owner," said Richard with a glint in his eye.

"Well," said Kate, holding out her hand. "Thank you very much for your help. You are officially my hero!"

Richard took her hand in his large paw and kissed it.

"You're more than welcome," he said. "Listen, obviously I don't have my phone right now, but do you think I could have your number? I'd like to take you on a belated first date."

"I'd like that," she said.

She leaned across the seat of the Mini and pulled a sketchpad—she never liked to be without a sketchpad—out of the glove compartment. She tore an unused page from the back and wrote her name and mobile number on it and handed it to Richard.

"I will call you," he said.

"Make sure you do," said Kate.

He closed her door and waited while she carefully maneuvered out of the snowy parking space. Kate looked back in her rearview mirror and was happy to see him still standing there watching as she pulled out onto the road.

The roads were better than Kate had expected. Apart from the quieter side roads, the gritting lorries had been out in force. Kate was tired, but the Mini's heating system was nowhere as effective as the one in Richard's SUV, and the chill kept her awake as she negotiated the icy roads.

She wished it weren't so late; she couldn't wait to tell Laura about meeting Richard. What were the chances? She smiled to herself. *Laura is going to love this!*

As Blexford hill came into view, it was clear the gritters hadn't been there yet. There was no way the Mini would make it up in the snow. *Bugger!* she thought. She parked at the bottom of the hill and wrapped the tartan blanket around her shoulders like a shawl.

Her phone blipped. It was a text from Matt. The time was from much earlier in the evening; she must have been out of signal range.

Hey dancing queen, don't forget I need the brownies
first thing in the morning for that breakfast party!
Hope you had a great night. M xxx

"Bugger and shit!" said Kate out loud. A passing cat meowed mournfully at her in response and padded off through the drifting snow. She'd been so engrossed in her work earlier that she'd completely forgotten Matt had asked for a double batch of brownies for the morning. The Blexford Primary PTA booked a breakfast meeting once a month at the Pear Tree and they always, always had breakfast pudding. *Women after my own heart,* thought Kate.

Blexford hill was steep, almost vertical steep. It was not for the faint-hearted. There was a bench halfway up on either side, and with good reason. Luckily Kate's love of hiking stood her in good stead, but even so, she was glad when she finally made it to the top of the first bend, where the incline lessened marginally enough to allow shallower breathing.

Blexford was asleep. Even Barry's light above the pub was off. The snow fell fat and white and silent, secretly cloaking the land while it slumbered, a secret only Kate was privy to: Kate and the owls and the foxes with whom she shared this night. The world would wake to a winter wonderland, but only Kate would watch the spell being woven.

Despite the time and her tiredness, Kate slowed her pace. She let the peace of Blexford at rest soak into her as though by osmosis. The stars were like silver studs in the black leather sky. The strings of lights draped over the old fir tree blinked lazily as the snow dappled them.

Pictures began to form behind her eyes: black cotton, a snowy owl on the wing, a sleeping chocolate-box cottage with a white roof and a fox investigating the garden, clouds parting to reveal a bulbous moon and winking stars. Kate shoved her hand into her pocket. *Dammit,* she thought; she'd left her pocket sketchbook in her other coat. She picked up her pace. She needed to get the essence of the idea roughed out; by morning the feeling would be diluted by sleep and dreams, and the jobs she had to do for the day ahead.

With frozen fingers she negotiated the key in the lock and pushed the front door closed and leaned back against it. She sighed. The grandfather clock in the hall showed that it was almost three thirty a.m. She desperately wanted to fall into bed. But she had to get her sketches down and she had brownies to bake. With another sigh she shuffled into the kitchen and switched on the oven.

Kate fixed herself a hot chocolate and as the warmth from the oven began to seep into the room, she grabbed her sketchbook and began to draw. An hour and a half later, with the brownies cooling on the rack and her late-night scribblings safely contained for posterity, she climbed wearily into bed.

Dates with Mates and Heartbreaks

The snow squeaked as it gave way under Kate's boots. A good three inches had fallen overnight, and Kate wasn't altogether convinced she'd be able to get her car up the hill today.

Drew had texted her to thank her for a lovely evening. He complained that his shins were aching and his hips were stiff. Kate told him about her car adventure. Drew texted her back immediately:

Why in God's name didn't you text me?

What could you have done? Kate texted back. Caught the train back and given me a piggyback?

That is the kind of facetious attitude that finds you sans a man! Drew wrote.

Harsh but fair, messaged Kate. Although I did get a date out of it.

Playing the damsel-in-distress card, Drew texted. How very sexist of you. Keep me posted on the man front, sexy mama. x

It was almost nine as Kate, laden with brownies, tramped through Potters Copse, a cut through from her house to the village square. She needed coffee. She'd had coffee, but she needed more. She'd set her radio alarm for eight a.m. If it hadn't been playing "Fairytale of New York"— her favorite Christmas song—she might have thrown a shoe at it.

Someone had taken it upon themselves to decorate a hawthorn tree in the copse with baubles and fairy lights, and the idea had apparently taken off. Now several trees, including a boisterous holly bush and a rowan tree, were bejeweled in Christmas apparel, and with snow adorning the branches and blanketing the ground, the place felt enchanted. Kate expected at any moment to spy a little wooden cabin with smoke curling out of the chimney and a jolly white bearded fellow busily working within.

She would come back later and take photographs for next Christmas's mood board. This year's Christmas fabric had been on sale since the beginning of November. She had submitted her final designs by September; she'd been sketching in earnest since July and gathering ideas before that.

The Christmas fabric was Kate's baby. There was a thrill to be had in each season's designs, an organic, slow-burning accumulation of inspirations and feelings, which drove each design to fruition. But it was the Christmas fabric that really excited her; there was something about it that fed her soul and warmed her bones from within.

When she'd first started at Liberty as apprentice to the art director, she'd bombarded him with so many Christmas design ideas that he'd let her design the festive paper napkins just to shut her up. They sold like a dream and the following year, he let her loose on the fabrics.

Kate banged her snowy boots off against the boot scraper outside the café door and went in. The Pear Tree was in full Christmas decorating mode. Christmas music belted out beneath the sound of the coffee machine. Matt shouted instructions while making coffee. Carla and an excitable throng of customers stood on chairs to pin red, gold, and green baubles to the wooden ceiling beams. Matt saw Kate and smiled.

"There's a free hot mince pie for everyone who helps with the decorations," he told her.

"Ah," said Kate. "That explains the enthusiasm."

"Cappuccino?" asked Matt.

Kate shook her head. "Flat white, double shot."

"Crikey!" said Matt. He continued, "I don't think you'll get your car up the hill today."

"How did you know my car was down there?" asked Kate.

Matt grinned and tapped his nose.

"How was the date?" he asked.

Kate yawned and then yawned again immediately.

"That good, huh?" said Matt.

"It's not what you think," said Kate, stifling yet another yawn. "The car wouldn't start. I had to be rescued."

"By who?" Matt asked.

"By the guy who stood me up on the first date," said Kate.

Matt pushed the coffee across the counter toward her, and Kate handed over the brownies. She plinked three lumps of brown sugar into the strong, dark liquid and swigged gratefully.

"Bit weird," said Matt as he carefully transferred the squidgy brownies to a large plate and handed them to the PTA chairwoman, who'd stood impatiently by like a politician waiting for an important document.

"It was, a bit," said Kate. "But in a good way."

She watched the chairwoman lower the plate onto the table. The PTA members pushed their breakfast plates aside and delved toward the brownies.

"What about your actual date?" asked Matt.

"What?" said Kate, watching a woman in a striped jumper slap another woman's hand away from an end piece of brownie. "Oh, he was brilliant!" said Kate, returning her attention to Matt.

"Wow," said Matt.

"And one hundred percent gay," said Kate. "But I'd definitely like to see him again. But with any luck I'll be seeing Richard, previous-no-show and now car-hero, in a more romantic capacity."

"Success all round, then," said Matt.

Kate smiled. A cardboard box full of all things jingle bells clattered to the floor, sending glittery objects skittering across the café.

"Need an extra pair of hands?" she asked.

Matt grimaced.

"There's as much coffee as you can handle in it if you would," he said.

"You can help me if you like," said Evelyn, wrestling a pythonlike garland out of a large cardboard box. "This needs to drape over the fireplace."

Kate helped Evelyn uncoil the greenery and secure it to the mantel shelf.

"Who's manning the shop?" asked Kate.

"I've put a note on the door," said Evelyn. "If anyone needs me, they'll come and get me."

"People have been decorating the trees in Potters Copse," said Kate, wrapping fairy lights around the garland.

"Yes," said Evelyn. "Your dad told me the other day. He brought a sprout tree in for me."

"Oh," said Kate. "That's nice. Well anyway, it looks really magical, especially with the snow, and I thought it might be a nice idea to add it into the caroling walk?"

Every year on Christmas Eve, the Blexford residents went on a caroling walk around the village. It had started back in the Second World War, as a treat for the children who'd been evacuated from London. The Women's Institute gathered all the children and they walked through the village singing carols. The residents would leave homemade gifts—paper airplanes, peg dolls, and knitted finger puppets—en route, hanging from branches or resting on garden walls, for the children to find as they went.

The tradition had endured, although these days the procession wasn't just for the children, and the gifts tended to be of the edible kind. But it got everyone in the Christmas mood and it was an excellent excuse to nose at people's outdoor decorations. Now there was a fair amount of unspoken competitiveness, which only made the village look even prettier.

"Good idea," said Evelyn. "I'll put it to the team."

With the garland secure and the lights evenly spaced, Kate and Evelyn tied baubles and wooden trinkets—rocking horses, little nutcracker soldiers, and ruby hearts—in among the leaves and pinecones and berries, until it looked as extravagant as a Fortnum & Mason display.

Carla disappeared from bauble duty into the kitchen and reappeared five minutes later with a Christmas-tree-shaped serving platter, laden with steaming mince pies. The customers fell gratefully upon them; Kate had two.

If the café had looked festive before—what with the giant gaudy tree hung with everything from toilet roll Santas to paper snowflakes—now it looked positively grotto-like. The fairy lights, which covered the walls, glinted off the sea of ceiling baubles, so that the whole place seemed to twinkle.

"Isn't it lovely." Kate sighed.

Evelyn nodded.

"His mum would've loved the way he runs this place," said Evelyn fondly.

Evelyn had been one of Matt's mum's oldest friends. Matt and Corinna's dad left when Matt was a baby without leaving a forwarding address. When Matt's mum died, her solicitor produced a letter, handwritten by her and witnessed, instructing that should anything happen to her, the children should be left in the care of Evelyn.

Matt hadn't always appreciated Evelyn's support, or her scoldings (Evelyn didn't suffer fools), when he'd been younger, but for the last decade or so she had woken up every Mother's Day to a card and a bouquet of flowers on her doorstep.

"Mince pie, Evelyn?" mumbled Matt through a mouthful of sweet shortcrust pastry.

He offered up the Christmas tree plate. Evelyn's hand hovered over the pies while she chose one.

"Don't talk with your mouth full!" she said.

Matt grinned.

"Right! I'm off," said Kate. "How much do I owe you?"

"As if you'd pay," said Matt. "Can you make me some more mince pies and a rocky road for Saturday? I'll pay you for the brownies at the same time."

"No problem," answered Kate.

Kate exited the Pear Tree grotto, shutting out Paul McCartney's "Wonderful Christmastime" as she pulled the door closed behind her.

The air was crisp and clean and the double shot in her flat white was having the desired effect. The sky had the laden look of more snow about it. Kate doubled back through Potters Copse and took photos while the light was still good and then dropped in on her dad, but he wasn't home. She guessed he was at her place tending the vegetable garden. She guessed right.

Kate poured hot soup into bowls and laid the table while her dad banged his boots off outside. He shrugged out of his overcoat and gloves and soon they were seated at the table. The log burner in the corner crackled and Mac cupped his hands around his soup bowl to warm them.

"How's your mum?" asked Mac.

"Do you really want to know?"

"We were married for thirty-four years. You care about someone for that long, it's hard to switch it off just because they're not around anymore," said Mac.

"She's good," said Kate. "She's in Barbados."

"Barbados!" said Mac. "Crikey! Holiday?"

"Work," said Kate. "Of sorts. She's selling a yacht out there and the owner is letting them stay on it over Christmas."

"Phew!" said Mac. "She has the life, eh? Well, that's good. I'm glad she's doing well."

"Oh, Dad," said Kate. "You're a better person than me. I'm not sure I would be so forgiving."

Her dad smiled.

"Really?" he said. "What about Matt?"

"What about Matt?" Kate asked.

"After the falling-out you two had," said Mac, "I thought you'd never speak again. And look at you now. Best mates, living in the same village, baking for him . . ."

"Well, that's different, isn't it," said Kate. "We weren't married with kids."

"True," said her dad. "But your feelings for Matt were . . ." He paused as he tried to find the right word. "Intense," he said finally. Kate shifted in her chair and Mac changed the subject. "I know your mum was no angel," he said.

"No angel?" said Kate, relieved to be on safer ground. "That's an understatement!"

"She was unhappy with herself," said Mac.

"There is no excuse for her behavior," said Kate. "I don't know why you stood for it. I'd have thrown her out after the first affair."

Her dad grimaced and Kate wished she hadn't said so much. She was always worried he might lapse back into depression.

"With someone like your mum," he said, "you always hope they'll change. Each time they come back they swear it'll never happen again, and my God you want to believe them so badly." He stopped; his eyes were fixed on a patch of wall behind Kate's head, but Kate could tell his mind was far away. He blinked and his reverie had passed. He looked at Kate, smiling.

"Maybe Gerry's the man to finally tame her," he said. "Good luck to him. He'll need it."

Kate's phone blipped and the screen lit up. It was a text message from Matt.

> On the fifth date of Shagmas my true love gave to me,
> One gay man dancing,
> One date of drinking,
> One fireman skating,
> One vegan weeping
> And a no-show outside the Pear Tree!

Kate shook her head and typed back:

> You are hilarious. Have you considered giving up catering and going into comedy?

Kate took her phone and shut it in a drawer in the dresser. "That man is the bane of my life."

"Matt?" asked Mac.

"The one and only."

"He brings out your sparkle," said Mac.

"That's not sparkle," Kate corrected. "It's rage-glitter."

Kate often felt that in Mac's eyes, Matt could do no wrong. With Matt's dad not around when they were kids, Mac had stepped in as a male influence, although Kate suspected this was less an altruistic gesture and more that he had a daughter who wasn't even slightly interested in football or cricket.

Sometimes on a Sunday, when Matt's mum was busy baking or doing the books, Mac would take Matt to watch the cricket; sometimes they'd play an inning. He'd energetically tried to engage Kate's interest in it but to no avail, and so it became something he and Matt would do together. Kate didn't begrudge either of them their time together; it kept her out of the stands and made her dad happy.

· · · · ·

"I liked Dan," said Mac, going off on his own tangent. "He was a good chap. A real go-getter. And I liked that other one too, what was his name? You sent back photos from Morocco?"

"Aaron," said Kate.

"That's the one. I could tell you liked him. But he didn't make you sparkle."

"I'm not looking for sparkle, Dad," said Kate. "I am on a grown-up-woman mission to find a suitable, sensible partner who has no improper pride and is perfectly amiable."

"Have you been watching *Pride and Prejudice* again?" asked Mac.

"Maybe," said Kate.

They ate the rest of their soup and crusty bread in companionable silence, while outside it began to snow again. After lunch her dad helped her clear up and Kate helped him in with the veg basket. He gathered up a few vegetables for himself and some for Evelyn and left the rest for Kate.

"I'll leave the rest in the ground, ready for Christmas dinner," said Mac as he left for home. The snow was coming down quite heavily and his footprints up to the vegetable patch had been all but filled in.

"Dad," said Kate. "Have you ever considered, you know, getting back out there again, you know, trying to meet someone?"

"I certainly have," said Mac, and he gave her a wink that she couldn't quite fathom.

Kate worked on her sketches until it was too dark, even with the lamps on, to get a clear sense of the colors. She rinsed out her brushes and laid some papery pressed flowers along the top of the table, ready for the morning. Below them she placed an illustrated treasury of nursery rhymes. It was a large tattered book, passed down from her grandma. Kate used to spend hours as a child looking at the pictures of ruby toadstools and fairies hiding in flowers. Now she would use them as inspiration for her spring collection.

The phone rang.

"Don't hate me," said Laura.

"Why? What have you done?"

"Ben's been called away with work," said Laura. "I can't make it to your Dates with Mates night. I'm really sorry."

Kate was disappointed, but she only said, "That's okay. I've got a lot of work I want to get done anyway. Maybe I'll skip this one."

"You can't skip it!" said Laura. "I'll feel awful. You want to do all twelve dates, don't you? This could be *the one*! And besides, you've paid enough for it, you ought to get your money's worth."

Laura was right, she really ought to make the most of it since she was paying through the nose for it, and honestly, it got her out of the house.

Her relationship with Dan had been full on. Dan was an adrenaline junkie; every moment they weren't working was spent abseiling or kayaking or hiking or rock climbing. It was never quiet. Exciting but exhausting. And since they'd split up, Kate had found herself reveling in the calm of her life. But she had been reaching the point where she'd quite happily become a hermit.

Laura—ever determined once she had an idea in her head—had drawn Mac into her scheme to get Kate signed up for the Twelve Dates of Christmas:

"There's nothing wrong with staying in, if it makes you happy," said her dad. "But you're hiding. And that's not the same thing at all."

He was right. She had been hiding. Because it was easier to hide away and never meet anybody than to potentially meet someone only to have it fail again.

Dan had been great. They had fun. The sex was good. They'd just run their course and that was that. Kate wanted children and Dan didn't. Neither one had deceived the other; they'd known where they stood from the start, though each of them had hoped the other would come around to their way of thinking.

Kate was philosophical about it. Dan had been the only serious contender for her heart in a long time, but even with him she hadn't really felt invested. And when, as she'd known it would, their relationship had fizzled out, she was aware that she wasn't as heartbroken as she probably ought to have been.

As for the rest of the flings she'd had over the last few years, they had been just that, flings: fun and frivolous but by no means life partner material.

If she did eventually want a family, she would need to either be more discriminating or sign up for IVF; she didn't mind which. She could more than capably raise a child alone. She would do this one thing to prove to everyone that she'd tried, and then she would go it alone.

Laura's pleading voice broke her reverie.

"Please say you'll still go," said Laura. "I'll feel terrible if you miss it. And Ben will too; I'll make sure of it."

"It's short notice to ask anyone else," said Kate.

"Ask Sarah!" said Laura, elated at her own genius. "She's always up for a laugh."

· · · · ·

Sarah normally dropped in to see Matt when she finished work. Kate arrived just after four o'clock and sure enough there she was, hugging a hot chocolate, the heat from the café curling her raven hair in just the right way.

"Wait a minute. Let me get this straight," said Matt. "You want to take *my* girlfriend with you on a date night, as *your* wing woman?"

"Yes," said Kate. "Although you make it sound creepy. The theme is Dates with Mates; it's just a chance for people to mingle in an informal way. It's a pub quiz, actually."

"Nice," said Sarah. "You know me and a pub quiz."

Sarah was very clever—as you'd expect from a headmistress—and fiercely competitive. Their pub team score had increased significantly since Sarah had joined them. The Pear Tree Perils were now a force to be reckoned with at the Duke's Head quiz nights.

"So, you haven't been assigned a shag . . . sorry, I mean *date* for this one," asked Matt.

"Give her a break, Matt," said Sarah. "You make it sound like Kate's the only person who's ever used a dating website. And I know for a fact that you were on one before we met."

Kate was aghast.

"You hypocrite!" she said. "You've been giving me grief this whole time."

"All right, all right." Matt held his hands up in defeat. "But still," he went on. "It's a bit weird, isn't it? I'm not sure I want you to go on a singles night, Sarah."

"It won't be like that," said Kate.

"And besides," said Sarah. "I do have a mind of my own. I'm not going to forget I've got a boyfriend just because there are men in the room. It's called self-control, Matt."

Matt was flustered; he rubbed his hand through his hair and it stayed stuck up in the air like the worst kind of bed hair.

"But this is set up with a view to people copping off," he said.

"At a pub quiz?" said Kate. "Are you this terrified at the Duke's Head quiz? Perhaps you think Sarah might pounce on Steve or Gavin?"

Matt looked sulky.

"What about Wally?" Sarah suggested.

"Wally *is* a hottie," admitted Kate.

"When he wipes the beer froth off his handlebar mustache it drives me wild," said Sarah.

"It's the eyebrow dandruff that does it for me," said Kate.

"All right! Fine!" said Matt. "You've made your point. But Kate, can you wear a sign or something so that people know you are *definitely* the date and not the mate?"

·····

Matt needn't have worried. The next morning Kate had an email from the dating site requesting that all "dates" wear a Christmas jumper to differentiate them from their "mates."

Kate had an embarrassing number of Christmas jumpers in an ottoman beneath her bedroom window, from full comedic with flashing lights, to sequin baubles, to embroidered snow and nativity scenes.

She picked out a pale green knitted sweater with felt sprigs of dark green holly and ruby berries across the front: one of the Knitting Sex Kittens' less avant-garde pieces.

Kate worked for a couple of hours on her spring collection. The winter sun streamed in through the window and illuminated the kitchen table and the dried flowers on it, as though wanting to inspire Kate to think spring thoughts.

She layered palest lemon paint onto her pencil primrose studies, slowly building to a more robust warm-butter shade toward the petal centers. The rough watercolor paper drank in the pigments. When she had a cluster of delicate yellow primroses on the page, she washed out her brushes and began to paint nodding bluebell heads in shades of periwinkle and lapis lazuli, letting the colors bleed into each other and the flowers come alive beneath her fingers.

Kate made herself a coffee and shook out her arms, turning her head from side to side to relieve the stiffness after such concentrated work. She leaned on the sink and looked out the window. The sky was blue for the first time in days, and already the warmth of the sun—scant though it was—was melting the snow on the grass. She'd opened the smallest window at the top a crack to stop the windows from steaming up, and through it she could hear the steady drip-drip-drip as the ice melted off the fascias.

. . . . .

Between the gritters and the sun, the hill to Blexford was clear enough
for Kate to retrieve her car from the bottom and bring it back up to the
village. She pulled up outside Matt's cottage and beeped the horn.
Sarah bounced out of the door and Matt followed, pulling her into an
embrace and kissing her sweetly. Kate pretended to stick two fingers
down her throat and Matt poked his tongue out at her.

"Put him down, Sarah!" she shouted. "You don't know where he's
been!"

Sarah laughed and Matt stuck two fingers up at Kate, grinning.

Sarah ran gingerly down the icy path to the car, looking impossibly
lovely even wrapped in a puffer jacket. And how did she get those delicate curls to caress her face like that? Kate's hair was corkscrew or frizz
with no in-between. When Kate's curls fell about her face, which they
did often, they looked like Medusa's serpents after a spell in a wind
tunnel.

"Hi!" said Sarah, as she bounced into the car. "You smell lovely."

"Thanks," said Kate. "How was work?"

"Busy," she said. "It's all Christmas play practice and party planning at the moment. And half of the old costumes are falling to
pieces, so we're spending all our lunchtimes sewing; it's like a nativity
stitch- 'n'-bitch."

"Why don't I ask Evelyn if the Knitting Sex Kittens can help you
out?" said Kate. "They can turn their hands to anything, they could
probably rustle you up some new costumes too."

"Oh my God. Would you?" said Sarah. "That would be amazing!
We need all the help we can get. The kids have worked so hard, it would
be a shame if their costumes let them down."

Kate promised to speak to Evelyn in the morning, and the

conversation continued to flow easily. Twenty minutes into the journey there was a lull; it wasn't uncomfortable particularly, but they didn't know each other well enough yet for it not to be a self-conscious quiet.

It was fully dark now, even though it was only seven o'clock. The snowbanks at the side of the road cast a dim glow into the car. Sarah fiddled absently with her ring finger, despite the absence of a ring. The old Mini engine seemed louder than usual.

"Can I ask you something?" said Sarah.

"Of course. Anything," said Kate.

"You know Matt better than anyone," Sarah said. "Would you say he's serious about me?"

"Absolutely," said Kate. "As serious as I've ever known him to be." She cast a glance at Sarah and smiled.

"Why do you ask?"

Sarah was quiet for a moment, as if choosing her words.

"It's just that sometimes I don't know where his head's at," said Sarah.

"Oh, I wouldn't worry about that," said Kate. "Nobody in the world knows how Matt's head works."

"You do," said Sarah.

"I think you're giving me more credit than I deserve," said Kate.

"I don't think I am," said Sarah. "You seem to get him. You sort of cut through all his . . ."

"Bullshit?" Kate inserted helpfully.

"I was going to say *layers*," said Sarah.

"Layers?" Kate laughed. "I don't think Matt's got enough depth for layers."

"Right there," said Sarah. "That. That's what I'm talking about. You have this way with each other."

"I'm just taking the mickey," said Kate. "It's what we do. We grew up annoying each other. He's like an irritating cousin . . . or a fungal infection you just can't get rid of."

"That's why I wanted to talk to you," said Sarah.

"Because I described your boyfriend as a fungal infection?"

"Because you know him well enough to liken him to one," said Sarah, smiling.

"Okay," said Kate. "What's up?"

"Don't get me wrong," said Sarah. "He's caring and thoughtful and demonstrative." She paused.

Out of the corner of her eye, Kate could see Sarah biting her lip.

"It's just that . . ." Sarah found her words. "Sometimes I get the feeling that he's holding something back."

"Like what?" Kate asked. Her interest was piqued.

"Well, that's just it," said Sarah. "I can't quite put my finger on it. It's more of a feeling, really. A sensation. Like there's always something on his mind, but he never quite spits it out."

"Oh, you know Matt," said Kate. "He's always got a hundred things on the go and a hundred more he's thinking about."

"I don't think that's it," said Sarah. "Not all of it, anyway."

Sarah closed her eyes as she tried to formulate her feelings into words. Kate kept her eyes on the road and waited patiently for Sarah. As someone who believed strongly in the power of female intuition, she wasn't about to pooh-pooh Sarah's.

"It's almost as if there's someone else," said Sarah.

Kate broke in. She was instantly protective of Matt; he was undoubtedly a twit on occasions but he was no cheater.

"Oh no," said Kate. "I can't believe that. That's not Matt at all. He would never cheat. I can tell you that much with absolute conviction."

"No no no," said Sarah, holding her hands up. "God no, you misunderstand me. I mean, it's like there's someone from before and their memory is preventing him from being fully invested with me; like he's dipping his toe in but can't go any further."

"Ahh," said Kate. Her chagrin evaporated. "Are we talking ghosts of girlfriends past here?"

"Yes," said Sarah. "We are. What can you tell me?"

Kate wondered if she ought to be divulging details about Matt's private life to Sarah. On the other hand, she could be helping him out. And besides—she reasoned—she didn't have to give details. And she would be a darn sight more discreet than some of the other Blexford residents.

"You know he was married?" Kate asked.

"Yes," said Sarah.

"I can't shed much light on that one," said Kate. "I never actually met her, though I don't think they were a match made in heaven, if you know what I mean."

"What about the one before me?" Sarah asked.

"Are you sure you want to talk about this?" Kate asked. "It feels a bit weird."

"I'm sure," said Sarah. "If Matt and I are to have any future together, I've got to understand his past."

"Maybe you should be asking Matt?" asked Kate.

"What, Mr. Squeamish?" Sarah laughed. "He can't talk about other women with me; he goes all red and blotchy and starts stuttering."

Kate laughed.

"I can imagine," she said. "Before you, there was a woman called Jessica; nice enough, but it didn't last long, so I doubt she's your ghost."

"Right," said Sarah. "And before her?"

Kate thought back.

"A couple of years ago there was Callie," said Kate. "She was nice. Professional tennis player; they met at a charity tennis match up at the manor. Matt was doing the catering. She traveled a lot and Matt was too busy to follow her around. I think it came to an amicable end, so I don't think she's your ghost either."

"No," said Sarah. "He's mentioned Callie before. What about Nadia?"

"Ah," said Kate. "Now Nadia was a bit more long-term. We—that is, the collective Blexford we—thought she might be the next Mrs. Matt Wells. But it wasn't to be."

"So it could be Nadia," Sarah mused.

"Could be," said Kate. "She cheated on Matt with her boss. I think she dented his pride more than his heart. His wife apparently cheated on him too, so I think Nadia was a double kick in the balls. And beyond that, I'm afraid, I can't help you. Matt and I lost contact for a long time, though I don't think he's been exactly prolific in the relationship department."

"Hmmm," Sarah mused. "That would explain his reticence, I suppose. Two cheating partners is enough to make anyone hold back a bit."

"I suppose so," said Kate. "But I don't think you've got anything to worry about. He's really into you, Sarah, I can tell."

Sarah smiled; she looked pleased, and Kate was suddenly engulfed by an inexplicable sadness. She swallowed thickly and pushed the sensation away.

"That whole marriage thing was a bit weird, though, wasn't it?" said Sarah.

Kate shook herself mentally.

"Bloody weird!" she agreed.

"Did you really have sex on the beach the other night?" asked Sarah.

And they both laughed. The kind of laughing that once you start you can't stop and which makes it very difficult to drive.

· · · · ·

The pub was one of those fairly-newly-built-but-built-to-look-old buildings, with ample parking and a pergola that ran the length of the front, dripping with ivy and fairy lights. Weather-beaten tables with wonky benches sat beneath it. Each table was adorned with a flickering tea light in a jam jar and a sprig of holly in a bottle.

Kate and Sarah walked through the gabled entrance with its crooked, knotty door frame, and the smell of wood smoke and hops enveloped them. Pinned to a large board by the inner door was a seating plan, the kind you find at weddings. Across from it was a fresh Christmas tree, clearly decorated by someone with control issues.

They scoured the seating plan for Kate's and Laura's names, finding them on a table at the far end of the pub, off to the right, near the kitchens.

They pushed through another set of doors and into the pub proper. It was a vast room but sectioned off into smaller, more intimate spaces by gnarled timber columns and half-structured frames. There were three enormous Tudor-style brick fireplaces, one at either end of the pub and one in the middle, which separated the bar area from the restaurant. Each hearth danced with crackling, snapping flames that could be heard above the Christmas music and the din of voices. Swags of rich juniper-green pine branches and ivy festooned the brickwork above the fireplaces and draped down from the ceiling above the bar.

"Drink?" asked Kate.

"Absolutely," replied Sarah.

They found a table close by and settled into cracked leather armchairs. Sarah admired the reclaimed floorboards while Kate surreptitiously took photographs of the garlands for her sketchbook. A nervous voice trembled out from the PA system for them to take their places at their allotted tables in ten minutes.

Kate and Sarah were playing a game of "who's going to pair off with who" by watching the mating dances of the men and women at the bar, when Sarah stiffened and all the color drained out of her face. Kate reached her hand out and touched her arm.

"Are you all right?" she asked.

"Don't look round," said Sarah through gritted teeth.

"Okay," said Kate. "Tell me what's wrong."

Sarah shifted herself down in her chair so that she was hidden from the bar by the high back of Kate's armchair. She beckoned Kate toward her and Kate dutifully leaned in.

"There was this guy," said Sarah. Kate noticed that Sarah's eyes had gone glassy. "*The* guy, actually. We were going to get married," she went on. "And then I got offered the head teacher position at Great Blexley Primary. I couldn't turn it down! I'd worked so hard. I'd been a deputy head for four years; this was my big chance to run a school the way I wanted it run."

She stopped and grappled a tissue out of her handbag.

"So, what happened?" asked Kate.

Sarah caught her breath. She hiccupped trying to hold back a sob.

"He didn't want to leave Bromley," said Sarah. "All his friends were there. His job. He didn't want to have to start again. So that was it. And now . . . now he's here."

Sarah looked at Kate with big brown eyes that welled with tears and overflowed, spilling down her cheeks. Kate's heart ached for her.

"Get me out of here," Sarah whispered. "Please."

"Of course," said Kate. "Tell me where he is. I'll casually make sure he's looking the other way and we'll make a break for it."

"He's over by the slot machine," said Sarah.

Kate looked over with what she hoped was nonchalance.

"The blond one or the one in the denim jacket?" asked Kate.

"No, no!" said Sarah. "The other slot machine. The tall Indian guy with the beard."

Kate moved her eyes across to the Test Your Knowledge machine.

"What? Oliver?" said Kate.

"You know him?" Sarah sniffed.

Kate grimaced.

"Kind of," she said.

Myriad hazy inappropriate images, hot kisses, and wandering hands flooded Kate's mind.

Oliver chose that moment to turn around. He locked eyes with Kate and grinned wolfishly. He waved and, after he'd drawn his friend's attention away from the machine, the two of them began to make their way across the pub.

"Shit! He's coming over!" Kate hissed through a tight smile.

"Oh God, no," said Sarah. "I can't see him. I can't. Don't let him see me!"

Kate was panicking. She half stood and sat down again and chewed her finger.

"What do you want me to do?" she asked.

"Anything!" said Sarah. Her tears had fled now; her eyes were wild, her cheeks red and blotchy. "Cause a distraction and I'll sneak out and meet you by the car."

Kate jumped up and kicked out at the table, sending it flying onto its side and the glasses rolling off along the bobbly floorboards, their contents splattering the legs of anyone in the vicinity. Sarah drop-rolled off the chair and onto her hands and knees, where she broke into a fast crawl, away from Oliver, swerving around chairs and table legs as she made for the exit.

"Whoa there!" Oliver laughed. He grabbed hold of Kate and hugged her, kissing her on the cheek. His scent made her blush.

"Hi!" said Kate. "I didn't know you'd be at this one."

"Yeah, it was a last-minute thing," he said as he righted the table and retrieved the now-spent glasses. "They had me down for the go-carting evening, but my brother's flying in from Edinburgh that night and I need to pick him up from the airport. So I swapped to pub quiz night."

"Great!" said Kate.

"I'm glad I did now," said Oliver.

Kate giggled girlishly; she didn't seem to be able to stop. Oliver's friend coughed loudly.

"Oh God, sorry, mate," said Oliver. "Kate, this is my friend Andy. Andy, Kate."

They exchanged hellos and shook hands awkwardly.

"Andy works with me in . . ." He stopped. He was staring over the top of Kate's head. Kate's heart sank. She turned slowly to follow his gaze. Sure enough, it was fixed on Sarah's bottom wiggling furiously as she navigated her way through a tight cluster of tables.

"Sarah?" he called above the noise. His deep voice carried across the pub. Sarah stopped, midcrawl. Frozen.

"Sarah!" he called again.

Kate bit her lip.

"Sarah?" said Kate. "Sarah who? I had an aunt Sarah, she was a terrible cook, she kept rats, or was it mice? I forget . . ."

Oliver wasn't listening. His eyes remained glued to Sarah's escaping backside. Kate gave it up. Sarah remained rooted to the spot. People were beginning to notice that there was a woman on the floor near the jukebox. Slowly and as casually as one can get up off all fours in a pub and retain any dignity, Sarah got to her feet. She held up a ten-pence piece.

"Found it!" she declared lamely.

· · · · ·

There followed awkward shrugs, lingering looks, brief but polite con-versations that simmered with unspoken truths, and far too many apologies before Kate and Sarah made a rushed and graceless retreat.

They were silent as Kate pulled out of the car park and onto the main road. She drove for about five minutes before turning off the main road and into a small hamlet. She continued down a narrow winding street until she found a quiet spot in front of a pair of thatched cottages and parked underneath a streetlamp.

Kate took off her seat belt and leaned her head back against the headrest. Sarah followed suit. They stayed quiet for a few minutes. Tak-ing stock. Just the sounds of their breathing and the tick of her dash-board clock.

There were a lot of questions whizzing around in Kate's mind. She had a sick feeling in her stomach. Did Matt know that Sarah still har-bored hurt from her breakup with Oliver? And if not, should Kate tell him? Was it her place to meddle? After all, everyone has baggage, espe-cially by the time you've reached your midthirties. And Sarah and Matt's affection for each other was clearly genuine.

And what of Sarah? Kate's recollection of her night with Oliver was sketchy, but she distinctly remembered him confiding that he regretted letting the love of his life go: the love of his life that, as it turns out, was Sarah. Should she tell Sarah? Should she tell Oliver that Sarah was still nursing a broken heart over him?

And then of course there was the rather awkward situation of Kate having gotten hot and heavy with Sarah's ex-partner. Kate thought that was definitely something best kept to herself.

Kate puffed out a long breath. Sarah made a squeaking noise and covered her face with her hands and Kate thought she might be crying.

But when she turned to look at her in the watery glow of the streetlamp, she saw that Sarah was trying to stifle her laughter.

It was infectious. The pub scene had been so utterly stressful that they hadn't had time to appreciate the full absurdity of the situation. Sarah's voice was a high-pitched squeal:

"I could hear you shouting from across the room, '*I had an aunt Sarah!*'"

"I didn't know what to do!" said Kate. "I turned around to see your bottom wiggling along the floor!"

They were both laughing uncontrollably now, holding their stomachs and covering their mouths. They laughed until their cheeks and sides ached.

"Stop!" squealed Sarah. "I've got a stitch."

"I'm going to wet myself!" Kate exclaimed, far too loudly.

But it only made them worse. Even when the curtains twitched up in one of the cottages. Even when a woman out walking her dog knocked on the window to see if they were all right.

"Oh God," said Kate as the woman marched back along the path. "She probably thinks we're drunk."

"Nope," said Sarah. "Just high on excruciating embarrassment."

Eventually the laughter died away and quiet contemplation ruled the car once more.

Kate started the engine and put the blowers on full and they rolled down their windows, despite the cold, to try to de-mist the windows.

"I don't want you to think my feelings for Matt are any less," said Sarah.

"I don't," said Kate.

"It's just that . . ." Sarah went on. "Oliver was my first true love. First man I ever lived with. First and only person I've ever been engaged to."

"You don't need to explain yourself to me," said Kate. A seed of unease was sprouting inside Kate's chest. It took root and she couldn't fathom its meaning.

"No, I do," said Sarah. "Because you mean the world to Matt and I know you care for him, and I don't want you to think that because I'm not ready to do a pub quiz with my ex, it means I'm not ready to get serious with Matt. Because I am serious about Matt. I promise you. Matt is everything I'm looking for in a man and more."

Kate looked at Sarah face on.

"I believe you," she said. The seedling sprouted tendrils that inexplicably curled themselves around her heart.

They drove home. And when Kate flopped into bed that night, her heart felt a little heavier than it had when she'd set out that evening. There was a nagging pulling at Kate's insides, like a kitten's claw caught in fabric. The idea of Matt getting hurt made Kate's breath catch. She rolled over in bed, pulling the duvet tightly round with her, but the feeling wouldn't go away, and when she did fall asleep, her dreams were abundant with ghosts of lovers past and farcical encounters of her trying to go to the toilet in clear glass cubicles.

· · · · ·

Hiking and Hickeys

"Eurgh!" said Laura. "Rather you than me."

"Well," said Kate. "You know me, I love a bit of nature."

They were sitting at the back of the Blexford Manor tearooms. It was Laura's lunch break and Kate had walked up to meet her. The tearoom was almost deserted; one elderly couple shared an Eccles cake and a pot of tea at the other end of the room.

The sound of hammering and a good deal of shouting could be heard from the courtyard, where the Christmas market stalls were being constructed for tomorrow. Then the tearoom would be full. Blexford Manor's Christmas fair always pulled in a crowd.

Laura was wearing her uniform: a navy blue skirt and blazer with her name badge pinned on her lapel. Her hair was tied back into a loose but smart chignon. She cut quite a different figure from the harassed mother of two, with mad hair and sick down her top, who went by the same name the other three days of the week.

Laura bit lovingly into her toasted brie-and-cranberry panini.

"I swear to God I come to work for a break," she said. "I get my food made for me. And my coffee. And nobody pulls on my legs or bites my nipples."

Kate winced.

"I should hope not!"

Laura wasn't listening.

"I'm going to have to give up breastfeeding," she said. "Charley's teeth are like little needles. It's agony."

"Laura, you're putting me off my lunch," said Kate.

"Sorry," said Laura. She took another bite of her lunch and moaned with delight. "Maybe I should come back to work full time."

"You'd miss the kids too much," said Kate.

"Maybe," Laura mused. "So anyway, how come you're hiking? I thought you were down for laser tag on this one."

"I was," said Kate. "But I emailed the rep and she said that Oliver was down for laser tag too. So I swapped."

Laura pulled a sad face.

"But you really liked him," she said.

"But he's still hung up on Sarah," said Kate. "The whole idea is just way too complicated. And you have to admit it's a bit icky: me with Sarah's ex-fiancé."

"Love weaves its magic in mysterious ways," said Laura, fluttering her hands in front of Kate's as though she might pull a stream of colored hankies from her sleeve.

"Yeah, well, I think I'll leave this mystery alone," said Kate.

"Not even for a bit of fun?" said Laura, making obscene gestures with her hands. "It's been a while, Kate. He could brush away the cobwebs for you!"

"Laura, you have no boundaries at the dinner table."

Laura grinned.

"Have a baby," she said. "Have seventeen people looking up your vagina and see how many boundaries you have left."

The tearooms were in what was the original banqueting hall. The ornately painted ceiling was so high that even with dozens of heaters pushing out hot air, the warmth was lost in its vastness.

The Pear Tree Bakery used to supply the manor with bread and still did until the late nineties, when they found a cheaper supplier out of town, a big bread manufacturer that could churn out bulk quickly and cheaply. It was this loss of business that encouraged the Harrisons to retire.

With the recent resurgence of homegrown produce and cottage industry, Matt had been approached by the manor and asked if he had any products to sell regularly in their farm shop. *Funny how things go around*, thought Kate. Though she suspected Laura might have influenced their interest.

And so Matt had a stall at the Blexford Manor Christmas fair. He'd spent a week in the autumn preserving fruits in brandy, just as his mother had, and stinking up the whole café with his spicy tomato chutneys and chili jams. They would be sold beside Carla's Christmas gingerbread men and Evelyn's miniature boozy Christmas cakes. Kate was going to start making chocolate truffle gift bags as soon as she got home after lunch.

"So where are you hiking to and from?" asked Laura. "Have you been assigned a date?"

"Through and around Epping Forest," said Kate. "We're meeting at one of the visitor centers at ten a.m. on Sunday. And yes, I've been assigned a date."

Kate reached for her phone before her friend even asked and flipped through to the picture of her next date:

"Phil. Forty. Owns an independent extreme sports store," said Kate, handing her phone to Laura.

Laura looked at the picture and nodded sagely.

"This," said Laura, stabbing her finger at the photo. "This is the one."

Phil's profile picture was him leaned up against a surfboard. He had matted salt-sea-spray hair and a deep tan, and he wore a wetsuit and a smile that implied complete confidence in the way he looked.

"Well, he won't be wearing a wet suit on Sunday, that's for sure," said Kate. "The weather forecast is minus two that day."

"Like I said," said Laura. "Rather you than me."

Laura scrolled through Phil's particulars and read them out loud as if Kate hadn't seen them yet.

"Never been married," she said. "One child. Loves his dogs. Looking for someone special to share his hobbies with. Awww, he sounds lovely." Laura swooned. "Let's hope he wasn't engaged to any of your friends!"

Kate snatched the phone back from Laura.

"Heard from Dick yet?" Laura asked.

"No," said Kate. "I haven't heard from *Richard* yet. He was the hero of the hour, you know," Kate went on. "You could cut him some slack."

"He did nothing more than any decent person would have," said Laura. "I'll call him Richard when he actually follows up on the lost date of Christmas. Until then," she said, using her finger to swipe some spilled cranberry sauce from her plate into her mouth, "he's a Dick."

Laura went back to work and Kate ambled back down the quiet roads toward home. The grass verges were still covered in snow, and with the day's cold clear sky it seemed unlikely they'd be thawing anytime soon.

She pulled her bobble hat down further over her ears. She was looking forward to the hike. She hadn't been to Epping Forest in years. And there was much less pressure to make conversation on a hike. She'd take her camera with her and if things were really dire, she'd bury herself in finding images for her mood boards and Phil would be none the wiser of her indifference toward him.

Her phone rang. It was a number she didn't recognize. She almost dismissed the call but curiosity got the better of her.

"Hello, Kate?" said a deep husky voice.

"Speaking," said Kate.

"It's Richard."

Kate's stomach leaped. *In your face, Laura!*

"Oh," said Kate, trying to keep the quiver out of her voice. "Hi!"

"Sorry it's taken me so long to get in touch," said Richard. "Turns out I hadn't left my phone at the club. It was nicked. I had to have a temporary phone for a couple of days and, well, I won't bore you with the details, you know how it is. Anyway, I'm calling to see if I can take you on that first date."

"Yes," said Kate. She didn't want to seem too keen, even though she felt like she wanted to climb down the phone and give him a good sniff. "Yes, you can."

"Great!" said Richard. "My treat. Do you know the Smugglers Arms in Great Blexley?"

They agreed to meet the following night outside the pub. Before she went home, Kate dropped in to see Evelyn to ask if the Sex Kittens could help Sarah's school with their costumes.

"Well, of course we will!" said Evelyn. "I don't know why she didn't ask me herself, silly girl."

"I don't think it occurred to her ask," said Kate.

"That's what you get from living in the Big Town," said Evelyn. "Big-town mentality! Every man's an island!"

Evelyn continued to vocalize her opinions on the failings of living in the Big Town while Kate puttered about the shop, gathering the ingredients she'd need for making truffles.

"Baking for Matt again?" asked Evelyn as Kate laid her shopping by the till.

"As always," said Kate.

"What would he do without you?" Evelyn mused.

"Find another mug to do it, I should think," said Kate.

· · · · ·

Tiny bubbles began to ripple beneath the surface of the double cream in the milk pan. Kate kept a steady eye on it, waiting for the first wave of a rolling boil. Laid out across the work surface were three deep glass bowls, each half filled with chopped dark chocolate.

Thick white bubbles broke the surface and began to rise up the pan. Kate whipped it off the heat and gently poured the hot cream over the chocolate in the first bowl. She gave it a moment and then gently stirred the mixture together, slowly and carefully, the dark chocolate melting into the pale cream in rich hickory stripes.

When the hot ganache mixture was fully combined, Kate dropped in some softened butter and two generous tablespoons of brandy and stirred again until she had a smooth glossy texture. The aroma was more than she could bear; her mouth watered. Luckily, she was prepared. She grabbed the extra bar from the cupboard, tore away the foil, and snapped off a glistening dark umber chunk of chocolate, making *mmmm* sounds to herself as it melted on her tongue.

She set the bowl aside to cool. When the ganache set, Kate would scoop out teaspoons of the mixture and roll it into balls before dipping each one in chopped hazelnuts or cocoa.

Her mind kept drifting to her impending date with Richard.

Though it went against her every feminist impulse, Kate found the idea of such a devoted father an appealing trait in a man. She had to keep reminding herself not to discount Phil, her hiking date for Sunday, just because some guy had made her ovaries swoon.

She washed the milk pan and poured in another tub of cream, ready to begin the process again. She would do the next batch with raspberry liqueur. She had some dried raspberries to toss them in when they were ready: delicate little buds of velvet puce. The last batch would be half cocoa and half icing-sugar-dusted whiskey truffles. She just had to make sure she got more in the bags than in her mouth. Not easy.

The phone rang as she set the fresh pan on the stove. It was Matt.

"Hi!" she said. "I'm up to my eyes in truffles for the market."

"Oh," said Matt. "Great. Yeah."

"You all right?" asked Kate.

Silence on the other end. She could hear him breathing. She sensed his hesitation. It wasn't like Matt to be indecisive. Not with her anyway. He was usually bold to the point of rude.

"Come on!" she said. "Spit it out."

"Did anything happen at the Dates with Mates night?" Matt asked.

Kate swallowed.

"Like what?" she asked brightly.

"I don't know," said Matt. "Just. I don't know."

"You'll need to be more specific," Kate said. Sarah had expressly asked her not to mention anything about Oliver to Matt, and she wasn't about to break her confidence. But at the same time, if Sarah had folded and told Matt of her own volition, then Kate needed to know before she denied all knowledge.

"It's just," said Matt. "These last few days. Sarah's been a bit . . . well, distant. And I wondered if you'd maybe said anything to her?"

Kate swirled the cream in the pan and set it back down on the heat.

"Like?" she asked.

She didn't like where this was going. She had a sudden feeling of nausea in the bottom of her stomach.

"I wondered if you might have said anything that might have put her off me," he said.

"Matt!" Kate was aghast. "As if I would."

"No, no," Matt broke in. "I don't mean it like that. I meant. Well. I didn't know if maybe, while you were bonding and being all girly-talky, you might have told her about the way I was with you, you know, at university and then how we didn't speak for . . . ten years."

Kate was silent.

The cream rose to a boil. Kate took it off the heat. She swallowed hard and cleared her throat. Her hand shook slightly as she mechanically poured the hot cream over the second bowl of chocolate.

"Kate?" he said.

"No, Matt," she said witheringly. "I didn't. But thank you for having such a low opinion of me, or such a high opinion of yourself, that you assume I would still be feeling wounded about a bust-up that happened thirteen years ago!"

"Kate," he said.

"Oh, it's all right." She took a breath. Her reaction had taken her by surprise. "I'm just being craggy. Sarah wanted my advice. She felt you might be holding something back."

"Holding something back?" Matt was incredulous. "Like what?"

"I don't know," said Kate truthfully. "She didn't know either, she just had a feeling."

Matt was quiet for a moment.

"I don't really know what to say to that," he said eventually. "I wasn't aware I was holding anything back."

"She suggested you have *layers*," said Kate.

"Crikey!" said Matt.

"Don't worry," said Kate. "I assured her you are far too shallow to have layers."

Matt laughed.

"Oh, I'm sorry, Kate," said Matt. "I feel like a shit now. So essentially each of us has bleated to you that the other is distant and/or holding back."

"Essentially, yes," said Kate.

"Right," said Matt. "It looks like Sarah and I need to work on our communication skills. I'm sorry about what I said earlier; I don't know what I was thinking."

"Yeah, well," said Kate. "I'm always telling you, you shouldn't do thinking. Your tiny brain can't handle it."

Matt laughed.

"I'll see you in the morning?" he asked.

"Of course you will," said Kate.

"Night," said Matt.

"Don't let the bed bugs bite," said Kate.

The call ended. The same strange unease prickled her insides. It was the same sensation she'd felt the other night with Sarah. Like coiling nettles.

Kate finished making the whiskey and raspberry ganache and placed all three bowls on a cold marble slab in the larder to set. She leafed through her sketches on the table, but she couldn't concentrate. Instead she went into the lounge and built a fire in the hearth and sat on the sofa with her bar of chocolate for company.

Kate and Laura had gone to Liverpool University together: Kate to study fine art and textiles and Laura, business and tourism. Matt went to Manchester to study accounting and finance.

It was inevitable, Kate had supposed, that they should drift a little from one another. What Kate hadn't expected was Matt's reluctance to keep *any* contact. On the rare occasions Kate managed to fix a weekend to meet up, Matt wasn't the same; he was distant, disdainful even. They bickered. Not so much Matt and Laura—they had never been as close—but oftentimes with Kate, it was as though he couldn't help but say things that would drive her further away.

One weekend Matt came down to Liverpool, grumpy as usual, to find Laura away visiting Ben and Kate nursing a wounded heart from a breakup with an intense classics student named John.

Kate and Matt went out drinking. They drank hard. One thing led to another.

They woke up the next morning in Kate's bed, awkward and embarrassed, a poster of Frida Kahlo glaring down at them from the sloping ceiling above the bed in her attic room. The smell of burning toast drifted up the staircase. Someone yelled something from the bedroom below. Matt couldn't get out of Kate's room and out of Liverpool quick enough.

After that their friendship quickly deteriorated. It wasn't that Kate had expected anything from Matt, but his dismissive attitude toward her was hurtful. She didn't want a declaration of love, just an acknowledgment that it had happened, so that they could move forward.

After three weeks of being treated like an infectious disease, Kate traveled to Manchester to have it out with him.

"I'm not saying it meant anything," said Kate. "But it was something. It did happen. And I think we should discuss it."

"Can't we just forget it ever happened?" asked Matt.

"Fine, then," said Kate. "Why don't we talk about what's going on with you instead? Even before this you were distant, I rarely see you anymore and when we *do* meet up, you're always moody!"

"Oh, I'm always moody," said Matt. "I wonder why that could be?"

"Yeah, I know," said Kate. "I know it's been horrific, but . . ."

"But what?" said Matt. "How do you know what's it been like for me? Is your family dead?"

"Matt, I . . ." Kate started, but Matt cut her off.

"Is your family dead?"

"No," said Kate. "But . . ."

"No," said Matt. "They're not. When they are, you can lecture me on mood swings."

Kate closed her eyes. "You're right that I can't even begin to imagine what you're going through, or how much pain you've been in. But your grief is not an excuse to behave like an arsehole, Matt! Sooner or later you've got to start taking responsibility for your actions."

"Ahh, there it is!" said Matt. "That's what this is really about: taking responsibility. So we had sex. So what? Now you want to be my girlfriend? You want to get married? What, Kate? What do you want from me?"

"I want you to stop being such a selfish twat!" Kate yelled.

"Shit happens," said Matt.

"Brilliant," said Kate. "Let's just sweep it under the carpet and pretend like everything's normal. For Christ's sake, Matt, I just want my friend back."

"But I don't want you," said Matt.

"What?" Kate asked. His statement knocked the wind out of her. "What are you talking about?"

"I don't want to be your friend," said Matt. "It's time to grow up, Kate. Did you really think we'd be best friends forever? Me, you, Ben, and Laura? All living in a big house together in Blexford like the fucking Brady Bunch?"

"I don't know what you're saying," said Kate. "We're too old to be friends anymore? That's stupid!"

"Stupid or not," said Matt, "that's the way it is."

He was as good as his word. He ignored Kate's phone calls and emails until she had no choice but to accept that they were indeed no longer friends.

It knocked her confidence. He'd always been there. And now suddenly he wasn't, like an annoying brother who you fought with all the time and then missed when he wasn't there to spar with.

It wasn't just Matt. It was Laura too. Kate leaned on them both. They were her support system. *But what if one day Laura disappeared too? What then?* Kate realized she needed to be good enough on her own. And the only way to do that was to put herself in a situation where *she* was all she had. Eventually Kate would look back at that time as a defining moment: the end of her childhood.

"You don't have to leave the country to find yourself!" Laura had said.

"Actually," said Kate, "that is precisely what I need to do."

Kate spent a lot of time going over it with Laura in the old Victorian town house they shared with three other girls. They sat in her bedroom, chain-smoking out of the window, the woodchip wallpaper peeled and the carpet threadbare.

"Will you write to me?" Laura asked.

"All the time," said Kate. "And we'll keep each other's letters and read them back when we're old."

Kate had saved enough money to last her for three months, by her own meticulous calculations but had blown it all on cheap beer, cigarettes, and nightclubs after two. So she found work. She pulled pints, instead of drinking them, in France and Belgium; and she waited tables in restaurants, across Germany, Austria, and Switzerland.

She stayed in youth hostels and occasionally in digs that came with the jobs. Kate absorbed her surroundings, felt the beating hearts of cities and towns, through their stone walls and dusty piazzas.

She took her sketchbook everywhere she went, and what she didn't get time to sketch, she photographed. Her mind became a library, collating the stories of strangers and new friends, alive and dead. And she made her own stories and lived them through her experiences.

Kate had only intended to spend six months traveling around Europe, but six months became a year and one year became a two-year globe-trotting adventure. When Laura had Skyped her to tell her that Matt had gotten married, Kate had barely flinched; her friendship with Matt had become just another jigsaw piece of her past . . . until her unanticipated move back to Blexford a decade later fetched it into her present.

· · · · ·

It was late by the time Kate dropped the last truffle into the last star-embossed cellophane bag and tied it with red and green ribbon. She stood all sixteen bags—each containing eight truffles—upright on the marble shelf and closed the larder door.

Over the course of the evening she'd received a dozen apology texts from Matt. In the end she'd stopped replying. She wasn't going to take responsibility for his guilt. He would have to work it out for himself. Perhaps he should try talking to his girlfriend instead.

The unease in Kate's stomach rolled to the surface, like a water snake coming up for air. Was Sarah having second thoughts about Matt? The idea of him being hurt made Kate's chest ache.

Kate lay in bed nursing worrisome thoughts that wouldn't let her sleep: Would Sarah leave Matt and go back to Oliver? How would Matt feel? What could she do to stop it from happening? Why was she worrying so much about it? It wasn't *her* heart that would be broken.

Kate flicked the lamp on. She shook herself, as if by doing so she could shake off the unwanted thoughts like a mosquito. *For goodness' sake!* she scolded herself. *Pull yourself together! This is not your problem; concentrate on your own love life!*

She tried to infuse her mind with thoughts of the deliciously scented Richard, but Matt's stupid puppy eyes kept ruining her fantasy. It was like being distracted by a stray cat meowing at the door; it wasn't her responsibility, but she couldn't ignore it either.

Surely Sarah wouldn't leave Matt and go back to Oliver? Kate remembered the adoring look Sarah had bestowed upon Matt that night in the snow; that was genuine. But so was the look of desperation when she'd seen Oliver at Dates with Mates night.

Kate gave herself a mental kick up the bum and slapped both her cheeks. "You are not responsible for Matt!" she said out loud. "He is big enough and ugly enough to look after himself."

But still a feeling of unease coiled around her chest.

Annoyed with herself, she padded downstairs in the darkness. In the scant light given off by the hob, she made herself a hot chocolate and sploshed in some brandy for medicinal purposes. Then she crept back upstairs, snuggled under the duvet, switched on the TV, and settled down with an old movie; the black-and-white images threw flickering shadows against the walls.

An unwanted thought swam into her mind and took root as she lay there, propped up against the pillows: Were her concerns for Matt born purely out of friendship? And if not, it raised the question: Was she so struck by Sarah's loving gaze at Matt because she longed for a love like theirs? Or because secretly, *she* longed to be loved by Matt?

At some point in the wee small hours, Kate had fallen asleep with the TV on and the empty mug still in her hand.

She woke early and got ready to meet Matt, making a conscious effort to forget her brandy-induced musings.

The Christmas fair opened at eleven a.m., but stallholders were allowed in to get set up from eight a.m. Kate had said she'd meet Matt at the café to help load the produce into the van. Carla would run the Pear Tree, and Petula was doing an extra shift to cover the busy lunch period.

Kate decided to ignore last night's awkward conversation and pretend it had never happened. Matt was obviously of the same mind.

"Here!" he said, thrusting a takeaway coffee into her hand as she reached the side entrance to the café. "Get this down your neck, or you'll be no good to man nor beast."

Kate took it and drank gratefully. The blue skies of yesterday had been overpowered by thick pewter clouds that threatened snow. She hoped it would hold off long enough for her to get to her date with Richard tonight. She also hoped they didn't cancel her hiking date tomorrow.

Sarah was noticeable by her absence.

"Where's Sarah?" Kate asked.

"She's gone to her mum's for the day," he said, heaving a crate full of jam jars into the back of the van. "Christmas stuff to organize, apparently."

"Oh," said Kate. "Who's helping you with the stall, then?"

Matt grinned.

"I was hoping you might," he said.

He flashed her a lost-puppy look and she almost caved, but instead she mentally slapped herself hard across the cheek and said, "Sorry, I'm busy today."

"What, getting ready for tomorrow's date?" asked Matt.

"Tonight's, actually," said Kate.

"You can't go hiking in the dark," said Matt.

"I'm not," Kate replied. "I'm hiking tomorrow. Tonight is a different date, not part of the twelve dates."

Matt blustered.

"What, two dates in two days?" he said.

"Since when did you become the date police?" asked Kate.

"It's that Richard bloke, isn't it," said Matt. "The one with the cauliflower ear."

"Not that it matters," said Kate. "But he doesn't have cauliflower ear. And yes, it is *that Richard bloke*: hero of the hour."

"Ooh, all hail Richard!" said Matt in a snarky voice.

"If he hadn't come to my rescue, I'd have had to call you," said Kate.

"I'd have let you freeze," said Matt.

"Then it's just as well Richard came along when he did," said Kate.

Matt grinned.

Carla called out from the café, "Do you need more coffee, Kate?"

"She hasn't done anything yet!" shouted Matt.

"Yes, please, Carla," called Kate sweetly.

Kate strode into the storeroom at the back of the kitchen and began to transport various crates and plastic containers filled with Christmas goodies to the van. At the back of the van, surrounded by rolled-up rugs—presumably for buffering during transit—was a coffee machine. *He's doing coffee as well!* thought Kate. *No wonder he asked for help.* When the van was thoroughly loaded, Kate laid the box containing her truffle bags gently on top of Evelyn's Christmas cakes.

"Sure I can't change your mind?" asked Matt.

"Quite sure," said Kate.

She waved Matt off as the van disappeared down the lane behind the café and joined the track to the manor. Then she went back in through the side door to get her second caffeine fix.

"It's going to be insane up there today," said Carla. "There's two coach companies running Christmas market visits from Chelmsford and Watford, and one from Calais! And that's before people coming by car."

"Ah," said Kate. "One second."

Kate pulled her phone out of her pocket and fired off a text to Matt.

> If it gets too busy give me a ring. I'll come and help.

Carla raised her eyebrows at Kate.

"You just caved and said you'd help him, didn't you," she said.

"Maybe," said Kate.

Carla shook her head laughing.

"You are such a sucker."

Kate was about to argue when the door chime jangled and continued to do so incessantly, as the café filled up with early-bird Christmas shoppers needing a fix before hitting the mall in Great Blexley. The noise level rose instantly from quiet to carnival.

"Oh my God!" Carla paled. "Petula's not in till half ten!"

Kate sighed.

"Give me a check pad and pen," she said.

Carla grinned and kissed her on the cheek.

"I wouldn't want you thinking I was only a sucker for Matt," said Kate.

Kate ran around taking orders and serving, while Carla worked up a head of steam at the coffee machine and doled out cakes. An hour passed by and they still hadn't stopped.

Christmas tunes belted out of the stereo, kids drew pictures on the steamy windows, and the Christmas tree jangled as friends jostled past it, greeting one another. Woolen hats and gloves were strewn across every table and the backs of chairs bulged with parkas and puffers and wax jackets.

At ten o'clock there was a short lull as the regulars left for their day of shopping mayhem. Kate and Carla attacked the clearing up; the dishwasher pushed out great clouds of steam.

At ten fifteen the café was besieged again, this time with townies dropping in for a pit stop on their way to the manor, having walked up the hill from Great Blexley. It was bedlam, but good-humored bedlam. Many remarked how they'd never been to the Pear Tree Café but that they'd definitely be back.

By eleven o'clock the Pear Tree was quiet again and Petula had arrived with a homemade roulade, a mincemeat tart, and a batch of spice biscuits, which was just as well as the chiller had been almost cleaned out already.

Petula whipped a tape measure out of her pocket and quick as a flash wrapped it around Kate's chest.

"I want to make sure these haven't grown since last year," she said, nodding at Kate's boobs. "I've come up with something this year that will blow your socks off!"

Kate laughed.

"I'm intrigued," she said. She genuinely was.

"It'll be ready in a couple of days," said Petula. "I had to order in more sequins."

Kate left just as the first snowflakes began to flurry around the green and squeezed herself through a hole in the fence behind the Duke's Head that led out near her dad's cottage.

"What'll you do if I ever get that fence fixed?" shouted Barry. Kate looked up. Barry was leaning over the top of the fire escape, with a steaming mug in one hand that read *The Boss* and a fat cigar in the other. Kate grinned and waved.

"Hi, Barry," she called.

"You're not too old for me to put you across my knee," he said.

"You'll have to catch me first!" she shouted back, and disappeared through the hole and into the alley on the other side.

"Say hello to Mac for me!" Barry bellowed after her. He chuckled and rubbed the back of his head with his cigar hand. "Some things never change," he said to himself.

· · · · ·

Kate knocked three times on her dad's front door and then let herself in with her key. His cottage was what she'd call chintzy; she never really understood why he didn't change it, but he said he didn't want it to lose its essence. William Morris wallpaper covered most of the walls and the furniture was Laura Ashley floral, as were the curtains. The carpet was a most luxurious weave with underlay so soft, your feet sank as you walked.

He rented it from Evelyn, who'd inherited it from her aunt, but Evelyn had always lived in the large flat above the shop and was determined to stay there. She liked being at the heart of everything that happened in the village, in mind, spirit, and body.

Kate kicked her boots off. The scent of fried smoked bacon wafted into the hallway. Her stomach growled.

"Hallo, love," Mac called from the kitchen. "I've just thrown a few more rashers in. I hope you're hungry."

They sat at the small table by the kitchen window and ate bacon doorstop sandwiches, hugging their mugs of tea, and watched the snow settle on the rhododendron leaves in the garden. A robin took shelter under the bird table roof.

"I've been thinking about Christmas," said Mac.

"Aha," said Kate, ripping off a crust with her teeth.

"I was thinking maybe we could have Christmas dinner here this year?"

Kate was surprised. They'd always had Christmas at her house.

"Because I'd like to invite someone," said Mac.

"You can invite someone to mine," said Kate. "You know you're always welcome to bring guests. It was your house before it was mine."

"But this is different," he said. "I would like this guest to not eat dinner in the house I used to share with your mother."

Kate spluttered into her tea.

"Dad, are we talking about a woman guest?"

Mac winced.

"How would you feel about that?" he asked, avoiding the question and Kate's eyes.

"Dad!" said Kate, reaching over and holding his hand. "I would feel brilliant about it! More than brilliant. I would be over the moon."

"Really?" said Mac. He visibly relaxed.

"Of course *really*," said Kate. "I'm so happy you've met someone. Who is she? Do I know her?"

Mac smiled.

"Evelyn," he said.

Kate slapped her forehead and laughed.

"How did I not see that coming?" she said. "Well, that settles it then. You, me, and Evelyn for Christmas dinner here! Oh, but what about Matt? He and Evelyn always spend Christmas Day together."

Mac put his hand on Kate's.

"I don't think Matt will be lonely, love," he said.

• • • • •

By two o'clock, Kate was ensconced in one of her dad's armchairs: legs stretched out across the ottoman feet toasting gently in the warmth of the fire, an old black-and-white movie with impossibly well-spoken actors on the TV.

Mac dozed in the chair opposite. Kate was just thinking she could blow off her date with Richard tonight and stay here, when her phone vibrated.

HELP! it read. It was from Matt.

Kate groaned. She considered ignoring the message. She'd seen a packet of crumpets in her dad's cupboard and had earmarked them for a hot buttery treat later. She glanced out the window. It was still snowing. Her dad snuffled in his sleep. She was so comfy.

The phone vibrated again.

PLEEEEAAAAASSSEEEEEE!

Kate puffed out in annoyance. Her dreams of a lazy afternoon popped like the champagne cork in the old movie.

On my way, she texted back, and reluctantly heaved herself out of the armchair.

· · · · ·

Laura called just as Kate was pulling her coat and boots on. She was on her lunch break and from the way she was talking—a mile a minute and slightly high-pitched—Kate guessed she was busy at the manor too. She wanted to know what she was wearing to her date with Richard.

"I haven't thought about it yet," said Kate. "I'm going to be pushed for time, though; now I've got to help Matt."

"Huh!" said Laura. "Sucker! At least I'm getting paid to be stressed."

"Eurgh," moaned Kate. "What's wrong with me? I hate that I can't just say no whenever he's in trouble."

"Funny," said Laura. "That's exactly what he said to me about you!"

· · · · ·

There was no point taking the car; if it was as busy up there as she anticipated, it would be a nightmare to park and if the snow kept up, she'd get a lift back with Matt in the van.

The cold air invigorated her and she felt her energy rising again after her afternoon slump. A humming snake of cars wound the lanes to the manor. Kate kept close in to the hedgerows.

Bronze-and-maroon-feathered pheasants bobbed up above the long grass of the fields, their claret heads bright against the snow. They flew like heavy cushions being thrown and landed just as ungracefully. Every now and again one would flap too close to the road and Kate winced. They didn't seem to be the cleverest of birds.

Snippets of Christmas music from car stereos whipped past her and Kate smiled to herself. She loved Christmas. Of all the holidays, Christmas was the one that replenished her soul and made her feel the most hopeful.

She saw smoke curl out of the tall chimneys above the tree line, long before the manor itself came into view. Round the next bend the path became gravel, forking off left and right for visitor parking and coach parties. From there, signposted paths led to the back of the manor, with its gardens and fountains and, for the next two days, the Christmas market.

Straight ahead was the long walk that led to the front of Blexford Manor. It was quieter here; only a few brave souls had chosen to walk in the snow. The path was wide enough for three cars, though it was only open to pedestrians most days. On either side were neatly cut lawns that ran to the edges of a pine forest. On quiet days wild deer meandered out from the trees to catch the sun on the lawn. But not today.

An ornate fountain—a later addition—with five scantily clad stone maidens holding a wide rimmed bowl above their heads stood before the manor, acting as both an opulent first impression and a sort of high-class roundabout.

The manor itself was an imposing building. The glass of the many leaded windows looked black against the pale stone and brick walls—the brickwork being the height of modernity for the time. One large gabled wing protruded from the center of the building, with another two at either end. And between these, several smaller coped gablets gave the impression of many long thin buildings having been squeezed together to form one big one.

Blexford Manor lent itself to every Jane Austen–esque fantasy Kate could imagine. The sheer romance of the architecture never failed to take her breath away, especially today with the gray clouds as moody back-drop and the snowflakes sticking to the slate roofs. Kate took out her camera and snapped some shots before heading round to the gardens.

She found Matt warming his hands by an electric fire in his allotted wooden hut, between serving customers. The coffee machine, which was usually housed in a closed trailer in the café garden—a throwback to when Matt used to work the festival scene before the café became so busy—was steaming happily on a heavy-duty butcher block.

"How on earth did you get that machine in here?" asked Kate.

"Sheer bloody-mindedness!" grinned Matt. "I may have sacrificed a couple of vertebrae in the process."

"Never mind," said Kate. "You've got more. I'm just going to have a quick look round and I'll be with you."

"Right you are," said Matt. He nodded and waved as a man in a green tweed jacket bent over the counter and inspected a bag of Carla's festive fudge.

The courtyard had been transformed overnight into a winter grotto, with rows of fairy-lit wooden huts standing side by side, selling everything from mulled wine and roasted chestnuts to stone-carved garden ornaments and Fair Isle jumpers.

Last year there had been a snow machine churning out snowflakes to help with the ambience; this year it wasn't necessary. The hut roofs were thickly white and though health and safety decreed that the courtyard be salted, the snow lay everywhere else it could; ceramic geese with blue bow ties wore snowy caps, as did the clay frogs and the laughing animatronic Santa, whose mirth shook the flakes from his shoulders, only for them to resettle a moment later. The branches of the conifers in beribboned pots drooped under the weight of their white blanketing.

Kate wandered the narrow lanes between the huts and soaked in the noises and smells. A Christmas market wasn't like a mall, where people went on a determined mission to attack their Christmas shopping, ticking off lists and snarling in queues. A Christmas market was a meandering affair, a gentle seeking of gift possibilities, melding pleasure with purchase.

The spicy Christmas aromas intoxicated Kate's senses and before she knew what had happened, she had purchased two cups of nonalcoholic mulled wine and a steaming bag of honey-roasted nuts and put dibs on a pair of Christmas embroidered cushions.

There was a queue outside Matt's hut and Kate could see that his stocks were depleted. She let herself into his hut through a door at the side and put her spoils down on one of the stools.

"Thank you *so* much for coming!" said Matt. "I really appreciate this."

He turned briefly to Kate and smiled as he handed change and a bulging paper bag with the Pear Tree Café logo over to a woman in a striped hat and scarf.

"I wasn't busy," said Kate.

A woman in a deerstalker hat picked up two jars of brandied fruit and a bag of Kate's alcoholic truffles. She ordered two gingerbread lattes and while she paid, a man in a matching hat joined her and took possession of her purchases. The woman touched her head to his in an unspoken mark of togetherness, and Kate was caught by such a pang of longing in her rib cage that she almost doubled over.

"That's the last of your truffles," said Matt as he turned to make the coffees.

"Really?" said Kate absently.

"Really," said Matt. "I've got more of everything else in the van, but I haven't been able to get away long enough to get it."

A young couple bought one of Evelyn's fruitcakes and a bag of gingerbread men and ordered cinnamon hot chocolates with whipped cream.

"And I'm dying for the toilet," he hissed in Kate's direction.

Kate took a swig of her mulled wine.

"Right," she said. "Finish these orders. Get yourself off to the loo and then replenish your stock. And grab yourself something to eat, while you're at it."

"But you can't make coffee," said Matt.

"I'll tell them its gifts only until you get back," said Kate. "Don't worry, I'm not going to touch your precious machine."

Matt grinned.

"Yes, ma'am," he said, and, hurling his money belt at Kate, he dashed out of the hut and disappeared among the Christmas shoppers.

Kate tied the belt around her waist and began to serve customers. A gospel choir sang "Carol of the Bells" under the tearoom's awning and as the afternoon light faded, Victorian-style streetlamps bloomed a golden glow between the snow-capped huts. Laura ran past the hut in her uniform; she ducked her head in as she went by and through a maniacal grin said:

"I haven't stopped all day. I want to kill absolutely everybody."

Then she ran off, waving and blowing kisses behind her at Kate as she went.

Kate had sold a good deal more of Matt's stock and assured several people that coffee would be back on the menu soon by the time he returned. He tottered into the hut with a large wooden crate and a brown bag containing hot crumpets with melted cheese on top.

They unloaded the stock onto the shelves and Kate sat on one of the stools to eat her crumpets while Matt took over serving.

"I've been thinking about the business," said Matt.

"You're always thinking about the business," said Kate.

"I wondered about getting the old coffee van up and running again," he said. "Laura reckons it would go down a storm here at weddings, and the vineyard has offered me a pitch at their food fair next summer. Maybe I could get a spot down the coast road too. What do you think?"

"Sounds good," said Kate.

"No, I mean, what *do you* think about doing it with me?" said Matt. "On your days off, I mean. Petula and Carla can handle the café. I thought it might be fun."

"Oughtn't you to be asking Sarah to do it with you?" Kate asked.

"Nah," said Matt. "It's not really her thing, she's not quite as outdoorsy as you. Not unless it involves a rooftop bar." He laughed. "Standing around in a wet field for eight hours isn't her idea of a good time."

"Oh, but it's mine, is it?" said Kate. "I happen to like rooftop bars too, you know."

"I've seen you on your dawn raids of Potters Copse," said Matt.

"Welly deep in mud, camera in hand. Sketchbook out when you think no one's watching. You love it."

Kate frowned.

"Think of all the inspiration for your designs," said Matt. "All that being out with nature but with coffee at your fingertips."

"You said yourself, I can't make coffee," said Kate.

"I'll teach you," said Matt. "Or you can take the money while I make the coffee. It'll be good to have the company. And an extra pair of hands."

Kate mulled it over. *It might be nice*, she thought. Weddings at the manor were a notoriously grand affair; she could stand to watch how the other half lived for a day. And there were worse ways to spend her days off than down by the sea. And it would be nice to be with Matt. He certainly never made for dull company; although there was always the risk that he might drive her crazy and she'd end up running him over with the trailer and leaving him for dead . . .

"I'll think about it," she said.

· · · · ·

By five o'clock they had sold out of everything, so they flipped the shutters down over the hatch and locked up for the night. It took three trips to carry all the empty crates back to the van. The fair was officially open until six thirty p.m., but already it was beginning to wind down since the snow wasn't letting up and people were anxious to get home.

It looked like a fairy-tale Christmas village in the dark. The carolers had packed up and left, and their joyous tones were replaced by a CD of *Christmas Hits* playing over the PA and a cluster of battery-operated singing Santas on a stall near the stables.

"Looks like I'll be up all night baking," said Matt. He was so transparent. "Good job I warned Evelyn and Carla to be on standby for more Christmas goodies."

Kate knew what was coming. *Don't do it*, she thought. *Say no!* She steeled herself to keep her resolve.

"I don't suppose you could . . ."

"I've got a date tonight, remember?" said Kate. "And another one first thing tomorrow morning. I really haven't got time. I'm sorry."

Matt looked at her with big amber-flecked eyes and she felt instantly guilty.

"That's all right," he said. "It was worth a try."

That made her feel even worse.

"Couldn't Sarah help?" she asked.

"She's staying at her mum's tonight; the weather's quite bad there, so she doesn't want to drive home in the dark," Matt replied.

"Look," said Kate. "I'll give you my truffle recipes."

Matt screwed his face up and ran his hand through his hair.

"What if I get stuck?" he said.

"You won't get stuck," said Kate. "I'll give you my ingredients as well and if you're really stumped you can call me."

Matt grinned.

"But only if you're *really* stumped," she reiterated. "Don't be calling me just to be a pain in the arse because you know I'm on a date."

"As if I would," said Matt, feigning a hurt expression.

"Shut up and drive me home," said Kate.

· · · · ·

With Matt loaded up with her foolproof truffle recipes and ingredients and on his way home, Kate began the task of getting ready for her date with Richard. She thought about wearing the tea dress she'd worn for their first ill-fated date, but she didn't want to jinx it.

In the end she settled for a pair of tight dark blue Levi's, a pair of biker boots—sexy and practical—and a bottle-green jumper with a gold-thread fleck running through it. Her hair was curly from having gone from damp to dry more times than she could mention that day, and so she swept it up and clipped it loosely, letting the shorter bits fall where they liked. A swish of lipstick, a hasty squirt of perfume, and she was off.

It was still snowing, but the roads were clear as she drove to Great Blexley. The Smugglers Arms was an old-fashioned pub. The walls retained their tobacco-yellow hue as a nod to the days when you could smoke in public houses. The velvet-covered chairs and sofas were threadbare on the seats and shiny at the backs, from years of greasy heads being rubbed against them. But the atmosphere was friendly, the landlord didn't mind if you kept throwing more logs onto the fire, and they served the best hot roast beef sandwiches this side of London.

Kate nervously scanned the low-lit bar. It had occurred to her, as she pulled into the car park, that she didn't really know anything about Richard, and she felt a sudden trepidation about meeting up with a perfect stranger outside the safety net of the Twelve Dates organization.

As if reading her mind, Laura had rung as she turned off the engine. "Kate, are you there yet?" she asked.

"I'm about to go in," said Kate.

"Listen," said Laura. "Are you sure this is a good idea? I told Ben about it and he went off the wall about how you don't know him and I realized, he's right! He could be a maniac! A cannibal!"

"Laura. You've got to calm down," said Kate, sounding braver than she felt. "I traveled around the world on my own. I think I can handle myself. And besides, he's a businessman; it's generally considered a poor show to eat the clients."

"But he's not exempt from having a cellar full of women in chains!"

"Laura."

"I know," said Laura. "I know. *You're a very independent woman.* But that doesn't mean you're impervious to serial killers."

Kate laughed off her friend's concerns, but she promised to keep her phone on, check in every hour, and text if they moved on to anywhere else. She also gave her most faithful assurances that she would text when she got home, no matter what time that might be.

· · · · ·

The bar was stuffy. Kate was too hot as soon as she walked in. She unwound her scarf and looked for Richard the potential serial killer.

Richard emerged as though he'd just teleported into the middle of the pub. He was very tall and his black hair caught the lights and reflected streaks of blue like a raven's wing. The punters parted like the Red Sea as he made his way through the crowded bar. He had a presence that could fill a room, and it wasn't just the width of his shoulders. A smile broke across his face and Kate felt the room get even hotter as he walked toward her. She tried to blow an errant twist of hair out of her eyes as she wiggled out of her jacket.

Richard held out his hand and Kate shook it. He bent and lightly brushed her cheek with a kiss. He smelled like pine forests and wood smoke. *Good God, he smells good.* Kate breathed him in; he made her feel tipsy.

"Kate," He said her name so smoothly she thought her knees would melt. "Thank you for giving me a second chance at a first date."

Richard placed one of his hands in the small of Kate's back and led her through the noisy pub, past the kitchen, the toilets, and the back bar. They headed down a darkened corridor and Kate began to wonder if she could dial 999 on her phone through her pocket, when the corridor opened out into an old timber-framed orangery.

Giant ferns brushed the glass roof and arched over their heads like fronded parasols. Orange and lemon trees were strung with fairy lights, and ivy climbed the wooden frames and splayed its leaves against the windowpanes. A wood burner flickered in the corner. And in the middle of the room, flanked by an olive tree, was a table set for two, complete with candles and a rose in a vase.

Kate drew a sharp intake of breath. She allowed herself to be guided to the table and seated. The pale snow drifted against the windows and made shallow banks against the French doors.

"It's beautiful," she said. "How did you do it?"

"My cousin owns the pub," said Richard. "I told him I had a lot of making up to do." He smiled and his eyes crinkled at the corners.

Kate laughed.

"Well, you've certainly made inroads with this," she said.

"Unfortunately, my cousin's repertoire only extends to beef sandwiches," said Richard. He whipped out his phone and texted something quickly before putting it back in his pocket. "So, I've had to make other arrangements."

At that moment a spotty youth in a tracksuit entered the orangery, carrying two rectangular paper parcels; he placed one on Kate's plate and the other on Richard's.

"Cheers, Trev," said Richard.

The unmistakable aroma of fish and chips wafted up from the paper. Kate's stomach growled loudly. Richard raised his eyebrows.

"No need to ask if you're hungry," he said.

Kate laughed.

"Bon appétit," said Richard.

He leaned down briefly beneath the table and came back up holding a champagne bucket filled with bottles of ketchup, salt, vinegar, and tartar sauce. He plonked it on the table and Kate clapped her hands in delight.

"Brilliant." She laughed and heaped a dollop of tartar sauce on the side of her plate.

Richard smiled warmly.

"Now," he said. "You can have any drink you'd like from the bar. Or, a mug of tea."

"A mug of builder's tea, please," said Kate.

Richard leaned back on his chair and hollered.

"Oi, Trev!"

Trev's voice squeaked back unseen.

"Two mugs of builder's tea, please, mate," called Richard.

Kate's eyebrows knitted together.

"Is Trev your cousin too?" she asked.

"Nah." Richard laughed. "Trev's my nephew. I'm paying him handsomely to be my slave tonight."

Richard grinned, showing all his teeth, and there was something devilish about him that made Kate's bones tickle.

As if the fish and chip supper and excellent muddy tea weren't enough, Trev produced two Cornettos for pudding and then cleared the table and brought out a game of Connect Four.

"I haven't played this in years!" said Kate.

"That's good," said Richard. " 'Cause I hate losing."

They played the best out of three and Kate won, so they made it the best out of five and Richard won, so Kate demanded they play best out of seven and Kate won fair and square.

"I thought you said you hadn't played in years." Richard laughed.

"Once a champ, always a champ," said Kate. "You don't lose a skill like Connect Four."

It was late now. The roar of the pub at the end of the long corridor had dwindled to a low hum by the time the bell rang for last orders at the bar.

"I'd better go," said Kate reluctantly.

The candles in their wine bottle holders had burned down to stubs. Kate played with the soft wax that spilled down the sides of the bottle.

Richard nodded.

"I'd better get young Trev back home to my sister," he said. "I'll walk you to your car."

Richard helped Kate into her coat and fixed her scarf around her neck. With his hand gently resting in the small of her back once more, he led her back along the corridors and through the quiet bar, and out into the snowy car park.

They stood by Kate's car. The snow was little more than white dust motes in the air. Kate looked up at Richard. Her stomach bounced with butterflies. She hated this part of dates: the anticipation. Would he want to see her again? Would he want to kiss her? Did she have haddock in her teeth?

"I had a lovely evening," said Kate. "Thank you."

"Me too," he said. "Thank you for giving me another chance."

After his confidence all evening and the easy way in which he had led their date, Kate was surprised to see that he looked nervous. If it was possible, this endeared him to her more.

"I'd like to see you again," said Richard quietly.

Kate stood on tiptoe and kissed him lightly on the lips. Richard's arms folded around her; he pulled her close against him and kissed her, gently at first and then more urgently. Kate actually felt herself swoon.

Kate's phone pinged loudly and they broke apart, breathless and starry-eyed. She remembered that it had been well over an hour since she last texted Laura to let her know she was still alive.

"Can I call you?" asked Richard.

"Please do," said Kate.

They kissed again, kisses hot enough to melt the snow. This time Kate's phone burst into a shrill ring. She extricated herself reluctantly from Richard's embrace.

"I've got to take this," said Kate. "She *will* call the army if I don't respond."

Richard laughed quietly and held up his hands in surrender.

Kate answered the phone.

"Hi, Laura, everything's fine, can I call you back?"

"I've got the air, land, and sea rescue services on speed dial," said Laura.

"Five minutes," Kate promised.

"Sorry," Kate said to Richard as she ended the call.

"Don't apologize," said Richard. "It's good to have friends that look out for you."

He pulled her to him and kissed her once more on the lips and then released her.

"I'll call you," he said.

"Make sure you do," said Kate. "Or I'll set my friend on you."

Richard laughed.

"I promise," he said.

Kate climbed into her car and wound down the window.

"I think this might be the best first date I've ever had," said Kate.

"I aim to please." Richard smiled.

Richard waited while she started the car, and she could see him still waving as she pulled out of the car park. Two minutes down the road she parked under a streetlamp and called Laura.

"Once an hour!" said Laura.

"I know, I know, I'm sorry. I was in the middle of a really big Connect Four contest," Kate explained.

"Obviously," said Laura.

"No, really," Kate said. "It was amazing!"

Kate briefly filled Laura in on the evening's events, and when she had satisfied her that Richard wasn't a maniac, she carefully drove home along the snowy roads. The hill to Blexford was well salted and soon Kate was letting herself into her house and making herself a mug of cocoa for bed.

Her phone blipped and she snapped it up, thinking it might be a message from Richard, but it was only a photograph of Christmas truffles from Matt. Kate pulled her warmest walking gear out of her wardrobe and laid it out, ready for the morning.

She climbed into bed and sipped her cocoa in the dark. She relived her kiss with Richard and her stomach flipped. Maybe Richard would be the balm to soothe the longing in her heart.

· · · · ·

It was freezing cold and bright blue skies as Kate wandered over the soft mossy floor in the forest clearing to meet the hiking group for the seventh date.

She'd woken up wondering whether she ought to tell Phil right away that she'd met someone. Would it be somehow immoral to pursue two men at the same time? But then she reasoned, surely out of twelve dates you were bound to meet more than one person with whom you made a connection. And she clearly recalled her nan telling her about how she used to go on lots of different dates, with a different man each night; she'd go dancing one night, to the cinema on another, maybe to a show. And if it was good enough for her nan, it was good enough for her.

The winter sun leaked through the spindly tangle of white-dusted branches overhead and cast a gray-blue light on the scene. The burnt umber of ancient tree trunks stood out starkly against their pale surroundings.

People wandered about trying to identify their dates beneath hats and scarves and winter coats. Two reps stood in the middle of the group, ticking off names and helping couples find one another.

By now some of the faces were becoming familiar, and Kate waved and smiled at the people she recognized from previous dates. There were at least two people from the salsa night, a tall blond woman from the cookery class, and a couple she vaguely remembered from cocktail making.

Kate made her way toward a rep in a plum-colored puffer jacket; the woman's teeth chattered as she tried to hold her pen steady between gloved fingers. Kate stated her name and a man in a deerstalker hat and a navy-blue parka turned round to join them.

"Kate!" he said. "There you are." It was Phil. "I wasn't sure if you'd make it. Quite a few people have dropped out of today."

Kate smiled.

"It would take more than a bit of snow to put me off," she said brightly. "Hi." She held out her gloved hand and Phil shook it, smiling.

"I'm glad to hear it," he said. He had a rich Australian accent and his teeth shone white against his tanned skin.

"Have you been on holiday?" asked Kate.

Phil laughed.

"I've just come back from a snowboarding trip in Canada; I guess I caught the sun," he said. "But my parents are Italian, so I really only have to look at the sun to get a tan."

"Lucky you," said Kate. "My skin has two states; pasty or burned."

The male rep called the group's attention.

"Okay, folks," he shouted. "I think everyone who's going to show up is here, so let's get moving before we freeze to the spot. We're going to do a ten-kilometer round trip, and we've got camps set up around the forest for refreshments. Everybody ready?"

The gaggle of hikers nodded and gave their assent. The reps went out in front to lead the way, although a few of the more competitive hikers were hot on their heels. Kate and Phil hung back and adopted a gentler pace; they both agreed they had nothing to prove. Kate could more than hold her own on a hike, and Phil could have given her ex-partner Dan a run for his money in the fitness stakes.

The snap of trampled twigs echoed through the crisp clear forest air. Brambles shivered as birds and other creatures scurried in and out of them, knocking the powdery snow from their thorny branches to dust the ground like icing sugar. Gray squirrels—not at all afraid of people—scaled tree trunks and darted to and fro across the forest path with jerky speed.

Phil was as easygoing as his looks suggested, and Kate quickly rubbed the idea of discounting him because of Richard from her head. He owned three extreme sports stores: one in his native Australia; one in Newquay; and his newest store in Surrey, which he planned to let his son manage.

"How old is your son?" asked Kate. She had imagined him to be no older than primary school age.

"He'll be twenty-two in the spring," he said. "He's been studying for a leisure and tourism degree back home and when he's done, he's going to be my business partner."

Phil smiled broadly. His face—already friendly and open—positively glowed when he talked about his son. Kate found herself basking in his sunny disposition and earmarking him as a possible sperm donor if she decided to go it alone.

"Wow," said Kate. "That's brilliant. I totally thought your son was about four years old." She laughed.

Phil chuckled.

"Yeah," he said. "I get that a lot. Me and his mum were really young when we had him. It didn't work out for us as a couple, but she's an amazing woman; she made sure I was a part of his life, even when I was being an idiot. If it weren't for her, I wouldn't have the relationship I do with my son. I probably wouldn't have the businesses either."

"She sounds like an inspiration," said Kate.

"Well," he said, "you could say that. But *formidable* suits her better. She's like a force of nature. She doesn't suffer fools; you shape up or you ship out. If I didn't want to ship out of my kid's life, I had to shape up."

"And she's happy for him to move to Britain?" asked Kate.

"Happy?" Phil laughed. "She's over the moon. It gives her an excuse to come to England with free accommodation."

Kate didn't find it hard to understand why Phil had never married. He was clearly in awe of his son's mother, even after all their years apart.

Kate and Phil ambled amiably together along the forest path. They talked about their travel experiences and Kate's brief foray into the world of extreme sports with her ex.

Phil told her about how a surfing trip to Fistral Beach when he was twenty-five was the start of a love affair between him and Cornwall. He intended to go back there to live when his son was safely ensconced in the Surrey shop. Kate pondered the potential for new fabric designs inspired by Cornwall. She'd been several times on holidays; could she envisage leaving Kent for Cornwall?

By now there was a clear demarcation around each couple in the hiking party and they walked in a queue like a primary school day trip.

"So, what made you decide now was the time to find a partner?" asked Kate.

"I could ask you the same," said Phil.

Kate was quiet for a moment. Why was she doing this? Why did she feel the need to find a partner? The ache in her chest gave a twinge and she remembered.

"I suppose I'm tired of bouncing in and out of relationships," said Kate. "I've reached the point where I'd rather be by myself than compromise. I'm giving this a go so that I can say I made the effort. And if nothing comes of it, then I will happily hang up my dating hat."

Phil nodded sagely, a rare expression of seriousness on his face.

"You might be the most emotionally intelligent person I've met on this merry-go-round!"

"Thank you," said Kate. "I think. Now you. What brings you to the Twelve Dates of Christmas?"

"The same as you, I guess," he said. "I've played around, done the love- 'em-and-leave- 'em thing. I'm tired of it. I lead a fulfilling life. I've got a great kid, a great business . . . every other aspect of my life is full, but my love life is pitifully shallow. I guess I want a relationship with a lover that's meaningful for a change."

Kate imagined herself ripping open her puffer jacket and yelling, *Take me now! I'll be your meaningful relationship!* but she kept her façade cool.

This wasn't what she'd expected. After the excitement of last night, Kate had imagined she would find Phil to be fun but ultimately not her type. Instead she found herself drawn to Phil's enthusiasm for life. He had a kind of Crocodile-Dundee-meets-Keanu-Reeves thing going on that made her feel like she wanted to giggle a lot and show him how she could do really good handstands.

After an hour they reached the first camp. Inside the pop-up yurt, bales of hay covered in sheepskins circled a portable fire pit. Most couples shared a bale: some looked as if they wouldn't be leaving the warmth of the yurt unless they were forced to. Conversations were lively but muted as the reps prepared mugs of instant coffee and hot chocolate from large catering urns and passed them round.

"Here it comes again!" said a woman in a faux-fur Russian hat, pointing through the gap in the yurt flaps. Phil got to his feet and pinned the flap back to get a better look.

"Wow," he said. "It's really coming down."

And it was. Big white flakes flurried around outside. Kate joined Phil and another couple at the entrance. The sky was pewter-gray; it must have been turning all morning, but Kate had been so engrossed in her conversation with Phil, she hadn't noticed.

Hugging her mug in her gloved hands, Kate stepped out into the clearing. There was something so peaceful about snow. Even the center of London was somehow subdued when it snowed.

Phil came out to join her. The forest sounds were muffled as though someone had turned the volume down. The ground was cold and hard and the snow accumulated immediately. The layering on the already dusted leaves and branches became thicker, whiter, and their dark undersides stood out in sharp relief.

Kate held out her hand and caught a snowflake. She held it close to her face and squinted. Six little points, like a star with icy frond arms. It held its glorious delicate shape for one long moment and then it was gone.

Kate wrestled her camera out from her inside pocket.

"I've got to get photos," she said, squidging her mug into the snowy forest floor.

She crouched down and let the flakes settle on her black jeans, snapping pictures of the tiny miracles before they dissolved from the scant heat of her thighs. Then she moved to the tree branches and the crisp fallen leaves on the ground and the crystals that clung to the guy ropes.

She became so engrossed in her work, she forgot she wasn't alone. It was all so beautiful, she had to capture the fleeting changes of scene. Each fresh layer altered the shapes in the microcosm.

Kate ducked under a snow-laden branch and pushed into the undergrowth. The snow was lighter here, drifting down through holes in the frosted canopy above, to rest butterfly-soft on the bracken. She leaned in close to a twisted knot in a tree trunk and focused her lens on the frosted spiral lines in the wood.

There was a snap behind her.

"Kate."

She spun round to see Phil smiling at her. He laughed softly.

"You've got snowflakes in your hair," he said.

He brushed his finger along the hair that had escaped her bobble hat.

"You are beautiful," he said, and bent down to kiss her on the lips. Kate kissed him back. A soft, tender kiss that made her forget how cold her feet were inside her stiff walking boots.

"They're moving on," Phil said, standing up straight and extending his hand to her. Kate took his hand, smiling, and let him lead her out of the undergrowth and back into the clearing, where the rest of the group was gathered for the next leg of the hike.

Crikey! Kate thought. *I've kissed two men in twenty-four hours. Does that make me a "loose woman"?* The idea made her smile, and the smile wouldn't be quashed as they pushed forward along the snowy track.

At the next refreshment stop the rep made an announcement. The snow had continued to fall heavily for the last hour and some people's phones had been bleeping amber weather warnings.

"Listen, guys," said the rep in the plum puffer. "The snow doesn't look as if it's going to let up, and I know some of you are worried about driving home."

People in the group nodded their agreement. Some had come from miles away, and Kate herself had come a fair distance.

"So we think it would be best to head back to the meeting point and call it a day," said the rep. "We'll get some hot drinks down us quickly and make a move."

Nobody argued. Kate had been having such a nice time with Phil that she'd pushed her worries about getting home in the Mini to the back of her mind, but now she was starting to feel nervous.

The fire pit in the yurt had already been extinguished. The hay bales were being neatly stacked to one side of the clearing and the sheepskins were being wrapped and stacked into the back of a Jeep. The hiking group huddled together outside and gratefully drank their hot chocolate.

The reps beetled about, packing things down and emptying the steaming urns onto the ground. A man carrying two bales of hay headed blindly toward a guy rope. Someone shouted, "Watch out!"

Too late. He caught his leg in the rope, and the force of his fall ripped the metal peg out of the ground. It whipped through the air toward where Kate and Phil stood. Phil saw it and quick as a flash pushed Kate to the ground and himself on top of her. The tent peg whipped above them and thwacked into a tree, taking a gouge out of the bark.

In the fall Phil's jacket zipper had pinched the skin on Kate's throat and made her yelp. As they untangled themselves, Phil assessed the damage and pulled a face.

"What?" asked Kate, "Am I bleeding?"

Phil shook his head.

"No," he said. "It hasn't broken the skin, but . . ."

"But what?" asked Kate, sitting up and rubbing her neck.

"Well," said Phil. "It looks like a giant hickey."

Kate laughed and groaned. "No! Really?"

A few of the group huddled round them to check that everything was okay. They laughed too.

"He's right, I'm afraid," said the woman in the Russian hat. "It's a proper purple hickey!"

"I can't even take the credit," said Phil.

"All the love bite and none of the fun," said someone else.

"I haven't had a love bite since the nineties," Kate protested.

"You have one now," said Phil.

Brilliant, thought Kate. She could just imagine the stick she was going to get from Matt when he saw it. There wasn't a chance in hell he'd believe it was a zipper injury.

The rep made many pleading apologies for the guy rope incident and begged Kate not to sue. Kate assured him she had no intention of suing the rep or Lightning Strikes for a fluke accident that had resulted in no harm at all.

· · · · ·

The snow didn't let up all the way back to the meeting point. All that remained at the site of the first refreshment stop was a shallow circle of new-fallen snow where the yurt had been.

By the time they reached the car park, Kate's gloves had frozen stiff with the snow. It became clear very quickly that Kate's Mini was not going anywhere. The car park floor was thick with snow and more-prepared people than her were setting to with shovels to clear paths around their wheels. Those with 4×4s looked on with concern at those without.

"I'll take you home," said Phil. His Range Rover engine ticked over with a deep purr while Phil helped to clear the car park.

"You can't do that," said Kate. "You live in Surrey! That's miles away."

"Don't worry about it," said Phil amiably. "I'm not going to leave you here, am I?"

"And what happens when you get stuck on your way home?" asked Kate.

"They're closing parts of the motorway," shouted a man in a brown wax jacket, waving his phone in the air.

"You see?" said Kate. "I'm an hour in the wrong direction from you."

Phil shook his head.

"I'm not leaving you," he said.

Kate thought for a moment.

"Is anyone going near Blexley?" she asked.

People shook their heads guiltily. The plum puffer rep piped up: "I'm going near the train station," she said. "I could drop you off if you could make it back from there?"

"That would be great," said Kate. "Thank you."

"I'll take you to the station," said Phil.

"It's no bother," said the rep.

"No, I know," said Phil. "But I'd like to do it."

The rep shrugged.

"If you're sure," she said.

Phil assured her he was. Around the car park, three other people who would be leaving their cars behind managed to get lifts either to their homes or very nearby. Kate wrote a scribbled note explaining the situation to any eagle-eyed traffic warden who might wander by and propped it up in her windscreen.

The last people pulled gingerly out of the car park, and Phil and Kate hit the road in the direction of the station.

"I'm paying for your ticket," he said.

"You are not," said Kate.

"You won't let me take you to your door; I'm paying to make sure someone else gets you there," he said.

"Do you always have to be the hero?" asked Kate.

"Only with women I've kissed in the snow," he replied, and winked at her.

Kate checked the train timetable on her phone as they drove.

"I can catch the 14:15 to Great Blexley," she said.

"What time does it get in?" asked Phil.

Kate checked. "15:20," she said.

Phil pressed a button on his dashboard control screen and used voice activation to call a taxi firm.

"Preston Taxis," a bodiless voice boomed through the speakers.

"Hi," said Phil. "I'd like to order a taxi to Great Blexley train station for 3:20, please."

Kate shook her head: slightly embarrassed, a little bit exasperated, and a fair amount chuffed to pieces. She tried to argue when he asked the woman to charge the journey to his business account, but it was no use.

"I want to be sure you're going to get home," was all Phil said to her protestations.

The traffic was slow going and they made it to the station with moments to spare. Of course, Phil paid for her ticket. He kissed her on the cheek and Kate promised she would call him as soon as she got home. She found a seat in an empty carriage and waved good-bye to Phil the Chivalrous.

The main roads in Great Blexley were mostly clear, and the taxi made it through the blizzard all the way to the bottom of the hill to Blexford, but the hill itself was impassable. The driver was apologetic and promised only to charge half the fare to Phil's account.

The hill was steep. The snow on the sidewalks covered a layer of ice beneath that was impossibly slippery, but the road itself was a white crisp layer and Kate's walking boots had good grips. Safe in the knowledge that no driver would be insane enough to drive up or down it, Kate walked up the middle of the road.

By the time she reached the first bend she was sweating inside her coat despite the cold, and breathing in the freezing air made her head hurt. On either side, lamps were being switched on in houses and curtains were being pulled tight against drafts. The snow was coming down so fast Kate could hardly see where she was going and her face was sore from the wind. She wished balaclavas didn't have such a negative reputation.

Wine Me, Dine Me . . .

It was dark by the time she reached the village square, quiet except for the hum of voices coming from the Duke's Head. The snow danced in the haze of the streetlamps. Kate was headed toward Potters Copse when she heard her name called from across the green.

"Kate?"

It was Matt. Kate turned and waved. Matt beckoned her over. The van was parked at the side of the café, lit dimly from the light spilling out from the kitchen. She sighed. She was about to become free labor again. What she really wanted to do was go home and get the kettle on. She struck a reluctant gait as she trudged over, in the hopes Matt would get the message.

"How was hiking?" asked Matt.

He was chirpy. Either he didn't notice Kate's effort at disinclination or he chose to ignore it. He held out a crate filled with jars and Kate took it with a look of resignation.

"It was lovely," she said. "Until snow stopped play. The Mini is still in the forest."

Matt stacked three crates and heaved them up. Kate followed him into the kitchen.

"How did you get home?" he asked.

"Train and taxi," Kate replied. "The hill is out of action, though."

"I'm not surprised," said Matt. "The Christmas market was really slow this afternoon; everyone wanted to get home before the roads closed."

They dumped the crates and went back out for the rest.

"Did you do all right, though?"

"Yeah," said Matt. "Not bad and it's good publicity for the café."

They finished emptying the van and Kate helped Matt empty the crates.

"This looks good," said Kate, holding a jar of mincemeat up to the light. The thick treacly mixture was bejeweled with whole crimson cherries.

"Cherry brandy mincemeat," said Matt. "A French lady was selling it; homemade. She didn't want to take them all home again, so I bought what she didn't sell at cost." He grinned at her. "Wanna help me make some mince pies with it, ready for the morning?"

"Ah, Matt," said Kate. "It's been a long day and I'm hungry and I've got to get myself organized for work . . ."

"Come on," said Matt. "Please. It'll be fun. I'll fire up the coffee machine. And I've got a bottle of Irish cream . . ."

"Where's Sarah?"

"She's staying at hers," said Matt. "She couldn't risk getting stuck up here and not being able to get to school."

"I really need to get back," said Kate. "And I'm hungry and . . ."

Matt held up his hand to stop her and delved into a cardboard box on the work surface. From it he produced two large jacket potatoes and a plastic tub of chili con carne. He switched on the oven and put the potatoes in.

"I picked us up some dinner from the market," he said. "The spuds will be reheated to perfection in twenty minutes, and the chili can go in the microwave! And we'll have boozy coffee as a starter. Pudding is anything you like from the chiller!"

Kate frowned.

"What do you mean you picked *us* up some dinner?" she said.

Matt looked sheepish.

"I was going to bring it to yours to butter you up so you'd help me, but you were already here."

Kate shook her head. It was game over. Carla was right. She was a sucker.

"Don't skimp on the booze," said Kate.

Matt smiled and went out to the café to get the coffee machine going.

By the time Matt returned with two very boozy Irish coffees, Kate had discarded her arctic weather attire and had already made a start on the first batch of pastry. Matt followed suit and when the disks of sweet pastry were laid in the fridge to rest, the jacket potatoes were hot and ready for their chili topping.

They pulled up two stools and sat opposite each other at the stainless-steel worktop. Bing Crosby was dreaming of a white Christmas through the speakers and the caffeine-alcohol combination had restored Kate's energy.

"What the hell is that?" Matt stopped midmouthful and pointed at Kate's neck.

Kate laughed.

"Oh, that," she said, touching her hand to her throat. "I caught it in my date's zipper."

"What?" Matt's fork clanged on the side of his plate. "Geez, Kate. Slow it down a bit, you met him like two hours ago."

"His jacket zipper!" said Kate. And she told Matt what had happened.

"It looks like a love bite," he said. Unconvinced.

"Well, it isn't," said Kate.

"Bit of an elaborate story, isn't it?" said Matt.

"That doesn't mean it didn't happen," said Kate. "It isn't a love bite."

"It looks like a love bite," he said again. He'd stopped eating.

"Even if it were a love bite, which it isn't, it would be none of your business," said Kate. "If every man I meet wants to suck on my neck, it would have nothing to do with you at all!"

Matt looked taken aback and then abashed.

"Sorry," he said. "You're absolutely right. I suppose I just feel protective toward you. I can't seem to get out of the habit."

"Well, that's very sweet," said Kate. "But I don't need protecting." And then as an aside she added, "And I don't need to be judged by you or anyone else about how I conduct my love life."

"I know," said Matt. "Sorry. Sometimes the words come out before I can edit them."

"Apology accepted," said Kate.

"So, what is this Phil-zipper like then?" asked Matt.

"He surfs and snowboards and owns three businesses and he was a perfect gentleman," said Kate.

"Apart from the hickey," said Matt.

Kate narrowed her eyes and threw a kidney bean at his face.

"What about the other one?" he asked.

"Richard?" said Kate. "He was lovely. It was a really good date." Kate felt her mind wander to Richard's warm embrace. "Really good," she murmured.

"Euuuhch," said Matt. "You've gone all doe-eyed. I wish I hadn't asked. Which one's your favorite?"

Kate eyed him quizzically.

"Don't look at me like that, Turner," said Matt. "One of them must be out in front."

"I think maybe Richard has the edge," said Kate. "But that could just be because I've spent more time with him."

"Kate Turner, the Blexford player," said Matt. "Who'd have thought it?"

. . . . .

It was, Kate had to admit, a lovely evening. It felt like a long time since it had just been the two of them, catching up, talking nonsense and being stupid. When the first batch of mince pies was in the oven, they had a pudding break, having by this time dispensed with the coffee element of the Irish coffee. Matt had a chunk of Victoria sponge and Kate had a slice of white chocolate cranberry cake.

Nat King Cole crooned about roasting chestnuts on an open fire as Kate spooned ruby-red cherries and brandied fruits into the next batch of pies and pressed pastry stars into their middles. Matt swished their tops with milk and encrusted them with granulated sugar. The kitchen was heady with the scent of buttery pastry, Christmas spices, and the mulled wine he had simmering on the stove.

Three hours later the worktops were a sea of golden-topped mince pies cooling on wire racks. They'd made enough to see the café through to New Year with plenty left over for handing out after the caroling. When they were cool, Matt would bag them up in small batches ready to get out when he needed them, though if the last two weeks had been anything to go by, he'd be needing at least a bag a day. Kate picked out eight for herself and let them cool separately.

"Wasn't free booze and dinner enough?" asked Matt.

"No," said Kate, shoveling a hot pie into her mouth and then hopping round the kitchen with her mouth open trying to cool it off.

They cleared up the kitchen in a haphazard drunken way via the medium of dance and song.

"Come with me," said Matt.

He handed Kate her coat and another steaming glass of orange-and-clove-scented mulled wine. He led her out into the garden and sat her down on one of the chairs on the veranda. Then he disappeared back into the kitchen. The blizzard had abated and left the world muffled; the sky was a clear, navy blue, punctuated by a million pinpricks of silver.

"Ready?" he called.

Kate opened her mouth to reply when the garden became awash with light. The gnarly old pear tree had been strung with hundreds of fairy lights. Its bare twisted branches fanned out across the width of the garden, its spindly fingers stretching up to reach the stars in the cold winter sky.

It was magical. Kate felt a lump in her throat as she imagined how much Matt's mum would have loved it. She sat for a long moment, cupping her wineglass with both hands and looking at the tree in awe. Matt came out and sat with her.

"Do you like it?" he asked.

Kate wasn't sure she could speak.

"It's beautiful," she whispered.

Matt smiled.

"I knew you'd like it," he said. "I was thinking of you when I did it. Me and you in this garden."

They were quiet for a long while. The snow lay in drifts against the legs of the garden furniture. The ground was covered in a thick layer of untrod snow that glittered in a million tiny tree lights. Matt scooched over and Kate laid her head against his shoulder.

"I think Mum would like it," said Matt.

"I know she would," said Kate.

"You were right," said Matt. "I should bring back the autumn pear parties. It's been long enough."

"I know a lot of people who will be very pleased about that," said Kate.

She didn't know why, but the idea that she could still get through to Matt after all these years made her chest feel warm. Or maybe it was the alcohol. She smiled to herself either way.

"Sarah has made me realize that I need to stop clinging on to the past," said Matt. "It's time to move forward."

And just like that the warm feeling inexplicably drained out of Kate's chest.

"Mum wouldn't want the tree kept as a shrine to her," Matt went on. "She'd want everyone to enjoy it."

"Mmm," Kate agreed.

But all she kept hearing in her head were the words *It's time to move forward*. What did he mean? Was he trying to tell her something? Was it code for *I'm going to propose to Sarah*? And why did she care?

"I need to go home," said Kate.

"What? Are you okay?"

"I'm fine," she said. And then, "I just feel a bit sick."

"Oh," said Matt. "Okay. Well, I'll walk you home."

"There's no need," said Kate. "I'm a big girl."

"You know, sometimes I think you argue with me out of pure habit," said Matt.

The village was asleep as they wandered home. Even the pub was dark and quiet. The bright moon lit their way as they made their marks on the virgin snow. The air was still now, as if it had worn itself out and the accumulating snow made the village feel somehow insulated from the cold.

They walked side by side, and the similarity between this scene and the one Kate had witnessed the other night between Matt and Sarah was not lost on her. But they would not wrap their arms around each other or kiss tenderly under the moon because that was not what friends did.

They reached Kate's house. It looked like a Christmas card. Her dad had placed two poinsettias in green clay pots on either side of the front door, protected by the gabled porch roof, white with a layer of gingerbread-house snow. Kate's footprints from that morning had been completely covered over.

"Thanks for your help tonight," said Matt. "I really appreciate it."

"You're welcome," said Kate. "I had a nice time."

"Me too," said Matt. "I miss that sometimes . . . you and me, just larking about."

"Me too," said Kate.

"Well," said Matt. "I'll be off. Early start as usual."

"Yep," said Kate.

Matt put his arms out and pulled Kate into a bear hug. He kissed her on the top of her head and trudged back down the garden path, pulling her gate closed behind him. He turned back and waved once as he wandered back down the snowy road and disappeared into Potters Copse. Kate watched him go and stood there a good while after he'd disappeared from view.

Later, Kate lay in bed thinking. She was thinking about Matt and Sarah getting married. She was thinking that her feelings about such a happy imagining weren't as joyful as they ought to be. Her phone blipped and the thoughts dropped away into the abyss. It was a text from Drew:

Steven the Home Office hottie is a heartbreaker! it said.

Oh no! texted Kate. What happened?

He's married, came the reply. To a woman.

Arsehole! Kate replied.

Totally. Drew responded. How about you?

Two great dates, two great kissers. Kate replied.

Slut! texted Drew, followed by I'm jealous! xxx

· · · · ·

"I can't believe it!" said Laura. "And you kissed both of them! Amazing! I'd have passed out from all the romance. I don't have romance anymore. Ben's idea of romance is not nodding off during sex."

Laura was spoon-feeding mashed banana to Charley for his breakfast, but she was wearing most of it down her T-shirt. Laura and Ben lived in one of a row of cottages that used to house the married servants of Blexford Manor; Laura enjoyed the historical juxtaposition of her life with that of the previous tenants.

The television was playing the children's channel; strange brightly colored creatures were singing nursery rhymes in a psychedelic woodland. Charley was transfixed. A gaudy Christmas tree, clearly decorated by Mina, dwarfed the tiny sitting room.

"So, did you hear from either of them yet?" Laura asked.

"Both," said Kate, grinning sheepishly.

"Oh my God," said Laura.

"Richard sent me flowers this morning," said Kate.

Laura clutched her hand to her heart and sucked in her breath.

"They're beautiful," Kate went on. "All winter blooms and Christmas foliage; he's really thought about it."

"Wow," said Laura in a dreamy voice. "Ben only buys me flowers when they've been marked down at the garage, or if he wants me to partake of some sexual deviance."

Kate pulled a face.

"But sadly, even that's not as often as it used to be," said Laura wistfully.

"Anyway," said Kate. "On the card in the flowers, it said: *Be ready at your gate for 9.30pm. I'm taking you out for a hot toddy. Wear layers.*"

"Oh my God," said Laura. "How are you still upright? I feel dizzy just hearing about it."

"And," Kate went on, "Phil and I have been texting back and forth quite a bit. He's hilarious, you'll love him, oh and he called me last night to arrange a date after Christmas."

"Blimey," said Laura. "They're like buses!"

Kate laughed. Charley shouted "BUS!" and slapped his hands on his highchair table, flicking banana in Laura's hair.

Ben's office had closed down for Christmas and he'd taken Mina out for a father-daughter breakfast at the Pear Tree, where they drank babyccinos and read princess magazines together.

"I popped into the café yesterday," said Laura. "Had one of your mince pies. You can tell which ones are yours," she said. "Matt's are somewhat rustic-looking. He said you had a love bite that you were trying to pass off as an accident."

"That man gossips like an old woman," said Kate.

"Are you doing the gingerbread house date at the manor?" Laura asked.

"Yes," Kate replied. "But first I've got that dinner date, tomorrow night, near Leicester Square. I'm going in to the office for a few hours during the day and then I'll head over. In fact, I'd better get off, I've got to be at the Pear Tree for half ten to help out with Petula's craft morning and then go home and do some work, and then go on a hot-toddy date."

"You are racking those men up," said Laura.

"It was a bit of a slow start," said Kate. "But it's certainly picking up speed now."

"Did you get your car back yet?" Laura asked.

"Patrick's bringing it back on the tow truck tomorrow," said Kate. "Poor old girl, she'll never make it up the hill in this."

· · · · ·

Kate left Laura's armed with a bag full of bay tree leaves freshly pinched from her garden and some dark green ivy she'd pulled from the back fence.

The roads were clear down in Great Blexley, but Blexford was still a winter wonderland. Most people were using being cut off by the hill as an excuse to start their Christmas holidays early. Parents pulled toddlers along on sledges, which doubled as handy shopping trolleys, and men whose summer rituals consisted of charring meat over hot coals now indulged their winter customs by lagging pipes and setting up Christmas laser-light projectors in their front gardens.

The Pear Tree was buzzing with activity, not least because of the three tables taken up at the back by Petula's crafters. Ben and Mina waved from the easy chairs; Ben was reading *National Geographic* and Mina was deeply involved in sticking unicorn stickers on her tights. Mina was sporting a chocolate Musketeer beard and mustache, which was transferring to her pink jumper from her chin in scuffs of brown that Kate felt sure Laura would disapprove of.

"Hello, stranger!" called Matt. "What strength coffee can I get you this fine morning? Rocket fuel or nuclear?"

"Nuclear, please," said Kate.

Matt was happiest when he was ridiculously busy; something about bedlam brought him out in deep joy.

Petula rushed at Kate and manhandled her to the craft area.

"Here she is!" Petula trilled. "Our very own Liberty designer."

Kate flushed as twelve curious crafters turned their eyes expectantly upon her. She was surprised to find that none of the faces were familiar; Petula must have been advertising her classes farther afield.

Kate surveyed the paraphernalia on the tables and added her own greenery to the mix. Some of the crafters were already inspired and concentrated on their projects, while others sifted through the festive bits and bobs with expressions of mild panic.

Matt brought her coffee over.

"I really enjoyed the other night," he said. "We ought to do it more often."

Kate felt the inquisitive ping of ears suddenly standing to attention all over the café.

"You can't say things like that," said Kate. "People will gossip."

"Let them." He grinned. "I'm well used to being sport for idle tongues; gossip is the Blexford currency."

"Don't I know it," said Kate.

"By the way," said Matt, raising his voice for the audience. "How's that love bite from the Aussie surf dude coming on?"

He lifted her hair and inspected the mauve bruise near her throat, making interested noises as he did so. Kate could swear she heard a collective intake of breath from the café. She slapped his hand away.

"There are times when I don't like you at all," she hissed.

Matt flashed her a wicked grin and went back to work. Kate pulled off her coat and jumper—leaving her scarf on—and fanned herself with a blank Christmas card from the table.

Kate pulled a chair to the end of the middle table and sat down. She plucked three large bay leaves from the middle of the table, positioned them together by their stalks in a fan arrangement, and tied the stalks securely with a piece of thread.

"The great thing about using nature for decorations is that Mother Nature has done all the hard work for us," said Kate. "And all we need do is add the slightest embellishments to make something that looks like we've got bags of style."

Kate took a length of raffia, wrapped it twice around the stalks, and knotted it. Two women at the table scrabbled about for bay leaves and followed suit, as did a man seated at the next table, craning his neck to see what Kate was doing.

Kate threaded a gold jingle bell onto the raffia lengths and pushed it up to the knot; she followed this with a small tartan bow and then another bell and then a slice of dried orange, before tying the raffia into a big bow to secure them all in place. She took a gold pen and wrote *Mina* in curly script along the length of the middle bay leaf.

"One place card," said Kate, holding the decoration up. "Or a fancy gift label," she added.

Kate went on to produce variations on this theme, using cinnamon sticks, star anise, dried apple slices, and sprigs of rosemary and trailing ivy. The crafters quickly caught on and produced their own adaptations.

Matt brought Kate over a piece of roulade and a gingerbread latte.

"Am I forgiven?" he asked.

Kate ate a forkful of roulade.

"Just," she said.

Ben and Mina came over to say good-bye. Mina's face was now chocolate free, but her jumper looked like the victim of a dirty protest.

"Laura's going to kill me!" said Ben.

Kate laughed.

"I'd say that's a fair assessment," she said.

Kate gave Mina her handcrafted name tag.

"You can put this outside your door on Christmas Eve so that Father Christmas knows which stocking is yours," said Kate.

Mina, who took all things Father Christmas related very seriously, considered the name tag with a look of such deep reverence that Kate had to stifle a giggle.

"Thank you, Aunty Kate," said Mina. "This is very good. Now I won't get Charley's baby toys. Because Charley's a baby and I am a big girl!"

An hour later and the class was over. The crafters left with bags of handmade treasures and stomachs full of cake. Kate helped Petula pack away her equipment into the plastic chests of drawers on wheels.

"Just put those out the back!" shouted Matt from behind the counter. "I'll drop them round to you later, Lula."

"Are you sure?" asked Petula.

"Absolutely," said Matt. "You can't be dragging those great things through the snow like some kind of craft-crazed hobo!"

Kate looked at her watch. The day was getting away from her and she really needed to get cracking on her work. She felt a familiar buzzing in her legs, the adrenaline running through them as she mentally calculated how much work she had to get done against how many hours there were left in the day.

"Go on with you," said Petula with a smile. "I can finish up here."

"It's no bother," said Kate.

"I can see you've got ants in your pants," said Petula. "You've got better things to do than hunt glue-stick lids!"

Kate kissed Petula on the cheek and gathered up her things. Through the steamed-up windows of the café, Kate could see that it had begun snowing again.

"You not staying for lunch?" asked Matt.

Kate shook her head.

"I've got to work," she said.

"Pity," he said. "I'm just about to go on my break, you could've kept me company."

Kate smiled.

"Maybe next time," she said.

· · · · ·

Back home, Kate got the log burner going in the kitchen and printed off the photographs from Epping Forest. She'd been sent a last-minute brief for a winter fabric to come out at the end of January, so she shelved her spring designs for the time being and set to work on some post-Christmas sketches.

She pulled an old tome from her bookshelf and began to leaf through the pages. It was an encyclopedia of flowers she had picked up in a secondhand bookshop: well-thumbed, with that musty attic scent that never leaves once it has impregnated the paper.

Kate found what she was looking for and settled down with paper and palette and began to sketch: dusky pink hellebores with tissue-thin petals and pale starburst middles. And Japanese quince flowers, the color of watermelon flesh: neat little bell-shaped blooms with sunshine centers. To these she added patches of snowy woodland backdrop, inspired by her photographs: frosted ferns and iced berries.

It was important to get the base color right; too red or too green and it risked looking like a Christmas design. Too pale and it would look cold and uninviting, when what she wanted to portray was the beauty of the wild, even in darkest winter. She needed a shade that would invoke warm blankets and comfort food and TV movies. She settled on a warm taupe, the color of deer in winter.

Late afternoon became early evening. Kate flicked on her desk lamp and continued to work as daylight left the world outside entirely and all that could be seen through the windows was darkness. A steady stream of coffee, mince pies, and crisps had kept her going. But now she was properly hungry.

She didn't feel like cooking. Her mind was too much on making sure she had her spring designs perfected and her last-minute winter brief completed ready for tomorrow. Instead, Kate made herself a very full cheese-and-pickle toasted sandwich and a mug of tea and went into the living room to eat it in front of the TV. She knew from bitter experience not to eat messy foods near her workspace.

Halfway through an episode of a Christmas baking show, Kate's phone bleeped. It was a text from Phil.

Can I call you? it said. Kate replied that he could. Two minutes later he called. There was something strange about his voice. He didn't sound like the happy-go-lucky man she'd kissed in the forest.

"I wanted to tell you that I've got to go back to Australia," he said. "I wanted to let you know because I thought we got on really well. And I wanted to see you again. And I didn't want you to think that I was just blocking you or anything like that."

"Is everything all right?" asked Kate. "You don't seem like, well, you!"

"My son called," said Phil. "His mum's sick. Like really sick. Suspected meningitis. I've gotta get over there."

"Of course you have," said Kate. "Absolutely, don't give it another thought. I hope she's okay. We can catch up when you get back."

"That's the thing," said Phil. "There won't be any catching up. When I heard she was sick I . . ."

"You realized you were still in love with her?" said Kate gently.

"I'm sorry," said Phil.

"For what?" asked Kate. "For being honest?"

"I'm sorry if you feel I led you on," said Phil.

"You have nothing to apologize for," said Kate. "When do you fly out?"

"Tonight."

"I'll be sending positive vibes your way," said Kate.

"In another time . . ." said Phil. "Things might have been different."

"In another time," said Kate. "They might have been."

"Take care of yourself, Kate."

"You too."

Kate felt a little pang of disappointment, but she wasn't entirely surprised; he had spoken about his ex with such reverence on their date that the only real surprise was Phil himself not realizing he was still in love with her.

Oh well, thought Kate. *That's one down . . .*

She finished her supper and went back to her sketches, a little wistful maybe but not altogether sad. She hoped Phil got the chance to tell his ex how he felt. *So many people looking for love*, she thought. She thought of her dad and Evelyn, and it made her smile. She hoped it would work out for them.

Kate worked until nine o'clock and then ran upstairs to squirt perfume, zhoosh her hair, and reapply makeup superfast. At 9:29 p.m. she stepped outside her front door. In the lamplight she realized she still had paint under her fingernails and was about to go back in and take a scrubbing brush to them when a black SUV pulled up outside her house.

Richard wound his window down.

"Hello, Kate," he said, smiling. "Ready?"

His voice was smooth; it reminded Kate of polished oak and freshly ground coffee. She smiled, a wide, toothy, excited smile, which she didn't seem able to switch off or even turn down to a sensible flirty smile; she was by all accounts looking as goofy as she felt.

She made her way ungracefully—slipping twice—to the passenger side and climbed in. The car smelled of Richard and it made Kate's bones go bendy.

"How was your day?" he asked.

"Busy," said Kate. "How was yours?"

"Dull," said Richard. "But improving by the minute!"

"Where are we going?" Kate asked.

"You'll be able to guess shortly," he replied.

Richard navigated the snowy maze of roads that led out of Blexford and even in the dark with no streetlights, Kate recognized the road to Blexford Manor.

"We're going to the manor?" Kate said.

Richard nodded and smiled.

"Well, it seemed only right," he said. "Now that we've had our second first date, we can enjoy our first second date where we should have had our first first date!"

"Blimey," said Kate.

The gated entrance was lit by several Victorian lampposts of differing heights, each adorned with a beribboned holly wreath. Instead of taking the turn for the car park, Richard drove slowly down the long walk and turned left at the fountain. They pulled round the back of the manor and parked in the staff car park.

"Are you allowed to park here?" Kate asked.

"You are if you're spending as much money as me," said Richard.

Bit showy, thought Kate, but she decided to let it go since she was having a very nice time.

Richard leaned across her and pulled a torch out of the glove compartment. He grinned at her.

"Come on," he said.

What the hell are we up to? Kate wondered.

Richard held his arm out and Kate linked her arm through his. It felt nice. Richard was confident, masterful, and Kate found herself feeling privileged to be the center of his attentions.

The dim, orangey glow from the manor's little bistro and adjoining bar lit their way as they crunched along the well-salted gravel. They stopped by a rough path cut into the grassland, which led away from the manor and into the black wall of trees that formed the forest's edge. Only the tips of the trees were identifiable: high above, backlit by the moon, like the spiky papercut scenery used in shadow puppetry.

Richard nodded toward the dark path.

"Shall we?" he said, and flicked on his torch.

The cutout path wasn't wide enough for two people, so Richard took the lead and Kate fell in behind him. It was freezing and Kate was glad of her layers, but when they reached the forest, the trees sheltered them from the sharpest bite of the breeze.

Kate took one last look back before plunging into the forest. The manor looked warm and inviting; its little leaded windows smiled amber warmth, and the smoke furling up through the many chimneys whispered tempting welcomes. Kate shivered and pressed on behind Richard. She didn't fancy being lost in the forest tonight.

Where the trees were most dense there was a mere smattering of snow on the ground, but in the clearings, the gaps in the green canopy let the snow in and the forest floor was thickly blanketed.

They tramped on along the rough frozen path, Richard's torch cutting holes in the dark. The night beasts were awake and screeching their annoyance at the two lumbering humans on their patch; scurrying creatures flickered past, fast, at the edges of Kate's vision.

Richard stopped abruptly and Kate, who was squinting into the trees to her left, bashed straight into his back.

"Whoops!" she said. "Sorry about that, I was trying to see what that scurrying thing was back there, could have been a fox, maybe a badger . . ."

Richard guided her round to his side and Kate stopped chattering and looked ahead.

Reaching up before them was an ornate stone tower, dark ivy coiled round and round, and at its top, a snowy turret, needle sharp, pierced the starry sky: the Blexford Folly.

Kate had been to the folly before but not for many years and never at night. The original lord of the manor had had it commissioned soon after the manor was built, but unlike many of its counterparts—stylish yet useless—Lord Milton Blexford had made his a functional folly. It was used as a place to entertain his hunting parties. It would have been a welcome respite for the party, with its grand fireplaces and comfortable surroundings but a nightmare for the staff, who would have had to trek the feast through the forest to the folly without being seen by or accidentally shot by the guests.

Its most recent incarnation was as a two-bedroom boutique hotel, with the ground floor serving as cozy bar and eatery. Kate hoped Richard hadn't taken it upon himself to book them a room. She had a lot to do tomorrow before she went to the office, and she hadn't shaved her bikini line in over a fortnight; it was less neat landing strip and more scrubby allotment.

"I promised you a hot toddy," said Richard, and he pushed open the heavy arched oak door to the folly. "After you," he said, and bowed slightly, which made Kate giggle like a schoolgirl.

The warmth from the giant stone fireplace enveloped Kate, and her frozen cheeks prickled as the heat hit them.

The room was circular; the flagstone floor—worn smooth and undulating slightly underfoot—was partially covered by a woven rug, so thick it could have been a blanket. And the walls were hung with lavish tapestries that picked out and complemented the deep reds, greens, and blues in the rug.

Opposite the entrance was the bar with a stone doorway on either side of it, offering glimpses of two spiral staircases disappearing off behind the wall. There were a couple of wingback chairs dotted about the room, and a luxuriant-looking sofa with a long, low coffee table made from the split trunk of a tree.

The deep stone recesses that framed the windows on either side of the door had been draped with rugs and piled with velvet and plaid cushions to make two comfortable window seats.

The one on the left was taken by a very honeymooning-looking couple, and Richard motioned that he and Kate should take the other. Aside from the four of them, there were no other customers in the bar. Choral music drifted out through hidden speakers, and the logs on the fire crackled and popped.

Kate slipped her boots off and hopped up onto the window seat, pulling her knees up to her chest and half wishing she were here with a good book. Richard climbed in opposite her; the frames were so big that even Richard was dwarfed by them.

"I feel like a kid in a giant's house," said Kate.

"They don't let kids have the kinds of drinks they serve here," said Richard with a wink.

The waiter came over and gave them each a cocktail menu, though Kate noted there were no Slippery Nipples on offer at Blexford Folly. Richard ordered a Blexford Hot Toddy and on his recommendation, Kate ordered the same.

"Have you been here before?" Kate asked.

"Once or twice," Richard replied, but he didn't elaborate.

Kate wondered if he'd brought other dates here, but then she supposed it didn't really matter; it seemed unfair to penalize a perfectly lovely location simply because he'd been here with someone else. *We've all got a past. And after all*, she thought, *it's me he's chosen to bring here tonight*, and she was very pleased he had.

Their drinks arrived; the soothing liqueur slipped down her throat like warm silk, hot with cloves and lemon and bourbon. By the time she'd finished her second toddy, Kate was feeling as warm on the inside as she was without. Richard had switched to virgin toddies as he was driving, but he seemed keen to promote Kate's consumption of their alcoholic counterparts.

He was playful and charming and Kate began to feel that if he had booked them a room, she might be tempted to partake, despite the unruly hedgerow in her pants.

"Okay, fine," said Kate when he coyly suggested a game of firsts, knowing full well she'd been goaded into it. "I'll play."

Richard chuckled darkly. Kate took another sip of her drink to try to quash the fluttery feeling in her stomach.

"First kiss," said Richard.

Kate's brain fizzled and her heart picked up speed.

"You first," she said.

"All right," said Richard, grinning wickedly. "Naomi Hall. In an old bomb shelter in the park. She was nine, I was ten. We were in the same class at primary school. Our teacher used to take us to the recreation ground on nature trails; we were supposed to be looking for dandelions."

He looked at Kate and raised his eyebrows. "Now you," he said.

A memory swam, warm and sepia-toned through her mind.

Strawberry-blond hair and freckles gone dark in the sun. Her breath caught as she remembered. The yearning took her by surprise and she squashed it quickly with another swig of hot bourbon. She tried to make her voice sound as removed as Richard's had been.

"Matt Wells," she said. "Behind a pear tree. We were both ten."

"And?" said Richard.

"And what?" Kate asked.

Richard leaned closer to her, his mouth near hers. His breath brushed her lips.

"And how did you know this Matt Wells?" he asked. "And why were you kissing him behind a pear tree?"

Richard could have no idea of the effect these memories were having on her, or the effect *he* was having on her. Kate was both confused and aroused, and she was unsure which sensation belonged to which effect. Memories of kissing Matt at another point in her history burst behind her eyes, and her heart hammered as though it wanted to be heard.

"He was my friend," said Kate, suppressing the feeling in her chest. "The pear tree was in his garden. And I don't know why we were kissing. You couldn't really call it *kissing*. He kissed me on the lips and I let him."

Richard leaned back, seemingly satisfied, and grinned. Kate let out a breath; Richard's proximity was more intoxicating than the toddy. This conversation felt strangely illicit.

"I'm going to say my first kiss was probably more exciting than yours," said Richard. "So that's a point to me."

"You're probably right," said Kate.

"Right then," Richard went on. "This next one's worth two points. First time you had sex!"

The memory of the boy with the strawberry-blond hair popped and was replaced by a dark-haired spotty youth. She smiled, relieved. She was on safer ground here. Her muscles relaxed.

"Rory Parker," she said triumphantly. "In the back of his car. I was seventeen, he was nineteen."

"What kind of car?" Richard asked.

Kate laughed loudly.

"That is such a *man* thing to ask," she said. "Not, was it tender? Was it romantic? Just what car was it?"

Richard grinned.

"Was it tender and romantic?" he asked.

"No," said Kate. "It was cramped and uncomfortable. He had a Ford Fiesta."

Richard nodded sagely as if he had had plenty of cramped sexual encounters in Ford Fiestas.

"Were you together long?" he asked.

"Six months," said Kate. "He joined the army. Got posted to Cyprus; I knew it wouldn't last."

"How pragmatic of you," said Richard.

His voice had become lower somehow, deeper, more intense. All this talk about sex was making the fluttering in her stomach travel south.

"What about you?" Kate asked.

"I was fourteen . . ."

"Fourteen!" Kate exclaimed.

"I was mature for my age," said Richard. "Cindy Jones. She went to an all-girls school. Her parents ran a B&B; they paid her to be the chambermaid."

"Let me guess," said Kate. "You had sex in a guest's bedroom."

Richard grinned and his eyes twinkled.

"I hope you changed the sheets after," said Kate.

"And that," said Richard. "Is such a *woman* thing to say; not, was it a good experience, just did we change the bed linen!"

Kate laughed.

"All right then," she said. "Was it good?"

"Very," Richard grinned. "Didn't last long, though . . ."

Kate spluttered.

"I *mean*," Richard continued. "The *relationship* didn't last long! Obviously, *I* can go for hours!"

"I'll bet you can," said Kate. It was her turn to switch on the sexy gaze. He picked it up instantly and something devilish flashed across his eyes.

"The *relationship* didn't last long because it turned out she had a penchant for relieving willing lads of their virginity; she'd had most of my gym class."

"Oh dear," said Kate. "Were you upset?"

"Nah," said Richard. "She was a nice girl. Showed me the ropes, as it were. I bumped into her years later in a bar in Westminster; she's a solicitor." He took a sip of his drink. "Did you ever see Rory again?"

"Oh God no!" said Kate.

"Were you never tempted to look him up on Facebook or Instagram?"

"Never," said Kate. "I don't like all that." She waved her arm in the air to encompass *all that*. "People confuse nostalgia with love and end up getting divorces or having affairs and all sorts. No, I think if you haven't kept in touch for twenty years there's probably a good reason."

"I met my ex-wife on Facebook," said Richard. "We went to school together but lost touch after. She found me, actually."

"Oh shit!" said Kate. "I'm so sorry. Trust me to put my big fat foot in my mouth."

"Don't worry about it." Richard laughed. Then he leaned in closer to Kate again. She could smell his cologne. He was looking straight at her. "I'm not interested in talking about my ex-wife," he said quietly. "I want to know more about your past sexual encounters."

He was so close to her now that his lips brushed hers as he spoke.

"Tell me what you like, Miss Turner," he breathed. "Tell me what makes you scream."

· · · · ·

It was still dark when Kate got up at five a.m. and set back to work. Her head spun lightly but not unpleasantly, with a dash of hangover and a heavy dose of last night's memories: Richard's mouth on hers, the taste of him, the feel of him pressed up against her, the cold hard of a tree at her back and the hot hard of Richard to her front.

He hadn't booked a room—more's the pity—and eventually the subzero temperature of the forest had enforced a literal cooling of their ardor, so that the evening ended on warm terms but minus consummation. In some ways Kate was pleased not to have had sex with Richard yet. What was her hurry? She always bowled into things without thinking and ultimately ended up single again. It was good to wait. It was good for her to wait.

Kate washed the brush out and blew on the red-painted toadstool to quicken its drying. She wanted to get the winter fabric designs ready to submit for approval today. The spring designs were already neatly stacked in her portfolio.

By seven forty-five a.m. the sun was just beginning to rise and the gray morning light spilled in through the kitchen windows. It hadn't snowed overnight but a thin dusting began to fall now, the flakes lightly scratching at the windows. Kate made herself another coffee and two rounds of hot buttery toast and ate them standing by the French doors.

A robin nibbled at the bird feeder and the sky looked low enough to bang your head on.

She'd just finished when Patrick knocked at the door with her car keys, her Mini safely restored to its spot outside the front gate. Kate thanked him and paid him cash.

"Evelyn tells me you're out on a date in London tonight," he said.

Honest to goodness! Kate thought. *Even the farmer knows about my love life.* But she smiled and said, "Yes, I am."

"You're not thinking of taking that, are you?" he asked, motioning with his head to her Mini.

"Not a chance," said Kate. "I don't think the old girl would make it in the snow."

"Well, I'm taking Evelyn up to Covent Garden market tonight to pick up a load of fresh Christmas trees," said Patrick. "So, if you finish late and you fancy a lift home, give us a call."

"Thanks, Patrick," said Kate. "I might just take you up on that."

By ten a.m. Kate was packed up and ready to go. She was taking a small pull-along case so that she could fit in her portfolio and a change of clothes for her date tonight; she could change at work. If she caught the half eleven train, she could be in the office by one o'clock and work until she needed to be at the restaurant by seven p.m.

She carried the case through Potters Copse, as the ground was too uneven to wheel it. The trend for decorating the trees in the copse had caught on and it didn't end with the trees. The hedgerows and brambles were dripping with baubles, and even the tree stumps were wound round with fairy lights. She determined to press Evelyn again about rerouting the caroling through this way.

Kate stopped in at the Pear Tree for a takeaway coffee, and Matt insisted on driving her to the station in his 4×4.

"There is no way you're going to get down that hill, in the ice, with a suitcase, and not fall arse over tit," he said.

Kate conceded that he was probably right.

"I need to go to the cash-and-carry anyway," he said. They left Carla and Petula holding the fort.

"So how is work going?" Matt asked.

"Good, thanks," said Kate. "I've got the first batch of spring designs ready and a last-minute winter one ready to submit."

"I'd like to see them sometime," said Matt. "I feel like I've been so busy recently, I haven't seen your work for ages."

"Well," said Kate. "It's good that the café's doing so well. And fabric's not greatly interesting to you, is it."

"I'm always interested in what you do," said Matt. He seemed strangely offended. "You're really talented, Kate. I've always admired your work."

Kate was a little taken aback.

"Oh," she said. "Thank you." She changed the subject. "How's Sarah?"

"She's great!" said Matt. "She's so busy with work at the moment, but the schools break up soon, so she'll be around a lot more."

"That'll be nice."

"I was thinking of cooking a pre-Christmas meal for us," he told her. "With you and Laura and Ben, and Sarah obviously. You could bring one of your Shagmas dates." He grinned.

Kate felt her chagrin rise, but she let it fall again. She would not give Matt the satisfaction. She wondered if it was too soon to invite Richard.

"I might have someone I could invite," she said.

"Who? The rugby player?" asked Matt.

"Yeah," said Kate. "Maybe."

"Getting along quite well with him, aren't you," said Matt. "Do you think it could be something?"

"Oh, it's definitely something." Kate smiled as last night's heavy petting session in the forest swam back into her mind. "I'm just not exactly sure what yet."

"Bring him along," said Matt. "And then I can grill him about his intentions."

"Oh, that's bound to encourage him to ask me out on further dates," said Kate.

Matt laughed.

"It'll be the first time all of us will have had partners at the same time," he said. "At least when we're all living in the same place."

· · · · ·

The train was packed. Kate only just managed to get a seat. She sat next to a man who picked his nose relentlessly and laughed out loud at the cartoons in his newspaper. Opposite were two women, off to do some last-minute Christmas shopping. They steeled themselves for the task by drinking gin and tonic out of plastic tumblers, which one of the women produced from a Harrods tote bag.

Moaning children were subdued with sweets and magazines, and sullen youths looked blankly out of the windows or kept their faces close to their phones; a *tst-tst-tst* sound emanated from their headphones. Most of the adults were no different; finger pads danced lightning fast over phones and tablets and laptops.

Kate watched the snowy landscape whoosh by. White roofs, white fields, white hills, the gray sky threatening more to come. They passed by a cemetery: flashes of red from poinsettias laid for the gone-but-not-forgotten. Lucky children on a snow day sledged down slopes, while sheep and cows huddled in groups respectively against the cold; a bright green tractor laden with hay bales chugged across the white terrain.

As they came closer to London the scenery changed. Snow-capped billboards enticed consumers with promises of a perfect Christmas. A sea of brick chimney stacks stretched as far as the eye could see, a maze of snowy streets below them, alive and buzzing with activity. Busy high streets with Christmas decorations strung above. Pubs on corners and tented market stalls that ran the length of town centers.

Closer still and the world morphed into a new kind of animal, a bigger, hungrier, more demanding creature. Here was a land of giants: towers that reached for the skies, power and poverty living side by side. Industrial blocks with mirrored windows and revolving restaurants in the clouds. Old stone and glinting steel; history and history in the making. The glorious muddle of a million humans rubbing along together.

Kate loved the city. She loved the grit and the grime and the streets paved with possibilities. If Blexford was her wife, then London was her mistress.

The station was bustling, the tube was rammed, and Carnaby Street was insanity, but it was worth every nudge, squeeze, and jostle to find herself outside her beloved Liberty at Christmas.

It bloomed, mirage-like at the top of Carnaby Street, in a carnival of Tudor resplendence. Christmas trees lined the balconies on the first floor and the leaded windows beckoned people in with glittering ribbons, vibrantly wrapped packages, and delicately constructed sugar plum wishes, plucked from the dreams of Christmas lovers everywhere.

Kate ambled through the festive decked halls and departments and soaked in the Christmas shop wonderland, adorned with more glitter and sparkle per square inch than the whole of Las Vegas put together. She picked out a few new baubles—to add to her already extensive collection—in anticipation of the tree Evelyn and Patrick would be picking up for her that night and made her way to the art department behind the scenes.

Her spring designs were approved, and she emailed them to the fabric printers. Her boss suggested one or two tweaks to the winter fabric and asked her to make an exact copy of the design on a different-colored background as well.

Kate made the required tweaks. She set up her easel and painted in some corkscrew ferns in frosted olive green between the hellebores and the quince, and dotted about clusters of pale brown honey fungus mushrooms. She scanned the final draft into the computer and made a copy with a duck-egg-blue background, so that she had one taupe and one blue fabric of the same design. Then she sent both to the printers.

It was dark by the time she'd finished, but the store beyond the studio was still frenzied with late-night shoppers. She slipped into the staff restroom and changed into her date clothes. She'd packed a racing-car-green knitted dress that had a pretty V-neck wrap-around top, long sleeves, and a tie belt and fell into soft pleats from the waist down. It was warm and flattering and went well with her practical knee-high tan leather boots. After a quick application of eyeliner and lipstick, she decreed herself date-ready.

Tonight she was meeting Jim. Jim was thirty-seven, divorced, with no children, and worked in the city; according to his profile he was something big in investments. His photograph showed him in a slick tailored suit; his hair was short and dirty-straw blond and he grinned in a way that was both charming and mischievous.

Kate stood almost cheek to cheek with the other commuters on the tube to Leicester Square and considered the phone call she'd had with Richard before she'd descended the stairs to the station and lost signal.

"I can't stand the idea of you meeting another man," said Richard.

"I want to get my money's worth," said Kate. "I've paid for this dinner, so I'm going to eat it. And anyway"—Kate laughed—"you're meeting other women! That is, after all, the nature of the twelve dates."

"But I'm thinking of you the whole time," he said.

"Really?" she said. "The whole time?"

"Scout's honor," he said.

Kate felt a little twinge of guilt about locking lips with Phil so soon after kissing Richard. She had to admit, it made life a lot simpler now that Phil had gone back to Australia; if he'd stayed, she wasn't sure she'd have been up to the task of choosing between them.

"Who's your date tonight?" Kate asked.

Richard was signed up for Bond Night at a casino. He'd sent her pictures of himself in his tux; he looked delicious and she'd made no bones about telling him so.

"Gerda," said Richard. "She works in accounts and plays netball and hockey."

"She sounds like your cup of tea," said Kate.

"I've found my cup of tea," said Richard. His voice was deep and smooth and Kate's stomach flipped.

Kate and Richard had spoken on the phone daily since their perfect date at the Smugglers Inn, sometimes more than once. They often texted several times a day: funny things they'd seen or heard, silly videos, thoughtful little texts that showed one was thinking of the other.

She'd woken to a text from him at five a.m. this morning, saying how much he'd enjoyed last night. It was, Kate had to admit, very romantic. Sometimes Kate had to remind herself that she'd only actually seen Richard three times in the flesh and one of those times was technically a rescue mission. It was easy to feel she knew him better than she actually did.

"It's like in the old days when people would fall in love with their pen pals," said Laura, swooning. "They fell in love over their letters without ever having met in real life."

"What? Like those women who write to men on death row?" Kate laughed.

"Exactly like that," said Laura. "But with less murder."

"It's moving so quickly," Kate mused. "I mean, it's fun and it's flirty, but sometimes it feels like we're beyond where we should be at. As if we've skipped a whole chapter."

"Well," said Laura, "just make sure you keep things at a pace you're happy with. A few saucy texts doesn't entitle him to the keys to your knickers—unless of course you want him to have them."

"It's been so long," said Kate. "I don't remember where the keys are!"

Though after last night's close call, she'd vowed to keep all her hairy bits shaved and trimmed, just in case the need for knicker keys should arise unexpectedly. However, she didn't expect to be needing them for tonight's date.

She had more or less decided that the dates from here on were just honoring her financial commitment to Lightning Strikes. The thrill in her chest every time she thought of Richard seemed to confirm that she had already found what she'd been searching for. She almost felt sorry for Jim, her dinner date for the evening.

· · · · ·

The restaurant was situated in a side road just off Leicester Square. It was low-lit and warm and smelled deeply of garlic and fresh bread. The walls were lined with dark oak boiserie paneling and the ceiling was ornately plastered to match the wood detail. Each table had a tea light in a burgundy-and-gold-patterned votive candle holder and a long-necked table lamp, with a smoked glass shade in the shape of a bluebell, which cast a warm glow over the table and kept its occupants in soft focus.

The building was narrow but went back a long way. A third of the tables were on the flat as you walked into the restaurant and the rest were up four steps, with a typical French bar to the right and the door to the kitchens at the far end. The sounds of Django Reinhardt's jazz guitar drifted around the restaurant and reminded Kate of summer evenings spent on the Left Bank in Paris.

Kate recognized the rep from her ill-fated cocktail-making date with Oliver and headed over.

"Hi, Kate!" said the rep. "Eighth date in. How's it going?" She ran her finger down a list of names on her clipboard, stopping at Kate's and drawing a line through it.

"It's going well," said Kate. "I've met some really nice people."

"Oh good," said the rep with a sigh of relief. "We've had a few teething problems," she went on. "But this is the first time we've ever offered something on such a large scale. We'll know better next time."

"What do you mean?" asked Kate.

"Well . . ." The rep bit her lip. "Not everyone has been completely honest about who they are, or their relationship status."

"Oh dear." Kate laughed. "I'll bet that's led to some awkward conversations."

"You have no idea." The rep's eyes were wide as if trying to communicate information she wasn't allowed to divulge. "We're going to have to improve our vetting process for next time."

"I've heard it referred to as 'the Twelve Shags of Christmas,'" said Kate.

"Yes," said the rep. She pursed her lips. "That's not been ideal either."

The rep pointed to a table by the window where Jim twizzled his glass of wine as he looked out of the window.

Kate made her way over.

"Jim," she said, smiling and holding out her hand.

"Kate." He smiled and stood and shook her hand, and then he hesitated for a moment and leaned forward and kissed her on both cheeks.

"When in France," he said. And then, "Oh God, that was awful." He laughed. "It sounded much smoother in my head. I never know how we're meant to greet each other."

Kate laughed too.

"Neither do I," she said. "It's so awkward, isn't it? Is a handshake too dismissive? Or is a kiss on the cheek too familiar?"

"And if you go for the cheek kiss," said Jim, "do you go for one cheek or two? If one of you goes for a two-er and the other for a one, the two-er is going to end up leaning in midair, all puckered up with nowhere to go."

"They really should design a standard etiquette procedure and have it on the website," said Kate. "It would save a lot of red faces."

"From now on I'm going in with a high five," said Jim. "It's the safest way."

"But what if they leave you hanging?" said Kate.

"Oh no!" said Jim covering his face in horror. "Oh, the shame of it!"

· · · · ·

The food was wonderful and Jim made very good company. He was confident and clever, yet self-effacing enough to be endearing and charming.

They started with French onion soup, rich with beef stock and topped with toasted Gruyère croutons. And for the main course, Jim went for the beef bourguignon and Kate had coq au vin.

The conversation flowed easily, too easily. Kate was beginning to wonder if the Lightning Strikes team were getting a bit too good at their jobs. At this rate she could end her Twelve Dates experience with more potential partners than she'd bargained for. With Phil out of the running, Richard was out in front, but Jim was looking like he could be a close second and she still had four more dates to go. Some of her confidence in her budding relationship with Richard had slipped a little after a couple of hours in the company of Jim.

Jim had been divorced for three years and hadn't had any serious relationships since.

"It's time I got back out there," he said. "I like being part of a team of two. I miss that. Does that sound too sappy?"

"Not at all!" said Kate. "I suppose we all want the same thing, or we wouldn't have signed up."

"I guess so," he said. "I don't know when it happened; I was living the life, out being a lad, drinking and chasing women, and then I woke up one morning and it's not enough anymore."

"I think that's called maturing," Kate said.

"What about you?" Jim asked.

"Oh, no such epiphany, I'm afraid," said Kate. "I am a walking cliché of *just haven't met the right man yet*. Boring, huh?"

"I don't think you're boring at all, Kate," said Jim. He leaned across the table conspiratorially and whispered, "I think you're quite the dark horse." He smiled and his eyes glinted something that made Kate's thighs feel hot.

They talked about London: their favorite restaurants, their favorite places to walk in the city, and their shared love for the South Bank of the Thames, and rather bizarrely, they had both frequented the same karaoke bar in Islington.

"I sing best when I'm horribly drunk," said Jim.

"Me too," said Kate. "It's amazing, the more cocktails I drink, the better singer I think I am."

"The people who work there must have to sign some sort of confidentiality clause, or there'd be videos of people like us all over the Internet," said Jim.

Kate covered her face.

"Oh God, can you imagine?" she said.

"I also think I'm a cross between Fred Astaire and Usher on the dance floor after a few pints," said Jim. "Unfortunately, I think the reality is more Mr. Blobby on acid."

"I take it you didn't sign up for any of the salsa dates, then?" said Kate.

"I'm trying to attract women," said Jim. "Not repel them."

Kate laughed. They'd finished their main courses and the waiter brought over more wine.

"Have you got work in the morning?" asked Kate. Jim had drunk twice as much as she had and it was starting to show.

"Nope," he said. "I booked the morning off. How about you?"

Kate shook her head.

"Well, in that case," said Jim with a smile, "we've got the whole night to get to know each other."

He poured Kate another glass of wine, which she determined not to drink.

· · · · ·

"Oh God," said Kate.

She'd excused herself from the table and was sitting in a toilet cubicle talking to Laura on the phone.

"I don't understand what the problem is," said Laura. "You signed up to this thing to help you meet men and that's exactly what it's done."

"Yes, but I didn't expect to like anyone else," said Kate. "What about Richard?"

"What *about* Richard?" Laura asked. "A couple of dates and a few cheeky phone calls does not an exclusive relationship make. Richard's tuned in to your horny wavelength, that's all."

"Oh, you're right." Kate sighed. "Of course you're right. I've just always been a one-man-at-a-time type of gal."

"Did you never watch *Sex and the City*?" asked Laura. "Dates are not relationships. Dates are the prelude to a relationship. You go on the dates first to see if it's worth pursuing as a relationship."

"You're absolutely right," said Kate. "I'm not being unfaithful to Richard because I'm not in a relationship with Richard."

"Precisely!" said Laura. "He's signed up too. And don't you go thinking he's not out there right now flirting with his Bond girl."

Kate's stomach squeezed. She didn't like the idea of Richard flirting with other women, but Laura was right; this was the nature of the Twelve Dates beast.

"So, get back out there quickly and enjoy your evening with sexy Jim, before you've been gone so long he thinks you're having a poo," said Laura.

· · · · ·

Kate wandered back through the restaurant. Several couples had already left. Kate wondered if maybe they hadn't hit it off. Then again, she thought, maybe they'd really hit it off!

Jim smiled at her as Kate took her seat and laid her napkin in her lap.

"So," said Kate.

"So," said Jim.

"Have you chosen a dessert?" Kate asked, picking up the menu and flicking through to the back page.

Jim smiled.

"I think we both know what's for dessert, Kate," he said.

"What?" asked Kate. She looked up from the menu to find Jim staring at her intently.

"I've got a room booked over near Kings Cross," said Jim.

"What?" Kate found herself repeating.

"Don't act coy, Kate," said Jim. "We both know why we're here."

"But," said Kate. "But."

She opened and closed her mouth a few times as she tried and failed to formulate a response. She'd dealt with creeps on numerous occasions but never one who hid his creepy under such a gentlemanly façade. She was trying to keep her temper, but it wasn't easy.

"I'm sorry if you got the wrong impression," said Kate. "But this is just a date. Nothing more."

"Oh, come on!" said Jim. "You're my number eight, I was on a roll. Don't make me miss my stride."

"Did you switch places with your evil twin while I was in the toilet?" Kate asked.

"I thought we were on the same wavelength," said Jim. "We've had a nice evening, we've got great chemistry, so why not?"

"Why not?" Kate blustered. "What about all that stuff about wanting to settle down and be in a team of two?"

"That was just to get you damp," he said.

"You're disgusting!" said Kate. Her temper was so hot she could feel her dinner roiling in her stomach.

"Oh great!" said Jim. "Just my luck. Another bird who watches romcoms! I'll let you in on a little secret. This is the Twelve *Shags* of Christmas, love! How did you think this was going to end?"

Kate blustered.

"With a good-night kiss and a second date," she hissed. "You misogynistic arsehole!"

"It's Christmas, darlin'," Jim drooled. "Loosen your corset a bit, treat yourself!"

"I am not your *darlin'*!" Kate hissed across the table. She didn't want to make a scene. "And sleeping with you is not my idea of treating myself!"

Jim seemed to be bringing out a Victorian side of her personality.

"You've got a high opinion of yourself, love," sneered Jim.

"And you've clearly got a split personality!" said Kate. "Somewhere between courses I've wound up with Mr. Hyde."

"I'd settle for an angry shag," said Jim. "I'm not proud."

"There is *nothing* that would induce me to have sex with you," said Kate.

"Right," said Jim.

He stood up and threw his napkin down on the table.

"Well, this has been a complete waste of time," he said. "I'm going to the bar to see if I can salvage a number eight. I've got money riding on this."

He strode through the emptying restaurant and up the steps and settled himself at the bar next to a woman in a sheer, skintight pink dress, with no demonstrable knickers and an umbrella in her cocktail glass.

Kate was about to go and warn the woman, when the rep came over and bent to Kate's ear.

"Can you come with me a moment?" she whispered.

Kate looked over at Jim to see him running his hand up the woman's back. The rep saw her looking.

"Don't worry about him," she said. "We've got his number."

Kate stood and followed the rep through a concealed door in the paneling, down a cramped corridor, and into a small, brightly lit office.

The rep motioned for Kate to sit and Kate did so, plonking herself down hard in one of the chairs at the paper-strewn desk.

"This relates to what we were talking about earlier," said the rep. "We need your help."

"Mine?" said Kate. "What with?"

"You see, most of the people who've signed up are genuine, like you," said the rep. "But there is a certain element who have formed a Twelve *Shags* of Christmas betting ring."

"Jim?" said Kate.

"Among others," said the rep. "We've been expelling the culprits as we discover them, but Jim has been hard to pin down. We can't take action until we have evidence and so far, all of Jim's dates have left with him willingly."

"Where do I sign?" said Kate. "He told me himself he had money riding on this."

The rep smiled and opened the laptop on the desk.

"If you could submit a complaint form, we can expel him from the Twelve Dates and any other forums across the Lightning Strikes website," said the rep.

"What about the woman outside?" Kate asked. "She seems too drunk to make good decisions."

"I've already called her a cab and the barman is going to make sure she gets in the car alone," said the rep. "The second you submit your form we can exclude Jim from the restaurant."

Kate was already filling in the complaint form.

"He is going to be so pissed," said Kate. She smiled broadly. "I wonder how much money he's got riding on getting a *full house*?"

"The last I heard," said the rep, "the jackpot was up to five grand. Each participant has to put two hundred pounds in the pot to join, and then they can bet more depending on how confident they are."

"Jim seemed pretty confident," said Kate. "I reckon he's bet himself high."

"We can only hope." The rep smiled.

Kate waited until Jim had been removed from the restaurant and been seen entering a taxi *alone* before slipping back out through the paneled door and out of the restaurant.

She grabbed herself a coffee from a late-night coffeehouse and sat outside beneath an awning heater and watched the theatergoers hurrying by after the evening performances and the tourists meandering along with spirits and cameras high.

She called Evelyn.

"What's wrong?" said Evelyn, ever astute. "Is everything all right?"

"Not really," said Kate.

She gave Evelyn a brief account of the evening's events.

"Get yourself over here," said Evelyn. "You know where we are, don't you?"

"New Covent Garden market," said Kate.

"That's the place," said Evelyn. "I'm getting ready to haggle with tree sellers! Call me when you arrive and I'll direct you to where we are."

Kate couldn't be bothered with the hassle of the tube, so she hailed a taxi and spent a small fortune on the ride to the gigantic marketplace. The market didn't open till midnight, but Evelyn would have made sure Patrick got them there at least an hour before it opened, so as to get a good parking spot and so that she was first in when the doors opened.

The taxi dropped her off near the fruit and veg entrance at eleven forty-five p.m. Traders had already begun to queue. It was going to be a busy night. Kate guessed there'd be a big rush on sprouts.

She called Evelyn.

"Where are you?" asked Evelyn.

"I'm at the entrance," said Kate.

"Which entrance?" Evelyn asked. "I can't see you."

It was hard to hear above the noise. Kate could make out a deep muffled voice near Evelyn; Patrick, she thought.

"I'm trying to find out!" Evelyn answered the voice. "Stop fussing!"

"The fruit and veg market entrance," said Kate.

"Oh, dash it all," said Evelyn. "Darling, we're at the flower market entrance. It's just across the way, you can't miss it."

More mumbling, quite grumpy mumbling from what Kate could make out.

"No, we will not go and meet her," said Evelyn to Grumpy. "I don't want to lose my place in the queue . . . She is perfectly capable of making it over here by herself . . . Oh, for heaven's sake, all right! Kate darling, stay where you are, the cavalry's coming!"

Evelyn hung up and Kate stood to the side of the haphazard queue and waited for Patrick to come and find her. Five minutes later the cavalry arrived.

Kate did a double take. Matt rubbed his hand through his messy hair when he spotted her. He looked serious. The collar and bottom of a checked shirt poked out from underneath his navy-blue fisherman's jumper, and his jeans were tucked into his old work boots.

Matt had a way of making scruffy look handsome; Kate always thought of his style as landscape-gardener-chic. He never really had to try. Clothes just sort of hung well on him, as if they were glad to be there. It was very annoying.

Kate's heart leaped at the sight of him, despite herself. She told herself she was just pleased to see a friendly face after her disastrous date, but the ache of longing in her chest was becoming harder to ignore.

"Hello," said Kate. "What are you doing here?"

"Are you all right?" Matt asked without preamble. "What happened?"

"I'm fine," said Kate. "Where's Patrick?"

"You didn't answer my question," said Matt.

"You didn't answer mine," said Kate.

"I swear to God, Kate, you drive me nuts," said Matt.

"Fair enough," said Kate. "Where's Patrick?"

"He twisted his knee on the ice, he can't drive," said Matt. "Anything could have happened, Kate. Anything!"

"No, it couldn't," said Kate. "I was in a restaurant."

"Yeah, but after that," said Matt.

"There was never going to be an *after that*," Kate assured him. "I had no intention of going anywhere other than to dinner. And I wish I hadn't bothered with that. The only consolation is that they've got one less arsehole on their books now."

"You don't know these people," said Matt. "They could be *anyone*."

"That could be said for any new person you meet," said Kate. "Everyone could be *anyone*, before you get to know them and ascertain that they're not."

Matt ran his hand through his hair again. It stood up on end like he'd plugged himself in.

"Well, I think you're putting yourself in unnecessary danger," said Matt.

"Well, *I* think this is by far the safest way I've ever dated," said Kate. "Organized dates with reps on standby throughout; it's hardly picking strangers up in seedy bars," she went on.

"I don't like it," said Matt.

"Then don't join."

"What if you meet another arsehole?" Matt pressed.

"Do you think this is the first time some bloke's pushed his luck with me?" Kate asked. "I'm a woman, Matt. Ask any woman you like; every one of us has had practice in dealing with unwanted sexual advances or expectations."

Matt put his arm round her and kissed the top of her head.

"That's really depressing," he said.

"You're telling me," said Kate. "Come on, you big dork. Take me to Christmas tree heaven."

Matt kept his arm protectively around her shoulder as they walked across to the flower market, and Kate let him. She leaned into him. She liked it. Just for a moment she let herself imagine: *This is what it would be like to be loved by Matt.* Another voice in her head whispered a warning: *Stop it, Kate, this path isn't for you.*

"So, you're saying even my great-granny Peggy would have experienced unwanted sexual advances?" said Matt.

"Undoubtedly," said Kate. "Granny Peg was a hot mama."

"It must have been those floral pinnies," said Matt.

"Thanks for worrying about me," said Kate.

"You're welcome," said Matt.

·····

Heaven was an understatement. The flower market was a full-scale attack on the senses. The perfume of so many blooms in one place was intoxicating; *if they could bottle this scent,* Kate thought, *they would make a fortune.*

Kate's arty-fingers were twitching; she was glad she'd brought her camera. She sighed with resignation; she was going to spend a lot of money here tonight.

And she did.

"Leave room for the Christmas trees," said Matt as Kate passed him with her loaded trolley.

Kate pulled a face at him and walked on; she wouldn't dignify that with an answer, she thought, as she nestled a large silver stag between two garlands of cypress, holly, and spruce, coiled like sleeping pythons and surrounded by bunches of frosted ruby berries.

Twenty-five Christmas trees and a veritable festive bounty later, Matt forced the doors of the van shut and the three of them clambered into the front seats, homeward bound.

"I need the window seat," said Evelyn.

"You're at the front of the van," said Matt. "They're all window seats."

"But I like to look out of the side window," said Evelyn. "And I don't want to be squished between you two bickering all the way home."

"I don't bicker," said Kate. "Matt is wrong a lot of the time and it's my duty to tell him so."

"Kate is a fantasist," said Matt. "She thinks she's always right."

"Get in the van," said Evelyn.

Evelyn was asleep with her face pressed against the side window, almost before they'd made it out of the car park. She snored quietly. Kate laid her coat over Evelyn, pulling it up around her shoulders and tucking it under her chin. Evelyn stirred but didn't wake.

"She's nice when she's asleep," said Matt. Kate stifled a giggle. "Come on, then," he said. "I've heard the condensed version, now tell me what actually happened with jump-yer-bones Jim."

There was no way to escape, so Kate gave in and told Matt what happened. She looked up at him occasionally as she talked and saw that his jaw was set; she could tell he was clamping his teeth together.

"It just worries me, Kate," Matt said when she had finished.

"But it shouldn't," said Kate. "Share my outrage by all means, but there's no need for you to worry."

"You're my friend," said Matt. "And you're out night after night with a different bloke; of course I'm going to worry."

"You make me sound like a hooker," said Kate.

Matt smiled wickedly.

"If the shoe fits," he said, grinning.

Kate flicked his ear hard.

"Ouch!" said Matt. "I'm trying to drive."

"Stop being a dick, then," she said.

They were quiet for a while. The fluorescent clock face on the van's dashboard read 3:45 a.m. The monotonous music of the tires on the road was strangely soothing.

Kate was warm and tired, and the temptation to rest her head on Matt's shoulder was almost irresistible. But resist she did. There was a time when she wouldn't have even thought about it, but here, next to him, in the warm dark, she felt suddenly and inexplicably self-conscious, as if her body language might divulge a secret she'd fought to keep even from herself.

The feeling in her chest was filling the small van; the voice in her head was shouting so loud she worried Matt would hear it. She felt she would burst from the pressure pushing against her ribs, her heart was so full: so full for him.

She looked at his long slender hands on the steering wheel. She glanced up at his profile, lit by the headlamps of cars on the other side of the motorway; he squinted slightly as he concentrated on the road. His hair was a shaggy mess of twists and curls. And Kate could no longer deny that she loved him. As impossible and implausible as that love might be, it was love and there was nothing to be done about it.

Kate stared out the window. It was just starting to snow again; the flakes flurried in the headlights like feathers from a burst pillow.

Unrequited love. This was to be her lot. The ache of it burned through her. This pain; this pain was why she'd tried so hard, for so long, to keep her feelings for Matt locked away.

She watched the snowflakes get bigger. They began to settle in fuzzy lines along the dark tarmac. In the dark van, with the smell of pine needles in her nose, she made a vow. She would never tell Matt her true feelings. And she would do everything in her power to make sure Sarah didn't, however unintentionally, break Matt's heart, because that's what people in love do; they protect the hearts of those they love, even if that love will never be returned.

· · · · ·

Patrick's son Pete was waiting for them out the back of Evelyn's shop as they pulled onto the drive. It was still dark. Kate gently woke Evelyn, who shivered visibly as Matt opened the van door and helped her out.

"Go on up to bed," said Matt.

"I'll be all right in a minute," said Evelyn. Her teeth chattered together. "I'll give you a hand."

Matt put his hands on Evelyn's shoulders. She looked very small, standing there in the dark shivering, and Kate noticed for the first time that Evelyn was getting old.

"We've got this, Evelyn," said Matt kindly. "Now get yourself off to bed."

Evelyn didn't argue. She nodded once and climbed the steps to her front door.

"Tally ho, chaps!" she said, and disappeared into her apartment above the shop.

The remaining three unloaded the Christmas trees and stood them up against the wall in Evelyn's yard. With the trees safely stowed, Pete waved cheerio and drove back to the farm in his Jeep; his day would be just beginning and it would be a long one too with Patrick incapacitated.

Five enormous bags stuffed full of Kate's Christmas fancies sat on the snowy path. They glittered beneath the streetlamp.

"Can I leave them in the van and pick them up later?" Kate yawned.

"I'll drop you back," said Matt. "And help you in with them."

"There's no need," said Kate. "I don't mind walking."

Matt shook his head.

"Get in the bloody van," he said. And Kate did as she was told.

· · · · ·

"What's the next date?" Matt asked, dumping the last bag in Kate's hallway.

"Escape room," said Kate. She was so tired now, she could barely focus.

"Crikey!" said Matt. "I hope your date's a patient man."

"What do you mean?" said Kate.

"Well, you're bossy at the best of times," said Matt. "I can't begin to imagine what you'll be like in a time-pressured environment."

Kate reached out to swipe him, but she was sleepy and her reflexes were slow. Matt dodged effortlessly out of her reach and out the front door. He waved at her as he trundled down the path and she stuck two fingers up and her tongue out at him and closed the door. She patted herself on the back. *He'll never know*, she thought.

. . . . .

Clashes, Kisses, and Bust-Ups

Kate didn't wake up until midday. The world outside her window was thickly blanketed in white once more and the weak sun looked as bleary as she felt.

At the bottom of the garden, Mac, welly deep in snow, tended the vegetable patch: tweed cap pulled on tight, his trusty wheelbarrow by his side. Kate knocked on the window and her dad looked up and smiled.

. . . . .

A quick shower later and she was padding down the stairs in her furry snowflake bed-socks with pompoms, a pair of elastic-waist tartan leisure trousers, and an old sweater she'd once borrowed from Dan and accidentally-on-purpose never returned.

Today was comfort day. Today was for decorating the house with the spoils from last night's shopping extravaganza. Today was for eating comfort food every hour, on the hour.

In time-honored tradition Laura would be over later with the kids to help decorate the house. Mina took this role very seriously; she had an eccentric decorating style, as most four-year-olds did. Kate was still finding last year's baubles in the most unusual places as late as this March.

She shuffled into the kitchen to find Matt sitting at the table, leafing through her drawings. Her portfolio lay open, the contents spread out across the table. Matt looked up at her and grinned sheepishly.

"Hello, sleeping beauty," he said. "You look cozy."

"What are you doing here?" Kate asked without preamble. She hadn't had coffee yet and she was hungry.

"I found another bag of your Christmas decorations in the van," he said. "Thought I'd drop them round."

"Oh," said Kate. "Thank you."

Matt went back to studying Kate's sketches, resting each one back carefully in its place before picking up another.

"These are incredible, Kate," he said.

"I wouldn't go that far," said Kate.

"No really," he said. "You blow my mind."

Kate blushed.

"Well. Thank you," she said.

"Oh, by the way," said Matt without looking up, "Richard called."

Kate thought her stomach might drop out through the bottom of her trousers. Her eyes darted to the worktop, where she had left her phone to charge last night. *Shit!* she thought. But she feigned nonchalance.

"I told him you were still in bed because you're a lazy cow," said Matt.

"Matt!" Kate rounded on him.

He threw his hands up in surrender.

"I'm kidding! I'm kidding!" he yelped. "I saw his name flash up on the screen, but I didn't answer it, I swear to God."

Kate snatched up her phone. Five missed calls and eleven messages. *Shit!* she thought again. *I hope he doesn't think I copped off with Jim last night.*

"Who's minding the shop?" Kate asked absent-mindedly as she scrolled through Richard's messages. They began chirpy—borderline cheeky—before descending into nervousness and finally deteriorating into panic and or disgruntlement. She would have to call him.

"Petula and Carla," said Matt. "I brought gifts," he said, and held up a brown paper bag with grease patches over it.

Kate instantly forgot about Richard's neuroses.

"Please tell me that's a loaded bacon doorstop slathered with butter and ketchup!"

Matt grinned up at her.

"It most certainly is!" he said. "It's a bit cold, you might want to—"

But Kate had already plucked the bag from his grip and was gratefully stuffing the contents into her face.

"Thank you, thank you, thank you," she said with her mouth full.

"I brought one for Mac too," he said. "He had his while it was hot."

Matt stood, crossed the kitchen, and pointed to a tall cardboard takeaway cup.

"And this," he said.

"Tell me," said Kate, ripping off a crust with her teeth.

"Large mocha," he said. "Triple shot with gingerbread syrup."

Kate moaned with delight.

"God, I love you," she blurted through a mouthful of bacon and bread.

She flustered. The words had just popped right out of her! *Way to go, Turner!* she shouted internally. *Geez, you couldn't keep your mouth shut for one day!*

Would he know that she meant it? Would he think she was joking? Bloody hell, she hoped he'd think she was joking!

The bacon sandwich stuck in her throat. *Keep it together!* she thought. *Act casual!* She swallowed hard, then coughed as the sandwich went down her suddenly dry throat.

"In a cupboard love sort of way, obviously," she added quickly.

"Yeah, I know," said Matt. "I used to have a cat like you; only wanted me for food."

Matt seemed unmoved by her outburst; she dearly hoped this meant she was in the clear.

"When did you have a cat?" asked Kate, glad of the distraction.

"When you were off globe-trotting," he replied wryly.

"What happened to it?" asked Kate.

"Maria took it when we divorced," said Matt.

Kate stopped chewing.

"Oh," she said. "Sorry."

Kate's armpits were prickling with sweat. She didn't know how to behave. Her heart raced. Externally she chewed her food and continued to chat casually with Matt, while internally she tried to hammer nails back into the box of feelings that had just exploded all over her kitchen.

"It's all right," said Matt. "It was a long time ago."

This was the first time Matt had even mentioned his marriage to her. *This is good*, thought Kate. *Move the focus totally away from me telling Matt that I love him.*

"Do you ever hear from her?" Kate asked.

"No," said Matt. "We were entirely and completely incompatible. Once the divorce settlement was finalized there was really no need for our paths to ever cross again."

"I'm sorry," said Kate again, for want of something better to say. *I think I've gotten away with it,* she thought. She felt like a *Scooby-Doo* villain without the meddling kids.

"Don't be," he said. "It was an impulse thing. A reflex reaction. Marry in haste, repent at leisure. Isn't that what they say?"

"I don't know," said Kate. "I've never paid too much attention to what *they* say."

Matt smiled.

"No," he said. "You haven't, have you?"

"Do you think you'd ever get married again?" asked Kate. *Oh God!* she thought. *Stupid stupid woman, why would you ask that?*

"I wouldn't rule it out," said Matt. "For the right woman. What about you?"

"I wouldn't rule it out either," said Kate. "But I'm not going to bet all my chips on it!"

Matt picked up the takeaway cup.

"Shall I stick this in the microwave, then?" he asked.

"Mmm, yes please," said Kate.

Kate excused herself and took her freshly microwaved mocha up to her bedroom, where she internally punched herself repeatedly in the face. Her phone blipped. Another message from Richard. She would have to call him and explain why she'd been offline for so long.

She concentrated on slowing her breathing down and pushed Richard and his handsome face and sexy aroma to the front of her mind and banished Matt to a far corner, with spiders and skeletons of old boyfriends.

Kate scrolled down to Richard's number and pressed dial. It rang almost to voice mail before he picked up; *Playing it cool,* thought Kate.

"Hello," said Richard.

There was a formality to his voice that Kate hadn't heard before. *So, this is what a Richard-perturbed sounds like.* His tone made her feel nervous and instead of explaining herself succinctly, she instantly began to babble.

"Hi!" she said. "I'm so sorry I didn't pick up your messages; I had my phone on silent and it was such a long night, and partial disaster—although it turned out all right in the end, and I didn't get in until well after five a.m. and then I was just knackered and I went straight to bed."

There was silence on the line for a few moments.

"Sounds like you had a busy night," said Richard tersely.

Kate didn't like the vibes she was getting through the ether.

"Well, yes I did, actually," said Kate. "But the date itself was a total nightmare."

Richard instantly brightened.

"Really?" he asked. "How so?"

Kate explained.

"What an arsehole!" said Richard.

"Indeed," said Kate.

"Would you like me to have him tracked down and pulled naked through the streets of London by a donkey?" Richard asked.

"If it wouldn't be too much bother," said Kate.

"None at all," said Richard. "I'll get someone on it right away."

"Much obliged," said Kate. "So how was your Bond night?" she asked.

"Oh, you know," said Richard, suddenly vague. "It was one of those awkward, nothing-to-talk-about dates. She looked the part, but there was nothing going on behind the eyes, if you know what I mean."

Richard had also signed up for the escape room date, but they had already been paired with different people so Richard suggested they meet for a drink first.

By the time the call ended, Richard was back to his usual charming self. Kate flopped back onto her bed. That was one drama averted. Now she had to work out how to be casual around Matt without making a complete twit of herself.

She lay there for a while looking at the ceiling. The sound of her dad snoring in the sitting room below rumbled through the house. She would throw herself into this *whatever it was* with Richard. She liked Richard, she really did. She certainly lusted after him. There were worse positions from which to start a relationship. It definitely had the potential to become something if she just gave it a chance. She refused to be one of those drippy heartsick women with hundreds of cats; she would hurl herself into the path of true love so that it couldn't possibly not hit her!

Kate dragged the rest of her Christmas decorations down from the attic. There were a lot. She couldn't seem to pass a Christmas display without making a purchase, and after a decade of such behavior, her Christmas collection was becoming obscene. When she added the musty boxes and bags to her haul from the market, it almost filled the kitchen.

At three o'clock Laura and the kids came round to help decorate the house. Her dad, refreshed after his nap, took charge of entertaining Charley, while Mina—dressed in a Rudolph onesie—raided the boxes and ran about the house hanging baubles on door and drawer handles and anything else she could reach.

Kate and Laura were bejeweling a garland draped over the fireplace in the sitting room. The one resting on the mantelpiece over the wood burner in the kitchen had all manner of sparkly Christmas ornaments thrown at it: teal reindeer, glittered doves, purple Christmas trees, candy canes, and baubles covered in multicolored shiny buttons. But for the sitting room, Kate kept it classic: reds, golds, and greens. Matt was delivering all the Christmas trees later for Evelyn, and the tree would go in here too, in the bay window.

It would feel strange not having Christmas dinner here, Kate thought. But she was happy that her dad had found someone to care for, and she was even happier that it was Evelyn.

"So, tomorrow is?" Laura asked, attaching a porcelain kitten in a red-and-white-striped stocking to a piece of spruce.

"The escape room," said Kate.

"Cripes!" said Laura. "Who's your date?"

"Edward. An IT guy from Ipswich; he's forty, never married, no kids, traveled the world, and writes graphic novels in his spare time."

Kate was struggling to unravel a string of lights for the garland.

"Handy in a PC crisis *and* creative!" said Laura. "And he's well-traveled. At least you won't be stuck for conversation. You can swap diarrhea disaster stories about India!"

"You know, sometimes I wish I didn't tell you *everything*," said Kate.

"Sorry. But he sounds good anyway. Just who you want with you in an escape room."

"Yeah well, I'm meeting Richard before we go in and probably afterward too," said Kate.

"Sounds to me like you've already written Edward off," said Laura.

"Oh, I don't know," Kate replied. "I really like Richard. And I don't want to be closed off to other possibilities. It's just that . . ."

She stopped, wondering how much to divulge to her best friend. She was scared that if she said the words out loud, then they would become real. They would be out there, out in the world, and she could never lock them back in again. Equally, she would need Laura's counsel if she was going to get over Matt and forge ahead with Richard.

"Yes?" Laura said.

"The thing is," said Kate hesitantly. "The thing is, I'm fairly sure I'm in love with someone else."

"Someone else?" said Laura. "Who?"

Kate took a deep breath. "Matt."

"Matt who?" Laura asked.

"Matt Wells!" said Kate.

"Our Matt!" spluttered Laura, dropping the gold bell she'd been twiddling. Kate made movements with her arms to indicate to Laura to keep her voice down.

"Yes," she hissed. "Our Matt."

Laura opened and closed her mouth like a hooked fish.

"For how long?" she asked.

"I don't know exactly," said Kate. "A while, I think. Maybe always? Or maybe not. I don't really know. It's been coming on slowly for a long time."

"Like black ceiling mold," said Laura.

Kate nodded. "And equally hard to get rid of," she said.

"And you didn't tell me?" Laura was affronted.

"There was nothing to tell!" said Kate. "I didn't truly know myself until last night, and then this morning he brought me a gingerbread mocha . . ."

"Wow," said Laura. "You really are easy, aren't you. Ever thought about holding out for something a bit more substantial, diamonds maybe?"

"Obviously it wasn't only the mocha," said Kate.

"Glad to hear it," said Laura.

"There was a bacon sandwich too," said Kate.

"Slapper," said Laura.

Kate laughed and then covered her face with her hands.

"Oh God!" she moaned. "Why him?"

"What are you going to do about it?" Laura asked.

"Nothing," said Kate. "What can I do? He's with Sarah and I wouldn't want to ruin that and I wouldn't want to ruin our friendship either."

Laura looked hard at her friend.

"Are you sure," said Laura, "that this isn't you self-sabotaging again? You know what you're like. A good thing comes along and you pick holes in it until it falls apart. You're on the cusp of something potentially serious with Richard and suddenly you're in love with Matt."

"Not suddenly," said Kate. "It doesn't feel sudden. I mean, it hit me suddenly, but then when I thought about it, it's like it's always been there, only I couldn't see it, like I've been wearing blinders and now I've taken them off and I can see that I do actually and truly love him."

"Bloody hell," said Laura. "You mean it, don't you? You really are in love with Matt."

Laura stumbled back into an armchair.

"Bloody hell," she said again.

"Yeah," said Kate.

"Matt?" said Laura. "Are you sure? I've got to be honest, this is grossing me out a bit."

"Oh," said Kate. "My apologies. I'm sorry my heartfelt confession has turned your stomach."

"Well, it's a bit of a shock."

"It kind of snuck up on me too," said Kate.

"You can't ignore this," Laura told her.

"I don't have a choice. I shall throw myself into this relationship with Richard. Who knows? Maybe it'll work out."

"It's not going to work out if you're in love with someone else!" said Laura.

"My options here are limited," said Kate. "I either take up the role of Matt's unrequited love slave and stay miserably single, or I make it work with Richard. After all, I really like him and he really turns me on; that's got to count for something!"

"God, Kate, I still can't believe it," said Laura. "You and Matt!"

"No," said Kate. "There is no *me and Matt*. There's me in love with Matt and there's Matt in love with Sarah."

"Is there any chance he might feel the same?" asked Laura.

"Absolutely none," said Kate. "He thinks of me like a sister. You remember what he was like after our Big Mistake at uni? He couldn't get gone quick enough; it was like he was disgusted by what he'd done."

"Kate," said Laura. "I want to tell you something . . ."

There were shouts from the kitchen and Mina came running into the sitting room yelling, "Charley pooed! It's weally bad, Mummy. Weally weally bad!"

Kate's dad wasn't far behind. He was holding Charley out at arm's length. Mustard-yellow stains bloomed up toward the chest of Charley's pale blue romper suit and down both legs.

"It's exploding out of everywhere!" said Mac. "It sounded like a lake of mud geyser eruptions!"

"Oh no!" said Laura. "I told Ben he shouldn't have given him all that butternut squash for lunch." She was laughing and wincing as she took her stinky son from Kate's dad. "Oh, Mac, I'm sorry!" she said.

"Not to worry," he said, although he was clearly relieved to have relinquished responsibility for Charley. "I've seen worse; you should have seen Kate when she was that age."

"Thanks for that, Dad," said Kate.

"Oh, Mac," Laura said, pointing at Kate's dad's shirt. "You might want to change your shirt!"

Kate's dad looked down at a large, slightly yellow wet patch on his shirt. When he looked back up he seemed a little queasy.

"I think I'll go home and change," said Mac.

"Come back round for dinner," said Kate.

· · · · ·

There was no alternative but to bathe Charley. Luckily Laura was the kind of mother who never left home without a suitcase of spare clothes for her children, and today she had also packed their pajamas since they were staying for dinner.

When Charley was fresh and talcum-powdered they bathed Mina, who insisted on having Aunty Kate's "lady bubbles" in her bath and slathering herself in Kate's body butter afterward. Several squirts of Kate's expensive perfume later, Mina sat on Kate's bed in her Christmas tree pj's having her hair blow-dried while Kate went downstairs to cook dinner.

Kate made pesto pasta and garlic bread and they all sat round the table to eat it. Mina grabbed a handful of grated cheese from the bowl on the table and dropped it onto her plate.

"Aunty Kate, where is your twee?" asked Mina.

"Uncle Matt is bringing it round later," said Kate. She felt her cheeks redden at the mention of his name and cast a glance at Laura, who raised her eyebrows at her.

"Can I help you decowate it?" she asked.

"I'm afraid you'll be at home, tucked up in bed by then," said Kate.

As much as she loved her goddaughter, there was no way she was going to let her decorate her tree.

"Oh," said Mina. "I decowated our twee at home."

"Yes," said Kate. "I've seen it!"

Laura's tree was an abomination.

"Charley did a poo on you, Uncle Mac," Mina said very seriously, as if he hadn't known.

238 · JENNY BAYLISS

· · · · ·

Dinner was done and dusted and the house was a-twinkle with fairy lights. Laura was cajoling her children into their coats, ready for the drive home.

"I think I'll push off too, love," said Mac.

"You don't have to, Dad," said Kate. "It's not even eight o'clock. Why don't you stay for a glass of wine?"

Dad shrugged into his overcoat.

"Thanks, love," he said. "But I said to Evelyn I'd drop in on my way home."

Kate saw Laura smile from under her pile of children.

There was a ferocious bang on the front door and they all jumped.

"What the hell?" said Kate, and she rushed to open the door.

"HELL! HELL! HELL!" shouted Mina.

Kate pulled the door open to find her Christmas tree lying horizontally across the doorstep, blocking the entrance, and Matt yanking the gate shut behind him.

"Matt?" Kate called.

Matt didn't answer. He carried on walking to his van. Kate jumped over the tree and padded up the path in her bed-socks.

"Matt!" she called again.

She yanked open the gate and followed him up the road.

"I don't want to talk to you, Kate," he said.

"Why not?" she asked. The snow was leaking through her socks and freezing her feet. "What's wrong?"

"Nothing I want to talk to you about," he said.

"I don't understand," said Kate, although the terrible sick feeling in her stomach belied her statement.

"Just leave it alone, Kate," said Matt. "I don't want to say something I might regret."

Matt reached his van, but so did Kate. She stood in front of his door.

"Get out of the way, Kate," he said. "I'm angry and I'm not in the mood."

"Clearly!" said Kate. "But you don't get to start a fight and then walk off before it's finished."

"Fine!" said Matt. "Sarah's just told me about your Dates with Mates night. About Oliver being there."

"Shit," said Kate.

"Yeah," said Matt. "Shit. Why didn't you tell me?"

"She asked me not to," said Kate.

"And she takes precedence over me, does she? Your loyalties lie with Sarah, do they?" He ran his hand through his hair. "I asked you, Kate. I rang you and asked if anything had happened and you said no. You bare-faced lied to me."

"I didn't lie," said Kate. "You asked me if I'd told her anything to put her off you and I said no. That was the truth!"

"You should have told me, Kate. You had no right to keep it from me."

"I didn't know what to do for the best," said Kate. "I only kept it from you because I thought it would do more harm than good to tell you. I thought it would be okay."

"Did you?" Matt's tone was acerbic. "Or did you know Oliver was going to be there and you took Sarah there on purpose?"

"Why the hell would I do that?"

"I don't know!" Matt's voice was getting louder. "Maybe you were jealous?"

"Jealous?" she shouted. "Why would I be jealous?"

"Because I'm happy and you're not!" said Matt.

"Don't be so stupid!" Kate yelled.

"I *am* stupid if I thought *you'd* have my back. Had a good laugh to yourself, did you? Stupid old Matt, chasing a woman who's in love with her old boyfriend!"

"I didn't know he was going to be there!" said Kate. "How could I? I didn't even know about him until Sarah told me that night."

"You found out," said Matt. "You found out somehow and you thought you'd screw me over."

"Oh right!" she said. "Because I'm so jealous?"

"Exactly," said Matt.

"Wow! What a high opinion you have of yourself," Kate jeered.

"You said it yourself, everyone's got someone except you. And you just couldn't stand it," said Matt.

"You're such an idiot! I wasn't trying to break you up; I thought by not saying anything I was helping to keep you together," said Kate.

"Fine job you did," he said.

"She was *fine* when she left me," said Kate.

"Clearly she wasn't *fine*," said Matt. "Because she's just told me we need some space."

"Well, blaming me won't help. It's not my fault you can't keep a girlfriend!" said Kate.

"Oh, I disagree," said Matt. "I lay the blame for this firmly at your door."

"Typical!" said Kate. "You never take responsibility for anything; it's always someone else's fault. Poor blameless Matt! Wake up to yourself!"

"Stay out of my love life and stay the hell away from me!" said Matt.

"Fine," said Kate. "Find yourself another scapegoat because I'm done."

"I won't need one when you stop poisoning my life."

"Is that the kind of person you think I am?" Kate asked. "You really think I'm that spiteful?"

"If the shoe fits."

"Piss off, Matt!"

"I was trying to, but you came chasing after me."

"Yeah, well, don't worry," said Kate. "I won't come chasing after you again."

"Good!" Matt yelled.

"Good!" Kate yelled.

Kate moved away from the driver's door and stomped back through the snow, her arms folded tight across her chest, her feet numb with cold, and her heart beating furiously. She heard the van door slam and the engine roar to life, but she didn't look back.

Her dad and Laura stood in the hallway, worried expressions on their faces. The tree was resting against the wall in the hall. There was no way they hadn't heard all that. The whole neighborhood would have heard all that.

"Shall I get Ben to pick the kids up and I'll stay awhile?" Laura asked.

Kate shook her head. She still hugged her chest with her arms. She was shaking all over and uncontrollably.

"No, thanks," she said. "I'll be fine."

"I can call Evelyn," said Mac. "Tell her I won't make it round tonight?"

"Honestly, thanks, both of you, but I'm fine," Kate said.

She wasn't fine. But she knew she was about to lose her self-control and she was too proud to have an audience while she did it. She felt light-headed.

"I don't think you should be alone," said Laura. And her dad agreed.

"Please," Kate implored them. "Please. I need to be on my own. Please, I love you, but you have to go. I'll be okay."

Laura scooped up her children.

"You call me," she said. "Anytime. I can be here in five minutes."

"Same goes for me," said Mac.

"Thank you. Thank you for a lovely day,"

Kate was on autopilot now. Her head pounded. She couldn't form cohesive thoughts. Her words came robotically.

At last they left. Kate's phone blipped and she saw a message from Sarah.

> Hi Kate, I've just had a long talk with Matt. I've told
> him about us bumping into Oliver. I had to explain to
> him how I was feeling. In truth, I'm not the only one
> with a past that isn't finished. Anyway, I hope it
> doesn't make things awkward between you two. Just
> thought I'd give you a heads-up. xxx

Kate collapsed onto the sofa and cried for a long, long time.

• • • • •

She didn't hear from Matt. Nor did she expect or wish to. Her dad and Laura had texted and Kate had assured them both again that she was okay. She wasn't okay. She was sad on so many levels she didn't know which one to deal with first.

She was sad that she was in love with Matt and she was sad because she knew that the feeling was far from mutual. And she was sad that their friendship was over. She had gone to bed sick with sadness, slept fitfully, and woken in the morning with a sadness so crushing she couldn't breathe. She lay in bed and watched the cold morning light eke dismally into the room, touching everything with gray.

She was consumed with thoughts of Matt. The bottle had been uncorked and now every smile, every grimace, every touch, every word, kind and unkind, that had ever fallen from his lips cascaded through her mind unfettered. Her chest ached. Her head ached. She was hollow.

There was nothing for it. She would have to leave Blexford. If anything, the argument had done her a favor, opened her eyes. She'd been a fool to think she could feel the way she did about Matt and stay; she would be living a lie and she refused to subject herself to that. She had moved back to nurse her dad through his heartache, but he was well now, better than well; he had found love again, and Kate could leave him in Evelyn's more than capable hands.

Her dad wouldn't like it. Laura would like it even less. But they would respect her decision, she was sure of that. She had friends in London whom she could stay with until she found a place of her own. Her job was in London, and she'd lived in London for years before, so it wouldn't be like starting over, more like going back after a sabbatical.

Yes. She had decided. She would stay for Christmas and be gone before New Year's. The decision gave her strength. All she had to do was get through the next two weeks. She could do that. She could avoid the Pear Tree; it wasn't like Matt was going to ask her to bake for him now. She would lay low and she would leave quietly.

She showered and got dressed. She looked at her reflection in the mirror. Her eyes were red-ringed. She applied makeup mechanically. She swept concealer under her eyes to hide the bags that had settled there. And all the while she recited the mantra over and again, "Just two weeks, just two weeks, just two weeks." Until eventually she felt enough of herself return that she could function in the world again.

She didn't want to meet Richard tonight. And she certainly didn't want to be stuck in an escape room with a group of hopeful strangers. But she was not prepared to let her feelings for Matt—before or after the argument—dictate her plans. She would go out. And she would make the best of it. Kate Turner was nothing if not stubborn to the point of ridiculous.

Kate wandered from room to room. Since taking over the mortgage from her parents, she had completely renovated the house. She hadn't wanted to feel bound by nostalgia, she wanted it to feel like her own, so she'd dug straight in and ripped the guts out of it and started again. She would be sad to leave it. She'd rent it out for a while and when she felt brave enough, she would sell it.

She spent the day moping in the Christmas wonderland they'd created yesterday. The shine had rubbed off. Neither the bright knitted stockings, nor the wooden nutcracker dolls, nor the red-berried wreaths incited the childlike joy they usually did in Kate. Perhaps it was time to grow up.

The Christmas tree still leaned against the wall in the hall, the branches constrained neatly within the mesh. She wrestled it back out the front door and around to the back garden, where she sawed off the bottom of the trunk and plonked the tree in a bucket of water to soak.

Richard texted to confirm their meeting place and Kate began the process of layering the pieces of herself together. The hill down to Great Blexley had been cleared, but Kate decided to leave the Mini where it was; she didn't want to risk getting it stuck again this close to the holidays. It was a long walk but she decided she needed it. She needed to stretch out and she needed to clear her mind, and a long cold walk was just the thing to do it.

The pub was like walking into a wall of noise when Kate pushed the door open, red-cheeked and exhilarated by the cold. She looked around and recognized plenty of faces from previous activities; clearly lots of people had decided to stop in for some liquid courage before the date started. She hoped her date for tonight wasn't one of them; she wouldn't like to be spotted having a cozy tête-à-tête with someone else. It didn't seem very sporting.

Richard must have seen her through the crowd because after a moment he appeared in front of her. He bent and kissed her hello, a slow tender kiss that Kate found herself leaning into with more enthusiasm than she'd have thought possible this morning.

Richard was attentive and tactile and Kate was surprised by how receptive she was to his advances. And the way he gently rubbed his hand up and down her back as they sat side by side on the corner sofa was not at all unwelcome. Perhaps Richard was just the man to distract her.

"I wish we could just blow this escape room thing off and get merrily and deliciously drunk together," Richard said quietly into her ear.

He ran his finger along Kate's jawbone and Kate found herself moved to kiss him, tentatively at first and then with a hunger that she could barely contain. Richard broke away first.

"Wow," he said. "Well, that's me done in for the evening. I won't be able to concentrate on escaping anything now."

Kate laughed.

"It's all part of my master plan," she said. "Disabling the other team so that my team wins." She grinned.

"I had no idea you were so competitive," said Richard.

"You don't know the half of it," said Kate.

All too soon it was time for them to move next door to the escape rooms.

"So who is your date tonight?" asked Kate.

"Her name is Echo," said Richard. "She's a dance teacher."

"Echo," said Kate. "What a fantastic name."

"I prefer the name Kate," said Richard. And Kate felt warmth returning to her cold bones.

· · · · ·

The escape rooms were housed in an old music hall that had been saved from demolition; the quirky floorplans were just what the company required to create a maze of rooms. Moulin Rouge–style bars dotted each floor, low-lit with voluptuous trappings, tassels, and silk and crimson draperies.

The reception hall boasted a stage framed with red velvet swags. The Lightning Strikes reps stood—looking uncomfortable in the glare of the spotlights—on the stage with their clipboards.

The hopeful daters formed two orderly queues beside the staircases at either end and took turns mounting the stage to be given their team name. Richard discreetly took Kate's hand and squeezed it before letting it drop so that they could ease into the crowd separately to be partnered up.

Kate checked her phone for the picture of Edward. He had a tall wiry frame, an amiable smile that showed laugh lines around his eyes, and a shaved head, the shadow of which insinuated light brown hair. The spotlights were hot and when it was Kate's turn to take to the stage, she realized the reps were glistening with sweat.

Kate's team was called the Snow Leopards and when she found Edward, he was already with the other members. Mandy and Todd had taken an instant shine to each other; they grinned maniacally at each other and everyone else in the room.

Mandy explained—while Todd held both of her hands and gazed at her dreamily as if every word that fell from her lips were the greatest thing he'd ever heard—that they had seen each other on the first date and felt an instant connection. From then on, they had been on all the same dates but had never been paired with each other until tonight. The reps hadn't been able to divulge their personal information, and both Mandy and Todd had been too shy to approach each other personally.

"We just kept locking eyes across the room," said Mandy, looking at Todd.

"It was like we were drawn to one another," said Todd, looking at Mandy.

"Like star-crossed lovers!" Mandy said.

And with that they began kissing in a way that didn't seem appropriate outside the bedroom.

"Blimey," said Kate to Edward. "Looks like escaping these rooms is going to be down to us."

Edward looked embarrassed and alarmed, and he smiled nervously at Kate as if she might actually be a snow leopard and was planning to devour him. *Crikey!* Kate thought. *I must be unwittingly giving off terrifying sex vibes tonight.*

Entry into the escape rooms was staggered. Kate's team was due to start in forty-five minutes, so they took themselves off to one of the bars.

"Would you like a drink?" Kate asked.

Edward bit his lip. "Would you?"

"Yes," said Kate. "I'm going to get a drink. Would you like one?"

"Oh yes, of course, um, yes please, I'd like a drink. Thank you," said Edward.

"What would you like?"

"What are you having?"

"I'm going to have a white wine," said Kate.

"Okay," said Edward. "I'll have a white wine too, please."

Kate turned to ask if Todd and Mandy would like a drink, but they were already mid-discussion about it.

"I'm going for a fruit cider," said Todd.

"Oh my God," said Mandy, "I was just thinking I fancied a fruit cider."

"Wow!" said Todd. "You were?"

"I swear to God!" said Mandy.

"We're just so in tune with each other," said Todd.

And the tonsil hockey tournament resumed.

Kate ordered two white wines and handed one to Edward, who was perched uneasily on the end of a banquette, looking like a baby bird about to fledge.

"So," said Kate. "IT, that's interesting. How often do you have to tell people to turn their computers on and off again?"

Kate had thought a little mild teasing might break the ice, but Edward only smiled meekly in a way that suggested that the joke was well worn and unfunny.

"Sometimes that's what's needed to reboot the system," he said.

"Yes," said Kate. "Of course. Graphic novels, though," she tried again. "That's an interesting hobby. Very creative."

"Yes," said Edward.

"Do you find it hard to come up with new ideas?" she asked. "It's quite an art, writing a novel with minimal prose."

"Yes," said Edward. "I have a lot of ideas."

Kate perused the busy bar. There seemed to be a lot more flirting in this group, and she wondered if it was down to the sensual décor or whether nine dates in, people were feeling more relaxed about the whole thing, although that didn't seem to be the case with Edward.

It was a long forty-five minutes. Kate drank another glass of wine and Edward eyed her as a monk might view a lush. She tried to draw

Mandy and Todd into the conversation, but every question seemed to result in more snogging. Kate wondered if Mandy had thought to bring some lip balm; she was going to need it.

At last their number was called. Mandy unwrapped her leg from around Todd; by now the pair were almost horizontal across the banquette and Edward looked more than ever as though he wanted to run screaming from the venue.

They were led into a small wallpapered room. The door slammed shut behind them. There was no handle on the inside and Edward stared hard at the space where one should be for over a minute, as if trying to open it with his mind.

Against one wall, a floral standard lamp stood next to an end table, on which stood a box with a combination lock. On the other side of the room was a metal step stool. At first Kate didn't think there was another door out of the room, until she spotted a gold keyhole on one wall near the ceiling and realized it was a hidden door, flush with the wall and wallpapered—as the rest of the wall—in a gold flock paper.

The wall with the table was papered in the same gold flock as the wall with the hidden door. That left two walls: one with a deep teal background, with a rain forest scene with birds and animals and brightly colored foliage, and the other—the one with the step stool— plain white except for a border of the same design as the rain forest wall running along the top.

Kate looked around the room. Then she felt around the walls for bumps or buttons or concealed cubbyholes that might hold a key or a clue about how to get out. She didn't find any.

"Any ideas?" Kate asked.

Todd, who stood behind Mandy with his arms around her waist, said, "I love lemurs."

"Oh my God," Mandy yelped. "I love lemurs too!"

"No way!" said Todd.

Mandy swiveled round to face him without breaking Todd's grip around her waist.

"I swear on my life!" Mandy said with such overblown sincerity that Kate felt sure she was being sarcastic.

But she was not. There followed two minutes of cooing at each other before they were lip-locked once more. Kate turned to Edward, who looked back at her blankly.

"What about you?" she asked hopefully. "Problem solving is your livelihood. What are your thoughts?"

"It must be in the wallpaper," said Edward.

Kate was deeply relieved to have any sort of proactive response.

"Yes," she said. "I think so too."

The two of them stood side by side, arms folded, staring at the rain forest.

"I don't fancy you," said Edward, his eyes remained fixed on the wall.

Kate was taken aback at the bluntness of a man who an hour ago couldn't choose his own drink.

"Fair enough," said Kate. "I don't think we could compete with Romeo and Juliet anyway."

Kate gave a nod in Todd and Mandy's direction. As she did so, Todd stumbled backward, still attached at the face to Mandy, and landed on the step stool, whereupon Mandy straddled him and the heavy breathing became obscene.

"I'm just grateful she's wearing jeans," said Kate.

"Romeo and Juliet both ended up dead," said Edward.

Kate tried to think of something funny to say but decided it would be lost on her companion.

She had an idea.

"What if we count how many there are of each animal," she said. "There are four types of animal and the chest is locked with a standard four-digit combination lock."

Edward nodded and the two of them began to count the creatures in the rain forest wallpaper while Todd and Mandy had trouser sex on a stool. There were nine parrots, six snakes, eight butterflies, and four lemurs on the wall.

"Okay," said Kate. "So now we just have to keep twiddling the numbers until we get the right combination. Simple! How many combinations can there be of four numbers?" she said brightly.

"Ten thousand," said Edward.

"Oh," said Kate.

She looked around the room and her gaze fell upon the border.

"There!" She tapped Edward's arm and he leaped away from her as though she'd stung him.

"Where?" he said.

Kate pointed to the border.

"They're in order," she said. "Lemur, butterfly, snake, parrot. That's the combo," she said. "I'll bet my granny on it!"

Edward gave a look that suggested she was just the type to gamble her grandmother away, but he nodded his agreement with her hypothesis.

"Would you like to do the honors?" said Kate, motioning toward the chest.

"Would you?" he asked.

"I don't mind," she said.

"I don't mind either," said Edward.

"You do it," said Kate.

She thought it might be good for Edward to do something assertive.

Edward used the combination and the lock clicked open. Inside the chest, the key to the concealed door lay on a purple velvet cushion. He took it out and held it up like he'd just discovered the Holy Grail.

Edward was tall but not tall enough to reach the lock without the stool. Clearly not wanting to be the one to break up the writhing couple on the stool, he handed the key to Kate.

"Smooth," she said, and raised her eyebrows.

After several tries at reasoning with them, Kate pushed at Mandy and Todd gently until they flopped off the stool, limbs locked around each other, and landed on the floor with a dull thud like a couple of sandbags. This did nothing to dampen their ardor; on the contrary, their rampant thrusting only increased.

Kate stood on tiptoes on the stool and slipped the key into the lock. The door clicked open and Edward was through it before Kate had even climbed down off the stool. She called to Todd and Mandy that they were going to the next room, but they didn't appear to hear her. *Oh well*, she thought. *That'll be a nice surprise for the next team.*

"And then there were two!" said Kate as the door snapped shut behind her.

Edward looked green.

The next room was furnished to look like a study, with bookshelves, a heavy mahogany writing desk and chair, table lamps, and a chaise longue. There were ornaments and trinkets above the fireplace and a crimson smoking jacket hanging on the back of the door, which was not concealed this time but made from the same oak as the paneling on the two walls free of bookcases.

A fleeting thought that Matt would love this room passed through her mind, and Kate banished it just as quickly and wondered instead how Richard was getting along with his date. She hoped he was having as much luck as she was.

At the end of the chaise stood an old leather-bound steamer trunk with Paris stickers all over it. It was locked, and Kate surmised that it was for this that they needed to find a key. The action of intent looking seemed to suit Edward, as it negated the need for conversation, and he became less jumpy.

They worked in amiable silence, Kate having written this date off as a complete nonstarter. Probably for the best, she thought; what with all the upheaval of moving, she would find it hard enough to find time for her budding relationship with Richard, let alone add another potential lover into her schedule.

Within the first couple of minutes Edward had found the first key in one of the desk drawers. The key didn't fit the lock. A moment later, Kate found another key in the smoking jacket pocket. That didn't fit either. The third key, which Edward found in a small gilded sarcophagus on the mantel shelf, did fit the lock, and they opened the trunk to find another smaller trunk inside.

Kate was beginning to enjoy herself. And without Todd and Mandy simulating sex in the corner, even Edward relaxed and became relatively chatty. One of the keys they already had fitted the second trunk, but the third key didn't open the third case—which was an old picnic basket with a parcel label tied to the handle and the words *A Moveable Feast* written on it.

Edward and Kate began an organized search—almost as if they were a team, Kate mused. Edward noticed a creaking floorboard beneath the tapestry rug in the center of the room. Carefully they rolled it back and found a floorboard that lifted easily. Kate reached her hand into the space and brought out a wooden box, which held the key to the picnic basket, and the key that Kate had found in the smoking jacket opened the fourth case housed within it.

The fourth case contained a small wooden box about the size of a jewelry box and, unlike the others, it also contained postcards, which, as they inspected them, were all black-and-white images of the Ritz in Paris in the 1920s.

"This must be the final box," said Kate, and Edward agreed.

They scanned the room.

"It must be hidden in the one of the books," said Edward, in a rare moment of assuredness.

Kate glanced at the floor-to-ceiling bookcases.

"Where do we even begin?" she asked as much of herself as of Edward.

Edward ran his finger along his lower lip.

"It can't be a random book," he announced. "The postcards must be a clue; look for any books pertaining to Paris."

Kate was suddenly excited. They took a bookcase each, working methodically along the shelves, pulling out anything that hinted at being at all connected to Paris. All the classics were there: Shakespeare, Dickens, Austen, the Brontës. All hardbacks and gold lettering like her dad's old *Reader's Digest* collection, in bottle green, red, and navy blue.

Kate reached the Hemingways and something in her memory clicked.

"*A Moveable Feast!*" she cried out. "It's Hemingway!"

Edward pushed a tome back into place.

"What?" he said.

Kate ran her finger along the row and picked out Ernest Hemingway's memoir, *A Moveable Feast*. She let it fall open and sure enough, the book was hollowed out through the middle, with a key sitting at the bottom.

"How on earth?" asked Edward, scratching his head.

"It was the steamer trunk," said Kate. "That was the first clue. Hemingway accidentally left a steamer trunk at the Ritz in Paris and they kept it for him in storage, and when he found it again later it was full of his old notebooks from the 1920s. That was the catalyst for his memoirs. I can't believe I remember that," she said more to herself than to Edward.

"*A Moveable Feast*," said Edward.

Kate grinned and offered the book to Edward. He shook his head.

"You do it," he said. "You found it. Well done."

He smiled at Kate. He really did have a lovely smile; what a shame it only made an appearance at the curtain call. Kate slipped the key into the lock on the final box and retrieved the key to the exit. Edward held out his hand and Kate shook it.

"It was lovely to meet you," said Edward quietly. "Under different circumstances . . ."

"What do you mean?" Kate asked.

"You can tell your boyfriend I didn't lay a finger on you," he said.

"My boyfriend?" Kate echoed.

But Edward gently lifted the key out of her palm, slipped it into the lock, and turned the key. The door clicked open and Edward slipped out through it and was gone before Kate could argue or get an answer.

Kate left the study and followed a corridor that led out into another bar. Edward wasn't in it. She approached the bar and ordered a drink.

"I seem to have lost my date," she said to the woman behind the bar.

The woman smiled.

"Happens to the best of us," she said.

"I don't suppose you saw a tall willowy chap in a blue stripy jumper pass through a moment ago?"

"Good-looking chap? Shaved head?"

"That's him!"

"He looked like he was in a hurry," said the woman. "Headed straight for the exit. Did you scare him off or chase him off?"

"Neither," said Kate. "I don't think."

But she had a horrid suspicion that Richard might have had something to do with it.

Kate took her drink and wandered through to the bar nearest the street exit. She sat and waited for Richard to finish. She hoped she was wrong about him. But who else would have said something to Edward? And what on earth must he have said to make Edward view her as though she were an infectious disease?

Twenty minutes later Richard's team entered the bar. Richard was making jokes and they were all laughing as though they'd been friends since college, not strangers on a date night. Richard's date seemed enthralled by whatever story he'd been telling, and she looked up at him doe-eyed and attentive. Kate fumed.

Richard spotted Kate and left his new friends—with much protestation on their part; he kissed Echo on the cheek, and with a wink that could have meant something or nothing he strode across the bar and plonked himself on a stool to face her.

"What say we get out of here and go somewhere a little more intimate," said Richard.

"You spoke to my date, didn't you?" said Kate. "Frightened him off."

For a moment Richard's face was a mask. Kate could imagine his thought processes: *Laugh it off? Play it cool? Be honest?* But he recovered his composure.

"It was just a bit of fun," said Richard. "I didn't mean anything by it!"

"By what?" asked Kate. "It wasn't a bit of fun to Edward; he looked bloody terrified to be near me!"

Kate thought she saw Richard's mouth twitch and repress a smile.

"Tell me the truth or I leave right now," said Kate.

"Babe!" he exclaimed. "Honestly, it was just a bit of a laugh."

Kate got up and started to put her coat on.

"All right! All right," Richard said. "I might've told him I'd rough him up if he got near you . . . or words to that effect."

He must have seen Kate's expression darken because he hastily added, "I didn't think he'd take me so seriously!"

"Well, he did," said Kate. "How dare you! How dare you presume the right to threaten a person on my behalf. You have no claim on me. None."

Kate was livid. She finished putting her coat on and left, despite Richard's pleading and calling after her. At one point he caught up with her on her the street; he blocked her path but one look from Kate and he stepped aside and let her pass. *Just you try it,* she thought.

She determined to write an apology email to Edward as soon as she got home. Hopefully the Lightning Strikes team would forward it along to him. Above all she felt embarrassed. What must Edward have thought of her? She was not some damsel who needed protecting, nor a gangster's moll to be possessed.

Kate walked through the town center with its Christmas windows and strings of lights, which looped back and forth above the shops from one end of the precinct to the other. There was hardly any snow here at all. She found a convenience store open and purchased several chocolate bars and a family-sized bag of kettle chips before jumping into a taxi at the rank and going home. "Two more weeks," she said to herself. "Just two more weeks."

THE TENTH DATE OF CHRISTMAS

· · · · ·

Gingerbread Tantrums and Secrets Outed

Kate cradled her coffee mug as she checked her emails the next morning. The printers had sent her a photograph of the winter fabric. She wouldn't get an actual sample until after the holidays, but she was happy with what she could see. They had a little more grace on the second phase of spring fabrics, so Kate didn't expect copies of those until maybe the second week of January, by which time, she thought, she'd be back in London.

The thought reminded her that she'd done nothing yet to facilitate such a move. She fired off a couple of emails to some friends who had spare rooms and wouldn't mind a bit of rent money coming in. She would need to tell her dad and Laura soon. Finding the right time wasn't going to be easy.

Also in her inbox was a reply the Lightning Strikes team had forwarded along from Edward. Kate had emailed a sincere apology as soon as she'd gotten home the night before.

Hi, Kate,

Thanks for your message. I guess we got off on the wrong footing.

I probably didn't handle the situation as well as I might have, but I've never been threatened like that before and it took me by surprise. I was also unsure as to whether you might have been a party to it in some way (I've had some strange experiences on this Twelve Dates merry-go-round). I am relieved to know that you weren't.

If you're ever in London, give me a call and we'll meet for a drink.

This probably isn't my place but I would advise caution where Richard is concerned. I don't think he's what he appears.

All the best
Edward

Kate decided to ignore Edward's parting comment. He'd only met Richard once; if she'd judged Edward against first appearances, he wouldn't have come out too favorably either. She probably would like to meet up with him for a drink sometime, though; *I'll be in London sooner than you think*, Kate mused.

It had snowed again last night and it was still snowing. Kate checked her phone. Several messages from Richard. Two from Laura. One from her dad. None from Matt. She looked out through the French doors to where her Christmas tree still sat in its bucket. *Can't put it off forever*, she thought.

Half an hour later the tree was in the bay window in the sitting room, screwed into its stand with a good glug of water in the bucket. Kate cut through the mesh, and the bendy boughs gently bounced down into their natural positions. It was a lovely tree. Matt might not like her at the moment, but at least he hadn't punished her with a shoddy tree. The branches were full with soft olive-green needles, and a smell of fresh pine perfumed the room.

Her collection of tree ornaments was as eclectic as it was large. She sourced baubles from anywhere and everywhere: from the places she had traveled like Venice, Greece, and New York, and from anywhere where a Christmas display would catch her eye. And of course there was Liberty: so many, many purchases from Liberty.

Laura came round having left the children with Ben and sat and watched Kate finish the tree; she knew better than to try to help.

"Have you spoken to Matt?" Laura asked.

"Nope," said Kate.

"It'll blow over," said Laura. "He never stays angry for long."

"I don't care either way," said Kate.

"Really?" Laura asked.

"What do you think?" said Kate.

When the tree was finished Kate made them each an Irish coffee and they toasted the light switching on.

"Don't skimp on the Irish bit," said Laura. "I've given up breastfeeding. Happy Christmas to me!"

"It's not even lunchtime," said Kate. "And you haven't drunk in over a year; are you sure you want that much booze?"

"Didn't anyone tell you it's Christmas?" asked Laura. "None of the usual alcohol rules apply. Also, Ben's home with the children. And also, I just got my boobs back; no more nibbled nipples! Now hit me with booze, baby."

The tree was lovely. The lights twinkled through the branches and danced off the surfaces of the baubles. It was barely midday, but the sky outside was so dark that the tree didn't look out of place being lit.

Kate told Laura about Richard.

"I don't like the sound of it," said Laura.

"He's got this work hard, play hard thing going on," said Kate. "You know, with all the rugby and stuff, I think he thought it was just banter and that Edward wouldn't take him seriously."

"I don't buy that for a second," said Laura.

Kate put her head in her hands.

"Oh God!" she said, her voice muffled beneath her hands. "You're completely right. The old me wouldn't buy it either. But this me is . . ."

"Desperate?" said Laura. "Pathetic?"

"I was going to say *hopeful*," said Kate. "I really felt like we might have had something, you know? I'm not sure I'm ready to give up on him just because he got a bit overzealous."

Laura stayed for another hour and another Irish coffee with extra Irish and a bit more Irish, before walking in zigzags home.

"I'll see you at the manor tomorrow," she called from the end of the path. "I bloody love you, Kate!"

Kate nodded and waved.

Tomorrow was the Twelve Dates gingerbread house competition. It was being held at Blexford Manor, in one of the dining rooms. After last night's debacle, Kate had little enthusiasm for meeting any man again. Ever. But the twelve dates were almost at an end and she wanted to see it through, just to be sure she was giving fate a fair chance.

Her date was called Adam; he was forty-five, he had three children, and he was divorced. Adam was an architect and belonged to a rowing club. This all sounded very promising, Kate thought, and it couldn't hurt to have an architect on hand when putting together a gingerbread house.

Kate scrolled through her phone to Adam's photograph. Adam stood beside his kayak, grinning proudly as he held aloft a trophy. He was wearing a wet suit, and a kayak and two discarded paddles lay at his feet. He had shoulder-length brown hair shot through with streaks of gray and a gingery-colored beard.

Kate wondered why so many of her dates had used sporty photographs of themselves; was it a chance to show off their physiques in their scanty hobby attire? She had submitted a picture of herself in a winter coat, grinning maniacally at last year's caroling procession, with a glass of mulled wine raised to the camera and a sprig of holly in her hair. Perhaps she should have sent in a photo of herself rock wall climbing in tight leggings and a Lycra vest top.

Her phone blipped. It was Richard. Again.

> Kate, I got it wrong. I'm sorry. It was a stupid thing to do. I'd had a few drinks and then I'd seen you and you looked so hot and I couldn't stand the idea of someone else putting their hands on you. There's no excuse. I was a jealous idiot. Rxx

Kate sighed. Part of her agreed with Laura, and ordinarily behavior like his last night would have spelled the end of any man for her, but right now she needed something, anything, to take her mind off Matt. She knew Richard wasn't the cure, but maybe he could numb the pain for a little while: a human paracetamol. Kate messaged back:

> Consider yourself out on parole. x

He messaged back immediately:

Dinner tonight? My treat.

Kate flopped about the house for the remainder of the afternoon. She couldn't settle on anything. Films didn't hold her attention and she wasn't in the mood for baking or painting. Ordinarily an afternoon like this would have found her ensconced in the Pear Tree, sipping coffee and organizing mood boards for work, and annoying Matt. Matt, Matt, Matt. It all came down to Matt. She stood by the French windows and watched the snowflakes tumble down. "Two more weeks," she said to herself. "Just two more weeks."

A knock at the door provided a welcome distraction from the morose turnings of her mind. It was Petula. She had a potted poinsettia plant in her hand and a tissue paper package tucked under her arm.

Kate smiled.

"Is that what I think it is?" she asked, nodding toward the package.

Petula smiled with something like sympathy in her eyes.

"Put the kettle on and we'll find out, shall we?" she said.

They took tea in the sitting room. Petula handed the package to Kate and sat on the edge of the armchair, her hands clasped in her lap in anticipation. Kate gently unstuck the tabs that held the tissue paper in place and let the sheets fall open.

Kate gasped. It was a thick knit: black with flecks of gold running through it, as soft as cotton wool balls and so smooth it shone in the light given off by the Christmas tree.

Kate held it up in front of her. It felt like silk in her hands. Across the front, in a mixture of knit and appliqué, was a village snow scene: tartan fir trees interspersed with brightly colored patchwork buildings;

tall town houses beside squat cottages, with snow-clad roofs and chimneys curling out spirals of silver smoke. White snow banked up against the front walls. Tiny sequin stars dotted the sky around one large gold star with gold-thread-and-sequin beams that stretched to the edges of the scene.

"Oh, Petula," said Kate. "This is beautiful. It's your best ever."

Petula beamed.

"Thank you so much," Kate continued. "I absolutely love it! You've made my day."

And with that Kate began to cry. Petula went to her and put her arms around her.

"There, there," said Petula, patting Kate's back. "He'll come round."

"He won't," said Kate. "Not this time."

"Oh, *tsk*!" said Petula. "Such nonsense. Him moping around the café like a wet dishcloth and you dripping all over the place. What's it all about, eh? Lot of silly nonsense."

Kate recovered herself.

"You're right, of course," said Kate, giving away none of her plans. "Thank you for the jumper, I love it."

"Perhaps you should wear it on one of your dates," said Petula.

"Oh, I will," said Kate. "As a matter of fact, I have a date tonight."

"Well then," said Petula. "You'd better blow your nose and start getting ready."

· · · · ·

Kate and Richard had arranged to meet at a gastropub on the outskirts of Great Blexley, just round the corner from the bottom of Blexford hill. Kate walked down, because she couldn't be bothered to dig the car out of the snow, and the hill was becoming dangerous, despite the salt on the road.

She was wearing her new jumper over the top of a silk camisole; the wool felt warm and soft against her skin. She'd taken the time to curl her hair back off her face; it meant she couldn't wear a hat without ruining the effect, but she decided to forgo warm ears for good hair. She had slathered herself in some expensive perfumed body lotion her mum had sent over, and even through her thick coat, she got wafts of it as she walked.

Kate used to come to this pub when she was younger—much younger, trying her luck at buying drinks underage and frequently getting served. The pub had gone through many incarnations since then and two years ago a chef from London bought it, renamed it the Tipsy Goose, and put it and Great Blexley on the culinary map. It was almost impossible to get a table without booking weeks in advance, and Kate wondered what Richard had had to do get one at such short notice.

Richard stood at the bar, opposite the door, and he smiled appreciatively when Kate walked in. Kate was pleased. She could do with the ego boost.

"Kate," he said, laying a warm kiss on her frozen cheek. "You look lovely. I'm so glad you agreed to see me."

"Well," said Kate breezily. "Far be it from me to turn down a swanky dinner. You normally have to put your name down at birth to get a table."

"I have connections," said Richard. His confidence made Kate's stomach flip, and she had to rein in the urge to toss her hair about and giggle.

As it turned out, Richard knew the restaurant manager—Richard seemed to know a lot of people; they played rugby together on Sundays and the manager owed Richard a favor.

The pub was old and had been restored sensitively. Dried hops hung from the oak ceiling beams, and the floors and door frames were as reassuringly wonky as Kate remembered.

They sat at the bar and Kate bought the first round. They talked amiably enough, consciously ignoring Richard's major faux pas with Edward, although Kate determined she would broach the subject before the evening was out.

"Both the kids have got parts in their Christmas plays," said Richard. "Plus, they've each got matinees and evening performances and you can't not have someone in the audience for each one, so me and their mum are on a kind of mad shift rotation all next week, dashing between school and preschool."

"Never a dull moment," said Kate.

"Chance would be a fine thing," said Richard.

"You get along well with your ex, then?" Kate asked.

"Oh God yeah, amazingly well," said Richard. "I mean you've got to really, haven't you, for the kids. It's not their fault their parents fucked it up."

"I've met three fathers on the dates so far, all of whom get on really well with their exes," said Kate. "It's been a revelation; I have a newfound respect for single fathers."

"Well, I don't say we're the norm," said Richard. "I suppose it's down to maturity. And, you know, social evolution: men not having to be stiff-upper-lipped anymore."

Kate was about ready to throw her knickers at Richard-the-new-age-father when a waitress came and ushered them to a table near the open fire. Kate noticed the way the waitress looked at Richard: all hooded eyes and suggestive red lips that pouted whenever he spoke to her. Kate was gratified to note that this peacocking was lost on Richard. In fact he seemed to take every opportunity to touch Kate in a way that announced to everyone that she was his sole focus: his hand on the small of her back as they walked, a brush of her hand with his, a touch to her cheek, gentle fingers that teased her hair back off her face.

They sat down and perused the handwritten menus.

"Kate," said Richard. "About Edward."

"We don't have to talk about that now," said Kate, whose mind was weighing up the creamy garlic mushrooms on sourdough toast against the salt-and-pepper calamari to start.

"I don't it want it hanging in the air above our heads," said Richard.

Kate reluctantly put the menu down. *All right then*, she thought, *we are doing this now.*

"I don't usually behave like that," said Richard.

"Good," said Kate. "I wasn't impressed. Macho bullshit has never done it for me, I'm afraid."

"At the time," said Richard, "I suppose I thought it was a bit of a romantic gesture?"

"Threatening someone with violence is not my idea of romance," said Kate. "It smacks of being a stalker. I won't lie to you, I seriously considered giving us a miss after that performance."

"I know," said Richard. "And you'd have had every right to. I don't know what I was thinking. But I want you to know it will never happen again and I'm sorry."

Kate looked at him. His expression was contrite, his dark eyes genuine, pleading.

"Apology accepted," said Kate.

"Does this mean I'm off probation?" he asked.

"Let's leave that in place until we've gone a couple more dates without you threatening to maim anyone," said Kate.

"Fair enough," said Richard.

Kate went for the calamari followed by the slow-roasted pork belly. Richard had pâté crostini to start and pan-fried duck breasts with cherries for his main course.

The conversation between them was easy now that he had allayed her fears, and Kate's mind wandered to an imaginary dinner table where Richard regaled their guests with the funny story of how they got together, against the odds, despite his having to stand Kate up on their first date.

Kate was shoveling in her last spoonful of an unctuously treacly sticky toffee pudding when Richard said:

"Why don't I come back to yours for a nightcap?"

Kate froze. She tried to play it cool, chewing for longer than she needed to, intimating to him with her face and hands that she'd answer him as soon as she had swallowed. She didn't know what to do. She hadn't had sex in a really long time and she didn't doubt that Richard would be a great lover. And my goodness, she'd like to. But still.

"Maybe not tonight," she found herself saying. "The house is a mess"—it wasn't—"and I've got a ton of work to do"—she didn't—"and I'll be burning the midnight oil as it is!"—she wouldn't.

Really, mouth! Kate chastised herself. *Why would you go and say that? We could have had sex! Actual sex!* But her mouth seemed to carry on regardless.

"Would you take a rain check?" she went on. "It's just tonight's not a good night."

Richard smiled. He leaned toward her and lightly kissed her sticky toffee lips.

"Another night, then," he said. "I can wait."

Kate smiled and licked her lips involuntarily. *Damn you, sensible mouth!* She had a distinct sense she had just passed over the chance for a very splendid night indeed.

She called Laura when she reached the top of the hill, having assured Richard she didn't need to be walked home. Aside from anything else, she wasn't sure she could have Richard outside her house and not be tempted to ask him in.

"Well, good," said Laura. "I think you made the right decision. There's no need to rush into anything."

"I'm a grown woman," said Kate. "I should be able to have sex with someone I like and not worry if it leads to something or it doesn't. What's wrong with me?"

"Maybe you're subconsciously biding your time until you've finished all twelve dates, just in case you meet Mr. Right on the last one?" Laura suggested.

Kate was considering this as she turned in to the village square when she spotted Matt and Sarah going into the darkened café.

"Shit!" she hissed down the phone. "It's Matt and Sarah."

"Where?" asked Laura.

Kate ducked down behind a holly bush out of sight.

"What are you doing?" asked Laura. "I can hear rustling."

"I'm hiding," whispered Kate.

"In a paper bag?"

"In a bush," Kate hissed.

"We're not back to that, are we?" asked Laura. "It took years for the hedges of Blexford to stop being Kate-shaped!"

"I don't want to see him!" said Kate.

"You're going to bump into him sooner or later," said Laura. "This is a small village, you can't avoid him forever."

Kate took a deep breath, keeping one eye on Matt and Sarah

through a hole in the bush. The café lights flicked off again and they emerged from the café carrying two shopping bags each and headed toward Matt's house; clearly Sarah had had enough *space*.

"Actually, I can avoid him forever," said Kate, still crouched in the snow.

"What do you mean?" said Laura.

"I'm leaving Blexford," said Kate. "After Christmas."

There was silence on the line for a few seconds.

"But you can't!" said Laura. "I'll miss you."

"I'll miss you too. But I have to go."

"But why?" asked Laura. "It was just a stupid argument, you two will get over it, you always do."

"You know that's not the reason," said Kate.

More silence on the other end of the line.

"What about your house? You love your house," said Laura.

"I'll rent it out."

"I can't believe you're going to leave Blexford," said Laura. "Couldn't you just avoid Matt for a while and then see how you feel in a month or so? Why rush into a decision you might regret in a little while? You and Richard might become a thing. You might forget all about Matt."

"I'm in love with him, Laura," said Kate. "I don't want to be, but I am. And I can't stay here and see him every day and know that he doesn't love me back. I can't do it."

Laura was quiet again. Kate could hear her breathing on the end of the line. Laura gave a long sigh.

"I know," she said. "I know. And I do understand. But that doesn't mean I have to like it."

Now that Laura knew, all that remained was to tell her dad. The rest of the village would find out soon enough. But not until she was already gone, far enough away that she wouldn't have to face the inevitable on-slaught of questions.

· · · · ·

The gingerbread house challenge was being held in the afternoon, and what a gray afternoon it was. It was snowing again. It had stopped over-night and begun again late morning, so that yesterday's snow had had time to harden, making a perfect surface for the next deluge to lie on.

The dining hall was paneled in dark wood to half its height, with the remainder of the exposed walls painted dark green. Coats of arms and ancestral portraits of men, women, and children with foreboding expressions lined the walls.

The long banqueting table that ran the length of the room—usually mocked up to look as it would for an Elizabethan feast—was covered in thick white paper tablecloths. There were twenty-five places laid, each with a flat-pack gingerbread kit house, ready to be constructed and all the icing and bowls of sweets required to do the job.

Each workstation had place cards, as though they were about to sit down to a wedding breakfast. Kate found hers and Adam's and sat down. Only four other people had arrived so far; they smiled ner-vously at one another down the vast table. Even the reps were nowhere to be seen.

Laura marched in wearing her uniform, looking very prim.

"Don't worry, folks," she said brightly. "The reps are out on the road directing the traffic in. The highways agency closed Blexford hill and diverted the traffic and everyone got lost!"

The faces around the table relaxed.

"I've got my kitchen slaves rustling up vats of extremely alcoholic and alcohol-free mulled wine," Laura trilled.

The faces around the table looked positively chipper. Laura made her way over to Kate and sat down.

"Can I talk to you later?" she asked.

"You won't change my mind," said Kate.

"I know," said Laura. "But I need to talk to you all the same. Can you wait for me after this? I'll give you a lift home."

Kate agreed. Laura bit her lip and smiled weakly. Kate imagined she must be taking her news worse than she'd expected. The rest of the dates began to shuffle into the hall, and Laura excused herself and left.

Adam caught sight of Kate immediately. He smiled and walked over, shrugging out of his parka and pulling off his scarf as he walked.

"Kate!" He grinned when he reached her. "Nice to meet you."

He had a strong Scottish accent, which, had Kate been in a different frame of mind, would absolutely have set her knickers on fire.

"You too," said Kate.

Adam had the look of a slightly grizzled pop star. He was handsome in a sort of Alaskan pioneer way; Kate could very well imagine him living in a log cabin and chopping his own wood for the fire. His long hair curled at the ends where the snow had gotten to it, and the knitted stag's head on his chunky sweater did nothing to dampen the image Kate had formed of him.

When everyone who was likely to arrive was seated and furnished with a goblet of mulled wine, the reps explained the fairly self-explanatory challenge. Each couple had two and a half hours to build their gingerbread house and decorate it, and the winners would win an all-expenses-paid meal out in London.

Kate had built enough gingerbread houses in her time to feel confident that she had this challenge in the bag. What she hadn't reckoned on was an architect with a highly competitive nature and a hatred for all things conformist.

"But a gingerbread house is a fairly traditional build," reasoned Kate. "And they have only provided us with a traditional gingerbread template."

This held no water with Adam. He insisted on leaving the back wall of the house off the structure, as this would be a glass feature wall. When Kate flagged up that they didn't have any glass for the glass feature wall, Adam produced a piece of clear Perspex and a craft knife from his satchel and proceeded to cut it to the house dimensions.

Kate pointed out that the structure was supposed to be entirely edible, but Adam only laughed and said, "Did no one ever teach you to stretch the boundaries of your imagination? Call yourself an artist?"

"They did actually," said Kate. "And I do call myself an artist. Working to brief is part of my job, and this brief says that a gingerbread house should be edible."

It made no difference. Extra windows were cut into the front wall, and a balcony—fashioned from part of the redundant back wall—was fixed beneath them and ran the length of the house.

Kate looked round and caught the eye of the couple next to her. They opened their eyes wide and pulled *eek* faces toward Adam. The couple opposite did the same. On the other side a woman with close-cropped pink hair gave her a sympathetic smile.

The front door was made bigger and a Velux window was chiseled out of one of the roof panels and filled in with more Perspex. The chimney pot was discarded and used to make a chiminea, which sat on the decking at the back of the house, formed from the remnants of the back wall, after the balcony was constructed.

Annoyingly, it did look good. When Kate voiced an idea or suggestion, based on her long history of gingerbread-house-making experience, she was met with terse rebuttals.

At one point Kate took matters into her own hands; she built a gable for the oversized front door and was about to stick it on with white icing when Adam saw what she was doing and slapped her hand away.

"Did you actually just do that?" Kate was astounded.

"Gables are last century," Adam said by means of explanation.

"Are you overly competitive or a just a maniacal control freak?"

Adam looked at her straight on.

"Both," he said. And added: "I don't like to lose, and I abhor the ordinary."

"People like tradition," said Kate. "If they didn't they wouldn't keep doing it."

"People are stupid," said Adam. "They don't know what they want until you give it to them."

In addition to the Velux window in the roof, four mirrored rectangles were attached. These, Kate was informed, were to serve as the solar panels.

By this time Kate had pretty much given up on the construction side of things and busied herself with sorting through the array of sweets provided for decoration. She looked around the room to find all the other couples having more fun than she was.

The girl with pink hair offered for Kate to come and work with them. They were having an absolute scream trying to get their house to stay upright. Every time it collapsed, they were helpless with laughter. Kate had the feeling those two would be seeing each other again. Kate was grateful but declined their offer.

The gingerbread houses around the hall ranged from fairly secure to subsidence and in some cases total destruction. The noise levels had grown now that the initial shyness had been overcome and the atmosphere was relaxed. It made the concentrated silence between Kate and Adam conspicuous.

"I'm going to start decorating," said Kate, blobbing a globule of icing onto the front wall.

Adam reared back in horror as if she had vomited on the veranda.

"We haven't discussed décor yet!" he said.

"We didn't discuss the design of the house, but it happened anyway," said Kate.

"But I have a vision," he said.

"I thought you might," said Kate.

"I want only white sweets on it," he said. "And the front of the house is to be cladded," he added, as if this were a perfectly normal state for a gingerbread house. "We can use cocktail sticks to create the woodgrain effect."

Kate stared at Adam for a long moment. And then attached a large red jelly sweet to the icing blob on the wall. Adam looked from the sweet to Kate and back again.

"I'm blowing your mind, aren't I?" said Kate.

She grabbed the tube of icing, drizzled a line along the roof edge—avoiding the window and solar panels—and sprinkled a handful of multicolored sugar glitter onto it. Adam stood up; his chair made an ugly grinding noise. Kate wondered what he was going to do.

Adam's mouth opened and closed as he tried to form words. Kate took the tube and squirted icing in up and down zigzags around the base of the wall and stuck green chewing sweets to it.

"That," she said, pointing at the sweets, "is grass and ivy."

She whirled the icing around the door frame and pressed pink and red candy into it.

"Rambling roses," she said. "Every cottage needs a rambling rose."

Adam looked on with revulsion. He held a small clear Perspex box in his hand, which he'd told Kate matter-of-factly was the observatory tower, which would sit on the roof instead of the chimney.

Kate smiled sweetly at him and continued to haphazardly squirt icing at the house and stick gaudy mismatched sweets to it.

Ordinarily Kate would take her gingerbread house decorating rather more seriously; she liked to have rows of sweets in complementary shades and shapes. She would, as Adam would say, have *a vision* of how she wanted it to look. But Adam's attitude had pressed a devilish button in her and she found herself unable to stop throwing every glittery, sugary, jellified, luminously colored confection at his grand design.

The hanging of green-and-white-striped candy canes along the balcony proved to be a step too far. Adam gripped the observatory until his knuckles turned white and then used it to smash the gingerbread house to pieces.

The entire room stopped to stare. The reps stared. Custodians and tour guides, hearing the racket, came into the room and stared. Everyone stared at the grown man smashing a gingerbread house to smithereens with his bare hands.

Kate covered her mouth to stifle her laughter. When the house was nothing but a pile of soft rubble and tiny solar panels, Adam stood back. Kate picked up a piece of decking and popped it in her mouth.

"Mmmm," she said.

Adam looked around the stunned, silent dining hall. He flicked his hair back and stalked out of the room with his nose in the air. Kate grinned. The other couples grinned back.

"Do you think I'm still in with a chance?" she asked.

The hall exploded into laughter. Kate found herself the recipient of a round of applause.

With her date showing no sign of returning, Kate left the dining hall and went in search of Laura.

She found her organizing a smaller, luxuriant dining room. The long table was laid with a heavy white damask cloth. Ornate silver bowls on filigree stands overflowed with fresh foliage: blood-red roses and poinsettias, ivy, holly laden with berries, bronze chrysanthemums, and white freesias, which cascaded down the stems of the bowls and spilled out across the table center. These were interspersed with candelabras as tall as four-year-olds and frosted fruits clustered together in pyramid triangles.

Each table setting had four sets of cutlery laid to attention beside gold-flute-edged dinner plates topped with matching miniature soup tureens.

"Wow!" said Kate. "This looks amazing."

Laura wiped her brow and stood back, her hands on her hips. She fired off a couple of instructions to her staff and came to stand with Kate. She was surprised that the gingerbread house challenge was over so soon. Kate explained that it was only over for her; the rest of the dates were still bonding over edible walls.

Laura looked stressed. Lady Blexford had long seen the value of Kate's friend and relied on her to organize things personally when they had guests. Laura often joked that she could run an entire manor house and one hundred twenty-five staff but couldn't handle two small children.

"Lord and Lady Blexford are spending Christmas at the manor," said Laura. "With their family and friends. We've got formal dinners every night till the twenty-seventh."

"Crikey!" said Kate.

"Yeah," said Laura. "The chef's gone crazy. He's drawn up a 'Christmas Dinner through the Ages' menu. You wouldn't believe the things I've had to order in for him: pheasant, partridge, grouse, woodcock! I couldn't even order that, I've got some guy shooting them for me on the estate! Wild boar, venison . . ."

"They're going to leave here with gout," said Kate.

"And diabetes," said Laura. "You should see the sweets menu. And don't get me started on the alcohol."

"What do I have to do to get invited to this shindig?" asked Kate.

"Sleep with Lord Blexford," said Laura.

"Done!" said Kate. "For that menu I'd sleep with old Wally."

Laura pulled a face.

Kate grabbed a coffee and sat in the tearooms waiting for Laura to finish work. The tearooms closed at four thirty, but they knew Laura and the staff would be around all evening, working the restaurant next door, so they let Kate sit with her coffee and her thoughts.

She could cross off date number ten, she mused. She was sure the desire not to ever see each other again was mutual. She'd been looking forward to the gingerbread house challenge too.

Her mind drifted to Matt as she watched the snow fall outside. Just a week or so before they'd been laughing and joking together at the Christmas market. She would never have believed then that she'd be planning to leave Blexford altogether by now. *What a difference a few days can make*, she thought.

Kate closed her eyes to stop the tears. Why did she have to love someone who didn't love her back? Why was life such a bitch sometimes?

She heard a chair scrape and opened her eyes to find Laura sitting opposite her. Laura's expression was concern and anxiety mixed. She chewed a fingernail and fidgeted.

"What's up with you?" Kate asked.

"I've got something to tell you," said Laura. She moved on to another fingernail.

"Are you pregnant again?" Kate asked.

"No!" exclaimed Laura. "Good God, no! This concerns you."

"Am *I* pregnant?" Kate joked. Laura didn't laugh.

"It's about Matt," said Laura.

"I don't want to talk about Matt," said Kate.

"Hear me out," said Laura. "You need to know this, in case it changes things."

"Unless Matt's undergoing a personality bypass, or you've got a potion to fix unrequited love, I doubt there is anything you can tell me that would *change things*."

Laura pursed her lips as if she were wondering whether whatever she was about to divulge was a good idea, but then she seemed to find her resolve. She set her jaw, took a deep breath, and began.

"About six months after you left to go traveling," Laura began, "Matt came to see me. He thought we were still living together. He didn't know you were out of the country, and, well . . ." She shrugged. "You know what he was like back then; I hadn't seen or heard from him to tell him. The thing is, Kate . . ." Laura stopped. She looked directly at Kate. "He told me he was in love with you."

Laura watched her friend, waiting for the words to settle in the air between them.

"I'm sorry," said Kate. "He what?"

"He told me he was in love with you," Laura repeated. "He'd come to Liverpool in a great rush of bravado, with flowers and this idea about professing his love, and then found you'd gone."

Laura was quiet. She looked at Kate, and Kate knew she was waiting for her to respond. But Kate didn't know how to respond. She was stunned. How had she never known this? A different life flashed before her eyes. *What*-ifs clattered through her mind.

"When he heard that you were intending to stay away longer, he told me to forget it," said Laura. "I told him to email you, tell you how he felt, apologize for being such a dick. But you know how stubborn he is. He got all angry, embarrassed probably, and he made me promise not to tell you. He said he never should have come in the first place."

Kate's mind reeled.

"Why didn't you tell me?" she asked.

"I didn't know what to do for the best," said Laura. "I'd promised Matt I wouldn't. But I told myself that if in your next email, you mentioned Matt, I'd tell you regardless. But you didn't. Your next email was all about Aaron or whatever his name was."

"It seems like quite a big thing to omit," said Kate.

"You were having such a great time," said Laura. "And Matt had been such a pain in the arse, and I know how upset you were with him and I guess I just thought, why bring him up when you're so happy? It would've just meant more Matt drama. And let's face it, he was good at bringing the drama back then."

"He told you he was in love with me?"

"I didn't know whether to believe him," said Laura. "And then he switched so quickly back to his default position of miserable bugger that I thought—well, I didn't know what to think."

"Why are you telling me this now?" asked Kate.

Laura blinked and bit at one of her nails.

"In case this changes things," said Laura. "If you love him, well, maybe he still loves you too and you're both too stubborn to admit it!"

"Clearly he is not harboring feelings of love for me," said Kate. "I'd say he's pretty well channeling the opposite right now."

"But if you just talked to him," said Laura.

"It's a little late for that," said Kate. "You should have told me when it could have made a difference."

Her voice was quiet. She was feeling so many things, but her overriding emotion was anger toward Laura. Her best friend, Laura. Her best friend, who hadn't bothered to tell her that Matt had been in love with her. How different might her life have been if she'd known?

"I promise you," Laura began, "that if I'd thought for one minute that the feeling was mutual, I would have told you straightaway, but you were all about Aaron!"

"You should have told me regardless," said Kate.

"Let's just say that I had," said Laura. "And you dropped everything and rushed back to find he'd changed his mind. It wasn't beyond the realms of possibility, Kate; he was up and down like a bloody yo-yo. He was married to someone else three months later, for God's sake! He wasn't exactly a reliable barometer of emotions back then."

Kate rose from her chair. Laura looked up at her, her eyes glassy with tears, a pleading expression on her face. Kate didn't care.

"I hope you feel better now that you've purged yourself of guilt," said Kate. "It must be a relief for you."

She left her friend sitting alone at the table in the deserted tearoom and set off into the cold dark evening.

· · · · ·

The cold wind bit at her cheeks but Kate hardly noticed. She'd been unfair to Laura and she knew it, but it didn't make her any less angry with her. And why tell her now? All these years later, when Matt hated her and she was leaving? Why now? Other than to assuage her own guilt.

The snow whipped at her face as she trudged down the lonely lane home. The snow was deep here, almost as deep as her boots. Sheep huddled together on the other side of the wire fence, ghostly forms on the landscape. The wild weather and bleak farmland echoed her mood.

Kate was struggling to understand what cosmic influences had found her at odds with the two people she considered to be her best friends in the world. She didn't know which betrayal stung more. How could Laura have kept something like that from her?

She found herself haunted by ghosts of a life that could have been. She saw Matt's arm round her shoulders in the snow instead of Sarah's. She saw anniversaries and Valentine's Days and Christmases and birthdays and holidays rushing past her eyes: a phantom life that might have been hers if only Laura had decided differently.

Kate arrived home to find a pie on the kitchen table with a note:

Kate,

Evelyn thought you might need cheering up, she's made you a steak and mushroom pie.

Love you. Dad xxx

It was still warm. Kate grabbed a fork and took the pie into the sitting room. She switched on the tree lights, built the fire, and put the TV on. If ever there was a time for pie, it was now, Kate thought.

· · · · ·

Kate's phone buzzed loudly on the coffee table, causing a fork that rested on a discarded plate next to it to vibrate. Kate jolted awake. The sitting room was dark except for the glowing embers in the fireplace and the flicker of an old black-and-white horror movie on the TV.

Kate leaned over and picked up her phone. The time said 5:17 a.m.

"Oh God." As she moved, a shower of pastry crumbs fluttered off her boobs and onto the carpet. She wiped her cheek; it was wet. She cast a glance at the cushion, where a wet mark stood out dark against the velvet.

"Oh, disgusting!" she moaned, realizing she'd been sleeping in a pool of her own dribble.

The phone buzzed in Kate's hand and she jumped, accidentally dropping it onto the carpet, where it glowed angrily, the word *Mum* lit up in red letters. Kate scrabbled about and got the phone to her ear.

"Mum?" she said. Still dazed and confused.

"Katy" her mum shrieked down the phone. Kate held the phone away from her ear. "Katy, thank God!" said her mum. "Something terrible has happened!"

"Are you all right?" asked Kate.

"No, I'm bloody not!" said her mum.

"Are you hurt?"

"No, I'm not hurt!" said her mum, as though this were a ludicrous idea. "I'm in prison!"

"What?" said Kate.

"I've been arrested!" said her mum. "It was all a scam. He didn't own the boat at all! It was stolen. He commissioned us to sell a stolen yacht for him. Well, we didn't know!" she went on indignantly. "And then the owner comes barging on board with the police and I got arrested!"

"Where's Gerry?" Kate asked.

"Gone," said her mum.

"What do you mean gone?"

"He left me," said her mum. "As soon as he saw the police, he jumped off the boat and ran away. The last I saw of him was his naked bottom mincing up the gangway like two white onions bobbing along in the moonlight!"

Kate tried to blink away the image.

"And you're in a Barbadian prison?" Kate asked.

"Well, I'm not exactly *in* prison," said her mum. "I'm being held in custody at the local police station, but the tea they served me was only lukewarm. The owner said he won't press charges provided I give the police all the information I have about the bogus seller and I leave the island immediately."

"Oh, thank God!" said Kate. "It could have been a lot worse—"

"I'd like to know how!" interrupted her mum. "I was bare-breasted when they burst in on us. It was pure luck I had a G-string on to cover my Aunty Mary. We've been working our way through the Kama Sutra . . ."

"Mum, please," said Kate. Her mum stopped with an audible *humph*. "Just get yourself on a plane back to Spain as soon as you can."

"Well, that's just it, darling," said her mum. "I can't. I haven't got any money."

"Didn't you take out travel insurance?" asked Kate.

"It doesn't cover repatriation when swindled by a career criminal, darling," said her mum testily.

Kate sucked in a breath.

"How much are the flights?" Kate asked.

"Seven hundred, give or take," said her mum.

"Seven hundred pounds?!"

"Well, it's Christmas and it's last minute," said her mum. "Just leave me here in a jail cell to rot if it's too much of a bother."

"It's not a bother, Mum," said Kate. "Of course it's not a bother. I would pay any amount to help you, you know that. It's just all come as bit of surprise, that's all."

"To you and me both, darling."

"Of course," said Kate. "It must have been a terrible shock for you."

"It's been an absolute trial," said her mum. "My nerves are quite shattered."

"What will you do about Gerry?"

"Gerry can fend for himself like he left me to do!" said her mum. "His passport's been seized and I've instructed the harbormaster to give all his clothes to charity. He won't get far," she went on. "A naked sexagenarian running around the island is bound to get noticed."

Kate had to agree.

"Leave it to me, Mum," said Kate. "I'll get you home."

Kate persuaded her mum to pass the phone to the officer in charge—who seemed very friendly and assured Kate that the tea had been hot when served—and acquired the relevant details before beginning the process of getting her mother safely back to Spain.

She didn't have seven hundred pounds *give or take*. She would have to whack it on the credit card and try to pay it back in the new year. If there was one thing Kate was sure of, it was that her mum would not consider this a loan.

Laura will love this, Kate thought, as she clicked confirm on the flight details. And then she remembered that she'd fallen out with her best friend and she felt sick to her stomach.

After phoning the Barbados police station and giving the details for her mother's swift departure—for which the officer sounded only too pleased—Kate got showered and dressed.

It was seven thirty a.m. and still dark outside. Kate grabbed her boots and threw on her coat and went to intercept her dad on his way back from getting his morning paper.

She found Mac wading through last night's fresh snowfall, cap fastened on his head, a thick tube of rolled-up newspaper under his arm. They were the only two people out in the street. Mac's face lit up when he saw Kate.

"Hallo, love," he said. "Are you out searching for inspiration?"

"Actually I was out searching for you," said Kate. "Fancy coming round for a coffee?"

As they walked arm in arm along the quiet road, Kate regaled her dad with her mum's latest adventures.

"I can't believe that Gerry is such a snake," said her dad.

"Can't you?" asked Kate. "I can well believe it."

"Well, you can't afford to pay out all that money by yourself," said Mac. "I'll give you half."

"No, Dad, it's fine, honestly . . ."

"Now don't go arguing with me about it," said Mac. "I'm paying half and that's the end of it."

"But she doesn't deserve it, Dad," said Kate. "Not from you. I have to help. I'm obliged by the unwritten law of daughterly responsibility."

"And I'm bound by the fatherly protection code," said Mac. "I'm not doing it to help your mother, I'm doing it to help you. And I won't take no for an answer," he went on. "You want to know where you get your stubbornness from? You're looking at it!"

Kate squeezed her dad's arm and reached up to kiss his cheek.

"Thanks, Dad," she said. "You're the best. Mum never did deserve you."

"Do you know something, my love," said Mac. "I think you might be right."

Kate smiled at him, already dreading having to ruin her dad's day by telling him she planned to leave Blexford. But it wasn't something she could put off. No action or expression was missed in the village; no roll of parcel tape purchased or cardboard box saved went unnoticed. It would only be a matter of time before tongues began to wag, and Kate couldn't bear the idea of her dad finding out from anyone else but her.

Lip-Smacking Wine and a Smack in the Chops

This was horrible. Awful. Kate looked at her dad and her dad looked back at her. He was getting old. It was easy to forget, he was so busy, so chirpy. But now as he sat at the table, holding his mug, looking from Kate to the table and back again, he looked his age. Worry lines crinkled his forehead and the lines under his eyes seemed more pronounced somehow; it was easy to miss them when he was smiling. He wasn't smiling now.

"So when are you leaving?" he asked.

"I heard back from Josie this morning," said Kate. "I can stay with her from the twenty-eighth. Just until I get myself sorted with my own place."

"Why the rush?" asked Mac.

"I think you know why, Dad," said Kate. "I think you knew before I did. I'm in love with Matt, and Matt is in love with Sarah, and it's a big mess. How can I stay?"

"I'll miss you," he said.

"I'll come and visit," said Kate. "And you can come and see me any-time. I'll book you into a nice hotel, and when I've found a place, you can stay with me."

"Don't you think this is a bit drastic?" asked Mac.

"It's not going to get any better," said Kate. "I love him, Dad. And he doesn't love me back and that's all there is to it."

Her dad sighed.

"I'm only surprised it took you this long to realize," said Mac. "You've loved that boy all your life. I could see it when you were twelve: the way you smiled when he called for you. And when you were sixteen; do you remember that bonfire night when you insisted on going to the fireworks with just that silly little denim jacket on and you ended up getting inside Matt's parka with him?"

Kate smiled at the memory. She'd had to stand flat against him so they could do the zip up. They'd spent the evening lolloping around like conjoined twins, laughing hysterically.

"I thought to myself that night," Mac went on, "*I've lost my girl to that there lad.* But I didn't mind so much. He was a good boy."

"Huh," said Kate, smiling at her dad. "I wish someone would've let *me* know."

"Like I said," said Mac, "he brings out your sparkle."

"Not anymore," said Kate. "What I need is a total Matt detox. I need to de-sparkle."

Mac rested his hand on Kate's.

"Have you patched things up with Laura yet?" he asked.

"No," said Kate.

"You know, as your father, I'd like to shake Laura's hand for what she did."

"Oh, thanks a lot, Judas!" said Kate.

Her dad shook his head and smiled.

"I'm serious," he said. "I would say Laura is the finest friend you could hope for. If she hadn't taken the decision not to tell you about Matt, you wouldn't have traveled the world, you wouldn't have been so driven in your work, you might not even be working for Liberty."

"I could have done all those things with Matt."

"Of course, you could have. But would you?" asked her dad. "Because sharing your life with someone will always mean compromise. You probably would have moved back to Blexford when Matt took over the shop. You might have taken a design job with a company closer to home. The things that define you would be different."

"But not wrong," said Kate.

"No," Mac agreed. "But different. You've always been strong-minded, Kate. If you're honest with yourself, I don't think you would want to change a thing."

Of course her dad was right. Dammit! In all probability, Kate would have dropped everything to be with Matt then. As much as she'd told herself—and everyone else—that their one-night stand was a meaningless mistake, deep inside, she'd wanted it to happen. How could she hold a friend in contempt whose decision had allowed her to flourish?

"I *am* lucky to have Laura," said Kate.

"Yep."

"I've been an idiot, haven't I?"

"Yep," said Mac. "But you don't have to stay one."

· · · · ·

Mac left. Kate made him promise he wouldn't tell Matt about her decision to leave and he reluctantly agreed; left to his own devices he would almost certainly try to fix things between them, and this was something that couldn't be fixed. Even if they made up after the argument, it would only solve half the problem.

Kate had convinced herself that being great friends with Matt was enough. But now she knew different. Now she'd listened to what her heart had been trying to tell her for so long: she would always yearn for being more than just good friends. She couldn't stay in a place where their lives were so intertwined; one way or another they always had been, and that was why she had to leave.

· · · · ·

Kate opened the larder and pulled out two bags of hazelnuts. She would need more. Laura's favorite bake of all time was a toasted hazelnut brownie. As a peace offering Kate planned to make her a batch and buy her a bottle of wine, and stand on her doorstep with her figurative cap in her hand and beg forgiveness. But first she needed more hazelnuts.

She wrapped up appropriately for the arctic temperature and made her way to Evelyn's shop. It had stopped snowing, but it was freezing cold and the wind was bitter. She cut through Potters Copse, where the foliage acted as a reasonable windbreaker.

There was barely a branch or bush that wasn't hung with baubles or tinsel now. People had started to leave larger decorations too. Through the trees, just off to the right, someone had deposited a wooden sleigh pulled by eight plastic reindeer. A nutcracker doll stood at attention by a hawthorn tree and several—some might say life-size—wooden elves were dotted along the snowy path.

A squirrel stopped to look at Kate, a nut clamped between its teeth, before scurrying up the nearest tree trunk. It paused at a shiny pink bauble that dangled from a twig and gave it a good sniff; then, satisfied that it hadn't missed out on a tasty morsel, it disappeared up into the spindly top branches.

Kate took out her phone and began to take photographs: the jolly Santa with his black boots in a tangle of snowy roots, the knitted owl that someone had perched in the hollow of a tree, and the fairy doll in the pink tutu, balanced where bough met trunk.

She lost herself for no little time in the magic of the quiet copse— until the spell was broken by a crow squawking angrily above her and a streak of a ginger cat landed in the snow next to her and slunk silently away, with no crow to show for his efforts. Kate pocketed her phone and continued on to the shop.

Of course Evelyn had hazelnuts. Not only that but she had the perfect wine to complement a hazelnut brownie.

She also had news: the caroling *would* take its route through Potters Copse this year and would then make its way back round to the Pear Tree for Christmas treats.

Kate didn't tell Evelyn that she wouldn't be attending the caroling, or any of the festivities thereafter. She had resigned herself to a quiet Christmas Eve this year. She would prep the veg for Christmas Day in front of the TV, with some mulled wine and a bag of truffles she had stashed in the fridge. It wouldn't be so bad. In truth, after so many dates of enforced conversation with strangers, she was quite looking forward to a bit of calm.

"I had a chap in earlier today that knows you," said Evelyn.

"Really?" said Kate.

"Lovely lad," said Evelyn. "Been in the Pear Tree asking after you. Said you told him it was the best coffee for miles. Was on his way to the manor."

Kate recalled there being a Christmas-tree-decorating competition as one of the Twelve Dates options. She hadn't realized it was up at the manor. Kate had opted for the wine-tasting tour at the local vineyard instead.

"Did you get his name?" Kate asked.

Evelyn closed her eyes and screwed up her nose as she thought.

"Daryl, Darrius, David . . ."

"Drew?" asked Kate helpfully.

Evelyn slapped her thigh.

"That's it!" said Evelyn. "Lovely chap, said you were a fine filly on the dance floor!"

Kate laughed. "That's Drew all right."

Kate stocked up on a few essentials while she was in the shop: a packet of Patrick's free-range bacon and a white crusty loaf. She had veg from the garden at home, so she picked up a pack of chopped steak from the fridge to make a stew. She grabbed some more suet for dumplings. She could slow-cook it today and there'd be enough for tomorrow as well—she would need something to line her stomach before the wine-tasting tomorrow afternoon.

Kate wandered around the shop. Evelyn put her glasses back on and went back to her book. It was the twentieth of December. The kids had broken up from school and the village suddenly seemed crowded.

Kate lingered by the deep rounded bay windows—filled with bargain romance novels, canned goods, and tinsel—and looked out across the green. The Pear Tree windows were steamed up as usual and a steady stream of families filed in and out. Kate could just hear the jingle of the bell above the café door. Her heart gave a twinge, and she felt a pang of longing. Longing to be in the Pear Tree, drinking coffee and being teased by Matt. Longing for things to be like they were before.

"We'll all be sad to see you go," said Evelyn without looking up from her book.

Kate might have guessed her dad would tell Evelyn her plans.

"Not everyone," said Kate.

"Some more than you might think," said Evelyn. "The world doesn't seem to sit right when you two are fighting."

"The world won't need to worry when I'm gone," said Kate.

Kate paid for her shopping.

"Don't leave on an argument," said Evelyn. "I know, he's proud and stupid, but don't do that to him. Give him a chance."

Kate smiled and nodded noncommittally. She *was* giving him a chance. She was giving them both a chance to get on with their lives.

· · · · ·

Kate pulled the toasted hazelnuts out of the oven, tipped them into a tea towel, and folded it up, rubbing the rough toweling furiously over the hot nuts. When she unwrapped the tea towel the hazelnuts were peeled and the towel was full of brown papery skins.

She chopped a third of the nuts roughly and ground the rest in the blender; these were flourless brownies—the best kind. She folded all the nuts into a thick mixture of melted dark chocolate, sugar, and eggs and poured the batter into a tin for baking.

She filled the slow cooker with the stew ingredients and left it to do its thing. She would make the dumplings later.

The house filled with the smell of hot chocolate praline. Laura would be at work today. Kate considered waiting until Laura was home, but then she thought she was less likely to throw her apology back in her face if Kate took her by surprise at work. Besides, she would quite like to see if she could bump into Drew.

Two hours later, armed with a batch of warm, very squidgy brownies and a bottle of Merlot, Kate set back out into the snow in search of salvation.

She heard Laura before she saw her. She was organizing the rehanging of a freshly polished chandelier in the ballroom. Two men stood atop a ladder each, with the chandelier held between them. Hundreds of crystal glass drops clinked merrily together as the men worked to reattach the light fitting to the ceiling rose.

"Steady now," Laura called. "A little to your left, Peter. Michael, there's a pendant hooked around your collar!"

Kate decided this was not the time to make a surprise entrance. She turned quietly and left the ballroom. She would find Laura later. She followed the signs instead for the Christmas tree decorating competition. Kate found herself in a corridor with blue fleur-de-lis carpet and framed pencil drawings of birds hung on the walls.

At the door to the room signposted *The Twelve Dates of Christmas*, Kate recognized the Lightning Strikes rep from her unfortunate dinner date in London. The rep looked up and smiled.

"Kate!" she said. "I didn't know you were doing this date."

"Oh, I'm not," said Kate. And she explained to the rep that she thought she might find Drew here.

The rep pointed to a tree in the farthest corner, where Drew looked astonishingly sexy in jeans, brogues, and a tweed jacket. He was untangling a string of gingerbread-man fairy lights with his date, who looked as if he couldn't believe his luck in being paired with Drew.

Kate thanked the rep.

"By the way," she said. "How did you get with your expulsion-of-arseholes mission?"

"Very well," said the rep. "After the infamous Jim, we managed to get rid of six more. We reckon they'd put about eighteen grand into the betting ring between them."

"Well done!" said Kate. "You should join the fraud squad."

· · · · ·

Kate wandered passed the other couples and their trees. As usual there was a mix of couples, some taking the competition very seriously, some making light of it; all of them flirting wildly.

When Drew saw Kate he dropped his fairy lights and got her into a bear hug. His date looked on with pursed lips.

"I'm so happy to see you," he said. "I had the most interesting chat with an intense man called Matt, in that coffee shop you kept on about."

Kate tried to look casual. Even the mention of his name made her wince.

"You were right about the coffee," he said. "Actually I was going to email you later about the twelfth date. Fancy it?"

There were two options for the twelfth date. The first was a "choose your own date" night; the idea was to pick your favorite date of the Twelve Dates experience and spend the final evening, the 23rd of December, with that person. The second option was the Lucky Dip Date, whereby your name would be put into a virtual hat and jiggled about and paired randomly with a wild card.

Kate had had enough surprises on this experience and had decided early on that she would not be partaking of the lucky dip.

She had considered asking Richard, but since it had been logged that he'd stood her up on their date, she'd thought it would look a bit odd. And actually, her date with Drew had been a fantastic night—before she got stranded in the car park . . . and even then . . .

"I'd love to," said Kate. "You haven't found Mr. Right either, then?"

Drew smiled wickedly and lowered his voice so that his date—who was feigning nonchalance but clearly straining to eavesdrop—wouldn't hear.

"Actually," he said. "I think I have. Only not on the Twelve Dates. I met him at the dry cleaners, of all places. They'd mixed up our dinner jackets. His name is Archie."

"Wow," said Kate. "That's great, Drew, I'm really pleased for you."

Drew sucked his cheeks in and tilted his head, looking smug.

"Anyway," he said, looking over at his date, who was beginning to tap his foot impatiently. "I'd better get back. But I will see *you* on the twenty-third for outdoor movie and chill."

Chill was the word! The final date was being held in Fitzwilliam Park on the edge of Great Blexley. It was an outdoor Christmas movie night—though how they would manage to prevent the participants from getting hypothermia was beyond Kate—and all the people from all the different dates were going to be there; hence the need to hire out a park. The film showing was *It's a Wonderful Life*, one of Kate's favorites, and she was looking forward to seeing it on the big screen.

But before that, Kate had to get through the wine-tasting date tomorrow with Thomas, the twice-divorced carpenter. And before that, she had to win her best friend back with brownies and booze.

Kate went back the way she had come and found Laura seated in a carved wooden throne, beneath a portrait of a portly, ruddy-faced man wearing velvet britches and a ruffled shirt beneath his matching coat. She was engrossed in the papers she held, running her finger down a list and stopping every now and again to mark a spot on the page with her pen.

"Hello," said Kate. Her voice sounded as small and pathetic as she felt in the big pompous room.

Laura looked up. She didn't speak. She just looked at Kate. And Kate looked back.

"I'm so sorry," said Kate. "You did absolutely the right thing for me and I was an ungrateful cow. I've brought hazelnut brownies and plonk as a peace offering."

Laura burst unceremoniously into tears. She held her papers up over her face, but it didn't hide her sobs. Kate crossed the room and knelt down beside the throne. She was crying too now.

"I'm really sorry," said Kate. "I know you were doing what you thought was best."

"I'm sorry toooooo," sobbed Laura. "If I'd told you sooner . . . It just kills me to think that you might be unhappy because of me."

Kate knelt up and put her arms around Laura's neck.

"I'm not unhappy!" said Kate. "I mean, yeah, I'm unhappily in love with Matt. But I'm not unhappy with the way my life turned out. I love my life!"

"I've been so worried you'd never want to speak to me again!" said Laura.

"That would never happen," said Kate. She leaned back onto her knees and took Laura's hands.

Michael walked into the room, saw the two friends crying and holding hands, and walked back out again scratching his head. Kate and Laura started laughing.

They sat themselves down on the floor, leaning up against the wall, and shared a large chunk of brownie. They left the wine in the bag, since Laura was still officially at work.

It was barely four o'clock, but the windows showed only dark outside.

Laura flapped her papers.

"I've got twelve live pheasants, thirty-six partridges, and two peacocks being delivered on the twenty-third, so the Lord and Lady can have live birds wandering around outside on Christmas Day," said Laura.

"Bloody hell!" said Kate. "You'd better tell Matt to steer clear of the manor for a while!"

"God only knows how we're supposed to stop them from flying away," Laura replied.

"It does seem extravagant," said Kate.

"This is the compromise!" said Laura. "They'd wanted flocks of geese and swans and a pack of wild boar let into the woods, but the groundsman said they were liable to attack the guests when they went out for their constitutionals."

Kate laughed. Laura wiped her brow.

"They like the juxtaposition between what they're eating and their live counterparts outside the window," Laura went on.

"Sickos."

"I've got enough dead animals hanging in the cold storage to entertain a taxidermists' convention!" said Laura.

She looked tired. The smudged mascara didn't help.

"Still," she said. "I sign out at five p.m. on the twenty-third and I'm not back till after the New Year."

They were both quiet for a moment. Reminded suddenly that one of them would be gone by then. Laura put her head on Kate's shoulder.

"What will I do without you?" she asked.

"You'll just have to have plenty of weekends away in London," said Kate. But they both knew it wouldn't be the same.

· · · · ·

Kate pushed her front door open and was greeted by the rich smell of beef stew. Her stomach growled. The house felt very warm after the bracing weather outside and Kate felt her cheeks stinging slightly as they thawed, chafed by the bitter wind.

She felt lighter now that she had made up with Laura. Kate wandered into the kitchen and caught sight of one of her packing boxes, half filled with art supplies, and a weight of sadness cloaked her shoulders once more. She sighed. It wasn't going to be easy to leave. But, she told herself, it wouldn't be the first time she'd started over; she could do it again.

· · · · ·

Her phone buzzed her out of her reverie. It was her mum.

"Hi, Mum," said Kate. "Are you safely home?"

"Yes, my darling," said her mum. "I am, thanks to you, Katy-Boo!"

"Dad went halves with me," said Kate.

Her mum went unusually quiet on the other end of the line.

"Did he, darling," she said after a moment. "He's a good man, your father."

"Yes," said Kate. "He is."

"I know you always thought he was too good for me, darling," said her mum.

"I never said that!" said Kate.

"You didn't need to," said her mum. "And, well, the truth of it is, he was. It wasn't that I didn't love him. I just didn't love him enough."

"Then why did you keep going back to him?" Kate asked.

"Because *he is* a good man," said her mum. "I could never match up. I could never love him like he loved me. I just haven't got it in me. You and your dad are cut from the same cloth; you're both sturdy, you can stand up to life and give it as good as it gets. I'm always just trying to stop it from blowing me away."

Kate was quiet. She'd never had such candid conversation from her mother. Was it possible there was more depth to her than Kate had given her credit for?

"Anyway," said her mum. "Enough of this nonsense! I bought a fabulous Chanel purse at the airport with Gerry's traveler's checks."

Maybe not.

"Mum, would you like to come back to England for Christmas?" Kate asked. "I don't like the idea of you being alone for the holidays."

Kate wasn't sure exactly how she would work such a scheme and keep everyone happy, but equally, she couldn't very well leave her mum stranded alone at Christmas.

"Alone?" trilled her mother. "Alone? I'm the life and soul of the complex, darling. I've had more offers of Christmas dinners than I know what to do with!"

"Have you heard from Gerry?" Kate asked.

"No," said her mum. "But while I was burning his clothes on the beach, I met a charming gentleman called Alejandro. Owns a bistro on the hillside. How I've not met him before I do not know!"

Kate rolled her eyes as her mum extolled the virtues of Spanish men of a certain age.

"Anyway, my darling," she said finally. "I have to go and get ready, as Alejandro is picking me up later so I can sample some of his delights."

Kate wasn't sure if Alejandro's *delights* were on the bistro menu or a euphemism for something else. Her mum rang off, none the worse, it seemed, for her ordeal with the Barbadian police force or her unwitting embroilment in multimillion-pound yacht theft.

By now Kate was really hungry. No sooner had Kate ladled a large helping of slow-cooked stew into her bowl than her phone blipped. It was Richard. He had a business meeting with some clients in Great Blexley that would finish at about half nine and would Kate like to meet up?

Kate didn't really want to turf out again. She'd already thawed her feet in front of the fire after she got back from Blexford Manor; she didn't want to be refrozen anytime soon. And the hill was still closed. And her little car was pretty well snowed into its parking spot outside the house.

Her phone blipped again:

Don't say no. I couldn't stand it. I want to see you.
Badly!
Rxxx

Kate pushed her fork into a dumpling. *Dammit*, she thought, but she knew the distraction would be good for her. If she stayed in, she'd spend the evening thinking about all the things she'd miss when she was back in London. Or worse, she'd spend the evening pining over Matt, and that would do her no good at all. Better to risk pneumonia than end up melancholic, she decided.

She messaged Richard and they arranged to meet in the Tipsy Goose. She took a taxi, which cost her a small fortune as it had to go the long way round—what with the hill being closed—past the manor and down the A-roads to finally end up at the pub. She consoled herself with the promise that she'd walk home later.

Richard had already had a few drinks. By all accounts his business meeting had gone well and he was in a celebratory mood. When he kissed Kate hello, it was with a hunger that took her by surprise. Their conversation was spirited; Richard's adrenaline was high from the deal he'd struck with some Norwegian investors, and Kate found his positivity infectious.

He was good to be around. Ambitious. Intelligent. His self-confidence could be described as arrogance, and his cocksure attitude might, under different circumstances, have been unappealing. But not tonight. Tonight she basked in it; he was fired up and *she* was the center of all his attentions. She needed this.

Everyone in the pub knew Richard. Everyone wanted to be his friend, but he only had eyes for Kate. *Me,* thought Kate, *he just wants me*. Kate was spellbound, flattered; she was intoxicated by the attention he lavished on her.

His kisses numbed the ache in her heart and silenced the siren that repeatedly wailed Matt's name through her brain. His hands found their way inside her jumper and wandered over her body in a way that was only just on the side of acceptable in public. Somewhere deep inside, a part of her that had been lying in wait stretched and woke up. And when Richard leaned into her neck and asked in a low deep whisper if he could come back to her place, Kate said yes.

They stumbled up the hill, laughing and slipping, pushing each other against garden walls and fences to steal hot kisses in the cold night. Chilled hands fumbled between layers of wool and cloth. Grasping and rubbing. Only the freezing temperature prevented them from dispensing with Kate's house to have sex in the nearby field. Richard was wild with lust and Kate was only too happy to reciprocate.

As they started along the lane that led to the green, Kate's inner self suddenly found its voice. Doubt began to fill her head and squeeze her stomach, but she pushed it away. Hard. She needed this. She needed to forget. Just let her forget for one night!

Kate hurried Richard across the green toward Potters Copse. The noise from the Duke's Head spilled out into the night. They had a live band playing. People stood outside, smoking and drinking. Richard tugged on Kate's hand.

"Hang on a minute, babe," he said. "I need to take a piss." He nodded toward the pub.

"We're literally five minutes from my house," said Kate.

"I can't wait," he said. "It's all those pints. I'll only be a second!"

Kate's inner voice got louder. Didn't he realize she had to do this before her sensible side took control again?

Richard disappeared into the pub and Kate followed behind. The splintering crash of drums and roar of sweaty-headed men hollering into microphones brought Kate's mind into sharp focus. She was instantly sober.

She scanned the pub in time to see Matt standing at the bar. He watched Richard go into the toilets. Something flickered across his face, a vague recognition, and then he spotted Kate.

Kate turned and walked smartly out of the pub. She wasn't going to fight with Matt and she certainly wasn't going to speak to him if she could help it. Indignation burned through her. She banished her inner self with its sensible suggestions to the farthest recesses of her mind. She was going to have sex with Richard tonight and it would be bloody brilliant!

She didn't recognize the people outside the pub. They must have come up for the band. Kate parked herself on one of the benches beneath a patio heater and waited.

There was a commotion inside the pub. Shouts that had nothing to do with the band. The music tapered off and died. Kate had a sense of foreboding. She could hear muffled voices trying to soothe the situation. Then Barry's voice over the din:

"Take it outside, fellas!"

Kate stood up and went to the door in time to see Richard storm through it.

"What the fuck is your problem, mate!" he yelled over his shoulder.

"Are you gonna tell her, or am I?" Matt shouted behind him.

Kate's stomach lurched. Richard was marching across the green, but Matt was on his heels. Kate followed. Richard was a big guy; she didn't want him to get into a fight with Matt. Matt was persistent.

"What's it to you?" Richard sneered.

"Tell her!" Matt shouted.

"Stay out of it, friend," said Richard. "You don't want to start with me!"

"I'm not your friend," said Matt.

Matt caught up with Richard and grabbed his jacket, spun him round. Richard swung a punch at Matt, but Matt ducked down swiftly and then back up and jabbed Richard hard in the face. Richard lost his balance and toppled backward.

Kate rushed over and knelt by Richard. His nose was bleeding.

"What the hell is the matter with you?" she yelled at Matt.

"Tell her!" said Matt.

Richard sat up, wiping his bloodied face with his hand.

"If you give so much of a shit, why don't *you* tell her?" Richard spluttered.

Matt looked from Kate to Richard and back again. The anger seemed to drain out of him.

"He's married, Kate," said Matt quietly. "I overheard him talking to his wife in the toilets. Giving her some bullshit about having to stay in town to close a deal. I think it's pretty clear *you're* the *deal*, Kate."

Matt turned and went back into the pub.

"Anything you need a hand with, Kate?" came a booming voice. It was Barry. He was standing by a picnic bench with his arms folded across his broad chest.

"I'm fine, thanks, Barry," said Kate.

"If you need anything, just holler," said Barry. "I'm good at putting the rubbish out. I've dispatched bigger things than that shower of shite!"

He looked pointedly at Richard as he said it. Big as he was, Richard was wise enough not to pick a fight with Barry.

"Thanks, Barry," said Kate. "I've got this."

"Okay, folks," said Barry. "Let's let the lady have some privacy."

The small crowd that had come outside to watch the show filtered back into the pub after Barry, leaving Kate and Richard sitting in the snow.

Kate was dumbfounded. She had a sick feeling in her stomach. Richard dabbed at his nose. Kate's jeans were wet through, her legs freezing where she knelt. Her head reeled.

"You're married?" Kate asked.

Richard didn't say anything. He didn't look at her. She said it again.

"You're married!"

He looked at her then. There was no remorse in his expression, only annoyance that he'd been found out, a defiance in his countenance that spoke volumes.

"Yes," he said. "I'm married."

"Aren't you going to try to excuse yourself?" asked Kate. "Tell me your wife doesn't understand you? Tell me you lead separate lives?"

"Would you believe me if I did?" he asked.

"No," said Kate.

"Well, then," said Richard, as though that should be an end to it.

"Was it all a lie?" she asked. "Was your son even in hospital?"

"That part was true," he said.

"Your poor wife," said Kate.

She felt sick, imagining his wife sitting at home with the children while her husband was out *on business*. Kate recalled his hands on her body and shuddered. She didn't suppose she was his only conquest; she wondered how he managed to keep them all separate.

"Don't *you* worry about *my* wife," said Richard. "She has a nice life."

"You make her sound like a free-range chicken!" Kate shouted.

Richard started to get up. Kate couldn't believe him. Most of all she couldn't understand how he was the one in the wrong and she was the one being made to feel awkward.

"Why go to all that trouble?" Kate asked. "All the seduction? The meals, the cozy drinks together. The texts! All that bullshit about being jealous of my other dates. Why?"

Richard brushed the snow off his jeans; under the streetlamp the wet denim showed darker than the rest. Kate stood and tried to get Richard to look her in the eye. She searched his face for an iota of remorse. There was none.

He pulled his jacket around him and looked down at her.

"The thrill of the chase, baby!" he said.

Kate laughed mirthlessly.

"Are you kidding me?" she said. "Who the hell do you think you are? A Wall Street trader from the eighties?"

He ran his hands through his hair and spat blood out onto the snow.

"I take it tonight's off, then?" he said.

"You make me sick," said Kate.

"Shame," he said. "We would have been hot together."

"Are you a sociopath?" Kate shouted. "Do you not feel any remorse at all?"

"Grow up, Kate," said Richard. "You think this little chocolate-box town is the real world? I'm out day after day, closing deals, making the kind of money you could only dream of . . ."

"Don't patronize me," said Kate. "Your business prowess has nothing to do with you being a lying arsehole! And cheating on your wife does not make you a grown-up. You used me."

"I didn't use you," said Richard. "You were a willing participant. You wanted it as much as I did."

"Not anymore," said Kate.

She turned and walked away. Richard didn't follow. Kate was relieved. She didn't want any more of a scene than they'd already created. If he did follow her, *she* was likely to punch him in the face as well. She felt dirty. Angry tears pricked at her eyes. "Idiot," she said to herself.

She marched through the copse, untouched by its nighttime beauty. She didn't see the little lights hanging in the trees. The secret Christmas wonderland was lost on her tonight. Creatures of the dark scurried out of reach of her stomping boots as she tore through the thicket.

It wasn't snowing, but the sky was full. The white paths glittered in the light of the cold round moon. Kate wanted to scrub herself. She wanted to find Richard's wife and tell her what kind of a man she was married to. She wanted to go back and find him and pummel him with her fists.

She was still livid as she turned into her street. As she marched toward her house she saw something move. Kate looked up. Laura was standing by her gate. Laura saw her and held up two family-sized bars of chocolate.

"Someone rang me and told me you might be in need," said Laura as Kate reached her.

"Who?" Kate asked.

"Who do you think?" said Laura. She turned slightly to the side and pushed her hip out. A bottle of wine protruded out of her deep duffle coat pocket. "Come on," she said. "Let's crack this bad boy open and you can tell me all about Dick!"

Kate had never been more grateful to see her friend. And what a friend she was: two small children at home who would be up at five a.m., but instead of getting an early night she was here, on a mercy mission at eleven o'clock at night. Kate wondered how she would manage without Laura when she moved away.

Laura listened while Kate lamented her fated romance and didn't say *I told you so* once. They curled up in the sitting room with just the light from the fire and the tree lights and talked and laughed, and ate chocolate until long after the witching hour.

Ben was at home with the children and Laura had a full night pass, and when they had exhausted all the unpleasant names they could think of to describe Richard, Laura settled into the spare room for a rare night of unbroken sleep.

Kate lay awake for a long time after. Her anger was exhausted, but the humiliation still stung. By morning everyone in the village would know. The thought of it made her cringe in the darkness. She was a fool. She wondered what lies Richard would conjure for his wife to explain his bloody nose.

She poked her arm from out under the duvet and grappled around her bedside table for her phone. Then, under the harsh glow of its light in the dark room, she systematically deleted every text and phone message from Richard, deleted his number from her phone, and blocked him from all possible social media avenues.

As the pale dawn light began to leak through the gap in the curtains and Kate had purged herself of feelings of revenge and resentment, telling herself that someone like Richard didn't deserve even her tiniest consideration, she finally fell asleep.

At ten o'clock Laura came in and woke Kate with breakfast in bed: hot buttery toast, boiled eggs, and tea in mugs the size of vases. Laura was showered and dressed, and they shared breakfast before she dashed back to her waiting family.

The wine-tasting date began at four p.m. The vineyard was half a mile north of Blexford Manor. In the snow she would have to allow an hour to walk there to be on the safe side.

She still had a few things she wanted to stock up on for Christmas, so she decided to spend the day making lists of what she'd need. She would pick up some wine at the vineyard, but she wouldn't go overboard, as Mac and Evelyn had been over to France a while back and returned home with as much booze as they could legally transport in one car.

Most of the vegetables for Christmas dinner would come from the garden, but there were some bits she needed besides. Patrick wasn't fully back on his feet yet, but two of his sons were managing the farm, and his wife and youngest son ran the farm shop.

Kate emailed a list of things she needed to the shop, and within ten minutes she had a reply telling her Andy would deliver it all to her door tomorrow. That took care of the extra veg, salad, sausages, bacon, and ham joint. She'd put her name down for a turkey weeks ago, and Andy would deliver that at the same time.

She checked the larder and noted down a few extras she could pick up at Evelyn's shop. She was aware that she would be gone in just a few days, but she was confident that any store-cupboard leftovers could be dished out between Laura and her dad.

In the back of the store cupboard were four large biscuit tins. Each held a Christmas cake that Kate had made on stir-up Sunday. She'd been feeding them with brandy ever since. One was for her and Mac. Two were orders for the café, and the last was for Matt.

Kate paused after she'd pulled them out and laid them on the worktop. What would she do with them? She would have to get them to the café somehow, but she *really* didn't want to see Matt. Even less so after last night's excruciating embarrassment. Now he would think she was pathetic as well as jealous! She decided she would leave them with Evelyn when she went in to get her shopping.

Lists complete, Kate set off for Evelyn's. The sky was a strange yellow-gray, bulbous with snow but keeping hold of it for now. The sun was thin and watery and without the wind of the last few days, it actually felt marginally warmer.

Kate took the long way round so she could drop some mince pies in at her dad's en route. She bumped into one or two people along the way and felt a niggling paranoia that they looked at her strangely.

She was acutely aware that she'd been unwittingly cast into the role of mistress. She hoped that if they did know about last night, they also knew she hadn't embarked on an affair with a married man on purpose. Perhaps she should wear a sign around her neck: *I didn't know he was married!*

She found Mac at his kitchen table doing the crossword. He invited her in for coffee but she didn't have time to stop, so instead he walked with her to the green and carried two of the Christmas cakes for her, which were surprisingly heavy.

"He was married then," he said.

Kate groaned.

"How did you hear?" she asked.

"I bumped into Barry when I was picking up my paper this morning," he said.

"I didn't know," said Kate.

" 'Course you didn't, love."

They reached the green.

"Why don't I take those into the café for you?" said Mac.

"Would you?" said Kate. "I'd really appreciate that. Thanks, Dad."

Mac smiled and Kate handed over the other cake.

"I don't suppose you'd get me coffee while you're in there?" Kate asked.

"Having withdrawals?" joked Mac.

Kate filled three shopping bags with groceries and managed to tick everything off her list and then some. There was no escaping the grilling from Evelyn about Richard, but Kate had been prepared for it.

"He'll get his!" said Evelyn eventually. "Dirty rat. They always come unstuck in the end."

Kate wasn't so sure about that. She suspected Richard was a professional philanderer. He probably had multiple phones, one for each woman.

"Matt's got quite a bruise across his knuckles," said Evelyn.

"Yeah, well, Richard took a swing at him," said Kate.

"I should think Matt would have wanted to punch him on the nose even if he hadn't swung first," said Evelyn.

Mac returned with three coffees.

"Leave those," he said to Kate as she hauled her shopping bags up and tried to balance her coffee. "I'll drop them round later," he said. "I want to check on the sprout trees."

"Are you sure?" asked Kate.

"Yes, love," said Mac. "Leave them with me."

Kate thanked him and left. Her dad showed no signs of leaving the shop anytime soon. Evelyn had pulled him up a chair next to hers by the counter. Kate looked back in through the window and saw her dad pull this morning's crossword out of his pocket and lay it out in front of them. Evelyn put her glasses on and the two of them leaned over the paper, sipping their coffees. Kate smiled to herself.

She looked over toward the Pear Tree and for a second, she could have sworn she saw Matt at the window looking back. But in another second he was gone; it must have been a trick of the light.

She walked home slowly, sipping her coffee and trying to soak in as much of this place as she could. She wished she could store it up in her soul, like charging a battery, so she could use it to sustain herself when she left.

· · · · ·

The vineyard was set on thirty-five acres of undulating slopes nestled in a deep valley; in the summer it caught the best of the sun all day long and you could easily be fooled into thinking you were in southern France.

Today the view was row upon row of snow-capped wooden stakes stretching far into the distance, like some great wooden army waiting for orders. The empty vines, like frozen hair, curled over and around the stakes in white, knotty tresses.

Forest-covered hills grew up on every side, with leaves of ice and pearl, like waves with white horses rising to the sky. The sky brooded, mirroring the metaphorical cloud that hung just above Kate's head.

The car park was at the top of the valley. Kate arrived on foot, puffed and red-cheeked, in time to jump into one of the Land Rovers that ferried the guests to the winery. It was a bumpy ride, but Kate was grateful for it; it was a darn sight better than walking.

The Lightning Strikes reps stood outside the shop with their clipboards, the daters by now well versed with the drill. Kate recognized her date immediately from his picture.

Thomas—a thirty-five-year-old, twice-divorced carpenter from Surrey—was a well-built chap, with a receding hairline and a strong jaw. He didn't look like the sort of man who was comfortable in casual attire and kept worrying at his suede desert boots, which were soaking up the snow like blotting paper.

Kate ticked them both off in the register—since the rep was having trouble holding the pen in her mittens—and went over to introduce herself. Thomas had the confident shrug of a car salesman and the accent of a man who'd tried very hard to lose his geezer roots.

"I'm not familiar with this neck of the woods," said Thomas. "Normally don't venture so far south of the big smoke."

"Well then, you're in for a treat," said Kate. "This is a very pretty part of the world."

Thomas looked unconvinced.

He kissed Kate on both cheeks, and Kate noticed he wore a tweed waistcoat and jacket under his Barbour coat. He was handsome *and* stylish. Kate found the flecks of gray at his temples and above his ears rather attractive. And his eyes were a striking shade of blue.

There must be something wrong with him, Kate thought, and then berated herself for being so cynical; Richard had left his mark on her.

"Do you *know* wine?" Thomas asked. "Or do you just drink it?"

"I like wine," said Kate. "And I know what wine I like to drink."

"I'll take that as a no," said Thomas.

"You may take it any way you wish," said Kate.

She smiled sweetly at him and decided it might be fun to spend the afternoon sparring with Thomas.

The wine-tasting experience began with a tour—albeit brief because of the freezing weather—of the vineyards, where their guide spoke about viticulture and how soil acidity and mineral levels in different regions affect the vines.

He talked about the challenges and perks of growing vines in England, and Thomas had an opinion on almost every point. Kate could see people rolling their eyes, and she felt embarrassed for Thomas and for herself as his date, as if having been assigned to him made her a know-it-all by proxy.

There followed a warmer tour around the winery itself. They found themselves in a large room with a mixture of large steel canisters and wooden barrels, which felt sterile against the wildness outside. The gleaming floor tiles and shiny steel tubes gave a strange science-fiction vibe to the ancient art of winemaking.

Thomas made *ahmmm* noises and said "Yes, yes" in agreement with the vintner as he talked. Kate noticed a space forming around them.

The guide explained the wine-making process, and Thomas helpfully added one or two tips of his own. The guide smiled and his left eye twitched. Thomas had been to several wineries in France and Italy, and he felt it was important to regale the group with the differences he'd found between them.

"Why don't we let the nice man tell us about *this* winery?" said Kate quietly.

"Knowledge should be shared," said Thomas. "I'm taking nothing away from this good man's expertise." He gestured to the vintner, who nodded and smiled graciously. "I'm just sharing what I know to enhance the experience."

He then went on to cast doubt over whether an English wine could really match those made in a more Mediterranean climate. The vintner's mouth thinned to a fine line, and Kate wondered if he was thinking about shoving Thomas into one of the steel barrels.

The winemaker led them down into a long, thin, brightly lit cellar with an arched ceiling and wine racks stretching its length. He gratefully passed the baton to the sommelier and left, shaking his head. Kate was glad for the winemaker that he was surrounded by alcohol; he looked like a man who needed a drink.

A long wooden bench ran down the center of the cellar and the group positioned themselves around it, though Kate noticed they left a fair gap around her and Thomas. Although she had barely spoken, it seemed Kate would be given as wide a berth as her date.

The sommelier walked reverentially up and down past the wine racks, pulling out bottles here and there and placing them carefully on the bench. There were rows of wineglasses on the bench and ten metal buckets on the stone floor, and Kate guessed these were for spitting out the wines tasted; she hoped the spitting out was optional.

The bottles were opened and an explanation given for each before they were poured. Kate followed the instructions for optimum appreciation; she swirled the wine around the glass and watched to see whether it lapped the sides thickly or swished without a trace and how fast the droplets rolled down the glass.

"It's all about the viscosity," said Thomas. "This is how we tell if a wine has legs or not."

The sommelier smiled graciously.

"Very good," he said. "I see we have a connoisseur in our midst."

Kate cringed. Thomas beamed.

"I dabble," he said. "I travel a lot with work, meet a lot of important people. It pays to know your Sauvignon from your Malbec."

Next was smelling the wine. Kate put her nose into the glass. It smelled like wine. Others in the group had a finer-tuned nose than hers. They threw out words like *lavender* and *black currants* and the sommelier smiled, pleased.

"Good," he said. "Blexford Manor grows lavender commercially nearby this estate, and the scent affects the vines. The same with the black currants; the hedgerows are full of them, and it all has an effect."

"I'm getting the sharp scent of buttercups in a beer garden," said Thomas. "And a hint of Victorian petticoat."

Kate laughed but saw that Thomas had his eyes closed, his nose thrust back into the glass again. She could see couples mouthing *Victorian petticoat* to one another and sniggering. She felt a bit sorry for Thomas. She sniffed at the wine again. It still smelled like wine.

They moved on to the actual tasting and Kate was confident that her sense of taste would be better than her sense of smell. As instructed, she sucked the wine in and let it sit on her tongue before swirling it around her mouth. She had swallowed her mouthful before she realized Thomas was chivalrously holding the bucket for her to spit into.

"Oh," she said, looking to the sommelier. "Sorry."

"Don't apologize," he said. "It doesn't feel natural to be spitting out a good wine, does it? Toothpaste is for spitting, wine is for swallowing."

There was a ripple of laughter in the cellar as several others confessed to having swallowed their wine too.

"If you're not driving," said the sommelier, "then fill your boots. It is Christmas, after all."

Another taste (followed by another swallow) and the sommelier asked for a response to what they'd tasted. A few people, including Kate, said berries, blackberries in particular. Some said apples; one person came up with baked plums, which delighted the sommelier as the estate had both an apple and a plum orchard.

"I'm sensing a floral petulance at the back of my tongue," Thomas announced. "Yes. I've come across it before in Italy. This is a rich wine; I'd drink it with steak or venison. That sour note of crushed dandelion leaves stops it from being too gaudy."

Kate drained her glass and prayed for drunkenness. The sommelier opened his mouth to speak and then closed it again, unable to summon a fitting response.

There were four more wines to taste and none of Kate's made it into the bucket. Thomas had a confident comment on each wine: the food it should be served with, the optimum serving temperature, and where else in the world he had experienced a wine similar.

His statements with regard to the aromas and flavor notes he detected in each wine were decisive and at times so surreal that Kate wondered if he'd eaten a stash of magic mushrooms before he'd arrived:

"Warm elastic bands around a postman's wrists."

"Poppy nectar on a bee's wing."

"Grass squashed beneath tent canvas with a cheeky note of quince jam."

And: "Cornflowers and Earl Grey tea spilled on hot tarmac at dusk."

"You should be a writer," said Kate. "You have a very vivid imagination."

"I know," said Thomas. "I've written seven books in my head. When I get the time I'll write them out and get them published."

"I'll be sure to look out for them," said Kate.

Despite his vast knowledge on every subject, Kate found him to be quite entertaining company. And she couldn't fault his manners. He was attentive and polite and made every effort to ensure that Kate was the benefactor of all his attentions; admittedly he spoke to her as though she were his favorite pet beagle, but he had served as diverting company for the afternoon and at this point in the Twelve Dates proceedings, she'd call that a win.

At the end of the tasting session they were led into the shop, where cheese and crackers—presumably to soak up some of the wine—had been laid out on tables dotted about the room. The shelves were wall to wall and wine laden.

Kate was a little giddy and a lot tipsy. She allowed Thomas to be gallant and take her around the shop and pick out six bottles of wine for her to buy for Christmas.

As they waited outside for the Land Rovers to take them back up the hill, Kate was comfortably warm in her wine jacket. Thomas offered to drive her home but Kate politely declined.

"Do you think I might see you again?" asked Thomas.

Kate smiled and patted his arm.

"I don't think so, Thomas," she said. "But thank you for a wonderful afternoon."

Thomas shrugged. He didn't seem overly upset.

One of the reps was heading to Blexford Manor to help clean up after another gingerbread house session, so Kate got a lift with her instead.

"How did it go?" asked the rep as they drove away from the vineyard.

"It was good fun," said Kate.

"Do you think you'll see him again?" she asked.

"No," said Kate. "He wasn't really my type."

"How about the twelfth date?" asked the rep. "Have you submitted your final choice yet?"

"Yes," said Kate. "All sorted."

"Ooh!" said the rep. "That sounds promising. Could he be the one?"

"Not unless I sprout testicles and a hairy chest between now and then," Kate replied.

THE TWELFTH DATE OF CHRISTMAS

·····

Endings and Beginnings

A sharp rap at the front door at seven a.m. found Kate stumbling down the stairs with her fluffy dressing gown pulled tightly around her. It was Andy with her grocery order. He beamed at her. He had the same crooked smile as his father that made the Knitting Sex Kittens swoon. Kate smiled back, making sure she didn't breathe morning breath over him.

"Morning, Kate!" said Andy. "Any chance of a coffee?"

"You're perky," said Kate.

She backed out of the doorway to let Andy in.

"I'm a farmer," said Andy by way of an explanation. "Early to you is nearly lunchtime to me."

Kate switched on the coffee machine and grabbed two mugs from the cupboard. Andy thrust his travel mug at her; the remnants of an earlier coffee coated the bottom of the mug.

"Are you begging coffee off all your customers?" Kate asked.

320 · JENNY BAYLISS

"Only the ones with coffee machines," said Andy. "I can't bear the instant stuff."

"You'll be high as a kite by the end of the day," said Kate.

"I'll need to be," said Andy. "The van can't get through the snow and I can't fit all the orders in the Land Rover. I'm going to be running up and down from the farm all day."

Kate looked out the window.

"Whoa," she said.

The sky had finally given up its load in the night. The snow reached the bowl of the birdbath in the garden. All that could be seen of her dad's sprout trees was their green petal tips. The world outside was still.

Kate put a double shot in Andy's mug. She paid him what she owed plus a tip for his troubles, handed him a large tin of biscuits from Liberty's for the family, and made him promise to drive carefully.

"I'll see you at the caroling!" Andy shouted over his shoulder.

Kate waved. Her smile was noncommittal.

She had just pulled on an oversized Christmas sweater—showcasing nine galloping reindeer pulling a very jolly Santa on his sleigh—and jeans, when the front door clicked shut and her dad called up the stairs.

Together they harvested the snow-clad vegetables, wrapped them in newspaper, and stashed them in wooden crates in the old coal shed, along with the veg Andy had delivered. Mac took a sled out of the shed and laid the turkey and the ham on it, ready to take back to his cottage.

"I don't suppose you'll be coming to the caroling this year?" he asked.

"No, Dad," said Kate.

"You know you two will have to make some sort of peace before you leave," he said.

"Have you been talking to Evelyn?"

"No," said Mac. "I'm just old enough to know when two intelligent people are being really stupid."

Mac left, pulling his sled of meat behind him.

Kate dragged a sack of Christmas presents into the sitting room and settled herself on the floor with sticky tape and shiny wrapping paper.

She'd bought Laura a silver charm bracelet, with two charms to get her started: a letter *M* and a letter *C* encrusted with cubic zirconia. She'd also gotten her a voucher for a spa day, which she knew her busy friend would appreciate.

Mina had a set of unicorn pajamas and a cuddly tiger, and Charley had a rainmaker and a set of bath toys. Kate carefully wrapped her gifts and put them into piles under the tree.

Mac's gifts were mostly books and clothes—he never bothered to buy himself clothes. And Evelyn had a set of lavender bath-and-pamper goodies, which Kate had purchased in the Blexford Manor gift shop.

At the bottom of the bag were some framed photographs. Kate had stumbled across some old prints months ago, when she was sorting through boxes in the loft. They were mostly family holidays and parties, but she'd found one of Matt grinning gormlessly on his fourteenth birthday, flanked by his mum and sister.

Kate had the photograph enlarged, printed in black and white, and framed, along with another picture of Matt, at ten years old, sitting on one of the branches in the pear tree. She had intended to give them to Matt for Christmas.

Kate held the picture of Matt in the tree. She remembered that day. She was sitting on the branch below Matt. Her dad had a taken a photograph of each of them separately and then a longer shot of the two of them, sitting like little elves in the branches.

Matt's mum called them in for tea and they clambered down from their perches. Kate had gone to run on ahead, but Matt caught hold of her hand and pulled her behind the pear tree and kissed her full on the lips.

She'd kissed a lot of boys since then. Hell, she'd kissed a lot of boys this month. But still, nothing ever quite matched that first stolen kiss behind the pear tree.

Kate put the pictures, with their memories and their old stories, back in the bag, unwrapped. Maybe she would leave them on Matt's doorstep as a peace offering when she left. Mac was right. It was stupid to leave on an argument.

She needed a distraction from her thoughts. She slipped into her wellies and coat, grabbed her camera, and went off in search of inspiration. Invariably she found herself in Potters Copse.

The Knitting Sex Kittens had been there; strings of crochet stars in gold-flecked wool crisscrossed above Kate's head, the ends tied to branches high up in the trees. Pompom baubles joined the myriad decorations that bespangled twigs, dangled from ivy-clad bushes, and bejeweled the spiky holly tree.

Kate's camera clicked over and over. A knitted wreath adorned with knitted snowmen, robins, and Christmas trees had been tacked onto a tree trunk. Another hung from a knotty bough; knitted toadstools and hedgehogs nestled in soft green knitted leaves.

Already Kate's mind was whirring with ideas for next year's fabrics. And she determined to show the Liberty buyers the Sex Kittens' handiwork; there was a place for these wreaths at Liberty, she was sure.

She had just zoomed her lens in on a set of glittery salt dough gingerbread women when the sounds of a commotion drifted into the copse. It was coming from the green.

Curious, Kate left the copse and stopped at the edge of the green. It looked as though half the village was in the square. There were yelps and screeches of fear and laughter as people tried to round up a flock of flapping, squawking birds.

A truck with its back fallen open, after what looked like a run-in with a postbox, was parked askew across the green. Several people were trying to heave it back onto the road. The crates from which the birds had escaped lay scattered on the ground.

Kate moved closer. She caught Andy's eye as he lumbered two long pieces of timber toward the van. He dropped them at the driver's feet and as the other men began to position them behind the back wheels, Andy dusted off his hands and walked over to Kate.

"Stupid arse got lost on his way to the manor," said Andy. "Thought this was a shortcut," he said. "Hadn't banked on the snow being quite so thick up here."

At that moment there was a shout:

"There's a partridge in the Pear Tree!"

There came a great flapping of arms and coats and whoops and shouts from the café, and the headache-inducing scrape and grind of forty-five chairs being scraped urgently across the floor.

The Pear Tree customers, who had been safely watching the ker-fuffle from behind the café windows, burst out of the door like they'd been ejected from a cannon and spilled out on to the green.

The green had become a sort of live poultry circus as fifty escapee partridges danced among men, women, and children in wellies and bobble hats.

Kate's mind instantly turned to Matt. She scanned the crowd of coats and brown feathers but saw no sign of him. She began to wade across the green, through snow and birds and people.

"Has anyone seen Matt?" she called as she went.

Nobody had.

Kate walked into the deserted café. The floor was muddy. Chairs had been upturned in the rush to escape and the tables were pushed crooked. A cup lay tipped onto its side, dripping latte onto the floor.

"Matt?" Kate called quietly.

No reply.

"Matt?" she hissed. "Are you in here?"

This time she caught a whisper of an answer, coming from behind the counter. Kate parted the plates of shortbread and mince pies and leaned over the counter.

There, crouched beneath the coffee machine and wedged between a giant bucket of hot chocolate powder and a box of takeaway cups, was Matt. He was pale. Paler even than usual.

He looked up at Kate pleadingly and nodded infinitesimally toward the shelf beneath the till, where a partridge was happily tucking into a piece of tiffin that Carla had stashed to nibble on while she worked. The partridge clucked contentedly.

Kate unzipped her coat as quietly as she could and slipped out of it. She walked gingerly around the counter, conscious of the squelch her wellies made, until she stood facing Matt. He was pressed hard against some shelves. If he could have fitted into one of them he would have. The till and the partridge sat directly to her left.

Kate held her coat open wide out in front of her, like a Spanish matador, and in one swift movement, she ducked down and threw the coat over the partridge and its tiffin and scooped them up.

She felt the bird flap as she hugged her coat gently to her, and her heart raced. Very carefully she walked out of the café and laid her coat on the ground, letting it flap open for the bemused partridge to escape. Then she stepped back into the café and closed the door.

Matt was shakily extricating himself from his stock behind the counter.

"Are you all right?" Kate asked.

For a moment Matt couldn't speak. His hands shook as he ran them through his hair.

"All right?" Kate asked again.

Matt nodded.

"Yeah," he said. Though he sounded uncertain. "Yeah, I'm fine. Thank you."

"All part of the service," said Kate.

She didn't know what else to say. She hadn't given a thought to what would happen after she got the bird away from Matt. She hadn't really thought at all.

Outside the crowd was beginning to thin. The birds—though a good many had made a successful bid for freedom—were being rounded up and put back into the undamaged crates, while John did a quick fix on the others outside his shop.

With the help of Andy's timbers the truck was backed off the snowy green and pointed in the direction of the manor. Andy offered to let the driver follow him up there, to prevent further mishaps.

Kate and Matt, meanwhile, stood awkwardly opposite each other.

"I mean it," said Matt. "Thank you." He added, "You know me and birds."

Kate did know *him and birds*. Matt had had a pathological fear of birds ever since he'd accidentally disturbed a magpie's nest as a kid and been pecked so ferociously, he'd fallen out of the tree. He still had one of the battle scars from the magpie's beak on his forehead; it shone silvery pink when he was stressed or angry. It shone silvery pink now.

Matt took a step forward and Kate froze.

"Kate," he said. "About Sarah. . . ."

"I don't want to get involved," Kate broke in. "I wish you both all the best. I really do."

Kate turned to leave, but Matt came up behind her and turned her back to face him.

"Don't go," he said.

"What?" said Kate.

"I don't mean now," he said. "Of course you can go now, you know, you can go out of the café. I mean . . ."

He held Kate gently by the arms.

"I mean, don't leave Blexford," he said.

Kate didn't know what to say. Her heart clamored in her chest. If anyone could entreat her to stay, it was him. And it would be the easiest thing in the world to stay and be near him and be like they were. Great friends. But Kate would always be wanting. Always longing. Her heart always breaking a little every time she saw Matt share a tender moment with Sarah. Always secretly wishing they were *her* moments.

She went to pull away, but he tightened his grip on her arms.

"Please stay," he said.

She looked up at him; the lights on the tree behind her picked out flecks of amber in his brown eyes, framed by long sandy lashes. Her eyes wandered over the freckles that dotted his cheeks and eyelids.

Matt leaned toward her and she didn't stop him. Their lips met. Soft and tentative, so familiar yet uncharted, like a promise waiting for fulfillment. Kate's skin tingled. Her stomach thrilled. A carousel of memories flickered behind her closed eyelids. Longing. Such painful longing. Matt pulled her into a close embrace and Kate melted into him. She wanted to be here so badly. She wanted more than anything for this to be what he wanted too.

The truck outside backfired and Kate was brought abruptly to her senses. She pushed Matt away.

"I can't," she said. "I can't do this. What about Sarah?"

She couldn't be the *other* woman, not twice in one week.

Kate dashed out of the café, leaving her camera on the counter and the Pear Tree bell jangling furiously behind her. She didn't stop to pick her coat up off the floor. She didn't stop to say to hello to the people who called out to her.

She walked as fast as she could through the thick snow, across the green, through the copse and down the lane. She didn't stop until she reached her front door. She jabbed the key into the lock, slammed the door behind her, and threw herself, wellies and all, across the sofa by the kitchen window.

She lay there for a long time. Thinking. Her head was in a whirl. Had he meant to kiss her? Or was it a reaction to his close encounter with the partridge? What did he mean when he said, *Don't go*? Don't go because he wanted to keep his old friend around? Or don't go because he felt more than friendship?

She couldn't let herself think that. She just couldn't. The fall to earth if she allowed herself to hope and it came to nothing would be too much.

"That's enough, Kate Turner," she said to herself.

She pulled her face out of the cushion and stood up.

"No more of this."

·····

Kate wiggled her largest portfolio case out of the under-stairs cupboard and laid it open on the kitchen floor. Next to the dresser was a large chest of drawers that Kate used to store her work. With methodical diligence she worked her way through the drawers, dropping sketches and mood boards into the case, ready for the move.

The kiss kept invading her mind, unbidden, causing her heart to leap and her stomach to thrill. It would catch her unawares and steal her breath, scrambling her mind. She'd drop papers and lose her train of thought. It was a heroic effort just to keep working.

She sifted through folders and old handmade books. Kate picked up a book bound with scraps of William Morris fabric; the paper was thick, good quality, beginning to yellow at the edges with age.

It was a book of leaf studies: photographs, sketches in pencil, charcoal and ink. Some washed over with color. Some vibrant with oil pastels; an old waxy smell rose up from the pages. Actual leaves stuck in with glue crumbled to russet dust as Kate turned the pages.

A third of the way through, the sketches became all about one tree. The pear tree. Watercolors and photographs. Dried leaves and pressed blossoms. Blossoms taken from the spring, before Matt's family were killed. Kate sighed. No matter how much distance Kate put between herself and Matt, the roots of that pear tree would always be tugging at her soul, pulling her back to him. She closed the book and put it back in the drawer. And went to bed.

· · · · ·

Kate woke up early; it was still dark. She remembered being in Matt's arms, recalled the taste of lips. The dark was full of Matt. She flung the curtains open, switched on the lights, and began to pack in earnest.

By lunchtime she had filled several packing cases, ready to be moved into storage. She had also written out a rental advertisement, which she would place with the local paper after Christmas.

Kate turned her attentions to her Christmas cake. Keeping busy was the only way to keep her mind from lingering on Matt's lips. And his crazy hair. And his brown and gold eyes. And his slim athletic body . . .

Stop it, she berated herself. *It didn't mean anything. He has a girlfriend.*

She kneaded the marzipan until it was almost too warm and soft to work with. Her woes of the previous day had transformed overnight into a kind of wild hopeful excitement; it was, she knew, completely inappropriate and yet she didn't seem to have control over her own thoughts.

She quite rationally put much of this down to being sex-starved and feeling trepidation about leaving Blexford. But she'd still had to hoover the house twice while listening to Christmas hits and singing along loudly, just to keep her mind from wandering.

It would have been easier if he'd just stayed mad at her. Then at least she could feel angry and wronged. She could leave feeling she had the moral high ground. But the kiss had turned everything on its head.

She'd dusted the whole house and scrubbed the bathroom until she was in danger of removing the enamel. She'd changed the sheets on her bed and washed the old ones. If she was burgled now, she could rest easy that the robbers would have no alternative than to declare her house-keeping skills a triumph.

She felt like someone had switched her controls to fast forward. Perpetual motion was all that stood between her and the abyss.

Kate started to get ready for her final date: the Twelfth Date of Christmas. She was meeting Drew at Fitzwilliam Park at six thirty p.m. by the Palace Royale coffee house. She watched *A Christmas Carol* in the bedroom as she dressed. There was no point dressing up too much as it was going to be freezing. She slipped on her best dark navy jeans and Petula's latest creation. She pulled on a pair of thick hiking socks and blow-dried her hair, pulling it up into a loose bun and pinning it, so that little curly straggles of hair fell about her face and neck.

By four o'clock she was perfumed and lipsticked and ready to go. She decided she would take a slow walk to the park and drink coffee in the Palace Royale until it was time to meet Drew. She shoved a book in her handbag—an Agatha Christie; she couldn't risk anything with ro-mance at the moment—and headed out into the snowy dusk.

In her haste to escape Matt the day before, Kate had left her warmest coat in a heap on the floor. She wore instead a gray three-quarter-length duffle coat and wrapped a stripy scarf in pastel peach, green, and pink twice around her neck.

Blexford hill, steep at the best of times, was impossible to get down without a sledge and even then, only the impossibly brave or the impossibly stupid would try it. Kate wasn't chancing a broken leg before Christmas, so she took the long way down.

A series of footpaths trickled down to Great Blexley through the hillside in a zigzag, alongside fields and garden fences. In places the snow reached the top of Kate's boots.

It was a quiet route and for the first time that day it gave Kate the unwelcome chance to be contemplative. The snow here was largely untouched but for the tracks left by dog walkers, and her only company were the sheep that baaed mournfully as she passed them, and the occasional surprised rabbit.

The paths were mostly lined by high hedgerows, but occasionally there was a gap and here the world seemed to fall sharply away to reveal the whole of Great Blexley sprawled out down below: twinkling lights, white roofs, church spires, and the sea at the end of it all, a strip of navy blue reaching up to meet the charcoal sky.

It was already dark but the meager light from the out-of-the-way houses lit some of the way, and where there was none, Kate used her phone's torch.

She wondered what Matt was doing now. Regretting yesterday's emotional outburst, probably. Kate had half expected to get a text asking her to forget it ever happened, or at least to keep it quiet. But she'd had nothing. She told herself that if he'd really meant it, he would have followed her, tried harder. But he was too proud for that. He'd probably have proposed to Sarah by now, spurred on by Kate's rebuff.

She trudged on. It was freezing, her ears were aching, and Kate wished she'd worn a hat, but she stupidly hadn't wanted to ruin her hair. She pulled her scarf up higher around her face.

She reached the town and was glad of the shelter lent by the buildings against the wind. It was markedly warmer here. She followed the road round until she reached the iron gates to the park.

Patches of dark green showed where the snow had been dug out to make snowmen. Fat white blobby figures, with carrot noses and twiggy arms, dotted the park. There were snow animals too, and snow women with big round snow-boobs—one wore a string bikini. A striking snow Mr. Tumnus stood beneath one of the lampposts that lit the many paths and wooded walks through the park.

The park was alive with people; it reminded Kate of a Lowry painting. She made her way to the Palace Royale and ordered a gingerbread latte. She took a seat by the window and looked out.

From here she could see the outdoor cinema screen ready for the final Lightning Strikes date night. Kate wondered how many people had actually found love on their Twelve Dates journey; Todd and Mandy for sure.

Stretched out in front of the screen were hundreds of striped double deck chairs, with tartan blankets on their seats and parasols stuck into the ground behind them. Kate's book remained untouched as she people-watched from the warmth of the café.

To the sides of the cinema arena were rows of portable toilets—the swanky kind, like caravans, with vases of plastic flowers on each cistern and actual soap in the dispensers—and next to them were vans selling coffee, beer, chips, popcorn, and even curry. Kate's stomach growled.

Kate ordered another coffee, not wanting to be one of those customers who make one latte last for two hours. After a while people started to gather near the edges of the arena and the reps took their places at strategic points around the park.

It was fully dark now and the families drifted home. The waitresses began to lift chairs onto tables in the café, and Kate took this as her cue to leave. As she stood up she heard a voice behind her:

"Hello, sexy. Come here often?"

It was Drew. Kate threw her arms around him and he hugged her back, lifting her off the floor. The waitresses looked on with lust in their eyes. *Don't waste your time, girls,* thought Kate. He was wearing a long double-breasted tweed overcoat and a matching flat cap, with a plain teal scarf. He looked divine.

They left the café and the salivating waitresses and checked in with the reps. Kate bought herself and Drew a plastic tumbler of mulled cider each; she had decided she would probably need rather a lot of mulled cider this evening for medicinal purposes, as it was bitterly cold already. The deck chairs were beginning to fill up and Kate and Drew chose one toward the back, in the middle, where they had a good view and easy access to the food vans.

They settled themselves under the blankets and Drew reached into his rucksack and pulled out a large thermos and two hot-water bottles, which he filled, and handed one to Kate.

"Why did you have to be gay?" said Kate.

"Why did you have to be a woman?" he replied.

Kate hugged her hot-water bottle and Drew filled her in on his exciting new relationship with Archie. Kate told Drew about the abominable Richard, and he was suitably affronted on her behalf.

"I knew he was too good to be true," said Drew.

"You could have told me," said Kate.

"What kind of a friend would I be if I didn't let you make your own mistakes?"

"That mistake has branded me a scarlet woman!"

"The scarlet women are always the most alluring," he replied.

"Says the gay man."

"Who better to know what a man wants than a man?" asked Drew, and Kate couldn't argue with that.

The deck chairs were full now and the noise levels were high, until the floodlights slowly dimmed down to nothing and a low expectant hum vibrated through the audience.

As the opening credits appeared on the big screen, a cheer went up and Kate watched as the couples in front scooched up closer to one another.

"Do you want some chips?" whispered Drew.

"The film's just started!"

"I'm hungry," he said. "I can watch it from the van."

Before Kate had time to properly object, Drew had discarded his blanket and hot-water bottle and headed off into the darkness. Kate sighed and pulled her blanket closer around her.

Ten minutes later he was back. Kate didn't look over; she was transfixed by the film.

"That scarf makes you look like a tube of Swizzels," said a voice that wasn't Drew.

Kate turned abruptly. It was Matt. He smiled at her. The light from the screen showed the crinkles around his eyes. Kate stared at him, confused. She couldn't seem to formulate a sentence.

"We need to talk," said Matt.

"Where's Drew?" she asked.

Kate leaned around the deck chair to look at the chip van. Drew waved at her and smiled smugly. He was sharing a bag of chips with a man whom Kate recognized from Drew's description as Archie.

"What's going on?" said Kate, turning back to face Matt.

"You need to listen to what I have to say without interrupting," said Matt.

"Don't tell me what to—"

"Please, Kate," Matt implored. "For once in your life, don't argue with me."

Kate closed her mouth. She hugged the water bottle and sat facing the screen.

"Talk," she said.

"Sarah and I split up," he began. "We split up the night I delivered your tree."

"The night you accused me of ruining your relationship . . ." Kate couldn't help but interject.

"I was angry," said Matt. "I took it out on you because I was angry that I was still in love with you. Am in love with you. Have always been in love with you."

He said the words slowly and carefully, like a confession.

"Sarah knew it," Matt continued. "She recognized the signs; she was still in love with Oliver and I was in love with you, but she was the only one brave enough to admit it for the both of us."

Kate's head was spinning.

"But I saw you both the other night," Kate objected. "Carrying bags out of the café."

"You saw Sarah picking up the costumes for the school plays, which *you'd* asked the Sex Kittens to help her with," said Matt. "If you'd stuck around to spy on me a bit longer, you'd have seen Oliver come to meet Sarah and take her home."

"I wasn't spying!" said Kate. "I was just passing by."

"Why are we even talking about this?" said Matt. He ran his hand through his hair. "I'm trying to profess my love for you here!"

"But you got married," said Kate.

"What?" asked Matt.

"When I was traveling."

"That was thirteen years ago!"

"You still got married," said Kate.

"My heart was broken," said Matt. "I'd pushed you away. Out of the country, as it turned out. I'd lost you because of my own stupidity. So I threw myself at the first woman who'd have me."

"You didn't lose me," said Kate quietly. "Not really."

"I don't want to waste any more time," said Matt. "We've wasted enough already. I love you, Kate. And you bloody well love me too, I know you do. So stop being such a stubborn arse and—"

Kate leaned over and kissed the words right out of his mouth.

· · · · ·

Drew and Archie settled themselves into a double deck chair a few rows ahead of Kate and Matt. Kate smiled as Drew rested his head on Archie's shoulder. He'd sent her a text just moments before:

> Just call me your fairy godfather. You're welcome!
>
> xxx

Matt pulled Kate in close to him, his arm around her shoulder. Kate settled in; her head fit perfectly, just as it always had, in the curve between his chest and shoulder. They would talk later. For now, they watched *It's a Wonderful Life* wrapped around each other, wrapped in blankets.

· · · · ·

It was Christmas Eve. Kate woke up and stretched. She rolled over and met resistance. She smiled as she remembered. She flopped one arm across Matt's naked chest and looked up.

"Hello," said Matt.

"Hello," said Kate.

Matt shifted onto his side, propping himself up on his elbow.

"I really need to go to work," said Matt.

"Yes, you do," said Kate.

Matt grinned wickedly.

"I just want to check something first!" he said, pulling the duvet over their heads.

An hour later they were still in bed. Matt leaned up against the pillows and Kate had her head on his chest. Her arm was draped across him, while he drew lazy circles on her back with his fingers.

The front door slammed.

"Morning, love!" called Mac. "I've brought you a coffee. I thought Matt would have been in the café. Carla said she hasn't seen him this morning. You haven't heard from him, have you?"

Kate jumped up. Matt watched her darting about the bedroom for her discarded clothes and laughed.

"Kate?" called her dad again. "Are you all right?"

"Fine, Dad!" she yelled.

She got to the top of the stairs. Mac stood at the bottom looking up at her.

"You're up late!" he said.

Kate grimaced.

"You haven't heard from Matt, have you?" he asked. "I know you two have had a falling-out, but I still worry about the boy. It's not like him to miss work and not call in."

Kate felt Matt fall in behind her. She glanced back and was relieved to see that he was dressed. Mac's eyes grew wide when he saw Matt, and then he recovered himself.

"I'm fine, Mac," said Matt. He rested his hands on Kate's shoulders. "More than fine, actually." He smiled.

Mac smiled too.

"Well, I never!" said Mac. "It's a Christmas miracle."

It was a busy day. Matt left for the café and Kate made breakfast while her dad brought the boxes of veg in from the coal shed, ready for prepping. Mac hugged her when he left.

"I'm so happy for you, Kate," he said. "This is a good thing. A really good thing."

He waved as he walked down the road and called: "I'll see you at the caroling."

Kate phoned Laura to tell her the news. She had to get in quick before someone else did. It only took one person to have seen Matt leave her house this morning in yesterday's clothes for it to become *village business*. Laura screeched down the phone for so long, Kate put her on speaker while she got on with something else. At first Laura wanted all the details, but then she changed her mind.

"Actually," she said. "I don't want to know. It's a bit like having my sister sleep with my brother."

"Better get used to it," said Kate.

"Ewwww!" said Laura.

But she was very happy that Kate was happy and even happier for herself that she got to keep her best friend in Blexford.

Kate had an awkward email to write to Josie, telling her that she wouldn't be needing the room after all, but she needn't have worried.

Ahh, my little country mouse!

The winter solstice magic has woven its spells around you! I'm so happy you've found your soul mate.

I needed to clear out that room anyway; all the clutter was messing with my feng shui! Luck and love, sweet girl, luck and love!

Kate wrapped Matt's presents and prepped the vegetables for tomorrow's dinner. Now there would be four of them in her dad's cottage for Christmas. Weirdly, after all the years they'd known one another, this would be the first time they'd actually spent a Christmas Day together.

She felt like she was in a sort of bubble. A good bubble, where she felt warm and cocooned. She had other moments where she didn't believe it was real. But then she'd get a text from Matt and be back in the bubble again.

I can't stop smiling! People are going to wonder what's wrong with me. M x

Last night was amazing. I love you. M x

This morning was quite good too!! M x

The caroling would begin when the children had finished their Christingle service in the church. Evelyn had organized the new route and everyone was to meet in the church yard at five p.m.

Matt had warned everyone that he was closing the café at three thirty p.m. today. When Kate arrived at three o'clock to help him get ready for the evening, the café was full. Lots of people—including Laura and Ben—had brought their children in for hot drinks before the church service.

Kate spotted Laura instantly and waved. Mina was in deep conversation with a giant cookie. Charley was sprawled across Ben's lap, rosy-cheeked and fast asleep. Carla called "Hello, Kate!" and Matt turned from the coffee machine. He smiled broadly when he saw her, and his cheeks flushed as red as Charley's.

"Gingerbread flat white?" Matt asked.

Kate nodded and slipped out of her duffle coat. She was wearing the floral tea dress she'd worn for the first of her twelve dates. Matt smiled wolfishly.

"And where might you be going?" he asked.

"I've got a hot date," said Kate.

Matt leaned across the counter.

"You want to be careful," he said conspiratorially. "I hear the owner has a big crush on you."

Kate grinned. She could almost feel her pupils dilate. She brushed her hands over her dress to make sure her thighs weren't actually smoldering.

Kate took herself out to the kitchen and started on tonight's food. She slipped on an apron and began with the orange chocolate chip shortbread. There would also be Marmite puff pastry pinwheels for the children and mince pies and mini Christmas pudding sweets for the adults.

On the hob, two catering-sized saucepans filled with red wine, orange peel, cloves, cinnamon, and bay leaves sat ready for heating later. And two giant slabs of gingerbread cake, which Kate recognized as Evelyn's handiwork, lay on the worktop, ready to be chopped into sticky fingers.

It seemed like every ten minutes Matt found an excuse to come into the kitchen and steal a kiss, and Kate was only too happy to oblige. Every kiss made her feel a little more confident that this was actually happening.

While the shortbread rested in the fridge, Kate got on with the sweets. She squished two shop-bought fruitcakes into a sticky crumbly mess in a large bowl and stirred in some melted dark chocolate and a good slosh of brandy. She dusted her hands with cocoa and took small bits of the mixture, rolled it into balls, and dropped it into petit four cases. When she had about a hundred walnut-sized sweets, she blobbed each one with white chocolate and topped it with a fleck of glacé cherry and stashed them in the fridge to set.

When the café was closed down and cleaned, Carla came out and helped Kate with the pinwheels while the shortbread baked. Matt nipped across to the shop to tell Evelyn about the two of them. He didn't want her hear it on the Blexford grapevine. Evelyn already knew. Of course she did. She probably knew they were going to get together even before they did.

Matt came back full of admiration for Evelyn's unparalleled powers of deduction and handed Kate her lost coat.

"Someone handed it in at the shop," he said. "Evelyn knew it was yours. She's washed it. Apparently it was covered in bird crap."

"I think that's supposed be lucky!" said Carla. She looked at Matt and then Kate and smiled. "I guess it worked."

The church was a short walk from the green, just down the lane past Mac's house. The candlelight from within lit the stained-glass windows without, so that the little church glowed like a beacon, welcoming the cold revelers.

The haunting sound of organ music drifted down the dark snowy lane as the villagers, Kate and Matt included, made their pilgrimage to the churchyard. As they got closer, they could hear voices accompanying the music.

They stood in the churchyard among the crumbling gravestones, some long forgotten, others adorned with fresh winter flowers and holly wreaths. Matt slipped his hand around Kate's and she felt a thrill of excitement; this was a public declaration. It didn't go unnoticed. Matt bent down and whispered in her ear.

"Let's make this official," he said.

He placed his finger under Kate's chin and tilted her face to meet his, then kissed her softly on the lips.

A ripple ran through the little crowd. Lips were bitten in an effort to contain the excitement of fresh gossip; there would be a race to spill the beans.

The Christingle service ended and the big wooden double doors opened, flooding the little churchyard with light. The children skipped out clutching glow sticks and oranges studded with fondant sweets.

Evelyn emerged and, with the help of her fellow Knitting Sex Kittens, handed carol sheets out to the gathering. Kate was surprised to see her dad walk out of the church behind Evelyn, though not as surprised as the vicar must have been, Kate thought.

They started with "Little Donkey." The first carol was always the quietest; people tended to hold back a little, because no one wanted to be the loudest voice in the procession. By the third song the group had found their confidence and their voices. And by the time they wended their way round the back of the Pear Tree Café, singing "Deck the Halls," the sounds of their voices rang through the village loud as church bells.

Just as in years past, people left treats on garden walls and hanging from fence posts. Foil-wrapped tree chocolates and knitted finger puppets delighted the youngsters, for whom the caroling was as much about the treasure hunt as the singing.

The throng gathered not only momentum but numbers too. As the procession passed by, people came out of their houses to join in the caroling. Barry temporarily closed the pub and he and the punters joined the revelers as they passed over the green and into Potters Copse.

A hush fell across those at the front of the procession as they entered the copse, and it rolled backward through the carolers as more people entered, until an awed quiet, broken only by gasps of delight, filled the woodland.

Thousands of tiny lights glittered like fireflies around the copse. They crisscrossed above the carolers' heads like dewy spiderwebs, and glinted through spiky holly leaves, and wrapped around spindly rowan tree branches. Every twig, branch, stump, and leaf was adorned with decorations that shone or twinkled.

The lower branches sagged under the weight of iced gingerbread angels and stars, which were deftly plucked and devoured by mittened children with round excited eyes.

Gnomes, stone foxes, rabbits, and ducks had joined the jolly Santa and his sleigh on the ground, while above, long-legged pixies and fairies sat in branches and dangled their pointed toes among the baubles. Knitted and embroidered stockings hung from the crowded hawthorn tree.

It was a place of magic. Kate had watched this enchanted woodland grow over the last few weeks, but for many people this was their first time. There was so much to see, so much to wonder at, everywhere you looked. Kate watched Matt's face as he took it all in. He caught her watching him and pulled her close.

Evelyn called the group to attention and flapped her carol sheet. There in the little copse, surrounded by twinkling lights and loved ones, they sang "Silent Night," "God Rest Ye Merry Gentlemen," and "The Holly and the Ivy."

As they began a rousing rendition of "The Twelve Days of Christmas," Kate and Matt slipped quietly out of Potters Copse and opened the café, ready for the cold carolers to arrive. Barry followed them out and gave a wave as he headed back to the Duke's Head.

Matt got the mulled wine heating and ran around turning on all the Christmas lights in the café. As Kate brought out the first tray of mince pies, the carolers were making their way across the green. She heard them before she saw them. They had reached "eleven pipers piping" and as the door burst open they had just begun "twelve drummers drumming."

The noise was deafening as eighty people, including Matt and Kate, finished the song with an earsplitting

"AND A PARTRIDGE IN A PEAR TREE!"

The wine was drunk and the nibbles nibbled, and after an hour or so the numbers began to dwindle. The families with young children were the first to leave; they had to settle excited offspring and hang stockings and put out milk, mince pies, and carrots for Father Christmas and Rudolph.

Laura hugged Kate tightly.

"I'm so happy for you," she said. "And I'm so pleased that you're staying. Life wouldn't have been half so much fun without you."

"I'm pleased too," said Kate. "I don't know what I'd do without you."

Ben shook Matt's hand.

"Good one, mate," he said. " 'Bout bloody time."

Then he gave Kate a squeeze.

"Thank God you're staying," he said. "Without you here for her to let off steam, my wife would have buried me in the back garden by now."

"There's still time," said Laura, handing Charley to him.

The rest of the revelers drained their glasses and slowly left for home or the Duke's Head. Carla and Petula helped to clear down the café, and then they too left. Matt turned the lights off in the café and joined Kate in the kitchen as she wrapped up the last of the mince pies.

He poured them each a mug of cocoa, grabbed a package wrapped in brown parcel paper, and led Kate out into the garden.

It was so peaceful. The snow in the garden was untouched, a deep undulating ocean of white. Matt swished some snow off one the tables and placed the mugs down on it. He motioned for Kate to sit and she did so. He joined her on the bench, looking out across the garden.

Matt handed the parcel to Kate.

"Open it," he said.

"But it's not Christmas yet," she protested.

"Just open it," said Matt.

Kate untied the string and the paper fell open. Kate looked. And then she looked again. Her eyes widened. It was a quilt. A quilt made from patches of all the fabrics she had designed.

Kate stood and shook the quilt out. They were all there: all her Liberty designs, scraps of old tote bags from before Liberty, swatches of lino prints and silk paintings, even designs printed on cotton tablecloths from her university days.

Kate turned to face Matt. She hugged the quilt to herself.

"How did you . . . ?"

"I commissioned Petula and Evelyn to make it back in the summer," said Matt. "I probably haven't got them all, but . . ."

"But how did you get hold of all these?" Kate asked. "Some of these designs are really old!"

"I had some of them already," said Matt. "Little pieces of you I kept, when I couldn't have the real thing. And the rest I sourced from Laura and your dad and the Internet."

He smiled nervously.

"Do you like it?" he asked.

"I love it," said Kate. "It's perfect. Thank you."

Kate sat back down and Matt tucked the quilt tightly around them both. They were quiet, the steam from their cocoa curling into the air, their histories and their futures entwined, as they always had been.

The old pear tree stretched its bony arms toward them, a million fairy lights twinkling in its naked winter branches.

"I love that pear tree," said Kate.

"Our pear tree," said Matt.

They kissed, as they had done all those years before, under the snowy boughs of the ancient tree and the watchful eye of the winter moon. And as Kate rested her head against Matt's shoulder, the snow began to fall again, soft white wisps that floated silently to the ground. Nothing stirred but for the sound of the lovers breathing and the beating of their two hearts made whole.

ACKNOWLEDGMENTS

·····

I am thankful to so many good people for making this book possible, in both the practical and the pastoral sense. It takes tens of dedicated book lovers, across many miles, to get one story to print, and it's been both an honor and a pleasure to meet so many of them along the way.

I will be forever grateful to Hayley Steed, my fabulous agent at the Madeleine Milburn Literary, TV and Film Agency, who saw a spark in my first draft and has been championing me ever since; thank you, Hayley, for taking a chance on me. You are a force of nature, and I adore how fiercely passionate you are about your authors. I'm so happy to be one of them. Thank you to Liane-Louise Smith, Georgina Simmonds, Georgia McVeigh, and Sophie Pelissier for all your hard work on the international rights front. And to the whole team at MM, I feel super lucky to have been welcomed so warmly into your lovely family; thank you all for being so generous with your time and for being endlessly patient when I ask all sorts of ridiculous questions.

Thank you to my British editor, Jayne Osborne, for always being nurturing and reassuring when I feel overwhelmed, and for being generally lovely in all situations; your enthusiasm positively radiates. Thanks also to my American editor, Margo Lipschultz at Putnam, for supporting me across the ocean, coming up with great ideas, and being so excited about this book.

And to the rest of the editorial team, in particular Sam Fletcher and Lorraine Green, thank you for expertly guiding me through the editing process and noticing all the things that didn't quite add up. My Thanks to El Gibbons for her amazing marketing skills and to Rosie Wilson for beautifully handling my manuscript's publicity. To all the lovely sales and marketing folks on both sides of the ocean, thank you for getting *Twelve Dates* out into the world.

I have to thank Mel Four, who designed the book cover for my UK jacket, and Sandra Chiu for designing my American jacket; I love them both. They are so different and yet each one epitomizes Christmas and captures the essence of the story.

Thanks, Mum and Dad, for being the proudest parents ever and remembering every story I've written since I was five. Dad, your quiet faith and explosive laughter fills my heart. Huge thanks to my brilliant siblings, Lindsay and Simon, and my heart-sisters, who have spent years reading my stories and encouraging me to keep going: Aileen, Jo, Adele, Tammy, and Sue, I'm looking at you! And to Bev, Jayne, and Helen, my wonder women, who live near and far but are always in my heart.

Dom, thank you for your unending love and patience and for being ever-ready to provide takeaways when required. And to my boys, Jack and Will, the lights of my life; I finally did it!

I feel thankful every day for the wonderful people in my life; I don't know what I did to get so lucky, but I will never take any of you for granted.

The Twelve Dates of Christmas

JENNY BAYLISS

Discussion Guide

Recipes

BOOK
ENDS

PUTNAM
— EST. 1838 —

DISCUSSION GUIDE

. . . . .

1. *The Twelve Dates of Christmas* is written in twelve chapters, each devoted to one of Kate's dates. How did that help in the development of the narrative arc and the consistent introduction of new characters?

2. Did you connect with Kate's cynical view of dating at the beginning of the novel? How did her outlook on love and second chances change throughout?

3. One of the book's themes is opening oneself up to new experiences. Why does Kate decide to go through with the Twelve Dates of Christmas? Discuss what Kate's various experiences can teach us about the trials and tribulations of modern love.

4. Which of the dates was the most entertaining for you to read? How do you think Kate handled herself through some of the mishaps and misunderstandings?

5. Like Kate, author Jenny Bayliss lives in a small British town and is a baker too. What did you think of the fictional town of Blexford? In what ways do you think the story would have been different if it took place in a metropolitan city like London?

6. How do Kate's feelings towards Blexford and her past there change over the course of the novel? Why does she consider leaving, and what ultimately encourages her to stay?

7. Kate's best friend, Laura, is a welcome and consistent presence in the novel. What role does she play in Kate's love life, both past and present? What can their friendship tell us about the value of women supporting each other?

8. The magical spirit of the holidays is an important theme in *The Twelve Dates of Christmas*. What part does Christmas play in the story, and why is it an important time of year for Kate?

9. At its heart, *The Twelve Dates of Christmas* is a story of discovering the love that was in front of Kate all along. What were your thoughts about the ending?

RECIGES

. . . . .

Laura's Toasted Hazelnut Make-Up Brownies

MAKES 18 GOOD SLICES

These brownies are so unctuously squidgy that they are almost a pudding; in fact, they would go exceedingly well with a generous helping of vanilla ice cream. But I like to eat them with a large, strong coffee. Beware, finger licking will be required.

These brownies are gluten-free, and if you use a dairy-free butter and dairy-free chocolate, they are also lactose-free.

Don't try to cut them until they are bone-cold, or you will end up with a heap of chocolate lava; I'm not saying this is a bad thing, just that a bowl and spoon will be required!

2 cups 70% dark chocolate

1⅓ cups sunflower butter

1½ cups granulated sugar

1 tablespoon vanilla extract

4 large eggs, beaten

2 cups ground toasted hazelnuts

1½ cups chopped toasted hazelnuts

Preheat the oven to 350 degrees (convection oven). If using a non-convection oven, preheat to 375 degrees. Line the bottom and sides of a 9x11-inch baking pan with parchment paper.

Bring a saucepan of water to a simmer, and place the chocolate and sunflower butter in a heatproof bowl. Place the bowl over the saucepan, making sure the water does not touch the bottom of the bowl, and stir occasionally, until the chocolate has melted and the ingredients are fully combined. If you don't have a heatproof bowl, you can use the microwave (like I do). Place the chocolate and sunflower butter in a microwave-safe bowl and, using the 60% power option, microwave in short bursts, stirring often to ensure the mixture doesn't burn.

Mix the sugar and vanilla extract into the chocolate mixture. Allow the mixture to cool slightly if the bowl feels more than just lukewarm to your hands (you don't want scrambled eggs) before beating in the eggs and all of the nuts, until fully combined. There is no need to use an electric mixer for this; a thorough stir with a wooden spoon will suffice.

Pour the batter into the prepared baking pan and bake for 30 to 35 minutes, until the top is set and the brownie slab is just beginning to shrink away from the sides of the pan. Cool completely in the pan before slicing.

These brownies will keep at room temperature in an airtight container for up to 1 week. Don't be tempted to keep the brownies in the fridge, as they will dry out.

Christmas Ginger Tiffin

MAKES 12 SLICES

This tiffin offers the fiery heat of ginger and the soothing balm of dark chocolate and Lyles Golden Syrup. It works wonders with a cup of tea and is the perfect accompaniment to a rainy afternoon. I like to make these vegan friendly by using dairy-free biscuits, chocolate, and sunflower butter, but you may do as you wish; they are delicious either way. It is worth noting that if you can't get hold of Lyles Golden Syrup, corn syrup can be used in its place.

½ cup sunflower butter

1½ heaping tablespoons Lyles Golden Syrup
or light corn syrup

¼ cup hot chocolate mix

2 cups dark chocolate, chopped

2½ cups gingersnaps, crushed into a mixture
of large pieces and "sand"

¾ cup raisins

Gold sugar stars or Christmas-themed sprinkles,
for sprinkling

Line an 8x8-inch square baking pan with parchment paper, leaving it longer at the sides for easy lifting when set.

Combine the sunflower butter, Lyles Golden Syrup, hot chocolate mix, and ⅓ cup of the dark chocolate in medium-sized saucepan and melt over low heat. Stir continuously until the mixture is fully melted and combined.

Take the saucepan off the heat and add the crushed gingersnaps and raisins. Stir thoroughly to coat all of the cookie pieces with the chocolate mixture, and then tip it into the prepared pan. Smooth the mixture out evenly; the back a of metal spoon works best for this.

Bring a saucepan of water to a simmer, and place the remaining dark chocolate in a heatproof bowl. Place the bowl over the saucepan, making sure the water does not touch the bottom of the bowl, and stir occasionally, until the chocolate has melted. If you don't have a heatproof bowl, you can use the microwave. Place the chocolate in a microwave-safe bowl and, using the 60% power option, microwave in short bursts, stirring regularly to make sure the chocolate doesn't burn.

Pour the melted chocolate over the biscuit base, spread it into an even layer, and sprinkle with gold sugar stars or edible Christmas adornments of your choice. Place the tiffin in the fridge to set; chill for 2 hours before slicing into 12 comforting bars of wintery decadence.

This will keep in the fridge in an airtight container for up to 10 days . . . given the chance!

Christmas Spiced Biscuits

MAKES 30 BISCUITS

These chocolatey, orange spiced biscuits taste just like Christmas, and their comforting snap makes them perfect for dunking in a mug of hot chocolate when it's cold outside. As an extra bonus—as if more was needed on top of chocolate and orange—your home will be filled with the Christmas-y aroma of cinnamon and ginger while they bake.

I make these biscuits vegan by using dairy-free chocolate and sunflower spread.

⅔ cup sunflower butter

¾ cup granulated sugar

Zest of 1 large orange

1 cup all-purpose flour

1 cup self-rising flour

1 cup dark chocolate,
chopped into small chunks

2 teaspoons pumpkin pie spice

Preheat the oven to 375 degrees F (convection oven).

Line three large baking sheets with parchment paper. Using an electric mixer, beat the sunflower butter, sugar, and orange zest on high speed until it is light and fluffy. Stir in the flours, chopped chocolate, and pumpkin pie spice until fully combined.

The mixture will be quite soft. Using a spoon, scoop out scant walnut-sized chunks of the dough and roll it into balls using your hands. Space the balls evenly on the prepared baking sheets to give them room to spread; I recommend 10 balls per baking sheet. Lightly press down on each ball to flatten slightly.

Bake for about 15 minutes or until the edges have begun to turn a golden brown.

Remove from the oven and allow to cool for a few minutes before transferring to a wire rack to cool completely.

When cool, the biscuits can be stored in an airtight container for up to 1 week, but I've never yet had a batch last that long. This recipe makes approximately 30 biscuits, which sounds like a lot, but with my family these will be gone in about 2 days! In my experience, these little Christmas biscuits are usually being plucked from the rack by eager fingers and devoured whilst they are still warm!